Mahdis Marzooghian is cofounder and editor-in-chief of *Five on the Fifth*. She has a master's degree in professional writing from Towson University, and is a writer and editor based in McLean, Virginia. Her fiction and nonfiction have appeared in the *Miso for Life anthology*, *Heartwood Literary Magazine*, *Welter Literary Journal* (print)*, Mud Season Review*, *Adirondack Review*, *BULL Men's Fiction*, *Lunch Ticket*, *Arkana Literary Journal*, where her piece won the Editor's Choice Award, and most recently in *Nowruz Journal*. Mahdis is founding member of the PRWR Towson University Alumni Alliance Writers Retreat program at Still Point, WV.

To my amazing parents and brother, whose own experiences as Iranian immigrants inspired parts of the Nezami family's story. I would be nowhere without your endless love and support.

To the love of my life, Alireza. Your compassion for our homeland and her people has touched my heart more than you know. Your love for me is the kind I always read about…how lucky I am to now live it.

And to my beautiful birth country of Iran, in whose rich soil I sprouted my roots and grew into who I am today. My ties to you can never be severed no matter how far away I may be; you are in every part of me and in every part of this story. This is my love letter to you.

Mahdis Marzooghian

DEATH HAS NONE

AUSTIN MACAULEY PUBLISHERS™

LONDON * CAMBRIDGE * NEW YORK * SHARJAH

A CIP catalogue record for this title is available from the British Library.

ISBN 9781398470545 (Paperback)
ISBN 9781398470552 (ePub e-book)

www.austinmacauley.com

First Published 2023
Austin Macauley Publishers Ltd®
1 Canada Square
Canary Wharf
London
E14 5AA

I would like to express my sincere gratitude to Catrina Barquist for creating the stunning cover design that captures the essence of my book.

Prologue

Sometimes I talk more to the dead than I do the living, and the only thing that frightens me about it is how familiar and natural I find it.

I lead the way through the labyrinth of gravestones until I find the one I am looking for; the one I've visited hundreds of times and spoken to as if the person lying underneath it were alive and facing me, answering back.

It is the last grave I visit today.

I stop in front of the familiar headstone and look back, spotting my son and daughter walking close to their mother, warily stepping around the graves with the same fearful look in their eyes that I must have had when I was their age, overwhelmed by the heavy stillness surrounding them. They were probably wondering whether they had any right to be there; whether the dead were offended by their living presence. So they tiptoed in silence, careful not to breathe in the air too deeply or step on any graves and awaken anyone who did not wish to be woken.

They came up and stood next to me, shoulder to shoulder, waiting. At sixteen and fourteen, my son and daughter were almost as tall as me. This was the first time I had brought them here; they had reached an age where I could finally tell them everything. Perhaps they could not yet handle death, but they could handle my story.

"It's time for the both of you to know who your grandparents were and how we came to be who we are."

The gift of storytelling was in my blood and I was ready to tell the most important story of all.

Chapter One

"Have I ever told you the story about the leopard and the moon?" my father asked one night.

Before I had the chance to answer, he continued, "Once upon a time, the leopard used to be the vainest creature on earth, regarding himself the most powerful and the most beautiful of all. One night, he climbed up to the tallest tree branch in the jungle and upon seeing the moon high above him, glowing and beautiful, he was overcome by jealousy and foolishly stretched out his paw to grab the moon and bring it down. To his dismay, not only could he not reach the moon, but he also lost his balance and fell down from the tree, shattering his body and his arrogance."

My father's name is Sohrab Nezami and he passed down to me and my brother a grand inheritance: his stories.

The stories that raised us settled inside our bones and shaped us into the men we are today. I can still hear my father's voice pronouncing every word with care and caressing it with his breath, bringing them to life before us.

I remember the first day we visited him since he had been sent away. Aunt Maryam helped me and my brother Rostam get ready. We were all reluctant to go, still in shock and disbelief over the harrowing events of the past month. What would we even say to my father once we saw him?

No one really told us much, except that he had to be taken away and while we grappled with the pain of one loss, we had to deal with another. I was fifteen and suddenly found myself the man of the house in my father's absence. Aunt Maryam was so furious with him that she didn't even mention his name, and whenever she said, "Your father," it was as though she was spitting venom. She tried to put on a brave face for us during the day, but I could hear her crying at night and whispering her older sister's name over and over again.

"Oh Pari *jan,* what are we to do?" she asked the darkness.

But my mother was not there to wipe her tears or answer her questions.

Jan – or joon, the informal version – means "life" in Farsi, my mother tongue. We attach it to the names of our loved ones so that every time we call them, we remind them of their significance. Every time we call them, we're saying, "You're my life."

And when those loved ones depart, we still attach the *jan,* but it takes on a different meaning. Instead, we're saying, "You took a part of my life with you," carving out a space in our hearts and filling it with the ache of longing.

"We have to try and make an appearance, no matter how difficult it may be," Aunt Maryam said, trying to hold Rostam's head still as she brushed his unruly black curls. "You are as slippery as a fish, Rostam, always escaping my grasp."

I stood in front of the slender, dusty hallway mirror and slipped on the coat of the only suit I owned. The mirror reflected a melancholy boy with large, brown eyes staring back at me. My mother always said I had her eyes, but my prominent Persian nose, strong jaw, and straight, dark-brown hair pushed away from my face were all my Dad. So was my thin, lanky frame.

"You look handsome, Cyrus *jan,*" Aunt Maryam cooed. I knew I reminded her of my dad and suddenly felt ashamed.

"I guess you'll have to burn some *esfand* for me to ward off the Evil eye," I said, trying to lighten the mood. Persians believe burning *esfand,* or wild rue, keeps harm, bad luck, and negative energy away. While that's mostly rooted in superstitious thinking, I always thought that its loud crackling sound as it burned and pungent odor, which always made my eyes water as a child, are what helped keep those things away from you.

Khaleh Maryam smiled, reminding me so much of my mother. I don't ever remember a moment when my *Maman* Pari's lips weren't occupied with laughter or her signature lopsided grin and I wished Aunt Maryam would smile more. Although given the circumstances, I didn't really blame her. When Aunt Maryam smiled, I pretended my mother was alive. They had almost identical features and people mistook them for twins all the time.

We lived in Bristol, Virginia and Aunt Maryam moved here from Orlando about two years ago to be closer to us, especially my mother. She had come to the United States years ago on an F1 student visa and when she got a job and became a permanent resident, and later a citizen, she decided to stay on and build a life for herself. She wasn't married yet and liked her independence.

11

She did, however, hate the cold, claiming she could never get used to the weather in Virginia. "I miss the Florida sun," she always said. "The sun doesn't really shine here in Bristol."

I loved living in Virginia, where we had all four seasons. I would feel cheated if I lived in a place where it was just hot or cold year-round with no gradual transition.

The car ride to visit my father took about half an hour. Rostam, who was five, took great interest in the farm animals that whizzed past our windows in a blur of brown, white, and black, shouting, "Cows! Horses!" and stabbing the window with his index finger to point them out. I turned the volume up on my iPhone and closed my eyes, hoping the music blaring from my headphones would calm my anxiety. What would I say to my dad? I was also afraid of what Aunt Maryam would say or do once she was face-to-face with him.

* * *

My father looked ten years older and twenty pounds lighter than when I last saw him. His shoulders were slumped and his steps were slow as he made his way toward us.

"Cyrus! Rostam! It's so good to see you both!" he said, then upon seeing Aunt Maryam, his smile disappeared and dropping his eyes to the ground, mumbled, "*Salam,* Maryam *khanoom.*"

Aunt Maryam stared at him for a brief moment, nodded, and then looked away.

"*Baba!* Why won't you come home?" Rostam asked. I could tell Aunt Maryam was as relieved as I was when Rostam broke the silence and began chatting with my father as if we were meeting for a casual lunch date.

My little brother then began to relay the details of all that had happened at home and at school within the past month without pause. My father listened intently, but every so often he raised his eyes to look at me or Aunt Maryam, trying to figure out if we were going to be as forgiving as his youngest son. But Rostam was only five. He couldn't comprehend the situation or the gravity of what had brought my father to this place. He could only grasp things were different now; *Maman* was gone and *Baba* had done something bad and had to go away for a while. He couldn't possibly imagine what it was. There were no words for it in either Farsi or English and even if there were, my mouth could not shape them and my voice could not sound them out.

Grandpa Behruz and Uncle Eskandar said they were still too ashamed to come with us to visit my father. In the Persian culture, a man's worth is calculated by his reputation – or as we say in Farsi, *aberoo*. Once he loses it, it's like losing everything all at once because all he has is built on and a product of his reputation.

"A man's reputation is his sole foundation," Grandpa Behruz would say. "And what happens when a home's foundation is ruined? Everything comes toppling down."

In America, it's called "losing face," but for us, it's losing your whole self.

Baba-bozorg Behruz – we called him *Baba* Behruz, for short – first came to the United States in 1988 to start a career as an engineer and eventually move his family here. My father was twelve and *Amoo* Eskandar was fourteen at the time, so they stayed in Iran with Grandma Afsar. Finally, in 1992, their visas got approved and Eskandar got on the first flight to join his father. He had recently graduated high school and needed to either sign up for the two-year conscription all Iranian male citizens have to complete once they turn eighteen or start college. But having zero interest in attending college or military service, Eskandar was grateful for the fortuitous timing of their visas, which arrived a week before he turned eighteen.

Sohrab, on the other hand, was still a sophomore in high school and had no interest in going to America. He decided to stay with his mother and finish school. Like her youngest son, my grandmother could not be convinced to leave her country and travel halfway across the world to a foreign land where she had to start her life over. She told her husband she would stay with Sohrab and that was that. At first, Grandpa Behruz pushed back and tried to persuade her to go with them, but after a while, he gave up.

Unlike Uncle Eskandar, who never had any interest in school or academics, my father was a scholar at heart and excelled in school. He passed his concourse exam his senior year and placed top of his class, which earned him acceptances to the best universities in Tehran. He made up his mind to stay, despite his father and brother insisting he come to the U.S., and attended university in the fall.

My father went on to earn his M.D. in obstetrics and gynecology from the Tehran University of Medical Sciences. After his residency at an affiliated hospital, he was able to join a practice. My parents met in college and fell in love, but because my mother came from a humble family, Grandpa Behruz was against their marriage. His disapproval could be felt even from thousands of miles away. But Sohrab, ever the free-spirited son, went against his father's wishes and married Pari at the courthouse on a cold October morning with only his mother, Pari's parents, and a few of their mutual friends as witnesses. My grandfather and uncle used the long distance and travel expenses as an excuse not to attend. They didn't even call to congratulate my parents – a clear sign that they would never accept Pari as part of the family.

Grandpa Behruz even admonished my father from time to time for his choice, lamenting the fact that he could've had his pick of girls from wealthy, respectable families, but he turned a deaf ear to these comments and loved my mother enough to make up for the lack of love and attention from my grandpa and uncle. Grandma Afsar also loved my mother and tried her best to keep the peace within the family. It wasn't until we moved to the U.S. that Grandpa Behruz finally grew to accept my mother as his daughter-in-law and even became affectionate toward her. I guess some things just take time and patience.

* * *

Rostam eventually ran out of things to say and the room grew silent again. I could feel my dad's eyes on me and reluctantly looked up to meet his gaze.

"And how is my eldest son?" he asked, flashing his usual smile that looked out of place in his now-gaunt face. His voice sounded like it was coming from the bottom of a well.

Even as toddlers, Persians are taught to respect their elders, especially their parents, no matter what. Respect and modesty are ingrained in our bones. If you so much as talk back or make a disrespectful comment, it's considered insolence of the highest degree. No matter how angry or upset you might be, you never raise your voice to an elder; respect must always be maintained.

I remembered *Maman* Pari's words, "Respect is like a thin veil that surrounds each of our relationships, but once the veil is torn, it can never be sewn back together or look the way it did before."

I swallowed and took a deep breath.

"I'm alright, how are you?"

"My breath comes and goes, thank God."

14

"That's good," I said. My tongue felt too large for my mouth and I wanted to spit it out.

"How is school going?"

"Does it matter?" I felt my throat tightening and bit down on the inside of my lips to keep from crying.

"Of course it matters! Why would you think it doesn't matter?"

I couldn't bite down hard enough on my tongue to keep it from spilling out the words I wanted to say to my father for the past month.

"Because Mom's gone, you're here, none of this makes any sense, and you're asking me about school? School is the last thing on my mind right now!"

Aunt Maryam went over to Rostam, who was looking from my father to me and then back to my father with bewildered eyes, and started talking to him in a soothing voice to distract him.

"Actually, school should be your only focus right now," my father said in a calm voice. "Everything will work itself out in time, God willingly."

"I don't think even God can help this situation," I said.

"Don't say such things. You must always have faith."

"Well, I'm having a hard time doing that." The tears finally pushed their way out of my eyes and I wiped them away with the back of my hand.

My father was silent for a moment, his forehead creasing with a sudden thought.

"Son, do you know why we named you Cyrus?"

Chapter Two

I stared into my father's graying face, wondering if I had heard him correctly. His beard reminded me of Virginia Beach in December – the foamy, white water bleeding into the dull gray sky.

"I asked you a question, son."

"I'm not really sure how my name has anything to do with—"

"I'm certain you've heard of Cyrus the Great, founder of the Achaemenid Empire in 550 BCE," he cut me off, his voice taking on what Mom and I called his "storytelling tone."

"Yes, and it's obvious you named me after him. It's a pretty typical name for Persian boys."

"One would imagine, but you won't really understand why I named you after this great man or appreciate the reason until you learn about who he was," my father said with a smile. "After all, parents have their own special reasons for what they decide to name their children, no matter how prevalent the name may be."

"What else is there to know? He was a famous Persian king, and you named your firstborn son after him to show off your Persian heritage and pride," I said, folding my arms.

"That's a very small part of it, Cyrus. I need to tell you his story and maybe once you've heard it, everything will make a little bit more sense. Right now, stories are all I can give you, but believe me, they will be enough," he said, looking at me and then over at Rostam, who still looked puzzled.

"Okay, Dad," was all I could say.

"Did you know Cyrus' grandfather, King Astyages, wanted to have Cyrus killed as an infant?"

"Why would Cyrus' grandpa want him killed?" Rostam asked, already engrossed.

"Because, my son, sometimes even having the same blood can't dissuade some people from betraying their own kin," my father said with a sigh. "But as the story goes, Astyages was the king of the huge Median Empire, bordering ancient Persia, which was a small kingdom at the time. When his daughter Mandane married King Cambyses of Persia, there was a prophecy that their firstborn, Cyrus, would take Astyages' throne from him, so he ordered his right-hand man Harpagus to kill the infant."

"Asstages was mean!" Rostam cried.

"As-tee-ya-gees," my father said, sounding out the name for Rostam. "But Harpagus couldn't bring himself to do it and ordered a shepherd to kill the child instead. Little did anyone know that the shepherd and his wife had lost their baby during birth that same morning, so they risked their lives and came up with a plan to switch Cyrus' rich robes with the simple clothes of the stillborn child, making Cyrus out to be their own son and showing Harpagus the dead body of their actual child."

"Oh, because all babies look alike," I said, rolling my eyes.

"Then what happened?" Rostam asked.

"Cyrus was saved by the herdsman and his wife, who raised him as their own until he reached the age of ten. Around that same time, however, Astyages finds out by pure coincidence his grandson is alive after a fight takes place between Cyrus and a nobleman's son. When the nobleman complains to Astyages, the king calls for the herdsman and his son – who was Cyrus – to answer before him. When he questions the boy about his ill behavior toward the nobleman's son, Cyrus' manner of speak and countenance give him away almost immediately. Astyages knew right away the boy was his grandson, noticing how much Cyrus' face resembled his own. The old king was overjoyed to learn Cyrus was alive. For ten years, the guilt and regret of ordering his own grandson's death haunted him. And at the ripe age of ten, Cyrus was already proving himself an exceptional leader, winning over the heart of everyone, including Astyages."

"Boys, it's time to go," Aunt Maryam spoke up for the first time since we were there, and her voice startled me. I'd forgotten she was even with us.

"Well, it looks like that's all the time we have, gentlemen," my father said, trying to look cheerful, but his eyes gave him away. "We'll pick up where we left off next time."

Rostam was lost in my father's tale, forgetting where we were and why we were visiting him in the first place. He flashed Aunt Maryam a disappointed look,

17

but I knew she was relieved we were leaving. She sent another quick nod my father's way, her lips set in a straight line.

"*Khodahafez,*" my father called after us.

"Goodbye" in Farsi was a farewell and a prayer all in one: "May God protect you."

I, too, prayed God would protect him in that lonely place.

* * *

The ride back home felt even longer.

As Aunt Maryam drove in silence and Rostam slept in the back seat, I looked out the window and replayed my father's story in my head.

The earliest memories I have are of my father telling me stories. His stories have been with me since before I was even born.

Maman Pari used to get teary-eyed whenever she mentioned the time she was pregnant with me and how my father kneeled in front of her every night before bed, gently placing his hands on her swollen belly, to tell me stories in his deep, soothing voice.

"If you were kicking away in my belly, your father's stories would somehow calm you down and later when you were born, he could get you to stop crying with just the sound of his voice," my mother said with a grin. "It was like magic, like water over fire."

She told me when I started speaking, one of the first sentences I formed were, "*Baba, gheseh begoo!*"

"Dad, tell a story."

Baba Sohrab was most passionate about Persian history and almost all of his tales were about different historical events and figures from our history, which spanned thousands of year. He was always reading books about Persian history and culture. When he graduated from university, my father earned his bachelor's degree in both history and biology.

Indeed, his interest in medicine developed when *Maman-bozorgi* Afsar was diagnosed with stomach cancer two years after Grandpa Behruz and Uncle

Eskandar moved to the U.S. It was around the time that he got accepted at Tehran University. He took her to all of her doctor's appointments and became her full-time nurse, along with going to school and working, until she passed away five years later.

Grandpa Behruz and Uncle Eskandar only visited two or three times and never stayed long enough to really help my father with anything. Their only contribution was sending my father money every month to help support himself and Grandma Afsar and to pay for her expensive treatments and medications. Grandpa Behruz suggested she come to the U.S. for treatment, but again my grandmother refused, claiming Iran already had the best doctors and she needn't travel thousands of miles just for fancier medical equipment and doctors whose language she couldn't even understand.

"If they're going to tell me I'm dying, I'd prefer it be in my own language," Grandma Afsar insisted. And that was the end of the conversation; she had her way.

Deep down, I think my father resented them for going to America in the first place. He felt his father and older brother abandoned him and his mother.

After Grandma Afsar died, Grandpa and Uncle Eskandar started putting even more pressure on my father to move to the United States and help them with their thriving restaurant business, but he was on his way to becoming a successful physician in Iran and told them it would be foolish to move overseas and work at a restaurant instead.

My mother, however, dreamed about living in the U.S. since she was a little girl and when I was around nine years old and she was pregnant with Rostam, she finally convinced her husband that moving to America would give us more opportunities and that he could still be a physician there, too. Grandpa Behruz had already requested visas for us and when they were approved, Mom was ecstatic. Seeing her excitement, my father started making plans and getting everything in order for our big move. I started bragging to all my friends at school that we were going to America – the country whose very name rang with promise and evoked images of tall, golden buildings. It's the most tempting mirage, disappearing once you immigrate to it.

I remember *Maman* Pari wanted Dad to sell our home and all the furniture, then pack and take whatever else we could with us, but my father told her it would be wise to leave some things behind – things we could go back to, if needed. It's a gamble, choosing the life of an immigrant. You have to be prepared for a return if things don't work out.

Mom laughed and called him a pessimist, but respected his wishes.

"You should always keep the option of going back home open," he told her. "That's why we're going to leave something to return to. I don't want to burn the bridges of our old life here."

He didn't sell our house. It was his childhood home; where he had memories of Grandma Afsar and the first few years living with my mom as newlyweds and then as young parents, watching me grow up. He wanted to return to it someday, or at least be comforted by the knowledge that it was still there.

We have been living in Bristol, Virginia for six years now and became naturalized U.S. citizens about a year ago.

I now wonder if any of this would've happened if we hadn't come to America. Would my mother still be here? Would my father be taken away? Would we be living a completely different, yet happier life?

Misfortune can befall you no matter where in the world you live, but an immigrant feels doubly responsible, wondering if it was a mistake to leave his birth country and travel to a foreign one. Wondering if he would've gone through all this hardship if he hadn't immigrated.

I think it has to do with the fact that as an immigrant, there's so much more to lose. So much more at stake. You travel to another country holding so much promise in your heart, thinking all your sacrifices must be worthwhile. Of course, as a child you don't sacrifice much, but adult immigrants give up whole lives for just the promise of an opportunity. It must feel like the deepest betrayal when the promise isn't kept or fulfilled.

After we moved, my father spent about three years studying and taking a series of difficult exams to be able to practice medicine in the U.S. He spoke English fairly well, but there was still a language barrier and because he was a foreign medical graduate, he had to score a lot higher than his American counterparts. The interview process for residency took place every fall and he had to wait until March to find out where he matched for residency, which started on the first of July. Prior to that, while studying for his exams, Dad did a research internship at the hospital where he wanted to do his residency. The research was unpaid, so he had to help at the family restaurant to make money. He did his research internship and worked at the restaurant for about three years until he was able to get interviewed for the residency spot. By July 2014, he got accepted and started working at the hospital as a resident.

"You have to work hard for what you want in life because that way, you'll fight to hold on to it with everything you've got," he used to tell me.

His stories, his advice, everything he taught me and the way he lived his life until now – none of it makes sense anymore. I feel like I don't even know him now. I look at him and think, *who is this stranger I call "Baba"? Who is this stranger with the voice and stories that I've known since I came into existence?* The voice and stories that are as much a part of me as my DNA. The voice and stories that mingled in my marrow as I took form in my mother's womb. What he did goes against everything he stands for and the person I knew and loved all my life. But it's still just an accusation. Can it be proven otherwise?

Oh *Maman*, what are we to do?

She never answered me, either.

But maybe the answers to all these questions were with Cyrus, my namesake. I decided to be patient and hear Cyrus' story. I would give my father this chance to tell perhaps the most important story of his life.

In fact, his very life depended on it.

Chapter Three

"What the hell is that? It looks like cat vomit," George Mullins cried, making a disgusted face and poking a plastic spork at the food in my Tupperware.

"George, keep stuffing your face with shitty cafeteria pizza and mind your own business," Yiannis said, throwing the football he was holding at George and knocking the spork out of his hand. "I know this is news to you, but other countries exist in the world where they eat food other than just pizza and hamburgers."

"Whatever, bro," George mumbled and got back to harassing the two girls sitting at our table. They seemed to enjoy the attention.

I grinned at Yiannis and shoveled a spoonful of the *ghormeh-sabzi* Aunt Maryam had packed for me into my mouth; a dark-green, aromatic stew made with a medley of fresh, finely chopped herbs, kidney beans, dried lime, and lamb served over white saffron rice. It was a classic Persian dish.

Aunt Maryam refused to let us eat cafeteria food and woke up early every morning to pack us lunch. I could not go a day without someone at my lunch table making a comment about my food, but I was used to it by now. When I first started school here, the teasing bothered me so much I skipped lunch and waited until I got home to eat.

Yiannis Anastas, my only friend at John S. Battle High, was a short and stocky Greek boy whose specialty was sticking up for the minority in our high school and making smartass comments to anyone who tested him. He was a linebacker on the football team, which is why he was respected by the popular crowd. While we had also attended the same middle school, we didn't become close until high school. This was mainly due to the fact that we only had a science class together in seventh grade and I mostly saw him in the hallways or during lunch. But on the first day of high school, we sat next to each other in homeroom biology class and bonded over our middle school days. Yiannis was the first one to start talking, saying he remembered me from our seventh-grade science class and joking about how terrible our science teacher, Mrs. Roberts, was. He was easy to talk to and I warmed up to him.

"Remember when she'd only let us write in pen?" Yiannis said, making a face.

"Oh man, I used the erasable kind," I cried, laughing. "The worst was how we could only write in cursive otherwise she wouldn't grade our work, which was my worst nightmare because my cursive was God-awful."

"I mean, we were only in seventh grade! She must've been a drill sergeant in a past life."

"Or, she just loved torturing kids."

"And here we are again, high school freshmen, meeting again in a science class," Yiannis said.

"Hopefully our new teacher won't be as bad as Mrs. Roberts," I said.

"Yeah, I don't think I could handle that."

I probably wouldn't have survived my freshman year of high school if it wasn't for Yiannis. When a guy in class once called me a terrorist, Yiannis would have gotten into a fight with him if some of the other guys in the class hadn't held him back. The kid got suspended, but I think Yiannis's reaction scared him more and he never said a word to me again.

"I guess it's up to the Greek guy to save your Persian ass every time," Yiannis said afterwards with a smug grin, animating his pale green eyes.

"Yes, I know it's like the biggest privilege of your life."

"Please, you know damn well us Greeks creamed the Persians back in the day," he said with a playful punch on my arm. "Didn't your dad ever tell you how the Greeks beat the Persians, being a history buff and all?"

"Yeah, but he also told me it was the Greeks' fault for messing with us in the first place."

"In all seriousness though, it's pretty cool how similar our cultures are."

"Hey, don't change the subject when you know I'm right," I said with a grin.

"But I agree, and it amazes me that humans instead find those few subtle differences to fight about."

Yiannis nodded.

"So, do you like going by 'Persian' or 'Iranian'?" he asked. "I've noticed most of you refer to yourselves as 'Persian' and it's interesting because your country's no longer called 'Persia.'"

"I don't really have a preference, but I guess 'Persian' sounds more authentic than 'Iranian,' or maybe more bad-ass because it's associated with a period of time when we pretty much ruled the world," I said, folding my arms across my chest with an air of mocked haughtiness.

"Yeah, yeah, I'm sure it was fun while it lasted."

* * *

The American school system is very different than Iran's, but lucky for me, I came here when I was young enough to pick up English quickly and not struggle academic-wise. Socially, however, I still felt like an outsider and didn't quite belong to any of the groups or cliques at John S. Battle High. People went to parties every weekend, participated in different social events and school dances, joined various clubs and sports, and I was in the middle of it all, wondering where I fit. I interacted just fine with teachers and classmates, but only in regards to schoolwork and projects. My sole point of social contact was Yiannis; everyone else pretty much ignored me and being the introvert that I was, I didn't mind it.

Yiannis tried to get me to talk to girls, but they didn't seem interested. I didn't know how to make a move and none of them piqued my own interest enough for me to put in any real effort.

That is, until I met Tamara Jones.

As a Persian raised in a Muslim household, I wasn't allowed to think about girls or dating. Not until after I graduated college, anyway. Traditionally in Iran, when a young man is of marrying age, which is usually when he's earned his degree and has a steady job, it's custom for the boy's family to research and ask friends and family members if they know any nice, educated girls suitable for their son. The boy himself might also meet a girl at college or a social gathering and then he'll ask his parents or elders to intervene and accompany him on a *khastegari* – or proposal ceremony. The boy's family calls up the girl's family and sets up a time to go over their house with flowers and sweets to see if the two are a suitable match. If not, then they move on to the next prospective girl on their list. Normally, it's the boy's mother who takes the helm – she's the one who finds the matches, makes the calls, and sets the dates. It's a job she takes very seriously because as a Persian mother who adores her son, she's going to

24

make sure she has a say in who her future daughter-in-law – and rival for her son's affections – is going to be.

Once the girl and boy end up liking each other and the families decide they're a compatible match, they go out a few times to get to know each other, and when things get more serious between them, they'll move toward getting engaged after a few months. Then, the couple and their families start planning their wedding during the engagement period. Nowadays though, and with the less traditional and non-religious families, teens and young adults date around until they find a suitable partner for marriage, perhaps waiting a year or two and even living together before getting engaged, much like Western cultures.

Tamara immediately caught my eye when she walked into English class on the first day of school. I was still trying to learn my way around the school and was relieved when I found out Yiannis also had English, algebra, and the same lunch period as me. We compared class schedules earlier in biology.

"This friendship was meant to be," Yiannis beamed, smacking the back of his hand against the schedule he was holding. "Our schedules are practically the same."

He had to stop by the gym after biology to pick up his football jersey and said he'd meet me in English right after. I was eyeing the classroom entrance to see if I would spot him when I saw Tamara.

She was engrossed in conversation with a friend as she walked inside, waving her one free hand around. She was petite and seemed to walk on her tiptoes, like a ballerina. Her skin was caramel and her eyes were large and brown, framed with thick, curled lashes. Her brown hair was pulled back in a ponytail and she was wearing a pale pink dress that hugged her body in a way that made something tug at my insides. My face felt hot and I looked away.

"I cannot believe you said that to Danny, Tam!" her friend said, giggling behind her hand.

Tamara floated over to a desk a few rows in front of me, requiring no effort to carry around her delicate frame.

"He deserved it, thinking I'm the type of girl he could just play like that."

Her voice caught me off-guard – low and husky, like she was whispering a secret just between you and her.

"Well, he's looking like a fool now."

"Good riddance," Tamara said in that breathy whisper.

25

As the classroom filled up with more students, Tamara's voice was lost in the steady hum of other conversations. Yiannis was one of the last people to saunter into class, making his way to the back of the room to sit next to me. Judging from her demeanor, I could tell Mrs. Miller was going to be tough. I needed to pay extra attention in her class, but I liked English even though it was difficult for me sometimes.

"Why do you have such a lost look on your face? Oh God, are we getting a surprise grammar test on the first day?"

"What? No, I was just spacing out," I managed to say, but when I stole another glance at Tamara, Yiannis figured it out.

"Wait, you've got the hots for Tamara?" he whispered, running a hand through his thick, jet-black hair. "The guys told me she dumped her boyfriend a week before school started, so you're in the clear!"

"I have no idea what you're talking about," I said, pretending like I was paying attention to the roll call.

"Bro, you're smitten, who are you fooling?" Yiannis said with a smirk.

"Tamara Jones," Mrs. Miller called.

Tamara's hand shot up in a swift, fluid motion. "Here."

"She does seem nice," I looked over at her again. She was listening to Mrs. Miller as she called everyone's else's names. When my name was called, I raised my hand and kept my eyes on Tamara to see if she would look my way. She didn't.

"I've heard she's nice, but would your parents be okay with you dating a non-Persian?"

"I don't really care what anyone thinks and besides, my parents are open-minded," I said, avoiding eye contact.

"Well, that's good, then," Yiannis said. "Go for it."

I kept my eyes on Tamara for the duration of the class. She wasn't the most beautiful girl I had ever seen and I noticed there were prettier girls than her just in English class, but there was a fragility about her that intrigued me and made me want to get to know her. I spent the rest of class trying to come up with ways to talk to Tamara and it's been an ongoing struggle since that first day.

We were now about a month into the school year and I was still trying to work up the nerve to talk to her. It didn't help that I only had English and lunch with her and she sat nowhere near me in either period. It also wasn't the best timing with everything going on in my personal life.

"It's torture watching you drool over Tamara and not being able to do anything about it," Yiannis groaned. "Either let me help you or grow some balls and just talk to her, she's not going to bite you."

"I need to find the right moment."

"I hate to say it, man, but she's going to be snatched up by another dude, most likely an asshole, while you're over here trying to find the perfect moment. Just make a move!"

I knew Yiannis was right. I was about to eat another spoonful of *ghormeh-sabzi* when I felt a tap on my shoulder. I sighed and ignored it, thinking it was George again, or one of his buddies.

"Excuse me, are you Cyrus?"

The voice sounded like a whisper, like I was about to be let in on a big secret.

Chapter Four

I spun around and was face-to-face with Tamara. If Yiannis hadn't nudged me, I would have just stared at her.

"Yes, I'm Cyrus," I managed to say. "Sorry, I thought it was one of the guys messing around."

"It's okay, I'm Tamara," she said. "Nice to meet you."

"Nice to meet you, too. We have English together, right?"

She nodded.

"Sorry to interrupt your lunch, but I was wondering if I could ask you a favor," she said. Somehow, her voice was all I could hear in the noisy cafeteria.

"It's okay," I said, hoping to keep her at our table for as long as possible. "What's up?" I wondered what she could possibly need from me.

"Well, hope this isn't too weird, but we've started a project in my world history class where we have to research and present about an ancient culture," she said. "I've been assigned the Persian Empire and word around the street is that you're Persian, so I was wondering if I could ask you a few questions?"

"Sure, I'd be happy to help in any way I can."

I could see Yiannis grinning from the corner of my eye and ignored him, praying he wouldn't make a stupid comment.

"I really appreciate it! I can text you to set up a time we can meet up, sound good?"

"Sounds great."

She took her phone out of her book bag and handed it to me.

"Just enter your info and I'll text you so you'll have my number, too."

I typed my name and number into her phone with shaking fingers and gave it back to her.

"Thanks, I'll talk to you soon. Bye, guys," she said, then turned and walked away. Even with her book bag on her back, she seemed to float.

"So, you just let them come to you, is that it? Well played, my man," Yiannis cried, patting me across the back.

I rolled my eyes. "Yes, Yiannis, you got me. I even convinced her history teacher to assign them the project."

"You can't tell me you're that lucky!" Something about Yiannis's tone told me luck had nothing to do with this and suddenly remembered he had world history with Tamara.

"Wait a minute, you didn't have anything to do with this, did you?"

"If by 'anything' you mean I nonchalantly mentioned to her that you're Persian, then yeah, I did something to do with it, so I guess you can thank me," Yiannis said.

"I should've known you couldn't stay out of it."

"Not the 'thank you' I had in mind, but I'll take it."

The bell rang to signal the end of lunch and as we made our way out of the cafeteria to our next class, I felt my phone vibrate in my back pocket.

* * *

Aunt Maryam was sitting at our small dining room table drinking tea and looking out the window. She resembled *Maman* so much that it both comforted me and made me ache.

Our apartment was a modest three-bedroom in a medium-sized complex we shared with Uncle Eskandar and Grandpa Behruz; they lived in the downstairs unit. Grandpa Behruz owned the building and pointed out on several occasions what a smart investment it had been. He often advised me that owning your own home and business and making sound investments were the only ways to have financial stability in this country.

I was too young to understand or care about what he was saying, so I nodded and tucked his wisdom away for later. That's a familiar exercise between the old and the young. The older generation gives generous advice while the younger generation nods them away in a little corner until they're old and experienced enough to finally understand.

When my parents first came to the States, my dad was reluctant to live in a home owned by his father. He wanted to live separately from his family to cement his independence from the start. However, he was short on money and living here was the only option. As always, Mom reassured him it was for the best and that he should be grateful Grandpa Behruz was offering it to us in the first place. Even in the most hopeless situations, my mother found a way to be positive. But I doubted even she would be able to find anything hopeful about our current situation.

There's a Persian saying that the mother is the light of a home – *Madar noore khoonas*. My mother was the light of our lives; she was our *pari* – our angel. Of course there was nothing hopeful about this situation simply because she no longer existed. Our lighthouse had been extinguished, and we were lost ships crashing into each other in the dark.

"Hi, *Khaleh* Maryam."

"Hello, Cyrus *jan,* I didn't even hear you come in."

"Where's Rostam?"

"He's taking a nap in my room," she said, glancing over at her bedroom door. "He had another nightmare last night."

"I know, though I didn't wake up until I heard you coming in to comfort him," I said, feeling a little guilty. Most nights, I tried my best to wake up and rush over to him, shushing and soothing him back to sleep before Aunt Maryam heard him.

Rostam started having bad dreams about a week after Mom died. He could never remember what the nightmares were about, but he woke up crying and screaming almost every night, covered in sweat.

Still, I thought he was handling everything well, given what he was going through at his age, but Aunt Maryam was worried about him.

"I'm thinking about taking him to see a doctor," she said, sipping the last of her tea.

"It's just a phase, he'll get better with time," I told her, trying to sound reassuring. "He's been through a lot in the past month, we all have, and given everything that's happened, I should be thankful my five-year-old brother is only having nightmares."

"Maybe you're right, but the little guy suffers and it worries me."

I nodded and didn't say anything, lost in my own thoughts.

If it wasn't for Aunt Maryam, Rostam and I wouldn't have gotten through any of this.

"You can come to me for anything," she told us after Mom passed away. "I am no different than your mother and although I can never fill her shoes, I'll do my best."

No one could've filled our mother's absence the way she did.

"Go wash up and put on some clean clothes," Aunt Maryam said, getting up from the table to take her teacup into the kitchen. "*Agha* Behruz and *Agha* Eskandar are coming over for dinner."

"I thought they had shunned us," I said, trying to keep the bitterness out of my voice. Ever since my father had been taken away, it seemed Grandpa Behruz and especially Uncle Eskandar, whose relationship had always been strained with my father, were avoiding us.

"Well, they've shunned your father, not you guys," Aunt Maryam called from the kitchen. "Go on, I'll make you a quick snack while you get ready."

"Whatever you say," I said, rolling my eyes. I picked up my backpack from the floor and carried it to my room, wishing I could go to bed like Rostam.

* * *

Around 8 p.m., I heard feet shuffling on the stairs outside our door. When the doorbell rang, Aunt Maryam was busy in the kitchen and asked me to answer. I reluctantly greeted my grandpa and uncle at the entrance, nervous about how they would treat me post-incident. Would their disappointment in my father also extend over to me, his eldest son?

"Hello, *Baba-bozorg*, *Amoo jan*, welcome," I said, reaching my right hand out to take theirs and leaning in to kiss them once on each cheek, as was the customary Persian greeting.

"Cyrus, long time no see!" Grandpa Behruz cried in his booming voice. He acted the same as before and I was relieved. Taking slow steps inside, he leaned on his cane and surveyed the small living room, a strange, almost pained expression on his face. He then dabbed at his eyes with a tissue he pulled from his pocket and cleared his throat. "Where's my Rostam?"

"He's sleeping, he was tired when he got home from school." I didn't want to go into much detail about why Rostam was tired. The less they knew, the better.

"Well, I expect to see him at the dinner table," Grandpa Behruz said, which meant we had to wake Rostam up for dinner.

Aunt Maryam came out of the kitchen and greeted her sister's in-laws.

"Good to see you again, *Hajj-agha*, *Agha* Eskandar," she said and nodded toward them, but did not shake hands with them, as it was immodest for a Persian woman to have physical contact with a man she did not have immediate familial or marital ties with.

"Ah, Maryam *khanoom*, good to see you again, dear," Grandpa Behruz said, smiling.

Uncle Eskandar seemed much more reserved and only nodded at her.

"Welcome, make yourselves at home, please," Aunt Maryam gestured toward the sofa. "Tea will be ready soon."

When guests enter a Persian home, no matter the circumstances, they are treated with the utmost hospitality. It's customary to serve guests freshly brewed tea, an assortment of sweets, fresh fruit, and *ajil,* which is Persian-style trail mix.

While Aunt Maryam went to the kitchen to prepare the tea, I was left alone with our two guests. After about two minutes of excruciating silence, Grandpa Behruz spoke.

"How is school going, Cyrus *jan*?"

"It's going well, I'm liking a lot of my classes," I replied and as I looked from Grandpa Behruz to Uncle Eskandar, I noticed him staring at an area on the floor in front of the bookcase; it made me uncomfortable.

"*Amoo*, would you like some fruit?" I asked and his head shot up to face me, startled.

"No, thank you," he mumbled and proceeded to busy himself with his phone.

Just then, Aunt Maryam re-entered with the steaming tea tray and I thanked her in silence for saving me.

"Thank you, Maryam *khanoom*," Grandpa Behruz said as she served him the tea first.

"You're welcome, dinner should be ready in about half an hour."

"Smells delicious, what are we having?" Grandpa asked.

"Chicken with *zereshk-polo*."

"My favorite! How did you know?" Grandpa Behruz said with a wink.

Zereshk-polo, or barberry rice, was another traditional Persian dish. The barberries are cooked separately with butter, slivered almonds, and sugar until caramelized, then mixed in with the rice. The rice is usually served with chicken. It was my mother's specialty and one of our favorites growing up.

* * *

I sat at the table with Grandpa Behruz and Uncle Eskandar, the food sitting on the table between us and emitting steam, while Aunt Maryam went to coax Rostam out of bed. I wanted the steam to envelop me, make me disappear.

We heard Rostam's sleepy protests from Aunt Maryam's bedroom. I knew she felt bad waking him, but she didn't want to disrespect Grandpa.

After about five minutes, Aunt Maryam reappeared with a groggy, stumbling Rostam holding her hand and rubbing his eyes.

"There he is, come on over to *Baba* Behruz," Grandpa cried and opened his arms wide for Rostam. "This is no time for a nap, *pahlevoon*!" My dad and grandpa always called Rostam and me *pahlevoon*, which means "champ."

It made me feel invincible as a child.

Rostam let go of Aunt Maryam's hand and ran over to Grandpa Behruz.

"That's a good boy, give Grandpa a hug and kiss."

I sometimes envied Rostam. He had no responsibilities and no one expected anything from him. In fact, they pitied and coddled him. I wanted that, even for a day.

Rostam sat next to Grandpa Behruz for dinner and started chattering away about something that happened at school, sleep now the last thing on his mind. Even Uncle Eskandar seemed to warm up to him.

The adults ate in silence until Uncle Eskandar cleared his throat. You always knew he had something important to say when he cleared his throat; my father had the same habit and I think it was one of the few things they had in common.

"Well, I believe it's only right to pay our respects to Pari, who cannot be with us at this dinner table. May she rest in peace."

It was the first time my uncle had spoken that evening and I wasn't surprised to find it angered me, given my father and uncle's relationship. I couldn't keep my mouth shut.

"Thank you, *Amoo*, but it's not only my mother who cannot be here tonight," I said in a shaky voice. "*Baba* also cannot be with us."

I was furious with my father, sure, but I wasn't going to let anyone disrespect him in his own home and at his dinner table. I glanced over at Aunt Maryam, sitting to my right, but her head was bowed. She was not getting involved.

"I, for one, cannot bring myself to say he is missed," Uncle Eskandar said calmly, looking me straight in the eyes.

I took a drink of water to detach my tongue from the roof of my dry mouth.

"I apologize, *Amoo, bozorgtarami, ehteramet vajebe,* but I will not allow you to come into my father's home and disrespect him in his absence and in front of his children." My entire body was shaking.

Bozorgtarami, ehteramet vajebe translates to, "You are my elder, it's my duty to respect you." It's the respectful way to argue with an elder.

"Disrespect? Have I insulted him in any way? I am merely stating how I feel."

"You're assuming he's guilty before anything's been proven!"

"What would you have me do, hm? Praise him for what's he's done?"

"All right, enough!" Grandpa Behruz cried. "That's enough for tonight. Maryam *jan,* it's time we took our leave."

"So soon? I apologize, *Agha* Behruz, Cyrus didn't mean anything, he's young. Please stay for tea," Aunt Maryam pleaded, standing up and wringing her hands as she spoke.

"No, it's best we leave, thank you for the delicious dinner and for your hospitality."

Aunt Maryam shot a reproachful look my way and I lowered my head to avoid her eyes. I felt bad for ruining dinner, but not for what I said.

Grandpa Behruz hugged and kissed Rostam before getting up from the table. He then grabbed his cane, stood up with some effort, and ambled toward the entrance. It seemed this was my uncle's plan all along – to create a scene and then leave as soon as possible. He looked pretty happy with himself.

"Maryam *khanoom,* thank you for dinner," he said curtly and patted Rostam's head on his way to take Grandpa's arm.

"Have a good night," Aunt Maryam said in a dejected voice.

"Goodnight, *Baba-bozorg,*" I called, but he just grunted in reply.

Uncle Eskandar ignored me.

I didn't care. No matter my own issues with my father and no matter what he had done, it was my duty to stand up for him, especially when no one else would.

Forgive me, Maman. I had to.

Looking at Rostam, I once again wished we could trade places.

Chapter Five

Following the incident with Uncle Eskandar the night before, I planned on visiting my dad. I needed to speak with him alone, without Rostam and Aunt Maryam there.

When school let out for the day, I took the bus to the county jail where my father was being held while he awaited trial. I texted Aunt Maryam that I was staying after school to study at the library with Yiannis and would be getting a ride home from his mom. I felt bad about lying to her, but knew she would never allow me to visit my father by myself, even though I was on the jail's approved visitor's list for children under sixteen. Dad was allowed four visiting hours a month and we used the first one when we visited him last week.

After going through security, an officer led me down the long corridor toward the visiting area. The room appeared smaller than last time and I was even more nervous being there without Aunt Maryam and Rostam. I waited for about half-an-hour until they brought out my dad. He had a worried look on his face as he walked over to me.

"Cyrus, I wasn't expecting you! Is everything okay?" Giving me a quick hug, he pulled away and anxiously looked me up and down.

"Everything is fine, I just wanted to see you," I said, taking a seat on the blue plastic chair.

He wasn't convinced and looked at me, eyes narrowing.

"Are you sure? Where's Rostam and *Khaleh* Maryam?"

"I came here straight from school and I didn't tell *Khaleh* I was coming to visit you," I said.

"You must tell her where you're going at all times," he said, tapping the table with his index finger to emphasize each word. "She's your and Rostam's legal guardian now and you must do as she says."

"I knew she wouldn't let me come see you if I told her, so I said I was staying after school to study. I'll tell her I came to see you when I go home."

"Okay, well you're here now. What did you want to talk about?" he asked, leaning back in his chair and crossing his arms. I hated seeing him in the dull gray jail uniform. It matched the gray of his beard.

"*Baba-bozorg* and *Amoo* came over last night," I began. "*Amoo* started badmouthing you during dinner, so I told him he had no right to say those things about you in your house." I was afraid to look him in the eyes, so I just stared at my hands on the table, slick with sweat.

"You had no right to speak to your uncle like that, Cyrus."

I looked up, shocked.

"I didn't disrespect him, but I had to stick up for you."

"What has gotten into you, Cyrus? I didn't raise you to be disrespectful to your elders."

I couldn't believe my father was lecturing me right now, as if he had any right to. He needed to take a look at himself and where he was sitting before disapproving my actions. I bit my tongue and stayed silent.

"I know things are hard right now and I appreciate you sticking up for me," he said, his tone softening. Feeling guilty for my thoughts, I hung my head lower. I wanted to get up and run away from there, but I just sat on that chair, motionless. My father took my sweaty, limp hands in his.

"Look at me, *pesaram*." It felt good to hear my father call me "my son" again.

"I just miss her," I whispered, hot tears I could no longer hold back running down my face. I wiped them away with my sleeve.

"I do, too." My father's eyes glistened with tears, but they didn't fall to his cheeks.

Strong Persian men held their tears inside their eyes and never let them fall.

I looked up, anger getting the better of me again.

"And aren't you the cause of it all? You don't get to miss her when you took her away!"

"If my own son thinks I would do something so heinous, then I can't expect much from anyone else," my father said, putting his head in his hands. He was silent for a long time and then looked up, giving me a defeated look. "But I have faith the truth will come to light eventually." He wiped the corners of his eyes with his index finger and let out a deep sigh.

"Do you want me to leave?" I didn't know what else to say.

"No, I wanted to talk a little more about Cyrus the Great."

"Okay," I said, relieved by the subject change.

My father nodded, closed his eyes, and thought for a while before speaking.

"As you know, many rulers throughout history didn't marry for love, but had strategic marriages to strengthen their rule, gain heirs, and so on. There were, however, a few rulers who were actually in love with their queens, like Shah Jahan of India who built his Empress Mumtaz Mahal the Taj Mahal, and our very own Cyrus, who was so in love with Queen Cassandane Shahbanu that there was a long-lasting public mourning throughout the empire when she died."

"How did they meet?" I didn't really care, but felt obliged to say something and at least pretend like I was interested.

"Cassandane was a Persian noblewoman and it is said when Cyrus first saw her, he knew he had to make her his queen."

"So, what was so special about their love?"

"One day, shortly after Cyrus and Cassandane were married, Cyrus was scheduled to meet with important government officials and invited Cassandane to sit in on the meeting. Once all the officials had taken their seats, Cyrus and Cassandane both entered to sit at the head of the long table. All of a sudden, as soon as the men caught sight of Queen Cassandane, they began murmuring amongst themselves. Cyrus sat down, looked at the men, and asked, 'Gentlemen, what are you discussing in such hushed, yet alarmed tones before our meeting has even commenced?'"

"One of the older officials decided to speak up and said, 'O Great Cyrus, king of kings, we are respectfully questioning the presence of Queen Cassandane, though revered she is by us all, at such an important meeting of men. We do not believe this is the place for a woman, your majesty.'"

"Cyrus was silent for a moment as he contemplated his answer. He looked over at his regal queen who simply said, 'If it is your will, my king, I will leave.'"

"Cyrus then said, 'Listen well, gentlemen, for I will only say this once. It is my belief that without great women, there are no great men and that women should be treated as men's equals. It is as much my queen's right to be here as it is mine, so if you want her to leave, then I will also take my leave and you can carry on by yourselves. But if there are no further objections regarding this matter, let us begin our meeting.'"

"What did the officials say in response?" I asked.

"There was nothing to be said, and from that day forward, no one ever protested when the queen attended Cyrus' meetings with him."

"I guess she sounds pretty cool."

"Yes, but sadly Queen Cassandane passed away too soon. Cyrus never fully recovered from the grief of losing her and for nearly a decade after her death, he remained inactive."

"Did he remarry after Cassandane passed away?"

"No, they say the only cure for a heart in love is heartbreak, but there's really no cure for heartbreak except the passing of time," my father said, looking down at his hands. I knew he was thinking about Mom and he was hurting, like the rest of us.

"I'm sorry about what I said earlier," I mumbled. "You have as much right to miss her as we do and even though I don't know what happened between you two that day, I know you once loved Mom very much."

"I have never stopped loving her, not for a second."

"I wonder what she thinks of all this, looking down at us from heaven," I said, looking up at the low ceiling of the visitor's room in that stark building. Could she see us sitting there, her husband and her son, in a place where no one would have expected my father to end up?

There's a Persian saying, *Behesht zire paye madare*, meaning, "Heaven lies underneath the feet of the mother," but with Pari gone, we were far from it.

* * *

It started raining hard on the bus ride back and I prayed it wouldn't cause traffic and make me late getting home. To keep myself from stressing about the time and what Aunt Maryam was going to say, I tried to make sense of the conversation with my father.

I still couldn't figure out the connection between us and Cyrus' story. I knew Dad enjoyed telling stories, but even in this situation? Was it his way of coping? Of not having to speak about or face the truth? I wanted answers, but he gave me riddles. I thought maybe he'd be more willing to talk to me one-on-one and offer some sort of explanation, but instead I get ancient tales about people long gone. I could not break through his wall. All my life, my father used his stories to entertain, explain, and educate; to teach us life lessons. He used them to get closer to us. Now, he was using his stories to create distance and distract us. But distract us from what, exactly? The truth?

I was more confused now than I had been before the visit, but I couldn't give up on trying to understand. My father never did anything without a good reason or purpose, and no matter how hard it might be, I needed to be patient and have faith this would somehow lead me to answers. I felt the prick of tears and closed my eyes to keep them from falling.

When I was little, *Maman* used to tell me that when it rained, it meant all the angels in heaven were crying. She called raindrops *ashke pari*, or "angel tears." I wondered if some of the raindrops falling down now were her tears.

* * *

By the time I made it home, it was almost 7 p.m.

Although the distance from the bus stop to our building wasn't long, the rain slowed me down; I was dripping wet when I eventually walked inside the door, cold and exhausted. Aunt Maryam looked up from her phone and stopped typing.

"Cyrus! I was just texting you," she said, getting up from the dining room table where she sat across from Rostam. They were both in the middle of dinner.

"*Dadash* Cyrus is home!" Rostam cried with his mouth full, beating his spoon and fork together in celebration and getting food all over the seat and floor.

Aunt Maryam went over to the linen closet to get me a towel. "Where have you been and why are you soaking wet? Didn't Yiannis's mom drop you off? Change out of those clothes before you catch a cold."

She threw the towel over my head and started drying it vigorously. It reminded me of when I was younger and Mom used to towel-dry my hair after every bath or shower, humming softly to herself. Even though it kind of hurt, I didn't stop Aunt Maryam until she pulled the towel off my head and wrapped it around my shoulders.

"I'm sorry I'm late, *Khaleh*, but I didn't actually stay after school to study with Yiannis," I said, looking down at my soaked shoes when her expression changed from worry to anger. "I took the bus to visit *Baba*."

"By yourself? I told you to never go there alone, Cyrus! So, instead of listening, you lied?"

"I'm sorry, but I had to see *Baba* alone."

"I could've given you a ride and happily waited in the car while you visited with your father alone," she said, waving a hand up in exasperation. "You know I have no desire to visit him, anyway."

"I didn't want to trouble you and…" I began, but Aunt Maryam raised a hand to silence me.

39

"I don't want to hear excuses, Cyrus. I expected more from you as the man of the house. You're supposed to be your brother's role model."

"Well, I never asked for either of those roles!"

"Enough! Go change out of those wet clothes and come eat your supper."

"I'm not hungry," I said and grabbing my book bag off the floor, I walked out of the room.

* * *

After I changed, I sat at my desk and tried to focus on homework. With everything that was going on, my schoolwork was suffering and I was beginning to fall behind in classes. If it hadn't been for Aunt Maryam's insistence, I would have dropped out by now. It was only the beginning of the year and I had already lost all motivation and focus.

My teachers were also noticing the change and made comments either directly or on my work. I used to love school and was a straight-A student, but what did it matter now? Being an A student wouldn't bring my mother back from the grave or get my father out of jail.

But I knew I couldn't let Mom down; she had always been proud of my grades and how well I did in school. And no matter how much I hated the responsibility and pressure sometimes, I had to be better and if not for myself, then for Rostam. Amidst all this loss, I had to hold on to what remained.

Around 8:30, Aunt Maryam entered the room holding the hand of a sleepy Rostam. She helped him into his pajamas, tucked him into bed, and pulled the covers over him.

"Goodnight, *azizam*," she whispered, kissing Rostam's forehead. Without so much as a glance in my direction, she left the room.

Half an hour later, I was in the middle of struggling through my algebra homework when my phone vibrated. My heart began racing when I saw Tamara's name on my phone screen.

"Hey Cyrus, would you be able to meet me tomorrow after school for the interview?"

How could I make Aunt Maryam believe I was actually going to be staying after school this time after the stunt I pulled today? I thought for a few minutes, then started to type a response.

"Hey! Of course, but would it be alright if I let you know tomorrow where we can meet?"

My heart beat even faster while I waited for her response. Five minutes passed. Then ten.

Finally, my phone vibrated to life, bearing Tamara's name.

"Sure thing! See you then."

I had to apologize to Aunt Maryam and make peace with her if I wanted this interview to happen tomorrow. I threw aside my half-finished attempt at algebra and tiptoed out of the room. In the dark hallway, I made my way toward Aunt Maryam's bedroom, knowing she was still awake.

It was around this time that she had her nightly one-sided conversations with her dead sister.

Chapter Six

I listened outside the bedroom door for a few seconds before I knocked, praying she would answer.

There was a pause and then a muffled, "Come in." When I entered, Aunt Maryam was sitting up in bed, her back supported by a pillow, typing on her work laptop. Her glasses were perched on her nose, and looking up from the laptop screen, she stared at me from over the rims like an impatient schoolteacher.

"What is it, Cyrus? Is Rostam okay?" she asked.

"Rostam's fine, I just wanted to speak with you for a few minutes, *Khaleh*."

She was silent, waiting for me to go on.

"First, I wanted to say I'm sorry for lying to you today and promise it won't happen again," I said. "I'm sorry for how I acted tonight when I came home, too."

Aunt Maryam closed her laptop and folded her arms across her chest.

"I appreciate that, and you'll do your best to be honest with me from now on?" she asked, cocking her head to the side as a challenge.

"Yes, I'll do my best."

"Okay, apology accepted." I could see a faint smile pull at the sides of her mouth and knew this was my chance to tell her about Tamara and the interview.

"I wanted to also ask you if I could stay after school tomorrow for an actual school project," I braced myself as Aunt Maryam's eyes narrowed. "I know it's hard to believe me after what I did today, but I promise I'm telling the truth and I can even show you the texts between me and my partner."

"Let me see." She held out her hand for my phone, then hesitated and pulled it away. "Never mind, I hate asking you to show me evidence to prove your honesty, but you see what happens when you break my trust?"

I nodded and lowered my head to show her how sorry I was. "It won't happen again, *Khaleh*."

"It better not because I don't like being controlling," she said. "My parents used to treat me like that when I was a teenager and it made me resent them. I don't want the same thing to happen to us, *shir fahm shod*?"

This was the Farsi equivalent of "understood?" or "capisce?"

I nodded again.

"Now, instead of showing me your private texts, just tell me about your partner and this project."

I looked up at her and smiled to show how much I appreciated her trust in me. It made me all the more determined to never break it again. I then told her about Tamara and her project.

"Tam-ara? Is that a boy or girl name?" I tried to keep a straight face as she completely butchered the pronunciation of Tamara's name.

"Tamara's a girl name – she's a girl," I said, feeling my face getting hot. "She's my classmate and wants to interview me for her world history project, which is about the Persian culture."

"That's fine, but I think it would be better if you do the interview with her here," Aunt Maryam said. "I'm only showing one house tomorrow, so I'll be home by the time the school bus drops you both off."

I was afraid Tamara would think I was a loser if I had my aunt chaperone us while we worked on a school project. Then again, I didn't have much of a choice. It's not like I could tell Aunt Maryam I liked this girl and needed to make a good first impression. Not a chance in hell. I would just have to make the best of it and pray my aunt wouldn't embarrass me in front of Tamara.

"Okay, *Khaleh*, thank you."

"You're welcome," Aunt Maryam said. "*Shab bekheir.*"

"Goodnight."

* * *

I texted Tamara early the next morning, a Friday, asking if it would be okay for her to do the interview at my house after school. I checked my phone a number of times as I got ready, feeling nervous the longer she took to reply. Was she going to cancel, thinking I was weird or creepy?

As I headed out the door to catch the bus, I felt my phone vibrating in my pocket and opened the text without hesitation.

"Okay, no problem – I'm assuming I'll catch the bus home with you after school then?"

Smiling at the timeliness of her text, I waited until I got on the bus to text her back.

In biology, Yiannis would not stop talking about the interview.

"You have to try and remember everything I've taught you," Yiannis whispered excitedly, ignoring Mr. Becks's lecture on Punnett squares. "It has all come down to this day."

"Will you relax? We're doing the interview at my house," I said, rolling my eyes. "Nothing's happening."

"You still have to try to make some moves without your parents noticing."

"Yiannis, she's coming over for a school project, it's not a date! And I'm definitely not trying to come off as creepy or desperate."

"Mr. Anastas, Mr. Nezami, am I going to have to separate you two again?" Mr. Becks glared at us from the front of the room, his marker-wielding hand raised in mid-air, ready to scribble more notes on the dry-erase board. "Just so you're both aware, this is all going to be on this week's quiz, so I suggest you pay attention and start taking notes."

Yiannis made a face at me and started taking half-hearted, illegible notes while I distracted myself by jotting down everything Mr. Becks had put up on the board. I almost wanted the day to go by slower, feeling more and more like a fool for having accepted to do this whole thing in the first place.

The bus ride was less awkward than I thought. Tamara had this easy way about her that made it almost impossible to feel awkward when you were with her. She made effortless conversation and wanted to know me outside of just her project. I was careful not to mention anything about what was going on with my family – not now, anyway. What would she think if she found out? This was probably the worst time to become interested in a girl because once she finds out everything, she'll run off and I won't blame her.

"I hope you don't mind us doing the interview at my house," I said as we got off the bus.

"Not at all," Tamara said, with a wave of her hand. "It'll be nice to see where you live. The interview will have more of an authentic feel."

"Well, don't get too excited, it's nothing extravagant."

"I've been reading about how well-kept and tasteful Persian homes are, so don't even try to fool me," Tamara said with a grin.

"I hope our home lives up to your expectations, then."

"I'm sure it will."

When we entered the apartment, I could hear Aunt Maryam in the kitchen and realized introducing her would probably lead Tamara to ask where my mom was. It looked like I couldn't avoid talking about the situation altogether, so I figured if she did ask, I'd just say my mom passed away without getting into any specifics.

"Cyrus, is that you?" Aunt Maryam called from the kitchen.

"Hi, yes, we're here," I said and led Tamara toward the dining room table. Aunt Maryam emerged from the kitchen carrying a tray of tea and snacks and placed it on the table between us.

Tamara placed her book bag on the table and extended her hand to greet Aunt Maryam. "Hello, I'm Tamara, Mrs. Nezami, it's very nice to meet you." As I suspected, she naturally thought Aunt Maryam was my mother.

"Likewise, sweetheart. I'm Maryam, Cyrus' aunt," Aunt Maryam said, shaking Tamara's hand. There was a brief look of confusion on Tamara's face.

"Oh I'm sorry, I didn't realize…" she began, turning red.

"It's fine, I'm just like Cyrus' mother, it makes no difference. Anyway, I'll be in the kitchen if you need me. Good luck with your interview!" Aunt Maryam said with a smile and headed back to the kitchen. I breathed a sigh of relief. It went better than I thought.

But when Tamara turned to me with questioning eyes, I knew I had to offer her some explanation.

"I'm sorry I didn't tell you beforehand," I began, choosing my words carefully. "My mom passed away recently, so my aunt moved in with us." It felt strange to say the words, "My mother passed away." It was actually the first time I said it out loud and it felt unnatural. The knowledge of my mother being gone was one thing, but actually saying it – my larynx producing the sounds and my tongue forming the words – didn't feel right and I almost felt ashamed.

"Oh, I am so sorry to hear that, Cyrus," Tamara said, looking down at her hands.

"Thank you, it's fine," I said, avoiding her eyes. "I don't really like to talk about it much." I hoped by saying that, she wouldn't ask any further questions. I could tell she wanted to know more.

45

"Of course, I totally understand," she said, nodding her head. "Want to get started?"

"Definitely, but please eat something and drink your tea before it gets cold."

I then explained to her in detail the process of making traditional Persian tea and she was fascinated, taking notes and saying how perfectly it'll fit into her project. Tamara then asked about my family background, what it was like growing up in Iran, the challenges of being an immigrant, different aspects of our culture and traditions, our language, food, religious practices, and holidays.

I answered each question as best as I could. She had done her research and was very thorough; I was impressed.

I told her about our different quirks and personality traits, describing how expressive we are and how we make a lot of hand gestures when we talk. I even tried to explain and translate our many expressions and idioms.

"Half of Persian wisdom is in the accent alone; the way words are nuanced and enunciated. Particular syllables are emphasized and certain gestures are made that play into the meaning of their words. If you listen to someone with a thick accent, you'll know what I mean."

"Your aunt doesn't have an accent at all!" Tamara commented.

"Right, she's been here for a while and got her college degree here, but my father, uncle, and grandfather all have pretty thick accents."

Tamara asked a few more concluding questions to wrap up. It was almost 4:30 by the time we were done.

"This has been so great; I totally owe you!" Tamara said, gathering her things and putting them back in her bag. "You have an amazing culture, Cyrus, I'm so jealous!"

"I'm happy I could help, and thanks, but you really don't owe me anything," I said, still unable to hold her gaze.

"I think this was plenty of information, but if I need anything else, is it okay if we meet up again?" she asked, looking down to type into her phone.

"Of course, I'd love to," I said, sounding way too eager. "Do you need a ride home?"

"Nope, I just texted my mom. She should be here in about ten minutes or so."

"Great, I'll let my aunt know."

I was grateful to Aunt Maryam for having kept her distance and aside from bringing us a fresh supply of snacks, she stayed in the kitchen during most of the interview.

"*Khaleh,* Tamara is leaving," I announced, taking our snack tray over to the sink. Aunt Maryam was sitting at the little kitchen table chopping onions. Her eyes were wet and I couldn't tell if it was the onions or if she was actually crying.

"Okay, I'll be out in a minute," she said, wiping at her eyes with the back of her hand.

Tamara thanked Aunt Maryam for her hospitality and to my surprise, Aunt Maryam said she was welcome anytime, shook her hand, and walked us to the door.

Just as we walked out of the door to wait for Tamara's mom outside, we came face to face with Uncle Eskandar coming up the stairs.

"Hello, *Amoo,*" I mumbled, cursing my bad luck. He nodded his head at me and then stared at Tamara, scowling. "This is my classmate, Tamara."

The scowl didn't go away. He just looked at us with silent disapproval. Between him and my father, Uncle Eskandar was always the more conservative one.

"Hello," Tamara said and I could tell she was uncomfortable.

I wanted to dissolve into the hallway wall.

"This is my Uncle Eskandar, he lives with my grandpa in the downstairs unit," I said, desperate to ease the tension.

"Oh great, it's very nice to meet you, sir." Tamara seemed a little relieved to learn this stern-looking older man staring at her was related to me.

"Bringing girls over now, Cyrus," Uncle Eskandar finally spoke, shaking his head. "*Cheshme babat roshan.*" He was getting me back for the other night, but I'm glad he said the last sarcastic part – "Your father would be proud" – in Farsi. He knew I couldn't talk back to him now.

"We were working on a school project, but she's going to be late, so if you'll excuse us, we have to go," I said, and grabbing Tamara's hand, slid past my uncle's large frame on the stairs and climbed down to the main entrance.

"What was that all about?" Tamara asked, grinning.

"My uncle is a bit of a hard ass, don't worry about it," I said and realizing I was still holding onto her hand, loosened my grip and watched it swing back to her side. "I'm sorry for grabbing your hand like that."

"No biggie," she said. "Oh, and it looks like my mom's here already." She waved to a figure I couldn't make out in a parked silver minivan. "Thank you again for everything, Cyrus!"

I was surprised when she hugged me, remembering Yiannis telling me about the lingering hug rule and that if a girl hugged you for longer than three seconds, it meant it wasn't just a friendly hug – it meant she liked you.

I counted in my head, *one Mississippi, two Mississippi, three Mississippi, four Mississippi, five Mississippi*, and then she let go. Five seconds.

I waved as she got into the van, almost wishing my uncle had seen us hugging.

Chapter Seven

Because my father was in county jail, he was permitted to send emails to family members and every week, he sent me a new Cyrus story.

At first, I was a bit slow in reading his emails since he wrote in Finglish, which was typing out everything in Farsi using the English alphabet. It took a while to get used to, but it was the easiest way for us to communicate.

Despite my mother having taught me how to read and write in Farsi – which I now realize was one of the greatest gifts she could've given me, as it was a part of her, my mother tongue – I was still pretty rusty and preferred Finglish. Plus, I doubted the keyboards at the county jail had the Farsi alphabet.

I liked getting emails from my dad because it didn't involve the awkwardness of face-to-face visits and still allowed us to keep in touch. It was also nice to have a written record of his stories. Maybe if I read each one closely, I could find the answers to my questions.

"You have to read between the lines, Cyrus," my dad always told me.

I was going to take his advice.

His email that week intrigued me, and I read it up to three times, searching for clues.

Dear Cyrus,

I have another tale for you. I'm skipping ahead in the timeline of Cyrus' life a little, but I wanted to tell you this part of his story now. Read this one closely and if you have any questions, let me know.

– Baba

One day, Cyrus was returning home after a visit to his grandfather's kingdom. It was on this trip that Astyages revealed Cyrus' true heritage to him. He was warned prior to his trip that because many people now knew of his royal lineage, they would try and take advantage of him.

Along the way, Cyrus encountered three men. Two of them were bickering back and forth, while the third was sitting in isolation, minding his own business. Cyrus dismounted his horse and walked up to the men, asking if everything was alright. The two men ceased arguing and one of them said, "No, we have no food or money and because we are blind, we have no way of providing for ourselves. Could you please spare something to help us?"

Cyrus asked, "Do all blind men beg in groups?"

Then, the man sitting in isolation approached Cyrus and whispered in his ear, "The other two are not actually blind, but are taking advantage of my disability and the kindness of the travelers on this path. You should not give anything to them."

Cyrus thought for a moment and said, "Before I give any of you anything, I will find out who is blind and who is not." With their permission, he then proceeded to blindfold the three men. "I have three gold coins and I will place them at different points on the road. Only a true blind man can find the coins and bring them to me."

Cyrus removed all but three coins from his coin satchel and gave the rest to his travel companion, who was there for his protection. He walked to an area on the road and as he announced that he was placing the first coin, instead of actually placing it on the road, he put it back in his satchel. He walked to the second location and did the same with the second coin. Finally, he walked to the last spot on the road, made an announcement, and then dropped the coin back in his satchel.

Cyrus placed the satchel on his belt and walked back toward his horse. "The coins have all been placed. If you successfully bring me these coins, you will be rewarded with them," he said.

The two men who were bickering now began complaining. "How will we ever find these coins? We are blind and cannot see where you placed them." They began scouring the ground in random directions, feeling around for the coins.

Meanwhile, the third man, who was quiet all along, stood up and walked up to Cyrus. He reached his hand toward Cyrus' belt and said, "You did not place a single coin on the road." He grabbed Cyrus' satchel, reached in, and felt three coins. He gave the coins to Cyrus and said, "I believe these are the three coins you were referring to."

The other two men were amazed, but then their awe turned to anger. "How could you possibly have known he did that?"

The actual blind man responded, "I could hear the jangling of the coins in his satchel as he walked. The sound was not there after he supposedly placed the first coin, but once he announced placement of the second and third coins, the sound became apparent. Then with every step he made, I heard it get louder and louder until he stopped walking and told us all of the coins had been placed."

Cyrus was elated to find an honest man among the three. He offered him all of his coins, but the blind man respectfully declined and asked for just one coin, so he could have something to hold on to and remember Cyrus by. He promised he would never spend it. Cyrus agreed and placed one coin in the man's upturned palm, impressed by his valiant character.

From that day forward, Cyrus always stopped to have dinner with the blind man whenever he made the same journey, and each time the man would show Cyrus the coin he gave him as a symbol of their friendship, proving he was a man of honor and a man of his word.

After the third reading, I emailed my father back with some questions I had.

Hi Baba,

I read the story three times. I really enjoyed it, but wasn't able to figure out its significance. I know it has an important message about honesty, but other than that, I wasn't able to get much else from it. I know you're sending these stories to me for a reason, but I haven't been able to figure it out yet.

– Cyrus

My finger hovered over the mouse, unsure if I should send it or not. Would Dad be disappointed that I didn't grasp the story's deeper meaning or relevance? But he said I could ask questions and I was doing just that. I hit "send."

Instead of focusing on schoolwork, which I needed to catch up on, I kept refreshing my email every five minutes to see if Dad responded. After about half an hour, I got a new email from him:

Cyrus,

I wanted to share this story with you to show the importance of both honesty and judging people's character and to talk about an old family heirloom I was planning on giving you on your eighteenth birthday. It was passed down from my grandfather to Baba Behruz when he turned eighteen and then to me, right before he left for the U.S. It's an old gold coin from the Pahlavi era, but not quite as old as the coins in the story. It's in my bedside drawer and I want you to take it and keep it. It is yours now.

I think it'll be okay if I break with tradition a bit and give it to you a few years before your eighteenth birthday. Keep it as something to remember me by, especially now that I can't physically be with you. Look at it as a memento of happier times – a keepsake between father and son. And although it may have substantial monetary value, I want you to remember that some things are priceless and worth much more than money in this world.

This is something the actual blind man in our story knew and practiced well. Follow his example: don't seek the coin – or anything else for that matter – only for the coin's sake. Seek the deeper value behind it. Seek generosity over greed. Seek honesty over deceit. Seek justice and don't pass judgment until you know the whole truth. Always seek the honorable path and you'll be rewarded for it. The other two men wanted to deceive Cyrus and in turn, received nothing. The blind man was honest and humble and in turn earned Cyrus' trust and lifelong friendship.

Let me know if you can't find the coin in my drawer and I'll suggest a few other places you can look. I can't remember for sure where I put it.

– Baba

I figured I'd reply back once I found the coin.

Aunt Maryam had gone shopping with Rostam, so I had the whole apartment to myself for a while and could search for the coin in peace.

Although no one was home, I still tip-toed to my parents' room, which I avoided ever since my mother died. I wasn't sure I was prepared to enter it now.

Would I be ready to face the memories? What if it still smelled like her?

The spaces my mother occupied in our home were now filled with her absence and I sometimes felt unable to exist within them without her. Every inch of our small apartment – the living room, kitchen, dining room – all contained the imprint of her memories. The spaces she lived and breathed in now magnified her absence as if to mock us. Living and breathing in these spaces without her felt unnatural, like learning how to walk for the first time. It still baffled me that it was something I had to just get used to – having to go on existing without my mother. My mother, who was partly the source for my very existence, who carried me within herself, nourished me with her own being, and then pushed me into this world. Now I was just expected to live without my life-giver? How?

Even though it was hazy, I remember the two weeks following the incident and the week-long police investigation. Aunt Maryam had gone through my parents' bedroom and cleaned out my mother's belongings in anger.

She said it was no longer my mother's room.

"I don't want a scrap of her things in this room! How could you, Sohrab? My poor sister! My poor Pari!" she fumed as she tore clothes off hangers and threw them into black trash bags.

All of my mother's belongings were now sitting in seven trash bags in the corner of Aunt Maryam's room. She didn't have the heart to take them out or give them away, which I understood, but I also didn't like the idea of my mother's belongings in trash bags. I wanted to take her clothes out of the bags, breathe in her scent, and fold them as neatly as she folded our clothes countless times. I was afraid of forgetting her scent or what she looked like, but remembering was still too painful. It was almost therapeutic to forget. Forget she was forever gone and instead think she was on a long trip with an unknown return date.

I planned to ask Aunt Maryam if she needed help moving Mom's things into boxes or a storage unit. Or maybe she wanted to give them away. They just didn't belong in those hideous black bags.

Reaching the closed door of my parents' bedroom, I stood facing it for a few minutes, trying to convince myself to go inside. Aunt Maryam and Rostam would probably be home soon. I didn't have much time. I placed a shaking hand over the cold knob and turned it.

The room was dark. Still. I didn't want to turn on the lights and disturb anything. Feeling like an intruder, I went inside, leaving the door open for the hallway light to cast a dim pool inside the room. My parents' bed loomed in front of me like a black boulder. Forcing my eyes to focus only on my father's side, I walked over to his bedside table. Using my phone's flashlight, I opened the little drawer.

Inside the cluttered drawer were old pieces of notepaper, letters, and other miscellaneous objects. My father was a hoarder – he held on to everything, claiming they would someday be useful. He hated discarding things and referred to himself as a collector of stories.

"Everything has value, everything holds a memory," he would say. "Even the smallest, most seemingly useless object has a story to tell."

I shuffled around until I came across a small velvet jewelry box hidden underneath a pile of old letters. Placing my phone on the table, I opened the box and found a quarter-sized gold coin sitting on the white satin lining. I traced the golden head of the Shah with my finger, then held my phone up to the coin to get a closer look. It was a smooth, solid gold coin with the head of Shah Mohammad Reza Pahlavi on the front and on the flipside, the Pahlavi monarchy's *Shiro Khorshid* – the Lion and Sun – emblem, which depicts a lion brandishing a sword in its right paw with the sun shining behind it. I was lost in the intricate details of the coin until I glanced at the time on my phone screen. Aunt Maryam would be home any minute.

I placed the coin back inside the velvet box and closing it with a snap, shoved it in my back jean pocket. As I put the pile of letters back inside the drawer, my eyes caught sight of a line written in Farsi: *Taghdim be eshgham*, Pari.

"To my love, Pari."

I realized these were the letters my parents wrote to each other when they were still dating back in college. My mom once told me because their families were against their relationship, they planned secret meetings and exchanged long letters that they wrote to each other every week since they couldn't talk on the phone.

"Don't take this whole mobile phone and texting thing for granted, Cyrus," *Maman* once joked. "Your dad and I would've killed for that kind of technology when we were young."

Without thinking, I grabbed the bundle of letters, closed the drawer, and hurried out of the room, remembering to shut the door behind me. Just as I was walking back to me and Rostam's room, I heard the jingling of keys, so I hurried inside and shut the door. I didn't hear Rostam's voice when Aunt Maryam walked in and figured he had stayed outside to play with the neighbors' kids before it got dark, which was a good thing because he would've barged into our room by now asking me to play with him.

I felt a little guilty for wanting to read my parents' private letters, but maybe my father had meant for me to find them, too? Maybe they would provide some answers? Even though my Farsi was rusty, especially in reading, I was still grateful for it. *Maman* made sure both me and Rostam wouldn't forget our mother tongue when we came to the U.S. She brought stacks of Farsi workbooks with her and gave us lessons on the weekends. Since Rostam was too young for writing lessons, she gave him simple speaking exercises. When I asked why I had to write out dictations, *Maman* told me just knowing how to speak Farsi wasn't enough – that we had to learn how read and write it, as well – and that as soon as Rostam was older, he would also be getting writing lessons.

"You may look at this now as extra, unnecessary work and think it's unfair that I'm making you do this on your weekends, but believe me, it's necessary and you'll thank me later," *Maman* used to say whenever I complained about all the work and how it felt like I was going to two schools with double the schoolwork. But as always, she was patient with me.

"Cyrus, Farsi is your mother tongue, it's the language you were born to learn. You have to honor it and learn it properly."

I wish my mother were here now to scold me about learning Farsi. I'd give anything to sit with her if just for an hour and write as many dictations in Farsi as she wanted.

When I was sure Aunt Maryam had gone into the kitchen to start dinner, I walked over to my desk and tucked the velvet box all the way in the back of the top drawer. Once I made sure the coin was safely put away, I turned my attention to the letters. Heart pounding, I pulled the top letter out of the rubber-banded bundle and placed it in the middle of my open history textbook, so if Aunt Maryam walked in, she'd think I was doing homework.

Unfolding the lined paper, I was surprised to find the second-half of the letter was written in English and in my father's curved, delicate handwriting was a poem:

When she danced, time decelerated,
and I was captivated by the
movements translating her heart.
Synchronized to the beat of the tombak,
the metronome of her soul,
ticking back and forth and back.
Our first embrace was by chance,
just as Pluto chased Neptune's elusive dance,
with moves tracing my heart.
A crossing of two celestial paths,
the momentum of our souls,

moving back and forth and back.
I dream about our wedding day,
when we'll sway to the drumbeat
of our joined hearts.
This dance binds us as one,
merging fabrics of our souls,
weaving back and forth and back.

My mother majored in English in college and her passion for the language and for English literature was one of the reasons she wanted to live in the U.S. I was moved by the poem and smiled despite myself, as it was obvious Dad knew just how to impress her; his love for her was evident even in that first letter.

Something else was also evident.

A man who knew such beautiful words and wove them together to create beautiful sentences and stories was incapable of killing.

Chapter Eight

Yiannis couldn't hold back his enormous grin as I walked into biology Monday morning.

"Wow, you're actually early for once," I said, feigning surprise. I sat down next to him and waited for the interrogation to begin.

"I couldn't wait to hear all the dirty details of your little interview," Yiannis said, putting air quotes around "interview."

"As much as you'd like to think otherwise, it actually was an interview. For a school project. At my house. With my aunt in the kitchen, bringing us snacks. I mean, it was a regular porn flick setup."

"Okay whatever, so how was it?"

"It went really well and she said she'd let me know if she needs more information," I said. "And before she left, she gave me a long—"

"Oh my God, you guys kissed?" Yiannis interrupted.

"Keep your pants on, we just hugged."

"Well, that's the gateway to kissing territory, she totally wants you." Yiannis raised his hand for a high-five. I shook my head at him.

I was a bit worried Tamara wouldn't need to do another interview. And then what? Would I text her and ask if she wanted to hang out? Did she even want to be friends and interact beyond this project? I had zero experience dealing with girls. My only source of reference was Yiannis and that didn't reassure me much. He was mostly interested in a girl's looks and the physical interaction, and although I can't say that wasn't important to me, I more so wanted to get to know Tamara for now.

There was no reason to rush anything, especially with how complicated my life was at the moment. She hadn't texted me yet about meeting again and I didn't have much hope she would. Maybe it was for the best, but I couldn't help feeling disappointed.

After class was over, I was walking out of the room with Yiannis when Mr. Becks called my name.

"Could you hang back for a bit, Mr. Nezami?"

I told Yiannis he could go on and I'd catch up with him later. I knew what Mr. Becks wanted to talk to me about: my close-to-failing biology grade. I braced myself.

After shuffling a few papers around and waiting for the last student to leave, Mr. Becks removed his glasses and looked up at me.

"Cyrus, I'm a bit concerned about your performance in my class and I wanted to discuss it with you now while it's still early enough in the school year to bring up your grade."

Aside from Tamara, no one else at school knew what was going on with my family and even she knew very little. I hadn't even told Yiannis yet, but now that Tamara knew, it somehow felt like I was betraying him.

After it happened, I missed school for a week and asked Aunt Maryam to write an absence note saying I had a stomach bug. I even had her sign it in my mother's signature so no one would ask any questions. I didn't want to explain or worse, be pitied. We stayed at a nearby hotel for that entire week while the investigation took place and our house was taped off.

So, what could I say now? I didn't want to use my mother's death as an excuse, but the truth was I was burnt out and couldn't focus on school. I didn't want to come off as a slacker and wanted my teachers to understand I wasn't just being lazy or blowing off school for the hell of it. My mother was dead, my family was broken, and I was doing my best to just hold still while everything around me spun out of control.

"I understand, Mr. Becks, but I'm going through a lot with my family right now and it's been hard to keep up with school," I said, the words coming out before I knew what I was saying. "I'll try my best to catch up in class and raise my grade."

"Well, I'm sorry to hear that, is there anything I can do?" Mr. Becks placed his glasses back on the bridge of his nose, as if he could convey his concern to me more if his eyes were seeing better.

"No, but I appreciate it and if there's anything I can do to help my grade, please let me know," I said, picking up my book bag from the vacant desk I had placed it on to signal I was done with the conversation.

"I will and I hope everything works out with your family," Mr. Becks said, removing his glasses again.

"Thanks, have a good day." I hurried out, almost bumping into Yiannis on my way out.

"I said you could go ahead."

I didn't want to talk to anyone for the rest of the day and that included my best friend.

"I'll take any excuse to show up to class late," Yiannis said, throwing his book bag over his shoulder. "What did the Beckster want?"

"Oh, you know, just wondering why I'm failing his class."

"What'd you say? And what was that I heard about family problems?"

"Thanks for eavesdropping, man. Anyway, my mom passed away about a month ago, right after school started," I said, and it still felt strange to say it out loud. "So, as you can imagine, it's been a little difficult focusing on school."

Yiannis stopped walking and stared at me, stunned. It was probably the last thing he was expecting to hear.

"Cy, I had no idea—"

"Can we please not talk about it? And don't mention it to anyone," I said, quickening my pace.

"Sure, man."

We walked in silence for the rest of the way. I kept my head down as we entered Mrs. Miller's classroom, not wanting to make eye contact with Tamara or anyone else. I wanted to focus on the lesson and discussion. English was probably the only class I wasn't failing. Yet.

Reading and writing essays were never my forte, but I enjoyed English. I liked that there was never just one correct answer and you could interpret a literary theme or metaphor differently than someone else in a way that made sense to you. Last week, we started our Shakespeare unit and although I struggled to understand Shakespeare well, I tried my best to at least read the plays we were assigned. I did know the themes of mistaken identities and how nothing is as it seems were present in a lot of his works.

Just as I expected, Mrs. Miller was tough; we had already finished reading *Othello* and were discussing the final scene, where Othello kills Desdemona in a jealous rage, convinced she was being unfaithful to him. I had never hated a fictional character as much as I hated Iago. Here was an honorable man so in love with his wife and yet because of the poisonous words of a man he considered a trusted friend, he ended up killing his wife and then himself. Granted, I didn't read much, but the books I'd read hadn't impacted me as much as *Othello*. I think it's because I related to it, in a sense.

I only hoped I would eventually relate to my father's Cyrus stories as much as I did to *Othello*.

Yiannis kept his distance for the rest of class and once the bell rang, he gave me a quick nod goodbye and walked out. I didn't blame him; he sensed I didn't want to talk and gave me space until I was ready. Or maybe he didn't know what to say.

Deep in thought, I was dropping my stuff inside my backpack when I felt a gentle tap on my shoulder. I turned around, surprised to find Tamara facing me with a shy smile.

"Hey, Cyrus," she said, adjusting her book bag on her shoulders. "I just wanted to thank you again for helping me out with my project."

"Oh, sure thing, I was happy to do it."

I zipped up my bag and followed her out of the classroom.

"You might not be too happy though, 'cause I may need to interview you again, if that's okay," she said, pulling at the tip of her braid nervously.

I smiled. "Of course, I don't mind at all."

"Great, I'll text you about when we can meet. The project is due in two weeks, so we still have plenty of time."

"Sounds good, looking forward to it," I said, wondering where her next class was so I could offer to walk her.

"Yeah right, as if the first one didn't bore you to tears," Tamara laughed, her hand pulling at her braid again. It seemed to be a nervous tick. Was she nervous around me?

"No way! Where are you headed to next?" I slowed down so she could take the lead.

"Oh, it's just down the hall," she said, pointing. "Biology with Mr. Becks."

"He's my homeroom teacher," I said. "I can walk you over."

Before she went inside, Tamara gave me another hug.

* * *

When I got home, I was in a better mood, both from my encounter with Tamara and a text Yiannis sent at the end of the day. He said he was sorry for my loss and although he understood why, wished I had told him sooner, adding he was there for me if I needed anything or just to talk. I texted back thanking him and told him he was a good friend.

With my mind at ease, I grabbed a snack from the kitchen and sat in front of my laptop to respond to my dad's email.

Dear Baba,

Thank you for your explanation – it really resonated with me. I also wanted to let you know I found the Pahlavi coin. Thank you for trusting me with it. I promise to take good care of it. Looking forward to more stories.

My fingers hovered over the keyboard and I debated whether I should tell him about the letters I found along with the coin. How would I even word it?

By the way, I'm reading your and Mom's private letters. Maybe they'll help me figure out why you killed her.

I decided to keep it to myself for now and figured I could always tell him later, ending the email with inquiries about his health and if he needed anything.

Just as I closed my laptop, I heard the front door slam and raised voices in the living room. It sounded like Rostam was crying and Aunt Maryam was trying to calm him down. I hurried out to see what was going on.

"Hey, what's wrong? You okay, Rostam?" I walked over to the living room couch where Aunt Maryam was sitting, her coat and shoes still on, holding Rostam and rubbing his back. He had his face buried in her chest and his tiny frame shook from the loud sobs.

"Don't worry, Cyrus, he's fine," Aunt Maryam said, kissing the top of Rostam's hair-matted forehead. "Some of his classmates teased him a bit today, that's all." I could tell Aunt Maryam was putting on a brave face for us, but her own eyes were teary.

"Who was it? And what did they say?" I felt my ears getting hot.

"It was Mikey!" Rostam yelled, jerking his head around, his face red. "He told me I smelled bad and then asked why my mom wasn't bathing me, so I told him she was gone and he said it was probably because she was sick of me and then everyone laughed."

I was tempted to call Mikey's parents right then. But seeing my little brother sitting in my aunt's lap, sobbing and shaking, broke my heart and I realized I needed to comfort him first. I went over to him and kneeled down so we were face to face.

"Come here, *Dadashi*," I said, calling him by the nickname we used for each other. He climbed into my arms and buried his hot face in the crook of my neck. I rocked him back and forth while I contemplated what to say to him.

"You know, kids your age can say pretty hurtful things without knowing it," I began, not yet sure where I was going with it. "You'll always have me and *Khaleh* Maryam to take care of you and as for *Maman*, her going away had absolutely nothing to do with you. She loved you the most."

Rostam raised his head to look at me. "Really?" I could see a faint smile making its way to his lips.

I nodded.

"So, why did she leave? Where is she now?"

After the incident, Aunt Maryam told Rostam *Maman* Pari wasn't feeling well and had to go away for a while, like *Baba* Sohrab. Rostam cried for days, asking why Mom and Dad weren't coming back. Eventually, he calmed down and grew accustomed to our parents' absence, but his fears and questions transformed into frequent night terrors that made him bolt upright in bed, screaming and crying out for our mother.

Even though I didn't want to be the one to tell him, maybe it was time to at least give him some closure; make him understand Mom wasn't coming back. It was unfair and cruel of us to say nothing and keep him hoping that maybe someday she would come back.

I gave Aunt Maryam a reassuring look before answering my brother's question.

"Rostam, *Maman* is in heaven now, okay? Remember when Aunt Maryam told you she wasn't feeling good here? Well, God took her to heaven where she could feel good. And I'm sure she's looking down on you, on us, right now and missing us very much. So, even if you can't see her, she's around and can see you. Do you understand?"

Rostam gave a slow nod.

I continued, "God didn't have enough angels with him in heaven, so he asked if Mom wanted to be one of his angels. Her name means 'angel,' after all. She couldn't say 'no' to God and she wanted to feel better, so even though it was really, really hard for her to leave us, she had no choice. But that doesn't mean she loves us any less or doesn't miss being home with us. She knows we'll get to be with her in heaven one day."

Rostam's tear-stained eyes were now wide as he looked at me, blinking with every word I said as if it could help him understand better.

"She can hear us, too?" Rostam asked.

"Of course, you can tell her anything you want and she'll hear you," I said. "But since she's all the way up in heaven, it's hard for us to hear her, so if you ask her something and it seems like she's not answering, just know that she is and you just aren't able to hear her."

The faint smile on Rostam's lips grew. "I can talk to her every night and she'll listen?"

"She's always listening, *Dadashi*," I answered, kissing the top of his curly mass of hair. "And Aunt Maryam's going to speak with your teacher and Mikey's parents to make sure he won't tease you anymore, okay? Just promise me you won't cry like that again because we need to be strong for *Maman*."

"I promise," he mumbled, giving me a hug. When he pulled away, his face was lit up with a full smile.

"Now, go get changed and I'll make you a snack!" I handed him his book bag and he ran off to our room.

I looked up at Aunt Maryam and noticed she had tears in her eyes. I placed my hand on her shoulder and she pulled me into her arms.

"Thank you for being such a wonderful brother to Rostam," she whispered. "Pari would be proud."

"We're all he has now," I said, trying to fight back my own tears. "He shouldn't have to be dealing with any of this."

Aunt Maryam nodded, picked up her purse, and made her way to her own bedroom. "None of us should be dealing with this," she mumbled more to herself than to me.

I wondered if she knew I could hear her talking to my mother every night, asking her for guidance like she did when they were growing up. Aunt Maryam was seven years younger than my mother, who affectionately referred to Maryam as her *abji koochike,* or "little sister." They were very close despite the age difference and my mother often told us stories about them when they were young; about how she was always getting Maryam out of trouble.

"You were the troublemaker out of the two of us! Mom and Dad were constantly grounding you," Mom joked with her whenever Aunt Maryam visited us, or the two times we went to see her in Florida before she moved here.

"And you were their perfect angel," Aunt Maryam retorted. "No wonder they named you Pari, it's such a goody-two-shoes name."

"Oh, and Maryam isn't? You were only named after the Virgin Mary."

"They couldn't have been more wrong naming me after her!"

And they burst into laughter.

Mom never went into much detail, but the reason Aunt Maryam came to the United States was because of a falling out she had with their parents about a year after my mother and father got married. Maryam, ever the outgoing and flirtatious one, started dating at eighteen, and naturally, her parents didn't approve. She felt left out and lonely after my mother moved out, so when she got accepted at Tehran University, she met and fell in love with an older boy in one of her classes.

Naturally, her parents didn't approve. University is the only education system in Iran that's co-ed, making it easier for girls and boys to meet and date each other. My grandparents lived outside of Tehran and it was hard to keep an eye on Maryam once she left home for college.

One weekend, my grandparents paid Maryam a surprise visit and saw her with the boy. They had no idea who he was and seeing that he was a few years older than Maryam, my grandfather flew into a rage and forbade her from seeing him again, certain he was only taking advantage of his naive daughter. But Aunt Maryam, stubborn and headstrong, continued seeing him. When my grandparents found out, they decided the best solution was to send her to the U.S. so she could forget about him.

Excited for the chance to get away from her conservative parents and have complete freedom in a country where she could date whomever she wanted, Maryam became preoccupied with planning her trip and soon began ignoring her lover. When he realized how serious she was about moving away and got tired of getting the cold shoulder, he eventually stopped calling on her.

Whenever something goes wrong for a family in Iran, many of them think packing up and going abroad, especially to the U.S., will solve everything. They place all their hope in having a fresh start in a new country, hundreds of miles away from their ancient homeland that gives its people several thousand-year-old roots.

It took Maryam months to gather her documents and apply to a number of American universities. When the first one in Florida accepted her, she was able to easily acquire an F1 visa through some of her parents' family connections and on her last day, she sobbed in my mother's arms during the entire car ride to the airport.

She may have been ready to leave everything else, but she wasn't ready to leave her older sister.

The separation took an even bigger toll on my mother and when my parents were debating whether we should move to the U.S. or not, one of their main deciding factors was Mom's longing for Maryam.

* * *

Later that night, I was getting ready for bed when my phone vibrated with a text from Tamara.

"Hey! Interview round 2 next Saturday?" I smiled, noticing the smiley-face emoji she included with her text.

"Hey there, I don't know if that'll give me enough time to prepare. Just kidding, that sounds good. Looking forward to it." I reread the text about ten times before hitting "send."

"Haha, can't wait."

When I walked back to the bedroom after brushing my teeth, I heard Rostam's voice, still soft with childish fragility. At first, I thought he was talking to himself, but then realized he was addressing *Maman* Pari. I stood behind the door to listen.

"And I'm sorry I didn't talk to you sooner, but that's only 'cause Cyrus told me today about where you are and how you can still see me and hear me. I wish you weren't so far away, but I'm glad you're an angel now. It must be so cool to fly. I promise to talk to you every night and be a good boy, so we can come see you in heaven one day. I love you, *Maman, shab bekheir.*"

Through the crack in the door, I saw him kissing the palm of his little hand and then raising it toward the ceiling.

Rostam slept soundly the whole night.

Chapter Nine

My mother has been dead for forty days.

In the Persian culture, we honor the seventh – *haftom* – and fortieth – *chehelom* – days after a person's passing, as well as the one-year anniversary – *saal*. But the *chehelom* is the day we're supposed to officially say goodbye to our loved one and accept their passing.

Close family members of the deceased are expected to wear black until the one-year mark; however, it's custom for other family members and friends to bring them out of mourning on the fortieth day by gifting them bright-colored clothes to encourage changing out of their black or dark-colored ones.

Aunt Maryam didn't want me to wear black past the seventh day because of school. I told her I was going to continue wearing black until the one-year anniversary.

"Children aren't even expected to wear black like adults, it's not appropriate," my aunt argued.

"I'm not a child, *Khaleh*, she was my mother and I have to respect tradition."

"We no longer live in Iran where these traditions matter so much," she said, blinking rapidly – something she did whenever she was irritated. "No one's going to judge you for not wearing black and besides, I thought you didn't want anyone at school to know about this."

"Most people think black's the only color Persians own in their wardrobe, anyway, so I don't think anyone's going to notice."

Aunt Maryam sighed. "Fine, do what you want, but don't make a big show of it in front of Rostam. He's having a hard time with all this as it is."

I wore black for two weeks straight until I ran out of black or dark-hued shirts to wear and could no longer get away with wearing the same shirt a couple of days in a row.

I found out it was a lot harder to wear black for forty days straight and gave up, but I still avoided wearing anything too colorful. When Aunt Maryam noticed

I was wearing other colors again, she reassured me two weeks was more than enough and sometimes, it was hard even for her to stick to it.

Now that it was the fortieth day, I was giving my aunt a pale blue shirt I bought her to change out of her own dark clothes. The week before Mom's fortieth ceremony, I asked Yiannis if his mom could drive us to the mall after school so I could buy her the shirt. I wasn't sure if it was the right size or if she would like the style, but I tried to buy something similar to her clothing style and knew her favorite color was blue.

Per my father's request, Aunt Maryam gave me a weekly allowance of $20 for my expenses. I saved up two weeks' worth of allowance to make sure I had enough to buy the shirt. When I got home from the mall, I placed the shirt in a gift bag, put tissue paper over it, and hid it in my closet. I planned on giving it to her after the fortieth ceremony.

I woke up early that morning, a Saturday, to help Aunt Maryam with preparations. She was already up making *halva* – the traditional dessert for funerals and mourning – and the warm, nutty smell permeated the apartment. I wondered whether *halva* was chosen as the dessert for mourning because of its dark-brown color and the fact that when you hold a sticky piece of it between your fingers, whispering a prayer for the soul of the departed before eating it, would the prayer stick to it better and be transported safely to the person's soul?

Whenever we're eating something and missing a loved one who's passed away, we say, *"Berese be roohesh"* – "May it reach his or her soul."

It's yet another small comfort, a way of bridging the boundless gap between the dead and the living.

Our ceremony for Mom was going to be a small and quiet ordeal; around noon, Grandpa Behruz and Uncle Eskandar would come over for some tea and *halva* and then we were going to drive over to the cemetery to visit my mother's grave and pray for her.

When I walked into the living room, the first thing I spotted was the wooden frame with my mother's picture sitting on the dining room table next to the fresh trays of *halva* and a vase of delicate white flowers Aunt Maryam had probably bought last night. There was a thick, black ribbon taped around the top right-hand corner of the frame. My mother smiled at me from the picture. Her dark, curly hair framed her round face with the dimpled chin and large brown eyes. My mother must've been in her mid-twenties when the picture was taken.

I hadn't been back to the cemetery since the day we buried her. We'd decided to take Rostam to the funeral, but he wasn't exactly aware of what was going on. We didn't mention anything about Mom, but he did connect our parents' absence with the somber ceremony.

"Why is everyone crying? Why are they so sad?" he asked me several times that day.

It wasn't easy to explain the concept of death to a five-year-old. I wasn't sure even I understood it.

"Sometimes even grown-ups need to cry to feel better," was all I managed to say. I was still in a daze. It felt like everything was happening around me at lightning speed, pulling me along with it against my will.

"Is it because *Maman* is sick, like you said?" he persisted.

"Yes, everyone is praying for her to get better."

"Is *Baba* with her now?"

"Yes, Rostam." I was starting to lose patience.

"When will they come back?"

"I don't know, Rostam! Please, you have to be quiet."

* * *

My mother died on the first day of autumn, her passing like the leaves falling from the tree of our lives all at once. Leaves that will never grow back, leaving us barren and in a perpetual winter.

I've often thought one of man's greatest punishments is the ability to remember. Memories are a curse. Even if they're pleasant memories, they'll still leave you longing for things and people in the past, of moments long gone. The very act of remembering reminds us of loss.

The day it happened was a bright September morning. It was still warm, but I could smell fall in the air. For some reason, I was anxious to get home. Usually, Mom texted me every day around lunchtime to ask how my day was going, but I hadn't heard from her all day. It didn't worry me too much and I figured she had gotten busy with work.

Because of her excellent English, my mother had no trouble finding a job when we first moved here and worked for a company that offered various interpretation and translation services. Her job was contract-based and when she first applied to the company, they snatched her up as soon as they found out she was fluent in Farsi. Her assignments varied from offering interpretation services at local hospitals and clinics between patients and doctors to translating government documents. She loved her job, especially because it was flexible and she could work remotely most of the time.

When I got home, I thought the bus must've dropped me off at the wrong apartment building. Surely, the cop cars and ambulance weren't parked in front of my home and the yellow "Do Not Cross" police tape was meant for another building. There had to be a mistake. A false alarm. I was grateful Rostam was at his after-school program and wouldn't be home until later. Taking my phone out of my bag, I called my mom.

No answer.

I called again.

No answer.

My heart beat faster with every ring.

No answer.

I called my dad.

No answer.

I wasn't sure if I could go inside, but I couldn't just stand out there, either. A couple of our neighbors were peeking from windows or standing on terraces to find out what was happening at our building; I ignored them. I had just about made up my mind to go inside when I saw Grandpa Behruz coming out, speaking to a police officer. His eyes were looking around nervously until he saw me. He said something to the police officer, the officer nodded, and then he signaled for me to go over to them. I didn't want to believe it, but I already knew something terrible had happened from the look on Grandpa Behruz's face.

They had already taken my mother's body away by then. I remember Grandpa Behruz's lips moving, his mouth forming the words, "Your mother is dead," but I did not comprehend.

I kept shaking my head, saying, "No, no, no, no." I tried to push my way past the two cops holding me back, yelling that I needed to go inside to see my mom. When they threatened they'd have no choice but to handcuff me if I didn't stop, I finally gave up and sank down to the ground, my legs collapsing underneath me, as Grandpa patted my back. I didn't even get to see my father before they took him into custody.

It felt as though my parents disappeared from our lives in half a day and I had no say in the matter. Everything was explained to me and I had to accept them as facts: "Your mother is dead. Your father has been arrested."

How do you even begin to argue with that?

My entire body felt numb and all I could do was lay on the cold grass, yelling for my mother and father over and over until there was a ringing in my ears and everything went dark.

I awoke in a dimly-lit room with my head pounding and someone speaking softly to me. I opened my eyes and saw my mother's face.

It had been a nightmare after all, I thought. But it wasn't her voice I was hearing, and what she was saying didn't make any sense. After a few seconds passed, I realized it was Aunt Maryam, eyes red from crying. I had awoken to the nightmare and everything rushed back to me with such force that my head began spinning again, making me nauseous. I looked around the foreign room in a sudden panic.

"We're at a hotel, *azizam,*" Aunt Maryam whispered, blowing her nose. "The police have to investigate, so we're staying here for a week. Grandpa Behruz and Uncle Eskandar are in the room next to ours with Rostam so your grandpa can distract him. I didn't want the poor thing to see us like this."

More words that didn't make sense.

"Investigate what?" My own voice, coated by grief, startled me. It sounded as if I hadn't spoken for years. It pushed up from my tight throat, crammed inside my mouth, and spilled out in fragments. It felt as if everything inside my body was broken, even my voice.

"Pari was—" Aunt Maryam paused, trying to steady her voice and hold back her tears. She drew a deep breath and let it out slowly, then said, "Pari was killed and your father's the main suspect. He was sitting near her body when the police got to your house, covered in her blood – that's all they would tell me. I'm so sorry, Cyrus *jan.*" She buried her crumpling face into a crumbled-up piece of tissue.

I didn't know what I could possibly say – there was no room left inside my mouth for the heavy, boundless words of loss – so I stayed silent and cried in the arms of the woman who looked so much like my mother that it broke my heart even more.

* * *

70

The loud knock on our door pulled me away from my thoughts and I was glad for the distraction until I realized it was probably Grandpa Behruz and Uncle Eskandar. I hadn't seen or spoken to Uncle Eskandar since he ran into me and Tamara on the stairs. It was only 9:30 and they were supposed to be here at noon. Aunt Maryam came out of the kitchen looking confused and asked me to open the door.

I was confronted with Uncle Eskandar, standing alone in the hallway and looking flustered.

"Hello, Uncle," I said.

"I wanted to come over a little earlier to help your aunt," he announced, not even making eye contact with me. He walked inside, brushing past me.

"That's so kind of you, but I don't want you putting yourself to any trouble, Mr. Nezami," my aunt said, leading him to the living room. "I'm almost done with everything."

"It's no trouble, Pari was my sister-in-law and it's my duty to make sure her fortieth ceremony is done in a respectable manner, seeing as how Sohrab couldn't be here," he said, flaring his nostrils – something he did whenever he was boasting. "My father will be coming up around noon. He wasn't feeling too well, so I asked him to rest until then." He seemed nervous about something, shifting his weight until Aunt Maryam asked him to sit down.

Uncle Eskandar never cared much for my mother and it angered me to see him acting like such a loving brother-in-law all of a sudden. It was all for show and I wasn't going to let him get away with it.

"It's good to see my mother has finally won your affections, *Amoo*," I said, looking him straight in the eyes. In our culture, it was a sign of disrespect to make direct eye contact with elders, especially during an argument. I didn't care.

"Cyrus! That's no way to—" Aunt Maryam began, but was interrupted by my uncle's raised hand, signaling for her to not get involved. This was between him and his insolent nephew.

"It's a pity to see your manners have gone away along with your parents, Cyrus, but I'm glad they're not here to see it," Uncle Eskandar said. "I'll overlook it because I know you're going through a lot, but if it were under any other circumstances…" he trailed off, shaking his head.

Without saying another word, I turned my back to him and walked into the kitchen. I heard Aunt Maryam apologize and then excuse herself to get the tea. She followed me into the kitchen.

"What was that about, Cyrus? Why have you been so disrespectful toward your uncle lately? Are you trying to cause more drama?" The color had drained from her face and I felt bad for being the cause of it.

"I'm sorry, *Khaleh,* but he's so two-faced. He never approved of *Maman* when she was alive and now that she's dead, all of a sudden, she's his beloved sister-in-law," I whispered. "You can choose to close your eyes on it and stay silent, but I'm not going to."

"Be that as it may, he's probably feeling guilty now and trying to make up for how he acted in the past," she said, putting her hand on my shoulder. "At least he's here and willing to make amends. They're all the family we have here now and we have to respect them, whether we like it or not."

"Amends? All he's doing is making himself out to be the hero at the expense of my dad," I said. "But there's no point telling you because you're just like your sister – always seeing the good in people even if it's not there." With that, I walked out of the kitchen and without so much as a glance in my uncle's direction, headed to my room.

I worked on some schoolwork until around 11:30. Rostam was still fast asleep, and it took some coaxing to get him out of bed. He was sleeping a lot better lately and it made me happy to know I had something to do with it. These days, even a morsel of positivity felt like a huge victory. While Rostam was washing up in the bathroom, I set his clothes out on his bed and then remembering something, walked over to my desk. Opening the drawer, I took out my father's coin and put it in my pocket. I knew how much my father wanted to be here today and even though I still didn't know what happened the day my mother died, I believed a piece of him deserved to be with us.

I recalled what he said in a recent email: *Seek justice and don't pass judgment until you know all the facts.* I didn't know all the facts yet, so it was not my place to pass judgment on him. He was my father and I owed him that much.

It was almost noon by the time I got Rostam ready. Taking his hand, we walked into the living room together. Grandpa Behruz had just arrived, sipping his tea and saying a prayer for my mother before taking a bite of the *halva.* Rostam ran over to give him a hug and I followed behind him to shake my grandfather's already-shaking hand.

"*Khosh oomadin, Baba-bozorg,*" I said.

"At least somebody is welcome here," Uncle Eskandar said under his breath.

Grandpa Behruz gave him a puzzled look, but didn't say anything and drank the last of his tea. He then took out the rosary he always carried in his pocket to pray in silence. It was a beautiful rosary, with large, amber-colored glass beads and a light-green tassel. The beads sounded like he was carrying marbles in his pocket when he walked.

Uncle Eskandar gazed at my mother's picture sitting on the table to his right. His eyes grew wide as he stared at her photo, like something in it frightened him. To my surprise, he took out a tissue from his pocket and dabbed at his eyes. Aunt Maryam was sitting on a chair in the corner softly reading the Qur'an. Rostam looked at them in bewilderment, so I took his hand and led him to the kitchen.

"Let's get you something to eat, mister sleepyhead."

"Why do *Amoo, Baba-bozorg,* and *Khaleh* look so sad sitting next to Mommy's picture?" he asked.

I thought for a few minutes while I got milk and cereal out for him.

"Remember when I told you *Maman* is in heaven now? Well, since she's all the way up in heaven and we can't see her, it makes everyone sad because they miss her."

"Is it okay if I'm sad, too?"

"It's totally okay, but I don't want you getting sad over breakfast," I said, patting his mop of curly hair. "Now, eat up before your cereal gets soggy."

"Is being in heaven the same as being dead?" Rostam asked, hesitating before saying the word "dead," as if it were a curse word.

My little brother was getting too smart for me.

"I don't like to think of Mom like that," I began. "I like to think she's still here, and can see and hear us even if we can't see or hear her and that somehow helps to feel closer to her, don't you think?"

Rostam thought for a few seconds, then nodded in agreement. Satisfied with my answer, he started spooning cereal into his mouth.

While Rostam ate, I poured myself some tea and went into the living room for some *halva.* Aunt Maryam told me we would be leaving for the cemetery in about half an hour.

Would that give me enough time to prepare what I was going to say to my mother when we got there?

* * *

It was close to 1:30 when we made it to the cemetery. I wasn't quite sure how to explain this part to Rostam and was certain he was going to ask more questions. As we walked toward Mom's grave in silence, Rostam ran to catch up with me. I shifted the bouquet of flowers I was carrying to my other arm and took his hand.

"Why are we here?"

I sighed and figured it was best to get the questions out of the way now.
"If you remember, this is our second time coming here, and we're here to visit something special that'll remind us of *Maman*. You can speak to her here, too, and tell her whatever you want and she'll hear you even better than when you speak to her at home."

"What are we visiting?" he pushed.

"Do you see all of these stones sticking out of the ground everywhere?" I pointed to the various headstones surrounding us. Rostam nodded.

"When someone goes to heaven, like *Maman*, that person's loved ones put up these stones to forever remember the person back here on Earth and keep their memory alive. It helps when we miss them because we can come here, visit their stone, and talk to them whenever we want."

"And they'll hear us and talk back to us? Are they magic stones?" Rostam asked. He stopped by a random grave, patted the headstone and said, "Hello!" I couldn't help smiling, despite myself.

"Yes, *Dadashi*, in a way they're magic stones and yes, they can hear us, but we can't hear them because of the distance, remember? You'll know deep in your heart what they're going to say to you."

I tapped his chest.

"I want to see *Maman*! Can't she leave heaven and visit us just for a little bit?" I could tell he wanted to cry.

He was a child who missed his mother and the miracle of her physical existence: her embrace, her voice, and her warmth. No matter what I said or did, nothing could ever replace those things for him and it broke my heart that he was only allowed five short years to experience her love. This was the hardest part for me to accept in all this mess, the most tragic part. The fact that my five-year-old brother was robbed of his mother's existence and love so early on in his life. It was my job to never allow him to forget her and how much she loved him.

"No, Rostam, once you go to heaven, you can never leave," I said. "Besides, *Maman* is very happy there and even though she misses us, she doesn't want to leave, either."

Rostam simply nodded and dropped his head, his black curls bouncing as he walked. He had our mother's hair. Not only that, I realized how much he looked like her the older he got, with his dimpled chin and round cheeks, especially when he smiled. Rostam took after our mother's side while I mostly resembled our dad. But we both had her eyes. Dad used to say that he fell in love with *Maman* Pari the moment he looked into her eyes, not only because they were so beautiful, but also because they were the kindest eyes he'd ever seen. He knew right then and there that he wanted to marry her. He told her he wanted their children to have her eyes, no matter if they were boys or girls. When he first told us this story, she flashed him a playful smile and said, "Well, you certainly got your wish!"

We finally made it to Mom's grave, sitting alone on a small hill. It still felt surreal, seeing her name etched on the stone's gray face:

Parisa Moghadam Nezami
Beloved Daughter, Sister and Mother, Taken too Soon
April 10, 1975 – September 22, 2016

For the first time, I realized there was no mention of "beloved wife" on my mother's grave and figured it was probably Aunt Maryam's decision not to include it. I still recall the quiet rage in her voice when she called her parents in Iran to give them the news of my mother's death. We were still staying at the hotel and even though she went inside the bathroom and shut the door to speak to them, I could hear her talking about my father with such resounding hatred it frightened me.

We were never close to our maternal grandparents and only saw them once a year during Persian New Year. They lived in one of the northern cities of Iran and rarely traveled to Tehran, so we would make a weekend trip north on the winding *Chaloos* road – cut into the heart of Mount *Alborz* – to visit them. *Chaloos* is considered one of the most beautiful and busiest roads in Iran. It's also one of the most dangerous, due to its narrow, winding nature and mountainous terrain.

Our grandparents were nice to us and cordial to my father, but there was always a distance I felt even as a child. They knew they could never wholly be part of our lives or accepted by my father's side of the family. While Aunt Maryam still didn't have the best relationship with them, she later told me that giving the news of her sister's death to her parents was one of the hardest things she ever had to do in her life.

My grandfather sobbed quietly into the receiver and said nothing after Aunt Maryam told him he had lost his eldest daughter. But my grandmother was beside herself with grief, and a few hours after receiving the horrible news, she experienced severe chest pains. Fearing it was a heart attack, my grandfather rushed her to the hospital. They were told she was actually suffering from something called Broken Heart Syndrome.

My grandparents both knew they wouldn't be able to attend their daughter's funeral to mourn and say goodbye to her. My grandfather, however, refused to believe my father had anything to do with his daughter's death. We never found out what my grandmother thought; after she was released from the hospital, she never spoke again.

Aunt Maryam explained that my grandparents held a small ceremony for my mother in their hometown and only invited a few close relatives, even though they didn't have her body to bury or grieve over. Their daughter was taken from them and they were unable to lay to rest the very body they had created and given life to. They never had closure.

I remember thinking how unfair it was, though what part of any of this was fair?

* * *

My little brother rubbed the top of my mother's headstone as if he could conjure her like a genie, and then casually asked her how she was doing in heaven.

Everyone else prayed and cried in hushed tones and in that moment, I felt like all five of us were so connected, even Uncle Eskandar. I said a prayer, asking God to help my mother's soul be at peace, and laid the flowers by her headstone. I then thought about what I wanted to say to her. There was so much that I didn't know where to start. Maybe she already knew everything I wanted to say and ask.

I wondered if she wished my father could be here and what he would do if he were with us right now. I couldn't imagine what he was going through, unable to visit his dead wife's grave because he was accused of having put her there. Only my mother knew the truth and she could only listen to our questions. I placed my hand in my pocket and feeling the cold coin against my palm, closed my fist around it; somehow, it comforted me.

As everyone started walking back to the car, I stayed behind. Kneeling in front of my mother's grave, I reached out to hold onto her headstone with both hands. I cried without restraint for the first time since the day of her death. It felt like I was back in her arms, crying until she made me feel better.

After death, the body is buried and held underneath mounds of dirt. But can the nagging, crushing weight of absence ever be buried?

It felt as though there was not enough soil on this earth to bury the burden of my loss.

Chapter Ten

Autumn used to be my favorite season. I looked forward to the upcoming holidays and school days off, but now, the beauty and meaning of the season is lost on me. Now, the leaves changing color doesn't thrill me. Instead, it fills me with a dread and sadness that saturates every dead leaf blanketing the sidewalks of my neighborhood.

Now, more than ever, I understand that this season is God's reminder of man's mortality; it isn't meant to be cruel, but a way to get us used to the idea year after year. So is the act of sleeping – we're practicing to eventually sleep forever, alone in the earth. It's all a preparation.

After we got home from the cemetery and Grandpa Behruz and Uncle Eskandar left, I went to my room to do homework and saw a new email from Dad sitting in my inbox. I was almost afraid to open it, but after a few seconds' hesitation, I clicked on it and began reading:

Dear Cyrus,

Let's get back to the part in Cyrus' tale where I last left off.

As I told you before, Astyages tried to have Cyrus killed as an infant to prevent the prophecy that Cyrus would one day overthrow him. I didn't go into much detail before, so let me elaborate a little more.

When Astyages' daughter Mandane was born, he had a dream that his daughter's urine would flood all of Asia. It was an alarming dream and he consulted his royal dream interpreters to explain its meaning. They told him it was a warning that Mandane's future son would overthrow his rule.

When she became of childbearing age, he arranged her marriage with a Persian king named Cambyses. Remember that at this time, the Persian Empire was small and weak. This was an attempt to thwart off the prophecy. No Persian ruler could possibly overthrow the great Median Empire.

When Mandane became pregnant with Cyrus, Astyages had another dream. This time, the dream revealed a vine growing from Mandane's womb and overtaking the entire world. Again he went to the dream interpreters, who reiterated that her son would overthrow him.

Terrified of the double prophecy, he ordered his most loyal nobleman, Harpagus, to have Cyrus killed. And as I told you before, Harpagus could not bring himself to sacrifice the baby, so he gave the child to a shepherd and ordered him to carry out the king's bidding. The shepherd, too, was unable to kill the child and instead, became determined to raise him as his own after having lost his biological son in childbirth that very morning. It was fate, he told his wife. The kind-hearted shepherd switched Cyrus' royal robes with the simple clothes of his dead infant and was able to trick Harpagus into thinking the royal baby was dead. Harpagus then went to Astyages and told him the deed was done.

To refresh your memory, Astyages found out his grandson was still alive by coincidence, after a fight took place between Cyrus and a nobleman's son ten years later. When the nobleman complained to Astyages, the king called for the herdsman and his son – who was Cyrus – to answer before him. When he questioned the boy about his ill behavior toward the nobleman's son, Cyrus' manner of speak and countenance immediately gave him away. Something deep down told Astyages the boy standing before him was his grandson.

On the one hand, he was happy to see his grandson, but on the other hand, he was afraid for his throne and angered that Harpagus had betrayed his order and trust. However, poor Harpagus never found out that the dead infant wasn't Cyrus and believed he had still carried out his king's orders regardless of not being able to kill Cyrus himself. In fact, Astyages was so furious with the man that in order to teach him a lesson and ensure he'd never betray him again, he ordered Harpagus' son to be killed. But he didn't just stop there. Inviting Harpagus over for a banquet, the cruel ruler had his royal chefs cook Harpagus' dead son and serve him in a stew to his poor, unsuspecting father. After Harpagus finished eating, Astyages calmly explained to the shocked man what he had just unknowingly done as punishment for betraying the king's trust. I'm sure you can imagine Harpagus' devastation. Many rulers were heartless in those days, but Cyrus was not one of them and it's fortunate he did not inherit his grandfather's brutality.

Astyages, no matter how cruel, could not help but take a liking to Cyrus and all of the great traits he possessed. He helped raise his grandson despite his own fears and turned him into the great leader he would soon become. He figured that raising Cyrus under his own influence and gaining his love and trust ensured Cyrus would never betray him. In fact, he could prove to be a powerful asset and an eventual heir when the time came rather than a dangerous rival.

Upon entering adolescence, Cyrus often found himself admiring a certain girl when he had some time away from his royal duties. Her name was Cassandane, an Achaemenian Persian Shahbanu consort. She grew up in the noble court in Persia and impressed Cyrus with her dignity, beauty, free spirit, and strong will. Cyrus was under constant supervision, but he frequently snuck off late at night to take her out into the woods where they spent hours talking and staring into the star-filled night sky together. As you can imagine, they soon fell in love, but he wouldn't marry her until years later. We'll get to that, but first it's important to mention what became of Astyages once Cyrus rose to power.

You see, it's never wise to betray those closest to us. Over the years, Harpagus did not forget Astyages' cruelty and this grudge turned into vengeance when the opportunity revealed itself. Once Cyrus became ruler of Persia, Harpagus went to him with his troops and convinced Cyrus to take over the Median Empire, which was considered a mutiny against Astyages. Granted, Cyrus was reluctant at first, not wanting to come across as disloyal toward his grandfather, though some historical accounts claim it was Astyages who first launched an attack against Cyrus. Eventually, Cyrus agreed Harpagus' plan was the best move for his kingdom and peacefully marched his troops over to Media. Cyrus took over Astyages' empire, but still allowed his grandfather to live a lavish life in the Persian court until his death. To ascertain himself the successor of Astyages, Cyrus married Astyages' other daughter – and his aunt – Amytis. This was more a political marriage to legitimize his rule than anything else.

Cyrus grew quite fond of Amytis and was ever faithful to her, but in the back of his mind, he often thought about the girl he fell in love with in the woods years ago. Amytis was a bit older than Cyrus and passed away from an illness a few years after Cyrus ascended the Persian throne. She bore him no children.

Shortly after Amytis' death, Cyrus declared his lingering love for Cassandane and they were soon married. She bore him two sons, Cambyses II and Bardiya, as well as three daughters, Atossa, Artystone, and Roxane. He considered her his equal and they ruled side by side. It was with her support that Cyrus conquered empires and it was with her love that he showed compassion to the enemies he conquered. They loved each other so much that Cassandane is known to have said she found it more bitter to leave Cyrus than to depart her own life. When she passed away, all of the nations under Persian rule underwent a great mourning. Cyrus himself did not recover from her loss for nearly a decade.

Well, that's enough history for today and this email is already long, so I will say one last thing.

Son, your mother was the love of my life. I will never stop mourning her. Forty days isn't enough, one year isn't enough, a decade isn't enough. I will mourn her loss for as long as I live, until we're reunited in the afterlife. She made so many sacrifices for us that we didn't even know about because she never complained. Our families did not want us to be married and tried their best to keep us apart. She left everything she knew to start a new life with me. Although she made it seem like she always dreamed about coming to the U.S., her reasons for actually coming here were entirely selfless – she came for us and to be closer to Maryam, but being away from her parents and birth country took a toll on her. I will forever be grateful to her for her love and for giving me you and Rostam. It was more than I ever deserved and even now, I still consider myself lucky for the time I had with her and the two of you – our children. It was a privilege to be her husband and father to you and Rostam. I am lucky to have lived a life alongside you three. You and Rostam are living, breathing proofs of the love between me and your mother. Your mother loved fiercely and boundlessly and it's my hope that she passed down the same love to the both of you. It's a rare and special kind of love; a boundless gift to those lucky enough to receive it.

I know the fortieth day was hard for everyone, especially for you and Rostam. I wish I could have been there alongside you. Be strong and pray for me. I'll see you tomorrow.

– Baba

P.S. Be sure to share the rest of this Cyrus story with Rostam in a way that he'll understand – I remember he was eager to know what happened. And I do hope you'll pass down to your brother the other Cyrus stories I tell you, as well. I know he's young, but I'm sure he'll love to hear these stories, so share them with him whenever you can. It will mean a lot to me.

Even when my parents argued, which was rare, I never doubted their love for one another. They fought fair and took care not to hurt each other with their words. No matter how angry they were, they worked it out. Deep down, I could never believe my father was capable of taking a life, much less the life of the woman he loved so much. It went against all he was. There was no sign of deceit or falsehood in his words.

There's an old Persian expression, *Sare bigonah ta dame daar mire, ama balaye daar nemire.*

"An innocent man's head may go all the way to the gallows, but he won't be hanged." Would the same hold true for my father if he's innocent? I had to believe it would.

I had a hard time typing a reply to my father's email. Whatever I wrote sounded insincere and forced. I figured the shorter the better, especially since we were visiting him tomorrow, anyway. After struggling with it for about half-an-hour, I came up with something I could send:

Baba,

Thank you for your email. I enjoyed reading it. Maman's fortieth went well – I'm sure she would have wanted you there, as did Rostam and I.

I never doubted your love for Mom and that's why I'm so confused by everything that's happened. It feels like nothing makes sense anymore. Like I woke up one day and was told everything I knew to be true was a lie. It's a terrifying feeling. I'm doing my best to believe in your innocence and I pray we can all find answers soon. I worry Mom's soul won't be truly at peace until we do.

I look forward to seeing you tomorrow.

– Cyrus

* * *

We planned on arriving at the jail around two in the afternoon. Aunt Maryam made it clear she wasn't taking any of Mom's *halva* for Dad and that we weren't going to stay very long, either. It irritated me that she made decisions like this without taking into consideration how I felt about them. She already treated my father like a criminal and didn't stop and think for a second that maybe he was innocent.

She was so certain he killed my mother that when I worked up the nerve one time to ask her how she was so sure, she simply responded, "I know it's hard to believe, but when a lion stands over a lifeless gazelle with its mouth and paws bloody, do I question if another predator killed the gazelle? No, because all the evidence points to the lion, no matter how much he may have admired or loved the gazelle for its grace and beauty."

"You can't possibly think that's the same thing," I said, angry with her response. "My father loved Mom for a lot more than just her beauty."

"I know *azizam*, I'm just giving an example," she said, softening her tone. "They had a great love, but often something can go wrong in even the most passionate, pure, and loving relationships and that passion can turn into hatred… It only takes a moment."

"My parents had no cause to hate each other, none that I knew of, anyway."

"Exactly, none that you knew of and you're far too young to understand this, but adult relationships are complex and delicate and have many layers. No matter how many of those layers are good, it only takes one rotten layer to ruin the entire thing. It only takes one word or one action to incite anger and feelings of betrayal that turn into a hatred so powerful that it blinds you in the moment, causing you to destroy the very thing you loved most in the world. The line between love and hate can be so thin sometimes, Cyrus."

Maybe she knew something I didn't, but I didn't push any further. Aunt Maryam was stubborn, just like my mother, and when they both made up their minds about something, there was no changing it.

As the Persian saying goes, *Hata age zamino asemoono be ham bedoozi…*

"Even if you sewed the earth and the sky together," you couldn't change my mother's mind once it was made up. Aunt Maryam was the same.

Before we left for the jail, I gave my aunt the shirt I bought her in an effort to cheer her up a bit. I initially planned to give it to her last night after we came back from the cemetery, but she was still in a state of mourning and I figured it wasn't appropriate yet.

After I helped Rostam get ready, I grabbed the gift bag from our closet and tiptoeing out of the room, found Aunt Maryam sitting in the living room, occupied with her phone.

"*Khaleh*, this is for you," I said, holding the bag out to her. She looked up from her phone, surprised.

"What's this?" she said, smiling. She took the bag from me and peeking inside, pulled out the tissue paper with the shirt wrapped in it. She undid the tissue paper and held up the shirt.

"It's just something to bring you out of mourning," I said, nervous she wouldn't like it.

"Thank you so much, *azizam*, that was so thoughtful of you," she cried. "It's beautiful and my favorite color, too."

"I wasn't sure if it's the style you like, but I also liked the color," I said.

"No, I love it, it's perfect," she said, opening her arms for a hug. "I'm going to wear it to work tomorrow."

Aunt Maryam was a real estate agent and always got dressed up for work. I was glad she thought the shirt was nice enough to wear to work.

On our way out to Aunt Maryam's car, we saw Uncle Eskandar sitting outside on the top step of the apartment building, smoking a cigarette. His back was to us and he sat still, the only movement being that of his arm rising up to his mouth and back down to his lap again, almost mechanic. He took a long pull at the cigarette balanced between his middle and index fingers and exhaled, a steady puff of smoke exiting his nostrils, dissolving into the air. As we passed him, he stood up.

"Hello, Mr. Nezami, are you well?" Aunt Maryam asked politely. I knew she hated his smoking habit. She complained whenever she saw his many cigarette butts littering the steps outside our apartment building. "The man smokes like a chimney," she mumbled under her breath each time, kicking the tan-and-white stubs into a corner with swift movements of her foot.

"Good, good, where are you three off to?" he asked, dropping the half-smoked cigarette and crushing it underneath his shoe.

Rostam giggled. "Uncle is blowing out smoke like a dragon!"

"Rostam, that's rude," Aunt Maryam scolded him. I tried to keep a straight face.

"I am a dragon and I'm going to eat you, you little rascal," Uncle Eskandar growled at Rostam, attempting to be playful. This was uncharacteristic of him and incited a look of confusion from Rostam.

"We're visiting your brother," Aunt Maryam said, her mouth set in a straight line. She placed emphasis on the words "your brother" as if to say it was his duty to visit my father and take us with him, not hers.

Uncle Eskandar looked down and nodded.

After a moment's silence, he said, "I appreciate you taking my nephews to visit my brother, I imagine it must not be easy for you." Like Aunt Maryam, he also wouldn't say my father's name, as if saying it would somehow deepen their shame.

"Don't you think it's about time you and your father visited him?" she asked. I was glad she wasn't letting him off easy.

"We'll visit when the time is right," he snapped. "I hope you understand how difficult it is for my father."

"This isn't easy for any of us, Mr. Nezami, but we've made sacrifices," Aunt Maryam said, her eyes lowered. She took Rostam's hand and signaled at me that it was time to go. "Anyway, it's getting late. Say hello to *Hajj-agha*."

"And you to your brother-in-law," Uncle Eskandar said.

I turned to glare at him, but his back was already to us, his foot making a swiveling motion again as he crushed the old cigarette butt deeper into the pavement before walking back inside.

The ride to the jail was always a silent one, but the conversation earlier between Aunt Maryam and Uncle Eskandar was bothering me and I had to talk to her about it. I took off my headphones and looked over at Aunt Maryam, who seemed to be deep in thought herself.

"*Khaleh,* if it's too hard for you to make these visits, I can always just go with Rostam," I said. "We can take the bus."

"Cyrus *jan*, I would do anything for you and Rostam, even if it's difficult for me," she said, taking her eyes off the road for a second to look at me. "Besides, I would never let you and Rostam ride the bus by yourselves."

"Well, I hope you know how much I appreciate it."

"I know."

The county jail building loomed ahead. After going through security and answering Rostam's many questions about the process, we followed the officer to the visiting room. We waited for about ten minutes until they brought my father out; he looked thinner than the last time I saw him, the jail uniform barely hanging on to his frail frame. There were prominent dark circles under his eyes, like he hadn't slept for days.

"Welcome! I'm so happy to see you all, thank you for coming," my dad greeted us and I was relieved to find his voice was still the same – strong and rich. The kind of voice that caressed every syllable of a word; a bard's voice. Aunt Maryam gave him another wordless nod and sat down. He wasn't his usual cheerful self and judging by his physical appearance, I could tell something was wrong.

As always, Rostam was the most excited to see Dad and wasted no time telling him all about school, how Mikey made him cry a couple of weeks ago, and that Aunt Maryam spoke with Mikey's mother and their teacher the next day. He also mentioned what I told him about being able to talk to *Maman* whenever he wanted and how we visited her magic stone yesterday. My father listened patiently, a faint smile on his face. However, his smile disappeared at Rostam's innocent mention of Mom's fortieth.

He looked up at me and his eyes were full of questions.

"It went really well, *Baba*," I said, trying to sound reassuring. I felt uncomfortable telling him about it with Aunt Maryam sitting right there. He seemed to understand and nodded. He asked about school and I told him I was doing my best to catch up.

After a moment's silence, he looked over at Aunt Maryam and she met his gaze without speaking.

"I'm sorry to trouble you, Maryam *khanoom*, but could you please take Rostam to the children's corner?" he said softly, pointing to a miniature table and chair set with some toys and coloring books to entertain small children accompanying visitors. "I need to talk to Cyrus in private, if you don't mind."

Aunt Maryam nodded and taking Rostam by the hand said, "Let's go see if you can color something special for your dad." Rostam eagerly followed her.

I expected him to ask me details about Mom's fortieth, or maybe he wanted to tell me something important about the coin, which I'd brought along with me.

Once they were out of hearing range, my father turned to me and said, "They've set a date for my trial."

He paused, gauging my reaction. I didn't know what to say, so I nodded for him to continue.

"Son, as you're aware, I've refused the prosecution's plea bargain and pled not guilty, so we're set to go to trial," Dad said. "Well, yesterday I found out the prosecution has requested the death penalty."

It felt as if someone dumped a bucket of ice water over my head.

"Death penalty?" my mouth formed the words and my voice gave sound to them, but they were foreign to me. Once again, I couldn't process why I was uttering these words in the first place.

"Yes, my lawyer said the trial is in two weeks, so we still have some time."

"Is he a good lawyer?" I had so many questions, but that's all I managed.

"He's decent enough, but there's only so much he can do," my father said. "The rest is in God's hands, so I'm not worried."

"No, it's in the hands of a jury, Dad," I cried. "He needs to come up with a good defense for you."

"I'm sure he's doing the best he can, given the circumstances of the case and the evidence against me."

"I can try to find you a better lawyer!"

"Listen, *pesaram*, it's going to be alright," he said, placing his hand on mine; it was ice-cold. He was probably more terrified than I was and instead of comforting him, I was giving him more cause to panic.

I nodded and took both his hands in mine. "I'm sure it will be."

"I know Grandpa Behruz and Uncle Eskandar don't want to see or speak to me right now, so I need you to tell them about the trial."

"I will."

I was so occupied with grieving over my mother's loss that I didn't think I could also lose my father, but now the thought of it knocked the breath right out of me. I imagined what I would do or say to him if he was found guilty. I pictured scenarios in my head where I yelled and told him I'd never forgive him for killing my mother and tearing our family apart, but in all those scenarios, he was always present. I pictured him behind bars for a long time, but the death penalty? It never crossed my naive mind.

As I grappled with the worst news I'd received since my mother's death, Rostam ran over to my father holding up a piece of paper.

"*Baba,* look what I drew you!" he squealed, handing his drawing to my father.

"Wow, what do we have here, *pahlevoon*?" He placed the drawing on the table for everyone to see.

There were six smiling stick figures standing next to a house and another stick figure with wings floating above them.

Rostam pointed to each one. "That's you, that's *Dadash* Cyrus, that's me, that's *Khaleh* Maryam, Grandpa Behruz, *Amoo* Eskandar, and that's *Maman* as an angel, looking at us all the way from heaven."

"It's beautiful, *pesaram*," Dad said, his voice quavering. "Thank you."

After a few minutes' silence, my father announced he wasn't feeling too well and wanted to rest a bit, so we left even earlier than planned.

On our way to the car, Aunt Maryam asked what my father and I talked about when she was with Rostam. I waited until my little brother ran a little ahead of us before answering her.

"He said his trial is in two weeks and they've requested the death penalty," I said in a low voice.

I could see the shock even in Aunt Maryam's face, but she only sighed and said nothing.

* * *

That night, I had a terrible nightmare. I dreamt I was in a large room with no doors or windows. The room was pitch black except for a dim light illuminating two giant platforms with guillotine-like contraptions fixed to them. I saw two people with black bags over their heads being dragged to the platforms by masked men. They were put in shackles and the bags removed from their heads, revealing the faces of my father and mother. When I tried to speak to them, no sound came out. When I tried to remove them from their shackles, my legs and arms would not move. I heard a voice from behind them reciting a prayer. It was Uncle Eskandar, who then emerged into the light with Rostam by his side and Aunt Maryam and *Baba* Behruz behind them. Uncle Eskandar ordered the ropes to be released and as the blades began to drop, I awoke and shot upright in bed, my heart beating against the still darkness.

I was unable to sleep the rest of the night, afraid if I closed my eyes, I'd see the horrible scene again and my parents' frightened faces, their eyes begging for my help.

Chapter Eleven

For the next two days following the visit with my dad, I debated how to deliver the news of the trial to my grandfather and uncle. How would they react? Plus, I much preferred to only tell Grandpa and have him share it with my uncle later.

I didn't want to do it at their home and decided the restaurant would be the best place. If my uncle was present when I told Grandpa, he wouldn't be able to show much of a reaction at their place of business. I texted Aunt Maryam and let her know I was going to the restaurant after school, which was located in downtown Bristol and about a thirty-minute ride away. I'd take the bus and walk the rest of the way.

My grandpa's restaurant, Persepolis Kabob, was always busy. They served different kinds of kabobs, Persian stews, and other traditional Persian and Mediterranean dishes. It was a fairly small place, with a limited seating area and about two to three servers. The kitchen and serving staff were always changing since my uncle was picky and wanted to hire the best he could find. The restaurant was his whole life and he worked long hours, especially with his wife and two kids still living in Iran.

We were never close with my aunt and cousins, either; my two cousins, Amir and Ali, were both a couple of years older than me and I'd only seen them a handful of times at family gatherings when we still lived in Iran. My uncle called them every Sunday and sent my aunt money at the end of every month.

It was around 3:30 p.m. when I walked into the restaurant. The lunch rush was over and only a few of the tables were occupied. I greeted one of the waiters and asked if he knew where my grandfather was. He told me he was in the back office. I thanked him and walked to the back of the restaurant where the cash register counter was located. To the left of the counter was a small office door with the sign, "Employees Only." I went up to the door and knocked.

"Come in!" said a muffled voice. I couldn't quite tell if it was my grandfather or my uncle; their voices sounded nearly the same. I opened the door and to my relief, it was Grandpa Behruz. He was sitting at the small desk that was overflowing with papers and receipts, his fingers tapping away at the noisy printing calculator in front of him, glasses sitting near the tip of his nose.

He looked up and smiled. "Cyrus! What a nice surprise."

I went over to give him a hug.

"Good to see you, Grandpa. Are you well?" I asked, shrugging my bookbag off and sitting down on the single chair facing the desk. He resumed his typing on the calculator.

"My breath comes and goes, *khodaroshokr*," he said. "Would you like some food? Tea?"

"No, Grandpa, thank you. I just came to tell you something and leave." I rubbed my sweaty palms against my jeans, thinking of how to word it. He stopped typing and looked up at me, waiting. His lined face held the worried, yet composed expression of a man who was accustomed to receiving bad news.

"Well, go on, is everything okay?" He pulled his rosary from his pocket and started fidgeting with it.

"Everything's okay, I have some news about Dad," I said. "*Amoo* probably told you we went to visit him yesterday."

"He did not, but go on, what's happened?" I could hear the slight panic in his voice. No matter how angry he was, my father was still his son.

"He's alright, don't worry, he just told me they've set the date for his trial."

"And?"

"It's in two weeks."

"Well, we knew this day would come, Cyrus *jan,*" he said. "Don't be upset, it's out of our hands and up to the will of God. But have faith, He will help us."

"There's more, *Baba-bozorg*." I looked up, unable to hold back my tears. "The prosecution's requested the death penalty."

The color drained from my grandfather's face.

"God have mercy," he murmured, removing his glasses and dropping them on the desk.

"Did you expect anything else? His own family has already labeled him a murderer, refusing to visit him or talk to him or even mention his name. What did you think they would do?" I tried to control my anger and keep my voice low. "And you're forgetting nothing's been proven yet. No one knows what happened that day and if Dad says he's not guilty, I think he at least deserves to be heard."

"You won't understand what I'm going through until you're a father yourself," he said. "You think it's easy watching my youngest son's life and family unraveling before my eyes? What would you do if they told you your son has murdered his wife, your daughter-in-law, the mother of your grandchildren? Huh? How else would you act?"

"I lost my mother and father on the same day, Grandpa," I said. "It hasn't been easy for any of us, but I've tried to put my own anger and doubts aside to be there for Dad and make sense of all this because at the end of the day, he's still my father and I won't just abandon him, even if there's a chance he might be the cause of all this misery."

"Then you're a better and stronger man than I am, Cyrus," *Baba* Behruz said, his voice tinged with sadness.

"It's not about being better or stronger, it's about doing what's right even if it's difficult." I went up to him and placed a hand on his slumped shoulder. "Please go visit him, Grandpa. You'll regret it for the rest of your life if you don't."

My grandfather gave me a strange look and said nothing.

"Well, it's getting late and I have a lot of homework to do, Grandpa," I said, picking up my bookbag and heading toward the office door. "Get home safely."

On the bus ride home, my mind drifted back to my childhood in Iran and memories of my mother, as I needed some respite from troubled thoughts. I recalled one morning when I was getting ready to go to kindergarten and how I almost missed the bus due to an incident with my shoes.

After putting on the brand-new sneakers Mom had bought me, I ran out the door to test them out and didn't wait for her to accompany me to the bus stop. When she yelled after me to wait for her, I stopped running and realized something was moving around in my right shoe. By that point, the bus driver had pulled up in front of our house and opened the door to the bus.

Screaming, I ran back up the stairs to the front door like I was on fire. The bus driver, seeing me in such a state, parked the bus and ran after me to see what was going on and if he could help. My poor mother kept asking me what was wrong until I pointed to my shoe and cried, "There's something in my shoe!"

Tearing at my laces, she yanked the shoe off my foot and to our horror, a giant flying cockroach – or *soosk*, as we call them in Iran – crawled out of my shoe.

I stomped on the cockroach with my other foot before it had a chance to crawl away. Mom burst out laughing, but my bus driver was not so amused. He shook his head and after waiting for Mom to help me put on my shoe, took my hand and walked me to the bus.

Ever since that incident, I've always checked the inside of my shoes before putting them on.

Another time, when I was in first grade, I recall being bored one weekend and whining about how there was nothing to do. My dad was at work and none of our neighbors' kids were available to play. No matter what my mom suggested, I would groan and dismiss it as too boring. Finally, she grabbed my hand and marched up to her room. Sitting me in front of her vanity mirror, she announced, "We're going to play dress-up!"

She picked up her red lipstick, turned me around to face her, and started drawing all over my face. Then, she picked up her hairbrush and hairspray and brushing my hair upward, she told me to close my eyes and sprayed my hair all over. Finally, she told me to stand up and tied a couple of her silk scarves around me.

"Okay, all done!" she chirped.

I stared at my reflection in the mirror and burst into laughter. My face was covered in red swirls, lines, and dots and my hair was sticking up from all sides. "Who am I supposed to be?"

"You're the Boredom Monster!" she said, as if it was an obvious fact.

"Who's that?"

"The Boredom Monster runs around gobbling up anything that's boring so no one will ever be bored, including yourself."

"Really?" I asked.

She nodded. "As long as you're dressed as the Boredom Monster, you won't be bored." While I was still gawking at myself in the mirror, she fetched her camera and asked me to strike a pose. Those photos of me in that ridiculous get-up are still in our old family album.

And as always, she was right – my boredom was cured for the rest of the day.

* * *

I arrived home at the same time as Aunt Maryam and saw her pulling into a parking spot in front of our building; the walk from the bus stop to the apartment was a short one. I waved to her and Rostam as they got out of the car and seeing my aunt taking groceries out of the back seat, ran over to help her with them.

"Hi *Khaleh*, let me get those," I said, grabbing the bags from her hands.

"Thank you, *azizam, pir beshi,* " she said.

Whenever Persian adults said this expression, meaning, "May you get old," it annoyed me as I used to think they were jealous of my youth and wanted me to age quickly. But as I got older, I realized it means, "May you reach old age and live a long life." I smiled, remembering all the times I complained when I heard it as a child.

Rostam was beaming as he took a brand-new basketball out of the back seat. "Look what *Khaleh* got me!"

"Wow, and it's a *Wilson,* too," I said, patting the ball with my free hand. "Aren't you lucky? Did you thank *Khaleh?* "

"I did, she's the best *khaleh* in the world!"

I turned to my aunt, who was smiling wide at her little nephew. "Thank you for making him happy."

"I want nothing more than to see you both happy and only wish I could do more, Cyrus *jan.* "

"*Dadash* Cyrus, will you shoot some hoops with me?" Rostam asked, hugging the basketball to his chest.

"We'll see, *Dadashi*," I said. "I have a lot of homework to do."

"Please? You haven't played with me in forever."

With everything on my mind, the last thing I wanted to do was play basketball, but I didn't have the heart to say no to my little brother. I didn't want his smile to fade.

"Okay, maybe for just half-an-hour, deal? Let me put the groceries in the kitchen and I'll be right out."

"Deal!" Rostam ran ahead of me to take his book bag inside.

Half-an-hour of basketball turned into almost two hours and it was dark by the time we went inside for dinner. Aunt Maryam had made pizza, per Rostam's request, and as the three of us sat around the dinner table, it almost felt like we were a normal family again.

"Rostam's getting a lot of special treatment tonight, what's the occasion?" I teased, picking up the steaming pizza slice from my plate and taking a big bite.

"I had a talk with Rostam's teacher today and she's been very pleased with how well he's doing, and he even earned a "Classmate of the Month" award for being so courteous toward everyone at school," Aunt Maryam said, patting Rostam's curly head.

"*Afarin*, Rostam, I'm so proud of you! You're well on your way to becoming a doctor like *Baba* someday."

"Speaking of school, hurry up and finish your dinner so you can get your homework done," Aunt Maryam said.

After dinner, I helped my aunt clear the table until she ordered me to go and get started on homework. Once I was in my room, it hit me just how tired I was – the visit to the restaurant and then the basketball with Rostam had drained me – but I pulled out the heavy textbooks from my bag and willed my body to get through the work.

I finished what I could around 11 p.m., unable to keep my eyes open any longer. Before going to bed, I decided to let my dad know I'd spoken with Grandpa Behruz, as promised.

Too lazy to get on my laptop, I got into bed and typed out a quick email on my phone:

Baba,

I hope you're doing well. Just wanted to let you know I visited Baba Behruz at the restaurant today and gave him the news about the trial. He was very distraught and assured me he'd let Amoo know, too.

We're all doing well – Rostam's teacher gave him an award today for doing well in school and she's very happy with his progress, so Khaleh got him a basketball.

I'll keep praying for you. Please take care of yourself.

– Cyrus

I still couldn't get used to the idea that my sole form of communication with my father, who was such a presence in our home with his deep voice and stories and laughter, was through email and occasional visits to a jail. This all felt so surreal, like I was worlds apart from the life I once knew and now longed for. It felt like I was living someone else's life, no longer recognizing who this new Cyrus was.

Chapter Twelve

I was so preoccupied with my personal life that my schoolwork, teachers, and classmates were pushed to the sideline and passed me by in a blur.

Some days I went through an entire day at school without interacting with anybody. Being an introvert, I never participated in anything by choice, but this isolation felt different. I could sense my pulling away from everything I once knew and hiding deeper into myself – a seclusion I both craved and detested at the same time.

The only thing that concerned me about my increasing isolation the most was my friendship with Yiannis. Ever since I told him my mom passed away, I'd distanced myself from him, as well. It wasn't intentional, but I didn't want him to treat me any differently or worse, to pity me. I was afraid him knowing about my mother would change our friendship. Since the last text he sent me, we hadn't talked much.

I knew the best thing to do was to swallow my Persian pride, which my father joked was twice the size of regular pride, and apologize to him. He was a good friend and I was in no position to lose his friendship.

The next day in biology, I prayed Yiannis would come to class a little earlier or at least on time so I could talk to him. When he walked in five minutes after me, I tried to think of what to say.

"Hey, man," I greeted him.

He nodded.

"Listen, I wanted to apologize for being such a jerk lately and I know it's no excuse, but things at home have been rough and—"

"It's alright, man, I understand," Yiannis said, interrupting me.

"I shouldn't have ignored you after telling you about my mom," I continued. "I know you just wanted to help."

"Well, I appreciate it. Takes a real man to admit he's been a jackass," he said, smirking and lightly punching my arm. To my relief, he was acting like the old Yiannis again.

"Yeah, I know it must have killed you not to talk to me these past couple of days," I said, grinning back.

"Not as much as it killed you, loser," he said, and then his expression turned serious. "But for real, man, how's your family doing?"

I panicked, not wanting to get into too many details.

"We're doing as well as we can, given the circumstances," I said. "Thanks for asking."

"I can imagine and sure thing, I'm here if you need anything."

"That means a lot, thanks, man."

On our way to English class, Yiannis teased me a bit about Tamara and this time, I was a good sport and let him have his fun. When we turned the corner, I noticed our guidance counselor, Mrs. Krasinski, waiting outside Mrs. Miller's classroom. Thinking nothing of it, I followed Yiannis inside.

"Cyrus Nezami?" Mrs. Krasinski called after me in a soft voice and I spun around. She smiled and beckoned me over to her with a curled index finger. She was a petite woman with short brown hair and dark eyes that were magnified by her thick glasses. Whenever I saw her walking around the school, she was almost always dressed in neutral-colored pantsuits and flat shoes. I couldn't imagine her wearing anything else, even at home.

"Hi, Mrs. Krasinski, is something wrong?" So many scenarios played out in my mind.

"No, everything's fine, I just wanted to chat with you for a few minutes, if that's okay?" she said, shifting the manila folders she was holding to her other arm. I wondered if one of them contained my student file.

"Sure, should I let Mrs. Miller know?"

"No need, I've already let her know I'm borrowing you," she said. "Let's walk over to my office."

On our way there, we made small talk as I wracked my brain trying to figure out what this was about. Maybe she wanted to tell me I was close to failing all of my classes and in danger of being kicked out.

Maybe she knew about Mom.

I followed Mrs. Krasinski inside the small office and she asked me to shut the door behind us. She placed all but one of the folders she was carrying inside an overstuffed filing cabinet and sat down behind her desk, placing the folder she kept out in front of her. She motioned for me to sit down on the chair facing her. I looked around the tiny room, its two walls covered with a number of those cringey motivational posters that only motivated you to roll your eyes at them than anything else.

"Do you know why I've asked to speak with you today, Cyrus?" she said, opening the folder and glancing over the papers inside.

"No, I was hoping you could tell me," I said, my mouth dry.

"Well, your biology teacher Mr. Becks asked me to speak with you after you mentioned to him that you're having some problems at home," she said, looking me straight in the eye. "He was especially concerned because it seems like whatever's going on is affecting your performance in school."

I should have known Mr. Becks had something to do with this. I remained silent.

"Of course, you don't have to disclose anything you're not comfortable with, but I think speaking to someone like me about what's going on will really help you both at home and at school, Cyrus," Mrs. Krasinski insisted. "And please understand, we're responsible for the safety and well-being of our students, and if their home life starts impacting their school life in a negative way, we have a right to know in order to help."

I had to give her something, but I had no interest to go in-depth about my family or what was going on. Granted, she was a trained counselor, but she knew nothing about me or my life except what was in the file in front of her. I didn't want to share my personal life with this woman I barely knew. She could be the best counselor in the world and a wonderful person, but it didn't mean I trusted her with the details of my life. Not yet, anyway.

I never understood how people could relay their entire life stories and problems to therapists and psychiatrists. For me, it went beyond doctor-patient confidentiality; it was more about truly knowing and trusting the person. I could never see myself opening up to a stranger. I wasn't yet comfortable telling my only friend about everything that's been going on, let alone Mrs. Krasinski. She blinked several times as she waited for me to speak, her eyes resembling those of a slow loris behind her thick frames.

I'd seen a picture of one in my biology textbook and thought they looked like the saddest creatures in the world, like their hearts were permanently broken. And maybe Mrs. Krasinski had a broken heart from having to listen to students' problems every day. She didn't need to add mine to her list, but I knew I wasn't going anywhere until I told her something.

"My mother recently passed away, so it's been hard on my family," I said, angry about having to disclose even that much. I avoided her gaze and looked down at my shoes.

"I am so sorry to hear that, Cyrus," she said, her voice softening even more. "I cannot imagine how hard it must be."

"Thanks," I mumbled.

She waited, willing me to go on with her sad loris eyes, but I was done sharing. The silence roared in my ears.

"Well, I won't press you to share any more than you have today, but please be aware that as this school's guidance counselor, it's my job to inquire about these matters and it's only because I care, not because I want to bug you," she said with a small smile, tapping the desk with the end of her pen. "I'll be checking in on you, so expect to hear from me again."

I nodded and stood up. "May I be excused?"

"Certainly," she said and without another word, I walked out of her office.

There were still twenty minutes left of class, but I didn't feel like going. Instead, I went to the bathroom and stayed there until the bell rang. I had one more class to get through – algebra – until lunchtime. I felt my phone vibrate in my pocket; it was Yiannis asking if everything was okay. I texted him saying everything was fine and I'd see him in math.

When I got to class, I told Yiannis about Mrs. Krasinski trying to intervene on me. He rolled his eyes.

"That woman looks like she was born to be a guidance counselor. Dude, remember her speech on the first day of school? 'I want you all to know you can come to me for anything. I'm here to listen,'" he said in a high-pitched voice, putting his hand over his chest to imitate Mrs. Krasinski. "What a load of crap."

I couldn't help but laugh. "Yeah, I need to come up with a plan to avoid her."

"More like an escape plan," Yiannis corrected me.

When we made it to lunch, I was surprised to find Tamara sitting at our table. For the past couple of days when I'd kept my distance from Yiannis, he ate his lunch at a spot everyone called "the beach," a small, closed-off lawn right outside of the cafeteria doors where a lot of the upperclassmen and popular kids hung out during lunch. While Yiannis and his football buddies ate their lunch out there,

I sat by myself at our table. When Tamara saw me and Yiannis together, she looked a little embarrassed. Yiannis nudged my elbow.

"Hey, sorry, I thought you'd be by yourself today," she said to me, standing up awkwardly.

"No, sadly he's decided he wants to hang out with me again," Yiannis said. "But I can leave if you'd like."

I glared at him and then looked over at Tamara, holding her lunch tray and looking uncomfortable. "What's up? Did you need to speak to me in private?"

"Oh no, I just wanted to double-check if we were still good for this weekend."

I blanked. "This weekend? Sorry, what's going on?"

Snickering, Yiannis swung his legs over the bench to sit down.

She smiled. "Good thing I came over to remind you, then. It's the second part of the interview for my project, which is due Monday."

"Oh, I'm sorry, I spaced for a second there. We're meeting at two, right?" I couldn't believe I'd forgotten about that.

"Yes, and it's totally fine, I texted you about it a while ago," she said, relaxing a little.

"Did you want to sit with us? There's plenty of room," I offered, sitting down next to Yiannis.

"Nah, I'll let you two catch up," she said, turning to leave. "I'll text you later."

"Damn, she's got it bad," Yiannis said once she was gone, taking a large bite of spaghetti.

"Oh, hush, she does not."

"Already acting like your girlfriend, texting you, coming over on the weekends," Yiannis said, shaking his head. "She's a stage-five clinger, my dude, watch out."

I rolled my eyes and started eating my lunch, glad to have Yiannis back at my lunch table.

* * *

That night, I asked Aunt Maryam if it would be okay for Tamara to come over Saturday to finish interviewing me. I was confident she'd be okay with it, having already met and seemingly liked Tamara, which is why I was surprised

99

when I saw her forehead crease in concern.

"I don't know, Cyrus, your uncle Eskandar gave me an earful the last time she came over," she said. "He said it's not right to have a young girl coming over to see you."

"Wow, *Khaleh*, it's not like we're doing anything wrong, it's for a school project, for God's sake!"

"I know, that's what I told him and I said I was home the whole time, but you know how he can be," she said, lowering her voice. "He's very old-fashioned, you know this."

"So, what do you suggest we do?"

"Meet her somewhere public, like a library or coffee shop? I can drive you."

"Really? And you're okay with it?" I asked, surprised a second time.

"Sure, she seems like a nice girl and it's just for school, right?"

"Right, thanks, I'll let her know."

On Saturday, Aunt Maryam drove me to a nearby Starbucks to meet with Tamara. I was excited and nervous even though I knew we were just meeting for her project.

"Is two hours enough time? I can pick you up at four," my aunt said, pulling into the Starbucks parking lot.

"That's great, I'll text you, thanks," I said, grabbing my things and rushing to climb out of my aunt's car. I didn't want Tamara to see me getting dropped off and even though she probably knew I wasn't driving yet, it still wasn't a good look.

I glanced around the parking lot and didn't see her anywhere. Aunt Maryam took her time pulling out of the parking space, waiting for a signal from me that it was okay to leave; I waved my hand at her impatiently and she drove away.

Walking over to the front of the Starbucks entrance, I stood there to wait and texted Tamara to let her know I'd arrived. She texted back right away, explaining she was running a little late and would be there soon. Noticing the rush of people, I went inside, ordered a drink, and grabbed a table before they all filled up.

Ten minutes later, a flustered Tamara walked inside the coffee shop. I waved at her and she smiled, floating over to my table in that effortless way she walked.

"I am so sorry, it took my mom forever to leave the house," she said, dumping her books on the table.

"It's fine, I understand Saturdays can be busy."

"Okay, I'll get a drink and we'll get started, yeah?"

"I got it, what would you like?" I stood up and headed toward the register.

"Oh, that's not necessary, I can get it," she said, blushing.

"No, I'd be happy to, really," I said and started fishing around my pockets for my wallet.

Tamara giggled and reached for my wallet, which in my hurry to pay, I'd forgotten to grab from the table. "Then, you might need this." She walked over and handed it to me; I felt my face burning.

"Oops, thanks."

"I appreciate it, but it's not necessary," Tamara insisted.

"Remember when I told you about the Persian tradition of *tarof* during our first interview, and how a big part of it is our insistence on treating everyone when we go out to eat to the point of fighting them over the bill? This is a perfect example of it, so there's really no use arguing or we'll be here all day."

Tarof is a nearly sacred custom to Persians – it is the delicate art of etiquette. The gentle tug-of-war of polite gestures and showering of pleasantries extending beyond social expectations.

Tamara laughed. "Well, I wouldn't want you to break tradition. I'll have a hot chocolate, please and thank you – or *mamnoonam*, I should say."

"Whoa, impressive!"

During the interview, I paid close attention to Tamara's body language and overall demeanor. She seemed even more comfortable than the first time we hung out and instead of just focusing on the interview questions, she went on tangents and asked me about things that had nothing to do with the project.

She had a small, barely visible mole just below her left eye, like a dark star that had fallen from the constellation of her dark-brown pupils and every time she blinked, her long, black lashes brushed against it, as if trying to sweep it back up to where it belonged.

Tamara wrapped up her questions around 3:30, so for the next half-hour, I asked her about herself. I learned she lived with her parents and younger sister, who had autism. I was surprised she trusted me enough to tell me about her sister and her family's struggles dealing with her condition.

I felt a bit guilty for being reserved about my own personal life when she was so open with hers, but then again, I had good reason to withhold some details. How would she react if she found out my father was accused of killing my mother and in jail awaiting trial? I didn't want to find out. I was enjoying getting to know her too much to jeopardize it in any way; maybe it was selfish, but I didn't care. When nearly everything I cared about had been taken from me, I deserved a little selfishness.

"So, we'll have to hang out again sometime," Tamara said, fingers grabbing at the ends of her hair.

"Oh yeah, definitely," I replied, glad she wanted to hang out again. I began entertaining the idea that maybe she was interested in me, too. I couldn't really tell until today.

We walked outside to wait for our rides. I was hoping Tamara's mom would pick her up first – I didn't want her to stand there by herself.

When Tamara's mother's van pulled into the parking lot a couple minutes later, I let out a sigh of relief.

"Thanks again, Cyrus," she said, pulling me into another hug. It amazed me that she could hug me so easily in front of her mother, whose eyes I imagined boring holes through my back. I don't think I could ever be overly affectionate with a girl in front of my family, even if we were married. It was something we didn't do in my culture and this made me realize there were a good number of disparities between our two cultures. My heart sank a little.

I told her I would see her soon and waved her off.

I looked at the time on my phone – it was a quarter past four. Aunt Maryam was usually on time.

Trying not to panic, I called her.

She didn't pick up.

I sent a text, waited five minutes.

No reply.

Not hearing back from someone I contacted gave me extreme anxiety, taking me back to the day my mother died. Even if a substantial amount of time hadn't yet passed since I'd called or texted them, I would still panic if I didn't get a reply right away.

Feeling nauseous, I called my aunt a second time.

No answer.

A third time.

No answer. The steady ring-back tone mocked me with its unhurried pace.

I couldn't believe this was happening again. It felt like I was reliving that horrific day. There was no reason for my aunt to be late or at least not answer her phone on a Saturday; something was wrong.

As I got ready to call *Baba* Behruz, my phone started vibrating with my aunt's name.

Bracing myself, I answered and expected the worst.

102

Chapter Thirteen

I mumbled a greeting into the phone, unsure if my aunt even heard me.

"Hello? Cyrus?" Aunt Maryam said and I didn't hear a sense of urgency in her voice.

"You're late, *Khaleh*, I got worried. What's going on?"

"I am so sorry, *azizam*, I was talking to Iran and lost track of time," she said. "I wanted to give my parents the news of your father's upcoming trial."

"Well, thanks for the heart attack," I joked, every muscle in my body relaxing.

"I'm so sorry, I'll be there in five minutes."

"It's fine, drive safe."

My legs still felt shaky after I hung up the phone, so I sat at one of the empty outdoor tables to wait for my aunt. Maybe it was worth speaking to someone like Mrs. Krasinski about all the recent anxiety I was having. I couldn't have panic attacks every time I didn't hear from someone right away.

People are busy, things come up, and it wasn't healthy to think something terrible must have happened to them if they don't respond when I need them to. Talking through it with an outside party might help. But I knew if I spoke with Mrs. Krasinski, I'd have to tell her everything and I wasn't ready to do that yet. For now, I'd have to cope with it on my own.

When Aunt Maryam picked me up, I noticed her eyes were a little red and she was quiet, barely saying a word to me when I got in the car.

"Is everything really okay?" I asked.

"Hm?" Aunt Maryam looked over at me for a second as if she was surprised to see me there, then she nodded. "I just received some upsetting news from my dad."

"What sort of news?"

"Grandma's not doing too well," she said.

"*Khaleh,* I'm so sorry to hear that. Is she still not speaking?"

"No, and her doctors believe she's showing signs of advanced Alzheimer's."

"Maybe they've misdiagnosed her because of her condition," I offered.

Aunt Maryam shook her head. "They've seen several specialists and they all agree it's Alzheimer's. I may have to make a trip out to see her, but I can't leave you and Rostam by yourselves."

"We'll be fine, *Baba* Behruz is here."

"He's busy with the restaurant and needs someone to take care of him."

We both knew better than to even suggest Uncle Eskandar.

"We'll manage somehow, and it's not like you'll be gone for too long," I said. "But you have to go see Grandma and I don't want us to be the reason for you not to go."

"We'll see, Cyrus *jan*, I haven't decided anything yet," she replied. "For the time being, misfortune keeps crawling up the walls and through every door and window, finding its way to us."

"Have faith, *Khaleh*. What did Grandpa say about the news of Dad's trial?" I asked, changing the topic from one misfortune to the next and thought maybe my aunt was right.

"You know how he feels about it," she said, and I sensed some anger in her tone. "He said it was all a farce and we should be ashamed of ourselves for following along. The conversation didn't last too long after that."

We were silent for the rest of the ride home and I wondered if my aunt was asking herself the same thing I was; how could we safeguard the doors, windows, and walls of our lives to keep more misfortune from finding a way in?

* * *

At school on Monday, I made sure to participate in biology a couple of times in an effort to convince Mr. Becks I did not need any counseling.

Yiannis caught on to my plan and chuckled under his breath, but Mr. Becks's face showed genuine surprise when I raised my hand to answer his question about natural selection.

"Well, isn't this a pleasant surprise?" he said. "The floor is yours, Cyrus."

Mr. Becks always dressed in suits. Today, he wore a lead-gray suit a size too small and it seemed at any moment, his large belly would pop right out from underneath the buttoned coat every time he raised his arm to write on the board. Even though he looked to be in his late fifties, he was square-shouldered, tall, and his large hands, which opened and closed into tight fists when he lectured, almost vibrated with a considerable amount of strength. He had steely eyes that peered out of thick glasses underneath an awning of bushy eyebrows and his thin lips were lost behind a jungle of spiky and unkempt gray whiskers. His head, however, was completely bald.

When I raised my hand a second time, he didn't hesitate to call on me again.

Yiannis coughed into his hand while saying, "Teacher's pet," and our entire row burst into laughter. I ignored them and answered the question.

As we were leaving class, Mr. Becks halted his furious whiteboard-erasing and looked over at me. "Keep up the good work, Mr. Nezami."

"Yes sir, I'll make sure he does," Yiannis said, doing a mock salute.

"And stay away from Mr. Anastas, he's trouble," Mr. Becks said, grinning when Yiannis feigned a hurt expression.

"I'll try. Have a good day, Mr. Becks," I said.

"You boys take care."

When we were out in the hallway, Yiannis started clapping his hands. "Well done, way to hustle to get the Beckster off your back so you can avoid seeing the school shrink."

"And that was a shitty move on your part calling me 'teacher's pet' in front of everyone."

"Come on, man, that was all in good fun," he said, putting his arm around my neck. "Now, let's forget all that and talk about what really matters, which is your coffee date this past Saturday with the lovely Miss Jones."

"I'm surprised you were actually able to hold yourself until after class to ask me about it," I said, removing his hand from my neck.

"Well?"

"Oh, you know, she may or may not have mentioned that we should hang out again."

"You're shitting me! She seriously asked if you could hang out again?" Yiannis stopped walking and yanked at my sleeve. "It just got way too real."

"Yeah, so you think she's interested?" I asked, wanting to be sure I hadn't read into it too much.

"For sure, but you definitely have to make the next move," Yiannis said. "Maybe ask her out to a movie next weekend?"

"Yeah, that'll take some serious planning," I muttered, already thinking about what I would tell Aunt Maryam.

I was excited Tamara wanted to see me again, but at the same time, the sinking feeling I got when we were saying goodbye lingered. Aside from the cultural differences, there was everything with my family. When she eventually finds out, would she even want to be friends? Should I continue getting closer to her or was it better to pull back before both of our feelings got involved? It wasn't right or fair to start something if I already thought it was doomed. But I liked her enough to at least give it a chance and knew if I walked away now, I'd regret it for a long time.

My mother always said, "*Yek sibo ke mindazi bala, hezarta charkh mikhore.*"

"When you throw an apple up in the air, it spins multiple times before coming back down."

This was yet another Persian idiom I didn't understand until I got older. It meant I couldn't possibly predict the many twists and turns of my life, so it was better to just leave it all to fate.

When I got home, I decided to get started on some schoolwork before my aunt and Rostam got home. Lately, I'd gotten into the habit of eating something and then taking a nap until dinner time. I wouldn't get started on homework until after dinner and some nights, if I was tired or just not up to it, I wouldn't even bother. But in a recent effort to catch up in the classes I was falling behind in, namely biology and algebra, I got to work as soon as I made it home. I grabbed a bite to eat and sat at my desk, putting my phone and laptop aside to avoid any distractions.

But as I tackled a tough set of math problems, I got distracted by my dad's gold coin sitting on the desk; I now took it everywhere with me as it offered a strange comfort. I liked the way it felt when I held it in my hand – solid, heavy, and perfectly round. Holding onto something tangible that was passed down within my family and belonged to my father was reassuring; being responsible for this family heirloom until it was time to pass it down to my own children gave me a sense of purpose. In a way, it was like I was guarding my family history and preventing us from getting lost.

A sudden sadness came over me. I often experienced it during solitary moments when I missed my parents with a crushing ache.

Memories of our life flooded my mind – like the nights when Dad came home exhausted from another brutal shift at the hospital and no matter how late it was, Mom stayed awake to make sure he made it home. As soon as she heard the jingle of his keys in the lock, she rushed to the kitchen to warm up his dinner.

He asked her countless times not to stay up for him and assured her he would warm up his dinner himself, but she insisted. No matter how tired she was, she couldn't fall asleep until she knew her husband was home safe and had a warm meal in his belly.

"What kind of wife would I be if I just went to bed and didn't care when my husband came home and whether he ate dinner or not?" she said in response to his protests. I often heard their hushed conversations and laughter if I was still awake, smiling to myself and falling asleep with the contentment and security only a child whose parents are in love feels.

These walls have witnessed all this love; they've listened to every late-night conversation and secret, every laughter. We humans have a strange relationship with the walls of the homes we live in – they are the mementos of people who once occupied them, who laughed and cried, breathed, loved, and dreamed within them. But these walls are not just mementos. Their white, blank faces are not so blank. Every shadow that falls on them evokes a distant memory that dances before our eyes and for only a moment, the lost are resurrected, as if their ghosts will fly out to us from the chalky surface at any moment, wanting to live again within the walls they used to call home. Yet, all we get are their memories and the pain of knowing they'll never again occupy these walls. We are the sacrifices of the walls we live in – our memories and soul fragments forever trapped inside them.

I figured reading one of my parents' letters would help ease my longing for them. Setting my math homework aside, I took out the bundle of letters still hidden in my desk drawer and pulled out the next one on the top of the pile:

Sohrab,

Thank you for the beautiful poem – it brought tears to my eyes. I didn't know I have my very own Romeo. I was surprised by it since you're not one to show much emotion – you're an Iranian man, after all. You know, it's funny how us Iranians always reference "Layla and Majnun" and talk about how Majnun (the Middle-Eastern Romeo) did so much in the name of love and so on, but the guy wasn't even Iranian. He was Arab!

How are your parents doing? Is your father still against our marriage? So is mine – what else is new? My father keeps telling me the same old things; that our families are on different social levels and your family will never accept me, that our marriage is doomed from the start, and so on.

But don't worry. I've told my parents either I marry Sohrab or I won't marry at all. That scared them a little, I think. Is it crazy that I knew I'd marry you the moment I met you? It's a feeling you get, you know?

I hate nearing the end of my letters to you. It feels as though our conversation is coming to a close and it saddens me. Even though it's just me talking – or writing, I should say – I imagine you're sitting in front of me, listening and smiling. I imagine your responses, too. Is that silly?

Okay, I have an English midterm to study for and really have to go. You are such a distraction, Sohrab Nezami.

Love,

– Pari

My mother's letter had me crying and laughing at the same time. She was always clever with her words and knew what to say in any situation. My father must have loved receiving and reading her letters; as he said in his last email, *"She loved fiercely and boundlessly."*

I felt that depth and strength in her motherly love, but I enjoyed learning about the romantic love between my parents and how it grew. Before, I never really cared about my parents' romance and like any other kid, I turned away whenever I was witness to an affectionate moment between them. But now, learning about their relationship felt almost necessary and I connected with it on a deeper level since meeting Tamara.

I was about to take the third letter out of the pile when I heard my aunt and brother entering the apartment. I put the letters back in the bundle and returned it to the drawer. I then heard another voice coming from the living room – it was either Grandpa Behruz or Uncle Eskandar; I could never distinguish between their voices.

Curious, I left my room to find out what was going on.

Grandpa Behruz was sitting on the living room couch, rosary in hand, as Rostam bounced around in front of him and excitedly chattered about the recent award he won at school. When he saw me, he hurriedly kissed Rostam on the top of the head and said, "Well done, Rostam *jan*, I'm so proud of you!"

I went over to greet him.

"Good to see you, *Baba-bozorg*," I said, bending down to take his hand and kiss his cheek.

"Ah, Cyrus, just the man I wanted to see," he said.

Rostam slumped down on the chair next to Grandpa, crossing him arms and pouting now that the spotlight had been taken off him.

Khaleh Maryam entered from the kitchen, carrying a tray of steaming tea. I took the tray from her and set it down on the table, the glasses clinking against their saucers as if shivering. We sat down, waiting to hear what my grandpa wanted.

"Please don't trouble yourself, Maryam *khanoom*, I'm only staying for a few minutes," Grandpa Behruz said.

"No trouble at all, it's just tea," my aunt said. "We'd be happy if you joined us for dinner."

"No, thank you, Eskandar is expecting me for dinner and then we're going to go over the restaurant's accounts right after. Do you mind if I speak to Cyrus in private for a few minutes?"

Aunt Maryam stood up. "Oh, of course! I was going to give Rostam a bath before dinner, anyway." She then turned to Rostam and held out her hand. "Come on, Rostam *jan*, let's go and give you a nice bath."

"But I wasn't done telling Grandpa about my award," Rostam whined.

"I'll still be here after your bath and you can finish telling me about it then, okay?" Grandpa Behruz said. "Right now, you need to listen and go with your *khaleh.*"

Without another word, Rostam took Aunt Maryam's hand and they left the room together.

I turned to face my grandfather and asked, "Is everything alright?"

He was silent and deep in thought, praying on his rosary. I loved hearing the soft rattle of the rosary beads as his fingers moved them along the delicate string; it was a comforting sound.

"I am really sorry if I upset you the other day," I said, taking his silence as a sign of disappointment.

He looked over as if he was seeing me for the first time, squinting to focus his eyes. "No apology is needed, you were right. That's why I'm here, I wanted to ask you a favor."

He spoke slowly, choosing his words.

"Sure, anything."

I waited. The lines on his forehead deepened and his lips quivered, as if he wanted to say something, but wasn't quite sure how to word it. A gleam of sweat coated his balding head, reflecting the ceiling light.

Finally, he turned to me and said, "I wanted to visit your father in jail. Will you go with me?"

I smiled. "Of course I'll go with you. Just let me know what day works for you, and I can arrange for us to go together."

He nodded and grabbing hold of his cane, pulled himself off the couch. "Apologize to Maryam *khanoom* and Rostam for me and tell them I had to go, but I'll visit again soon."

"I'll tell them," I said, standing up and accompanying him to the door. I held the door open for him and before he walked out, I placed my hand on his arm and squeezed. "Thank you so much for doing this, *Baba-bozorg.*"

He nodded again and walked out, descending the stairs with great care and patience; he never allowed us to help him, claiming that the day we help him walk is the day he'll be ready to die, alongside his pride.

Chapter Fourteen

When Dad emailed me the day after *Baba* Behruz asked me to accompany him to the jail, I wasn't sure if I should let him know his father wanted to visit him or keep it to myself.

We hadn't specified which day to go yet and I thought it best not to mention anything until I knew the definite date.

Dad's email was long and included another story, which I was looking forward to more and more:

Dear Cyrus,

I was very happy to hear Rostam's good news – please tell him how proud I am. How is he liking his new basketball?

Thank you for telling your grandpa and uncle about the trial.

I am well – I try my best to eat and keep my spirits up, but sometimes, it's not easy to do either in a place like this.

I have another Cyrus tale for you, so let's not waste any time and begin.

One day in Cyrus' court, a young servant boy was accused of stealing a sacred Zoroastrian amulet from one of the palace fire temples – known as ataskada, or "house of fire," in the ancient Persian tongue. During those days, theft was punishable by death, especially if something was stolen from the royal court or temple. The guards rushed to the servants' quarters and after placing the terrified boy under arrest, took him away to await execution. The boy begged them to reconsider, claiming it was a false accusation and that he had never stolen anything in his life. His pleas fell on deaf ears. The guards scoffed and said, "How could the accusation be false? The stolen item was found in your room!" The boy screamed he was framed, but the guards beat him and threw him in a cell to await his fate.

Three days prior, the keeper of the temple delivered the disturbing news of the missing amulet. Since hearing it, Cyrus had been unable to sleep and the

111

little bit of sleep he did get was riddled with troubled dreams. Thus, he ordered every guard in his court to find the amulet and the thief who stole it. Cyrus worried that Ahura Mazda, the Zoroastrian God, would be angered if the amulet was not found or even worse, that it was an ill omen.

Cyrus was beyond thrilled when his guards informed him the amulet had been found on the third day of their search, but upon learning about the arrest and the servant boy's plea of innocence, he grew concerned and decided to look into the matter at once.

Cyrus visited the young servant boy's cell and spoke with him, asking him to explain his side of the story in detail. After hearing what the servant boy had to say, Cyrus went back to his chambers to think. He was relieved the amulet was safe and sound, but something about the servant boy's claims and the entire incident bothered him. Punishing the wrong person for this crime would surely anger the God. This was no regular crime – it was the theft of a holy item and had to be handled with great care. Ahura Mazda himself was testing Cyrus and he had to pass this trial.

Meanwhile, Cassandane was worried about her husband and how much the theft of the amulet had affected him. She was sitting in their private chambers when Cyrus stormed in; he was in such deep thought he didn't notice her at first.

"What is wrong, Cyrus?" she asked him, walking over to where he was pacing back and forth like a caged lion.

"Forgive me, I did not see you," he said, startled. "The amulet has been found and I have just come from questioning the young servant boy accused of having stolen it. But he insists he's innocent and has been framed. What if he's right? What if someone else committed the act and is walking around freely while an innocent man pays for his despicable crime? God is testing me and I cannot fail!"

"Everyone knows you are a fair ruler and I have no doubt you will find the man responsible," Cassandane said, taking Cyrus' hand in hers. "You could question the keeper of the temple again, for is it not true he was the only person in the temple that night? How could he have not seen anyone enter and leave the temple?"

"You are right," Cyrus said. "He could be hiding something."

"He was perhaps paid by the actual thief to keep quiet," Cassandane suggested.

"So we're assuming the thief is a person of higher status, who can afford to pay someone to keep quiet?"

"It looks to be that way, my lord, otherwise why else would the keeper of the temple protect this person's identity?"

"I have a plan to make the keeper confess," Cyrus said and standing up, he took Cassandane's hand and kissed it. "Thank you, my queen."

With that, he rushed out of the room as quickly as he entered it, calling for his guards.

A few moments later, the guards brought the keeper to one of Cyrus' meeting chambers.

"Ah, keeper, I am sure by now you've heard the good news of the amulet's recovery," Cyrus said, smiling and gesturing for the keeper to sit down.

The keeper bowed and sat across from Cyrus. "Yes, my lord, thanks be to God."

"And you heard my guards arrested the thief?"

"Yes, your grace, it was Arshia, the servant boy," the keeper replied with a look of disdain. "I should've known."

"Why is that?" Cyrus asked.

"Well, I am sure he planned on selling it for money."

"But Arshia claims he is innocent," Cyrus said.

"It's clear as day he's lying," the keeper insisted.

"Why? Because he's a simple servant boy, then he must be lying?"

"Yes, my lord, he does not have the upbringing or social standing to know any better."

"Indeed. Keeper, why is it you didn't see anyone enter the temple and steal the amulet that night? Is it not your job to watch the temple?" Cyrus said, folding his arms and looking straight at the keeper, who dropped his gaze and looked down at his hands.

"I must have been distracted by my prayers and failed to notice Arshia entering the temple and taking the amulet," the keeper stuttered.

"It is a small temple, keeper, and the amulet is kept right in the middle, meaning it was in your line of vision no matter where you were sitting. In addition, you would have easily noticed someone slip into the temple and take the amulet, no matter how distracted you were by prayers." Cyrus' face seemed to be carved out of marble, with only his lips moving.

"But my lord—" the keeper began and Cyrus raised an arm to silence him.

"I know who stole the amulet and it is not Arshia the servant," Cyrus said, his voice low. "Your punishment will be a lot less severe if you confess everything to me now."

The keeper fell down to his knees in front of Cyrus and began sobbing. "Forgive me, my lord, but it was your advisor Jahan who tricked me and stole the amulet!"

"Go on."

"He entered the temple three nights ago to take the amulet, thinking I was asleep. When I confronted him, he threatened me and said if I kept my mouth shut and went along with his plan, I would be generously rewarded. Right then, he pulled out a bag of gold coins and dropped it in my hand. I was tempted and my greed overcame me, my lord, please forgive me!"

Cyrus was shocked to learn one of his closest advisors could betray his trust like this, but did his best to hide his surprise.

"It seems I have been blind all this time, trusting men who so easily betray me. Guards, take this traitor away and bring me Jahan."

"My lord, please have mercy on me!" the keeper cried, kissing Cyrus's feet before the guards dragged him away, screaming for forgiveness.

Cyrus shook with anger, but was able to calm down a little by the time the guards brought Jahan to him.

"Your grace, what has happened?" Jahan cried, his face bereft of all color.

"You tell me, Jahan," Cyrus said, signaling the guards to let him go. "Sit down."

Jahan sat down in the same chair his accomplice had occupied moments ago.

"I'm afraid I do not know why your guards have rushed into my chambers and dragged me here with such brute force."

"Oh, no? Perhaps it has something to do with stealing the amulet from the temple, paying the keeper to keep quiet, and then framing an innocent servant boy to take the fall for your crime," Cyrus said, slamming his hand down on the table in front of him. He was unable to control his anger any longer.

Jahan's face turned whiter.

"My lord, please allow me to explain—"

"What explanation could you possibly give to justify your actions? I trusted you like my eyes, Jahan, and you betrayed me."

"I was going to return it, I swear to God," Jahan said. "I only needed it for a few days."

"You know taking anything from the temple is forbidden," Cyrus said. "And not only that, but you bribed the temple's keeper and framed an innocent man. I cannot overlook these grave crimes."

"I needed it to pray for my sick son," Jahan said, bursting into tears. "I thought maybe the amulet would help and God would answer my prayers faster and cure him. Cyrus, I was desperate or else I would have never betrayed your trust like this."

"You were willing to let an innocent man take the fall for your crime," Cyrus yelled. "Nothing changes that! And instead of treachery, you could have come to me and I would have tried to help you."

"I made a terrible mistake, but in all my years of service, I've never once betrayed your trust," Jahan said. "I panicked seeing how distraught you became over news of the theft and I didn't know what else to do. I thought about returning it to the temple, but you had your guards surrounding it, and I knew I'd be caught. I eventually planted it in one of the servants' rooms."

"The crime of theft alone is punishable by death, but I am not one to forget your many years of loyal service and will instead demote you from your position immediately," Cyrus said. "I believe the embarrassment of that is punishment enough for your crimes."

"I would rather be executed than leave your side, Cyrus," Jahan cried. "Please reconsider."

"My mind is made up, Jahan," Cyrus said. "Either that, or you will leave the court for good. Guards, take him away and order the servants to clear his belongings from the palace chamber and move them to the servants' quarters. His wife and son, however, are permitted to remain in the palace. It would not be just to have them pay for the crimes of Jahan."

The guards took the humiliated man away.

Cyrus also ordered the servant boy Arshia to be freed at once and rewarded for his honesty. He was promoted as the new keeper of the temple while the former keeper and Jahan were forced to live in the servants' quarters. That same evening, Cyrus visited the temple with Cassandane to give thanks to Ahura Mazda for helping him pass this test and for returning the amulet to its rightful place. He even prayed for Jahan's sick son and planned to have his own physician pay the boy a visit.

So you see, my son, Cyrus proved himself to be a fair ruler once again. He showed his high regard for justice, making sure an innocent man wasn't falsely *accused and punished for a crime he did not commit, even if he was just a lowly servant. Always be fair and seek justice in life. Even when all the evidence seems to point you one way, don't forget to follow your heart and seek the truth no matter how inconvenient or impossible it may seem.*

Love,

– Baba

* * *

When I saw Grandpa Behruz on the stairs the next day after school, he told me he planned to visit Dad on Saturday.

Now that there was a set date, I told Dad about our visit in my reply email later that night.

Dear Baba,

I hope you're doing well. I enjoyed reading about Cyrus again. He could have just let the servant boy take the fall after the amulet was found, but he chose to find and punish the real culprit, even if it was one of his closest advisors. I'm starting to really like this Cyrus the Great guy.

I have some exciting news! Baba Behruz and I are planning on visiting you this Saturday. He's looking forward to seeing you.

Let me know if you need anything.

Take care,

– Cyrus

By Friday evening, Dad hadn't responded to my email yet and I was getting anxious. Was he upset *Baba* Behruz wanted to visit? Was he ashamed? I wished I had asked him first. It was too late now to reschedule or cancel; in fourteen hours, Grandpa Behruz would be showing up at our door to leave for the jail.

Maybe my father didn't say anything because there was nothing to say. He knew this day would eventually come – just like his trial date, then eventually his sentencing – and he would have to face it all in silence. He had no other choice. What can a man say when he's lost the ability to make choices? The right to choose and to have control is taken from a man imprisoned and aren't those two things the very formula for freedom?

Perhaps it's just punishment for a man whose wrong choices and lack of control led him to be imprisoned in the first place.

* * *

Grandpa Behruz was a man set in his ways.

Like any Persian, especially one who has seen many winters, he had an opinion about everything and you couldn't convince him otherwise. I was still getting ready when he showed up at our door fifteen minutes earlier than planned. Aunt Maryam was in the kitchen preparing breakfast and welcomed him inside. I told her earlier in the week about our plans to visit my dad. She nodded and said it was about time he visited. She knew better than to ask whether Uncle Eskandar was going.

Grandpa was seated at the dining room table sipping tea. When I said good morning, he nodded and then looked me up and down with one eyebrow raised.

"Cyrus, those pants are falling off your waist, please wear a belt," he said. "What's the point of wearing pants if they're not covering anything?"

I looked down at my loose khaki pants and without saying a word, walked back to my room. Grabbing the only belt I owned from a shelf in the closet, I threaded it through my pants, fastened it, and with a final look in the mirror, went back to the living room.

"Much better," Grandpa Behruz said with a nod. "Now, come eat some breakfast so we can get going."

Even though he was almost seventy-five years old and dependent on a cane when he walked, my grandpa insisted he was still capable of driving. We got inside his 2006 silver Chevy Malibu and I entered the address of the jail into my phone's GPS to navigate him.

We didn't talk for most of the car ride and instead listened to NPR; the radio host had a soothing voice that calmed my nerves. I tried to focus on his voice and the segment they were doing, which was on a married couple with different cultural and religious backgrounds. My ears perked up.

The host interviewing the couple asked them how they were able to hold on to their own separate traditions and beliefs and if they had any difficulties raising their child in a bicultural household. The couple spoke about balance, respect, and acceptance, of allowing their child to choose what she wanted to follow and believe from their two cultures and religions. They viewed it as something that brought them together more rather than something that divided them.

"The most important thing we can teach her is how to be a good person, and the rest will just fall into place," the wife told the radio host. I was so engrossed with the interview, I didn't realize Grandpa had asked me a question.

"Cyrus, did you hear me?"

"Sorry, Grandpa! What was that?" I asked, sitting up straight and turning down the stereo volume.

"I asked if you told Sohrab we're visiting him today," he said. I was surprised to hear Grandpa Behruz calling my father by his name.

"Yes, I emailed him earlier in the week and let him know," I replied.

"Good."

After a moment's silence, I asked, "Did you tell Uncle Eskandar you're visiting Dad?"

"I did, and he tried to convince me not to go."

"You told him they've set a trial date and requested the death penalty?"

"I did and it upset him, but I don't think he's ready to see your father yet," Grandpa said.

There were things I wanted to say, but knew better and held my tongue.

"He is stubborn, but he'll come around," Grandpa said.

When we arrived at the jail, I could sense my grandfather's discomfort and even though it went against his nature, he allowed me to hold on to his arm. After we went through security, one of the officers led us to the visitor's area. Grandpa Behruz walked slower than usual to keep a courteous distance from the tall, heavily-armed police officer. He looked around, taking in the somber, gray walls.

We waited almost twenty minutes until my father came out. When he was led into the visitor's room, his eyes scanned the room and once they found us, dropped to the floor. Every time we visited, he turned his back to us to have his handcuffs removed. Once his wrists were freed, he trudged over. We stood up when he approached us.

Without saying a word, my father bent down to kiss my grandpa's hand – the highest sign of respect for an elder in our culture. But Grandpa Behruz drew away his hand and pulled him up into an embrace. The two men stood like that for a whole minute without saying a word. It was as if they both already knew what the other wanted to say, apologies and explanations hanging from their lips like silent prayers.

Mom used to tell me I didn't need to say my prayers out loud if I didn't want to because God already knew everything I wanted to ask and could hear me even if I said my prayers to myself.

When father and son slowly pulled away from each other, I could see their eyes were glistening with the tears they wouldn't let fall. My dad cleared his throat and after hugging me, signaled for us to sit down.

"Thank you for coming," he said. "How is everyone? Eskandar?"

"All fine, Eskandar says hello," Grandpa said. "How are you doing? You're all skin and bones."

"I'm doing okay and eating well, but all the exercising they have us do makes me lose everything I eat," he said, trying to smile. "Eskandar couldn't come?"

"No, you know how he is with the restaurant, always busy," Grandpa said with a wave of his hand. "But really, do they treat you okay here? Do you need anything?"

As soon as he laid eyes on his son, it was as if every ounce of my grandfather's reservations, anger, and shame melted away and were replaced by fatherly love and concern.

"I'm fine, and you've done more than enough caring for the kids while I'm in here," my father said, lowering his eyes again.

"Their aunt is the one doing it all," Grandpa Behruz replied, pulling out his rosary from his pocket like a lifeline. "If it wasn't for her, I don't know what we'd do."

"Yes, she's been so gracious. I don't think I'll ever be able to repay her kindness, especially considering the circumstances."

Grandpa Behruz thumbed at half the rosary beads before speaking again.

"So, what can you tell us about the upcoming trial? Have you spoken with your lawyer?"

My father looked up, his expression a mix of surprise, as if he wasn't sure why my grandfather was asking him that question. It seemed the grave reality of his son's situation hadn't sunk in yet.

"It's really up to the jury and witness testimonies," he said with a sigh. "My lawyer doesn't have much to go on in regard to my defense. The evidence is against me."

"They will most likely call Eskandar to the witness stand," Grandpa said, pulling at the rosary beads faster.

"I am aware of this."

119

Before he spoke again, I saw the same look of struggle on my grandfather's face as when he told me he wanted to visit my father in jail.

"Sohrab, before your mother died, she made me promise to look after you and Eskandar, but I haven't been doing a good job of that lately. I dreamt of her a couple of nights ago; she was crying and turning her face away from me when I tried to comfort her. I know she's upset with me."

"It was just a dream," my father said. "I'm sure it doesn't mean anything."

"No, it was a sign. She told me to protect you and keep an eye on Eskandar, always worried his ambitions would get him into trouble. I've failed you both, with you in jail, your family shattered, and Eskandar's health suffering as he works himself to death in that restaurant. I've failed Afsar – I failed her when she was alive and I'm failing her now."

"You have not failed me; I have failed you. And you haven't failed Mom or Eskandar – you're doing the best you can. Some things are out of our hands."

"Sohrab, I'm visiting my youngest son in jail and talking about the poor health of my eldest son with him. How is that not failure? Part of the reason I'm here today is because I'm worried about Eskandar and don't know what to do anymore. He works long hours, doesn't look after himself, and his health issues have gotten worse with the stress of the restaurant and you being in jail," Grandpa Behruz said, wrapping the rosary around his index finger until the tip turned beet red.

"*Agha joon*, try not to worry so much, I'm sure it's mostly due to him being stressed," my father replied, but his face showed concern.

"You're a doctor, maybe you can figure out what's wrong with him."

"It's hard to tell without examining him, but what are some of his symptoms?" my father asked.

"He coughs a lot and I've noticed he's lost weight," Grandpa Behruz said.

"Is he still smoking?"

"Ooh, almost two packs a day."

"Try to convince him to go see a doctor and cut back on the smoking."

Grandpa nodded his head and said nothing. There was no point in saying what we already knew; no one could convince my stubborn uncle to do anything he didn't want to do. I wasn't too surprised to hear the news about his health. My uncle had never been one to take care of himself and ever since I could remember, he was a heavy smoker.

I recalled an amusing memory from my childhood, though it wasn't quite amusing at the time. One night, a few months after our move to the U.S., Uncle Eskandar and Grandpa were over for dinner when I spotted my uncle's packet of cigarettes sitting on the living room table and got a bright idea. While the adults were busy talking in the dining room after we'd eaten, I grabbed the cigarette packet and hugging it close to my chest, ran into the bathroom, dumped the cigarettes into the toilet, and flushed without a moment's hesitation. I was so proud of myself, thinking my heroic act would somehow convince my uncle never to smoke again. I threw the empty packet in the trash and ran back to the living room, heart pounding.

Once everyone made their way over to the living room moments later for tea, Uncle Eskandar started looking around for his cigarettes, as he loved to light one up whenever he drank tea. When I couldn't take the suspense any longer, I smiled and announced to everyone what I had done, thinking they would all praise me.

"You did what?" Uncle Eskandar asked, his face turning red.

I stopped smiling and innocently said, "I thought it would stop you from smoking. It's bad for you, *Amoo!*"

My mother started apologizing to my uncle while *Baba* Sohrab and Grandpa exchanged glances and tried not to laugh.

"Do you have any idea how expensive cigarettes are? Besides, my smoking is not your concern, young man."

I looked down at my feet, feeling stupid, and mumbled, "I'm sorry, *Amoo.*"

"Yes, he's very sorry, and we'll be sure to replace your cigarettes, *Agha* Eskandar," *Maman* Pari said as she shot me a stern look.

"There's no need, but please teach your son not to stick his nose where it doesn't belong."

He actually used the ever-popular Persian saying, "*Khodeto nokhode har ash nakon,*" which literally translates to, "Don't be a pea in every soup." A very creative way of saying, "Mind your own business."

My poor mother simply nodded and said nothing while Dad tried to change the subject.

My father's deep voice snapped me out of the past and brought me back to the stark room we were sitting in.

"I'm sure it's also hard not having his family – especially his wife – here to look after him," Dad said. Something in my father's tone made me feel sorry for Uncle Eskandar, despite myself.

My dad tried to console my grandfather some more, seeing how distressed the old man was.

When it was time to leave, I found it difficult to watch them say goodbye. My father embraced Grandpa Behruz tightly, as if he were a child again and needed his father to protect him and tell him it was going to be all right. In turn, my grandfather wrapped his arms around his youngest son and buried his face in the hollow of his neck, taking in his scent and regretting that he could no longer protect him from the troubles he faced.

Chapter Fifteen

When we moved to the U.S., I remember it was around *Nowruz*, the Persian New Year that fell on the spring equinox.

My mom was not only busy unpacking our things in our new home, but also getting everything ready for *Nowruz*. This included the annual spring cleaning, or *khooneh-takooni*, which literally translated to, "shaking up the house," to rid it of all the dust and clutter that had collected during the winter months.

Mom wasn't going to let the fact that she now lived in a different country change how she celebrated her country's biggest, most ancient holiday.

"It'll feel like we're back in Iran," she chirped.

Nowruz was her favorite time of the year, and she always said it made more sense to celebrate a new year in the spring rather than the winter. For us, *Nowruz* – meaning "new day" – was a time of spiritual renewal, so we celebrated it in the spring when everything blossomed and the earth birthed hyacinths and crocuses.

That week, Mom made trips to several stores to buy what she needed, including a few visits to Grandpa Behruz's restaurant for the special *Haft-Seen* table items regular grocery stores didn't carry.

Haft-Seen means, "Seven S's," which are the seven special items we decorate the *Nowruz* table with that each begins with the Persian letter, *seen*, similar to the letter "S" in the English alphabet. These items are *samanoo*, a kind of wheat pudding; *senjed*, which is dried lotus tree fruit; *sabzeh* – wheat, lentil, or barley sprouts grown in a dish; *somagh*, which is sumac seasoning; *serkeh* – vinegar; *seer*, which is garlic; and *seeb* – apples. In addition to the seven main items beginning with the letter *seen*, we add goldfish, gold coins, decorated hardboiled eggs, hyacinths and tulips, a mirror, candles, a medley of pastries, and either a collection of Hafez's poetry or the Qur'an.

Each of these items are symbolic of everything we celebrate during *Nowruz* and are hoping for in the new year: life, rebirth, nature, beauty, peace, good fortune, good health, family, and above all – love.

When *Maman* Pari went to the pet store to buy goldfish, the sales associate informed her she was the tenth person coming in to buy goldfish that day and she couldn't figure out why their goldfish sales had spiked all of a sudden in March. Mom told her about *Nowruz* and solved the mystery for the curious sales associate.

Most of the *Nowruz* goldfish die within a few weeks, but that year, one out of the three fish my mother had bought was still alive two months into the new year. Mom took this as a good omen and became attached to the little fish, changing its water every day and making sure to feed it once a day just as the pet store associate instructed. She swore the fish knew she was going to feed it by flipping its tail back and forth and trying to jump out of its bowl. *Maman* named the fish Tala, meaning "gold" in Farsi.

"Tala *khanoom*, it's time for dinner," she'd say in a sing-song voice each night, crunching the pungent fish flakes between her thumb and index finger and sprinkling them over the water's surface. Tala shot up to the surface and sucked in the soggy flakes.

One day, my mother came home from work to find the little fish dead on the kitchen floor.

It had most likely jumped a little too high and left the safety of the fish bowl, landing on the cold kitchen floor, its tiny gills taking in the poisonous air.

When I got home from school, I spotted Mom kneeling in front of the little garden beside our apartment's main entrance, crying and digging at the dirt with a spoon. Alarmed, I ran over and asked what was wrong.

"I should've covered the fish bowl with something, Tala had a tendency to jump," was all she said and using the spoon, she gently scooped up the dead fish out of the waterless fishbowl and placed it within the small hole she had dug in the garden. She was so heartbroken over the death of that tiny thing, whose burial took less than a minute. Maybe because it was spring and the time for rebirth, she found even the death of something so small impossible and out of place. Like a cruel joke.

"Perhaps it was God's will," she murmured and picking up the dirt-covered spoon and bowl, stood up and walked back inside. Later that night, Mom was cooking in the kitchen when she bumped against the table holding the fishbowl. It fell to the linoleum and broke into a hundred pieces, scattering all across the kitchen floor. My mother stood still and stared at the mess before her, her face a mixture of shock and resignation. In a calm voice, she told me to stay out of the kitchen until she cleaned up the glass shards and without saying another word, fetched her broom and dustpan.

She swept the kitchen floor with great patience, gathering the jagged, glistening pieces into a pile which she then transferred onto the dustpan with quick flicks of her wrist. I can recall the sound of the glass as it slid from the dustpan into the trash, making a sad, twinkling echo. I went to my room, realizing she needed to be alone. Twenty minutes later, she popped her head into my room to announce she was going to bed and that my dinner was on the table. Dad was at the restaurant with *Baba* Behruz and *Amoo* Eskandar and wouldn't be coming home till later.

Even in the dim light of the bedroom, I could tell she had been crying.

When my mother died in the fall and we buried her body, I wondered if she somehow planned it that way because it was autumn and the time for death. But losing her seemed impossible no matter what season, what day, or what time of year and it broke my heart beyond repair, like her fishbowl.

I tried to tell myself her death was God's will, but I couldn't believe it, no matter how hard I tried. No God of mine could have willed my mother's death. I could search my whole life and still find no rhyme or reason to convince or comfort me.

Maybe it was a cruel joke, after all; the workings of a malevolent god. The same god that willed my mother's goldfish to die that beautiful spring day. That was the day she realized celebrating her new year in the spring of a foreign land, where its people celebrated their new year in the winter, meant things would never be the same.

For her, Tala's death was the death of the old life she had known.

* * *

The first day of my father's trial approached with furious speed. It was a terrifying feeling knowing the fate of someone you loved rested in the hands of total strangers. People who didn't know about you, your life, or the people in your life. All they knew were facts, evidence, witness testimonies. A man's whole life and character defined by those two words: "guilty" or "not guilty."

I arrived at the court with Grandpa Behruz, Aunt Maryam, and Uncle Eskandar. It felt like I was having an out-of-body experience; everything within me refused to accept this reality.

We decided – my father included – that Rostam shouldn't be exposed to the trial and dropped him off at a trusted neighbor's house. They were a nice Turkish family and Rostam got along with their two kids. Since the trial was in the morning and would likely run until after Rostam got out of school, they were going to drop him off and pick him up from school. When Rostam asked where we were going and why he couldn't come, I simply said it wasn't a place for children, all of a sudden very conscious of my own ascent into adulthood.

My age felt heavier than it should, weighing my shoulders down. For a brief moment, I forgot how old I was. I couldn't possibly be fifteen; I felt much older. No matter how old your birth certificate says you are, it's your experiences that age you. Every line and wrinkle marks the cost of experience, of pains endured. I wondered how dented and grooved my heart was.

Walking into the courtroom and seeing my father looking so small and defeated physically hurt. I wanted to give him a reassuring look, but instead I bowed my head and focused on my feet making their way to our seats. I sensed him turn around to look at us and hoped our presence gave him some form of comfort. I was too much of a coward to look at him, afraid if we locked eyes, I would see something in his I could not handle. Or maybe he would see the fear and uncertainty in mine. Or maybe it would make all this too real.

When he turned back around, I looked up to get a glimpse at his lawyer, an overweight, middle-aged man with a full head of gray hair and a bulbous red nose. He looked more like those Santa Claus impersonators at the mall than a lawyer, but seeing him poring over the case documents and speaking into my dad's ear reassured me a little bit. Maybe he had a plan. Maybe he knew things I would never know.

When the judge entered and we all rose, everything started happening too fast. The first step of the trial was something the lawyers called the voir dire process, or jury selection, and most of the jury members that were selected were white, middle-class working males and would likely be biased against my father. A jury of his peers, indeed. The prosecution knew what they were doing and the case seemed to already be shifting in their favor with the jury selection.

After the voir dire, the district attorney – a short man with piercing blue eyes and rapid movements – walked up to the front of the courtroom to present his opening statement. As soon as he started speaking, I hated him. He had a lisp and spoke in a slow, dramatic fashion that juxtaposed with his quick physical movements.

During his statement, this little man would point to my father with his slender fingers, then turn to face the jury members with violent intensity, as if to say, "Here's your criminal, I've got him for you right here."

In that moment, it seemed as though I had lost my sense of hearing or the ability to comprehend words. Everything out of this man's mouth was gibberish to me, as if my body and mind were still rebelling – unable to accept any of this as reality. I could only register gestures and movements, trying desperately to follow along and know what the others knew. I tried to read the faces of the jury members, searching for a faint sign of pity or doubt.

Their faces were stone.

I glimpsed at the judge's face, but he only nodded every time the district attorney addressed him, every "Your Honor" slimier than the next. I didn't want to know what my father was thinking or feeling. I wanted to run away, but couldn't move.

When my dad's lawyer addressed the court, I remember him being up there for a much shorter period of time. His movements were slower, and his voice sounded like a low hum. When he spoke to the jury, I peered from face to face and this time, noticed some of the stone faces scowling, trying to make this less competent lawyer with almost no case understand he was defending a murderer and they wouldn't let him get away with it.

The state's sharp, quick-witted lawyer would bury him and they would back him up, voting in the name of justice to give this foreign murderer what he deserved. Hell, if he could murder his wife so easily, what would stop him from murdering strangers – hard-working American citizens like themselves?

It was as if I could read their minds.

After the two lawyers spoke, the judge called for a recess, but before he could leave, the district attorney hurried to the judge's stand and asked if he could approach the bench. After being granted permission, he said something to the judge in a low voice.

The judge nodded his head.

"At the prosecution's request, this court will reconvene at the next trial date for cross examination and witness testimonies. Court dismissed," the judge bellowed, banging the gavel. After the bailiff said, "All rise," everyone stood up collectively and then dispersed to go their own ways.

My dad's lawyer said something to him and patted him on the back, to which my father responded with a shrug. A police officer stood next to him, handcuffs in hand, waiting to take him away. We exited the courtroom before I could make eye contact with him. I looked back in time to catch a glimpse of his back – hunched over, small – getting swallowed up by men in suits and uniforms.

We walked toward the building exit in silence. I wondered why the district attorney asked to dismiss the court earlier. Did they need more time to gather evidence or witnesses? I looked up at my uncle walking beside me, wanting to ask him if he was one of those witnesses and if so, whether he'd be willing to testify against his own brother. I said nothing because I already knew the answer.

As soon as we were in the open air, Uncle Eskandar's hand flew to his pocket and produced a pack of cigarettes. Tapping the open end into the palm of his hand, he pulled out a slender white stick, inserted it between his lips, and lit it to life with his lighter. A cigarette seemed to always dangle from a corner of his mouth nowadays; I could see why *Baba* Behruz was worried. Aunt Maryam turned away and walked faster, trying to put some distance between herself and my uncle's cigarette smoke.

"That was a waste of time, they hardly did anything today," Uncle Eskandar said. As he spoke, the cigarette delicately bobbed and let out a steady thread of smoke, making his eyes water.

What was he expecting, a sentencing already? I bit my tongue.

"Everything in this country has a special process and it all takes time," my grandfather said, leaning heavily on his cane. Then, after a pause, "They'll call on you to testify."

Uncle Eskandar nodded and said nothing, taking a long drag on his cigarette as if he relied on it to breathe.

"Well?"

"I was subpoenaed, so I have to testify," he said, exhaling smoke. "But I'll tell them exactly what I saw. Nothing more, nothing less."

My grandfather said nothing. What could he say? His eldest son would be testifying against his youngest son.

Blood against blood.

There's a Persian saying, *Baradara gooshte hamo mikhoran, ama ostokhoone hamo door nemirizan.*

"Brothers may eat one another's flesh, but they won't throw away the bones."

I wasn't too sure about that. Uncle Eskandar seemed capable of both eating the flesh and throwing away the bones. I prayed I was wrong. I prayed somewhere deep down, he still loved his younger brother enough to protect him.

Aunt Maryam was silent the entire time and glimpsing over at her, I couldn't tell what she was thinking. It was a difficult position to be in; on the one hand, seeking justice for her sister and on the other, wishing that justice didn't come at the expense of her brother-in-law and the father of her nephews.

She must often feel like an outsider, my mother having been her closest relative. Now with my mother gone, she probably felt isolated. Her love for me and Rostam – her sister's mementos – was the only thing that kept her attached.

Chapter Sixteen

On our way home from the trial, Grandpa Behruz announced he was treating us to dinner from the restaurant, so he took our orders in the car and called to have the food prepared for pick-up. Even though I could tell Aunt Maryam wasn't in the mood for company, she invited them over to eat with us.

When we picked up Rostam from the neighbor's house, he sensed our somber demeanors and refrained from talking too much or asking questions. It saddened me to know this entire ordeal would eventually rob my little brother of his childhood, too. Like me, he would be forced to wonder at his age.

The smell of kabob and saffron filled the tense air of our small dining room and I realized I was starving. We ate in frenzied silence, filling our mouths with food so no words could escape. Words we didn't want or know how to say. Rostam was the only one who ate at a slower pace, stealing nervous glances at us and no doubt wondering where we'd been and why we didn't speak of it.

After finishing his dinner, my uncle pulled out his pack of cigarettes again. Seeing my aunt's expression, he cracked open the window behind him and lit the cigarette. Aunt Maryam looked down and said nothing. Uncle Eskandar tried to blow the smoke outside, but as soon as it filled the room, my aunt rose from her seat.

"Kids, help me clean up the table?" she asked, but I knew we didn't have a choice in the matter.

I shot up from my chair to pick up the rice Rostam had spilled all over his lap before he had a chance to get out of his seat. After cleaning up my brother, I gathered the empty Styrofoam carry-out containers for Rostam to take to the kitchen and grabbed the dishes and utensils myself. When we entered the kitchen, I could tell Aunt Maryam was upset. She took the dishes from me without a word and turned on the faucet. I helped Rostam throw the containers into the recycling and walked out for the rest of the dishes.

My uncle took a long drag on the dying cigarette and then crushed it into the uneaten tomato on his plate. "You can take this, Cyrus *jan*," he said, pointing to the plate covered in cigarette ashes. I nodded and took it, dumping the tomato into the trash and wiping away the ashes with a paper towel before handing it to my aunt.

When the dishes were done, Aunt Maryam prepared the tea and I put together a small bowl of fruit. Rostam looked bored, so I told him to go watch TV. I promised I'd join him soon, as I also didn't want him to hear anything about the trial; Uncle Eskandar was bound to make comments.

My grandfather was in deep thought and it was apparent he wasn't in the mood to speak; our presence was the only thing preventing him from becoming wholly lost to his thoughts and worries.

"*Hajj-agha*, you look tired," Aunt Maryam gently broke the silence. "Please feel free to take a nap in the kids' room once you finish your tea."

"Thank you, Maryam *jan*, but we'll be leaving soon," Grandpa Behruz said. "We've troubled you enough today."

"No trouble," my aunt replied. "*Khoone khodetoone*." This was a *tarof* to guests, translating to, "Our home is your home."

Uncle Eskandar cleared his throat and I braced myself. "From the looks of it, this case is not going to go in my brother's favor. We should not get our hopes up or fool ourselves."

With his testimony, he would make sure of it, I thought. It took everything within me to keep quiet.

He continued, "The unfortunate truth is whether by accident or intent, Sohrab ended Pari's life and has to face the consequences. We can't sit here and keep asking why this tragedy happened, what's done is done and we have to move on."

I couldn't believe what I was hearing. I looked over my shoulder and was relieved to find Rostam watching television, out of earshot of my uncle's words.

"We have to think about Cyrus and Rostam and as their legal guardians in the absence of their parents, we have to do right by them."

I looked over at my aunt and grandfather, but they remained silent. Were they in agreement with this nonsense?

"I'm sorry, *Amoo*, but I think it's up to the judge and jury to decide the case," I said, the trembling of my body spilling into my voice. "I would appreciate if you didn't talk about my father as if his fate has already been decided."

131

"There are some things you don't know, Cyrus," my uncle said with a wave of his hand. *"Dahanet boo shir mide."* Adults use this expression to chide the young who meddle in adult affairs, and it literally translates to, "Your breath still smells of your mother's milk." Or, the English equivalent, "You're still wet behind the ears."

"What don't I know?" I challenged him.

"Cyrus, enough," Aunt Maryam hissed, but I ignored her.

"No, it's fine, he should know," Uncle Eskandar said. "I was there that day; I saw your father – I saw everything! He's guilty, Cyrus, and whether it was by accident or not, Sohrab killed your mother."

I felt my face burning with anger and looked over again in Rostam's direction. He was distracted by our raised voices and looked over at us with wide, questioning eyes. I smiled at him and reassured him everything was okay. He turned his attention back to the television screen, but looked unsettled. Rostam was smart. Pretty soon, he'd start putting bits and pieces together and continue asking questions until he got a convincing answer.

I pictured him asking questions later tonight before we went to bed. *"Cyrus, what did Uncle mean when he said, 'Sohrab killed your mother'?"*

What could I possibly say to him?

"How can you claim you care about us when you talk about your own brother like this and can't be considerate about what you say around my five-year-old brother?" I spat at him. To my surprise, Uncle Eskandar's expression softened and he smiled.

"You're right, I'm sorry about that, but I am not sorry about telling you the truth, which Rostam will find out sooner or later," he said in a lower tone. "You and Rostam need a father figure, someone who will be there for you. All I'm trying to say is whatever happens, I'm here for the both of you."

"May God keep you for your own children, but we already have a father," I said. "And we also have *Baba* Behruz."

I wasn't going to let him have his way. As long as my grandfather was alive, I didn't consider my uncle as my guardian, let alone a father figure. We had Aunt Maryam, too, but I didn't mention that because I was irritated with her for never coming to my defense. Whenever I tried to stand up for my dad, she either silenced me or reproached me and I was getting tired of it, but for the time being, I ignored it and focused my anger back on Uncle Eskandar.

I wasn't buying this act he was pulling. Besides, he was hardly a father figure to his own children, let alone me and Rostam. Since childhood, my uncle had been in competition with his younger brother, wanting to be the best at everything. Now, for whatever reason, he wanted to prove he could be a better father to us than our own dad. My uncle was selfish and whenever he offered to do anyone a favor, he only did it if it benefitted him in some way.

"You can resist all you want and you may not believe me, Cyrus, but I want what's best for you and Rostam," Uncle Eskandar said.

"You have no idea what's best for us," I shot back.

"That's enough for today," *Baba* Behruz finally said, raising his hands in protest. "As if we don't have enough problems, I have to deal with the two of you always bickering. Enough! *Baseh dige!"*

I mumbled an apology and looked down at my hands. Uncle Eskandar said nothing. He tried to smoke another cigarette, but my grandpa signaled for him to put it away.

"Smoking, always smoking," *Baba* Behruz cried. "If you want to kill yourself, that's fine, but don't subject everyone else to it, especially not my grandchildren. I've told you a thousand times not to smoke near them."

Aunt Maryam excused herself to get more tea.

"Don't trouble yourself, Maryam *khanoom*, I think it's time for us to leave," my grandpa called after her, looking around for his cane. "This day has worn me out."

"Of course, thank you again for dinner, *Hajj-agha,"* Aunt Maryam said, coming back from the kitchen holding an empty tray.

"It was nothing, thank you for coming to the trial today."

Aunt Maryam nodded and didn't say anything. We accompanied my grandfather and uncle to the door. Grandpa Behruz waved a quick goodbye to Rostam on his way to the door, but my uncle stopped in front of my little brother and held out his arms.

I was stunned.

"Aren't you going to give your uncle a hug goodbye?" he said.

My oblivious brother smiled wide and jumped up into my uncle's outstretched arms. I couldn't hold it against Rostam; he didn't know of my uncle's selfish intentions and I knew he missed Dad. My uncle and father looked very similar, especially now that *Baba* had aged so much. Just as Aunt Maryam physically resembled *Maman* Pari, I could say the same for Uncle Eskandar and

Baba Sohrab. But whereas my aunt and mother actually shared a lot of the same qualities, my uncle and father did not.

The two brothers were like night and day.

While Rostam clung to him, my uncle turned around to look me straight in the eyes. Without breaking eye contact, he kissed the top of my brother's curly head.

When he put Rostam back down on the couch, he said, "If you continue to be a good boy, I'll have a special prize for you next time. Deal?"

Rostam smiled and nodded, thrilled his uncle was paying him some attention all of a sudden. Uncle Eskandar high-fived him and laughed, as if this is how his relationship had been with us our entire lives. Where was the stern, aloof uncle we'd always known, who was always frowning and giving orders?

Aunt Maryam placed her hand on my shoulder, silently begging me not to show a reaction. I listened to her this time.

When they left, I went to my room and shut the door, wanting to be alone. I thought about my dad and how he must be feeling after today's trial. Had he already lost hope? Despite everything, I still wanted to believe he could be innocent – that this was all a big mistake. I wanted to write him an email and offer some form of reassurance; I felt guilty for not being able to do that at the trial today. The image of him sitting in the courtroom, looking so alone and vulnerable, wouldn't go away.

Aunt Maryam came into the room twenty minutes later carrying a sleeping Rostam. I looked at the time on my laptop; it was half past ten. I didn't realize it was so late. After tucking my brother into bed, she turned around and looked at me with a strange expression.

"The day you were born, I was already living here, and your mother called to give me the good news," she said, smiling at the memory. "Her happiness was contagious as she described your every detail, but then she got quiet all of a sudden. Worried, I asked if everything was okay. She drew a deep breath and said, 'Maryam, I am mother to the most perfect boy.' She started crying and wouldn't stop, so I asked why she was sad. You know what she told me?"

I shook my head, my aunt's head swimming in the tears filling my eyes.

"I'll never forget it, she calmed down a little and said, 'Because I just realized never again will I be as happy as I am in this very moment.'"

Khaleh Maryam walked over to me and held my face between her hands, wiping my tears away with her thumb. "Pari loved you so much, and I know she's proud of the man you've become. Don't think I haven't noticed how well you've been handling everything and taking care of Rostam. I'm proud of you, too."

"Thanks, *Khaleh*," I whispered. "I just don't want anything to happen to him. I'm constantly afraid he'll be taken away from me, too, just like Mom and Dad, and I won't be able to do anything about it."

"Nothing is going to happen to him as long as he has you," she said. "Remember, you also have me and I'm not going anywhere, either. Don't worry about your uncle, he's just trying to show you he cares in his own way."

"I wish I could believe that," I mumbled, then I had a thought. "By the way, did you decide if you're going to make a trip to Iran to see Grandma?"

"I thought about it and I'm going to stay put for now."

"Why? Don't you want to see her?"

"It's complicated, Cyrus," she said in a defensive tone. "I'm needed here more and besides, she probably won't remember me or be able to talk to me, so what's the point? It'll be another pain I'll have to carry – another loss."

"But you're her daughter—" I began.

"No, I'm her disappointment. Her daughter is dead."

"What about Grandpa? I'm sure he'd love to see you."

"Cyrus, there's a lot you don't know," she said, pulling at a loose thread poking out of her blouse sleeve. "We would just argue the whole time. We don't see eye to eye on anything, and especially not on this current situation regarding your father."

It was pointless to argue, so I looked down at my hands and gave up trying to change her mind. Once her mind was made up, there was no use convincing her otherwise.

"Don't concern yourself with any of that, I'll figure it out," she said and kissing my forehead, wished me goodnight and left me alone with my own worries.

I cracked open the window facing my desk so the cool night air could keep me awake long enough to type up a quick email to my dad.

When I finished the email, which was a pathetic two-line attempt asking him how he was doing and that I was hopeful of the outcome of the trial, I closed my laptop and yawned. I felt like I'd been awake for days.

As I was getting ready to close the window, I heard the silvery click of a lighter outside and saw a cigarette sizzling to life in the dark street below, burning a glowing orange hole into the black fabric of night.

Chapter Seventeen

The following day at school, I was happy to be there for once; it was a much-needed distraction from the trial and everything else on my mind. Since I had to miss school the day before because of the trial, Aunt Maryam wrote me a sick note to hand in to Mr. Becks. I didn't need unexcused absences bringing down my already fragile grades.

After handing the note to Mr. Becks, I was about to walk away from his desk when he motioned for me to wait. He unfolded the piece of paper and glanced over it. When he finished reading, he raised his eyes at me questioningly, as if he wasn't convinced and expected an explanation from me.

"So, you're feeling better today, Mr. Nezami?" he asked, plucking his glasses off his nose and dropping them on the pile of papers in front of him.

"Yes, much better, thank you," I said, trying to maintain eye contact with him, but there was something about the way he looked at me that made me uneasy.

"Very well, but I should mention Mrs. Krasinski plans to speak with you later today," he said, crossing his arms across his huge chest.

It was just an absence, what was the big deal?

"Do you know what it's in regard to? Is it because of my absence yesterday?" I asked.

"Something like that, but I'm not inclined to discuss what she's going to speak to you about," he replied. "You'll find out from her soon enough."

I trudged over to my desk, heart ramming. Yiannis was absent for an away game, so I was on my own. On the way back to my desk, I got a couple of strange looks from some of my classmates, but I ignored them.

After the bell rang, I looked around the hallway on my way to English, paranoid that Mrs. Krasinski would pop out of nowhere and ask to talk to me. Why couldn't Mr. Becks mind his own damn business? I was doing the work for his class and participating more; my class performance was the only thing he needed to concern himself with. My personal life was nobody's business and I shouldn't be referred to the guidance counselor for missing one day of class.

When I made it to English without any run-ins with Mrs. Krasinski, I saw Tamara and waved, but she looked down as if she hadn't seen me. Dropping my hand, I made my way to my seat. I'd hoped school would be a sanctuary, but this day was turning out to be a nightmare. There were more stares and whispers from the kids in class.

It finally dawned on me that something was going on and it involved me.

My phone vibrated – a text from Tamara. I glanced up in her direction, but she didn't return my look. When I tapped on the screen to read her text under my desk, I already knew it couldn't be anything good.

"Why didn't you tell me?" was all her text said. I was so confused.

"Tell you what? What's going on with everyone today?" I texted back.

"You really don't know? It's what everyone's been talking about today! Your dad's trial, Cyrus. I know we're just starting to get to know each other, but I wish you'd have trusted me enough to tell me."

I was stunned, but everyone's weird behavior now made perfect sense.

"Wow, how did everyone find out? I'm sure you can understand it's not exactly something I want to share with anybody."

When I hit "send," I glanced over and saw Tamara's bent head as she read my text, then her fingers tapped at her phone screen without a moment's hesitation.

"I understand, but I thought we were friends. And it's a public trial, of course it's going to get covered in the news."

I was mortified and prayed the floor could open wide and swallow me whole. Now almost everybody in school knew about my father and what was going on with my family. I couldn't escape it. It never once occurred to me that news of the trial could come out and I'd no longer be able to keep it a secret.

I assumed when news of the shooting was first reported, it was at the beginning of the school year when no one knew me or my name. Since we were further into the year by now, people had figured out the trial's connection to the shooting a couple of months ago – and my family's involvement. Yiannis would probably give me an even harder time than Tamara for leaving out this huge detail. For the first time that day, I was glad he was absent.

"Look Tamara, I'm sorry, but you have to understand I was nervous to share this with you – it's been crazy, everything my family's been through these past few months and I didn't know what you'd think of me if you found out. I don't even know what I think of it yet. Like you said, we're just getting to know each other and I was afraid if I told you, you wouldn't want anything to do with me. That's the only reason I didn't tell you, not because I don't trust you."

She replied back, *"I understand where you're coming from, but I wish you had more faith in me than that. We all go through messed up shit, especially when it comes to family and if someone cares for you, they won't judge or blame you 'cause they know it's not something you can control. Instead of hiding it, you could've just told me and I would've understood or at least tried to understand. It would've been so much better to hear it from you than from somewhere or someone else like I did."*

Now I felt horrible for keeping this from my two closest friends. Tamara was right – it would've been much better coming from me. I had to tell Yiannis before he found out from the news or someone in school.

"You're right and I'm sorry. You've been a great friend and I should've told you. Are we okay?"

I stole another sideways glance at Tamara as she read my text and caught a faint smile.

"We're good and apology accepted. Also, if anyone says something ignorant, just ignore them. Their opinions don't matter."

Just as I was getting ready to reply back to Tamara, I heard Mrs. Miller calling my name.

"Cyrus, Mrs. Krasinski would like to see you, please."

I looked up and saw the guidance counselor standing at the front of the room next to Mrs. Miller, smiling at me. Now I understood why she wanted to see me. Everyone's heads turned in my direction. Ignoring their looks, I stood up, gathered my things, and walked to the front of the room followed by whispers.

Once we were out of the classroom, Mrs. Krasinski turned to me with concern in her eyes and asked, "How are you doing today, Cyrus?"

"I'm fine, just a little confused, I guess."

"Well, let's go to my office and we can discuss it there," she said, quickening her steps. I followed in silence until we made it to the claustrophobic room. I dropped my backpack next to the chair facing the desk and sat down.

"It looks like you haven't been completely honest with me, Cyrus," Mrs. Krasinski said, sitting down to face me.

"What about?"

"According to the news that's been circulating around the school today, it seems you're dealing with a lot more than just your mother's passing, Cyrus."

"With all due respect, Mrs. Krasinski, I don't think my personal life and what's going on in it are anybody's business," I replied, trying to keep a level tone.

"That's absolutely true and you have every right to your privacy, but when issues at home start affecting our students at school, then that's when it becomes the business of the school," Mrs. Krasinski said, placing emphasis on the word "school." Her high-pitched voice, combined with the large loris eyes, made her seem more like a cartoon character than a guidance counselor. I found it hard to take her seriously.

"I've tried my best to not let it affect my performance at school, and I've been doing better recently."

"I know, Mr. Becks has kept me updated on your improvement, but this is more than just how well you're doing in school," Mrs. Krasinski said. "Above all, we care about the well-being of our students. If there's a problem at school, home, or elsewhere, we try to help our students find a solution, which is why I'm here."

"I understand, but..." I began, interrupted by Mrs. Krasinski holding up a hand to stop me.

"Let me emphasize that you're not in any sort of trouble and given the circumstances, nobody expects you to be doing wonderfully at school or in general. We understand the severity of your situation and only want to make sure you're doing okay, that's all."

"Thank you," is all I could manage to say.

"Today must have been especially difficult, with the news of your father's trial circulating around the school," she continued. "It's part of the reason I wanted to see you today to discuss another important matter with you. As you know, some students can be much less sensitive or even cruel when it comes to this sort of thing, so if anybody makes any comments or does anything inappropriate, I want you to let me or any of your teachers know right away."

I nodded.

"Good," she said and then looked at me for a few seconds. Her eyes looked sadder than usual, if that were even possible. "I really am sorry about what you're going through, Cyrus. Just know I'm here if you need anything and my door is always open if you want to talk or use my office to get away and relax for a bit. You can come in, kick me out, and have the place all to yourself for a while."

"I appreciate it, thank you." And I meant it. I could tell she sincerely wanted to help.

"You're welcome, now is there anything else you'd like to talk about today before I let you go?"

"I think I'm good for now, thank you, Mrs. Krasinski," I said, standing up and picking up my backpack.

"Alright, and remember, my door is always open. Take care, Cyrus."

I nodded and said goodbye.

The rest of the day went by in a blur, much to my relief. At lunch, I sat with Tamara since Yiannis was absent, and I tried my best to pay no attention to the dirty looks I was getting from George Mullins and his posse a few tables away. Tamara and I talked about other things and she no longer seemed upset with me. I could tell she wanted to ask me about my family and the trial, but decided it wasn't the right time or place for it, which I appreciated.

"Listen, Tamara, I promise I'll explain everything to you soon, okay?" I said after a moment of silence.

She smiled and nodded, not saying anything. When the bell rang, I walked Tamara to her next class, wishing we didn't have to part ways; I didn't want to go through the rest of the day by myself. But thankfully, my family and I seemed to be old news closer to the end of the day. At least for the time being.

On the bus ride home, I called Yiannis. After some small talk and Yiannis joking about how I couldn't bear to be away from him for one day, I told him everything that's been going on with my family, how my mother died, and the trial. I told him news of the trial had spread around school and I wanted him to hear about it from me, not someone else. I explained my reasoning for not being completely honest and apologized.

After I finished talking, Yiannis was still silent. My heart beat so loudly in my ear I was afraid it would drown out Yiannis's voice when he eventually did speak.

"Say something, man," I said.

"I don't know what to say, Cy," Yiannis replied. "I can't imagine going through that. It's a lot."

"Yeah, and that's honestly the only reason I didn't get into the details. I didn't even know where to start or what you'd think of me and my family after I told you."

"Shit, I don't blame you," Yiannis said. "I would've done the same if I were in your shoes, but we all deal with family issues to a certain degree and I'd never judge you or ruin our friendship over it."

"That's pretty much what Tamara said."

"Oh man, she found out at school today, too, huh?"

"Yeah, she wasn't very happy with me for not telling her sooner, but I apologized and promised to explain everything to her soon."

"Well, if there's anything I can do, I'm here for you," Yiannis said. "I mean it, bro."

"Thanks, man, and thanks for understanding."

We said goodbye and hung up.

For the first time in a long time, I felt a little lighter.

Chapter Eighteen

Dear Cyrus,

Thank you for your email and for thinking about me – I will be fine, don't worry. I wanted to talk a little bit more about Cyrus the Great and the lesson we can take away from the last story I sent you. During Cyrus' rule, there were countless instances, similar to the last one, where his sense of justice was put to the test.

After the amulet was found, Cyrus could have very easily let the innocent servant boy take the fall instead of one of his most trusted advisors. As emperor, he could do anything he wanted, but his conscience kept him in check. You see, Cyrus, a good and honest man will always act based on his conscience, no matter how much power, wealth, and influence he has.

On the flip side of the coin, it's important to note no matter how damning the evidence against an innocent man is and no matter how little power, wealth, and influence he has, the truth will always come out. His innocence will be proven one way or the other. We must have faith that it will.

Although I felt bad for thinking this, I did wonder whether my dad was using the Cyrus stories to avoid facing the truth and addressing questions he didn't have answers to. Or didn't want to give answers to. Maybe insisting on his innocence and believing in it helped alleviate his guilt. I prayed to God to take years off my life if it meant my father wasn't guilty of what he was being accused of. I didn't want to lose another parent – or hate him forever because he was the cause of my mother's loss. And yet all of this insistence and escape from reality just made him look more guilty. I hoped I was wrong.

I continued reading:

I have to admit, though, my faith has not been very strong lately. I think to myself, what if justice is not served and no one believes I am innocent? What if I have to pay the price for someone else's crime? And the thought of someone doing that to your mother and me not being there to protect her and prevent it from happening torments me to no end. I'm supposed to be the protector of my family and yet I failed you all. I don't know if I ever apologized to you for that, but I am so sorry I couldn't protect your mother. I am so sorry I can't be there now to protect you and Rostam. If I make it through this nightmare, the shame of my shortcomings will weigh on my shoulders until my last breath.

But you know what tortures me the most, Cyrus? Not that I may rot in prison or be sentenced to death – no, those things are trivial in comparison to being found guilty of having ended the life of one whom I cherished and loved most in this world, one whom I vowed to protect – my wife and the mother of my children. Of having robbed my children of their mother. Of having brought such misery and shame upon my family. That's what tortures me the most. A man is nothing without his reputation and good name, and I would rather die than have anyone, especially my family, think I murdered my wife.

I wish I knew who did this to us. I wish I could prove to you and everyone else that it wasn't me. I don't know why anyone would want to hurt us, particularly your mother. I've gone over that hellish day thousands of times in my head. I've thought maybe it was a hate crime against us or a stranger trying to rob us. Horrible things happen every minute of every day without any explanation. Yet this person didn't leave a trace and I was the one who happened to show up at that moment. If only I'd showed up sooner or left for work later. If only I had a more convincing explanation. If only...

Cyrus, you have to promise me no matter what happens, you'll do your best to protect Rostam from all of this. I am so proud of what a great older brother you are to him. Promise me you'll always be that way – that you'll love and support your brother no matter what. I expect him to do the same because he has you as his role model. As you know, and this isn't easy for me to admit, I've never had that with your uncle Eskandar. Our relationship has always been complicated and it's become one of the biggest regrets of my life. I apologize for not setting a good example for you in this regard, but I ask you to be better than me and learn from my mistakes and shortcomings.

Over the years, Eskandar and I grew further apart and certain issues only widened the gap – issues that no longer seem important in hindsight. You may already know about some of our disputes and I am sorry for that. Either way, I want to tell you what happened. When Eskandar came to the U.S. with your grandpa, I was just starting college. The physical distance hurt our relationship even more and to be honest, I always resented him and my father for leaving, especially when Grandma got sick. I felt they had both abandoned us.

When we came to the U.S. years later, Eskandar helped me out by lending me a large sum of money since I wasn't working. I promised I'd pay him back as soon as I became financially stable. The main reason we had a falling out is I still haven't been able to pay back the debt I owe him. Not that I didn't want to, but with my low residency income and having to support a family, I haven't been able to afford it yet. I gave him my word, in writing, that I would pay him back the full amount I owed plus interest as soon as I started work at a practice. Well, your uncle felt he couldn't wait any longer, that he gave me more than enough time to pay him back and because I haven't been able to yet, I should instead give him my share of the restaurant to settle the debt. I disagreed with him, claiming it was unfair of him to ask for my share of the restaurant, which is my – and more importantly, your and Rostam's – rightful inheritance from your grandfather.

I know Eskandar is struggling financially and I hold myself accountable for not having paid him back yet, but your uncle's always been a little selfish. It's either all or nothing with him – there's no in-between. Sure, he's worked very hard in the restaurant for many years, more than I have, but I didn't think he deserved full ownership of it. And so we argued and fought for years, placing more importance on expendable, material things than on our brotherly bond. We lost sight of who we were. I admit, I was selfish, too. Maybe I could've paid him back little by little, but I chose not to. I kept making excuses and putting it off and building more resentment, more bitterness. And now, the worst part of all this is that he has to testify against me in court. My own brother, my own flesh and blood. How did it come to this? It saddens me to see how far we've fallen.

I don't want to burden you with any of this, but I needed you to know the truth and do better than I did. Be better. I ask that you take care of Rostam and not allow trivial things like this to ever come between you two. Money and property and jobs come and go, but you only have one brother. Family is irreplaceable. I learned all this when it was too late. Don't make my mistakes. Be better.

Love,

– Baba

I sensed the frustration in my father's email, along with a subtle desperation to persuade me with his words; to convince me he was innocent and being accused of something he hadn't done. He had never tried so hard to convince me before. More than anything, I wanted to believe he was innocent, but I couldn't shake off the nagging feeling that he was trying a little too hard.

I appreciated him giving me a straightforward, honest account of his relationship with my uncle instead of another Cyrus story, but there were parts of his email that troubled me and I couldn't put my finger on it. I almost wanted him to go back to telling stories again. His tone had shifted, as if the severity of his situation was just sinking in. It scared me that he was scared.

I sat in front of my laptop for a long time, trying to figure out what to say. I was afraid my words would further upset him, and his reaction would make me lose more faith in his innocence. I decided I wasn't ready to respond yet and closed my laptop.

* * *

From a young age, my parents taught me the importance of believing in something; of having faith. They never forced religion on me and instead, explained and encouraged.

They said having faith and believing in a higher power strengthened your conscience and the ability to choose between right and wrong. Neither of my parents were that religious, but they were firm believers in believing.

"I think it's a backwards belief that children have no choice but to take on and accept their parents' religion as their own," my father once said. "You should never blindly accept anything, especially religion, without first researching and learning about it. You have to fully understand what you're being asked to accept, so you can accept it with an open, willing heart. You have to question and have doubts and always seek to know more."

Unlike more traditional Persian families who practiced Islam, my parents never required me to pray or fast when I came of age; they told me it was not something you could be forced into. I was always curious and had a strong belief in God, but I was not one to follow rituals. I felt I could be closer to God amongst His creations, rather than reading from a book or visiting a mosque. I wasn't against doing any of those things and grew up experiencing them, especially since my grandpa and uncle were religious. But for me, witnessing a sunset was worship in the purest sense of the word.

My father used to recite us a quote by Rumi, his favorite of the Persian poets, that stuck with me:

If in thirst you drink water from a cup, you see God in it.
Those who are not in love with God will only see their faces in it.

I went for a walk around the neighborhood to pray. Standing underneath the dusking sky, the chill of late November licking at my bones, I closed my eyes to speak to God. Stuffing my cold hands inside the pockets of my coat, I found my dad's coin in the left one and closed my fist around it.

As I walked, my exhales produced fast, white puffs into the air, reminding me of when I was little and thought I was actually blowing smoke out of my mouth. It's funny how when we were children, we had all these elaborate, fantastical explanations for everything and yet life was much simpler; it made so much more sense back then. Now, the magic and fantasy are gone, but everything is somehow more complicated and makes less sense. I wondered if that was why my father preferred telling stories so much. Perhaps it was easier to explain life through stories.

When I reached the end of our block, I still didn't want to go back home and kept on walking. There was a small shopping center a few blocks up with a little coffee shop. I texted Aunt Maryam to let her know I'd be going there to study; glad I'd brought my backpack along with me. The coffee shop wasn't very crowded, so I bought a chai tea latte and grabbed an empty corner table near the window.

Occupied with my phone, I was about to take a careful sip from my drink when I heard a familiar whispering of my name, "Cyrus?"

It was Tamara.

Startled, I drank the hot tea too quickly and burnt my tongue. With watering eyes, I turned around to see where her voice was coming from. She'd just walked in, cheeks flushed from the cold air, wearing a white knit hat and a matching scarf loosely wrapped around her neck. In one hand, she was carrying a plastic shopping bag.

"Hey, Tamara!" I said, trying to ignore my burning tongue.

"Hey, what are you doing here? I saw you from the window and thought I'd say hi."

"I took a walk and wound up here, so I figured I'd stick around and study for a bit."

"Nice, well I needed to make an emergency run to the store for printing paper, which I realized we didn't have right when I got ready to print my essay for class tomorrow," she said, swinging the bag with the printing paper back and forth.

I chuckled. "Sounds about right. Are you in a hurry to get back home?"

"Nope, one of my friends dropped me off but had to leave, so I either have to walk back home or ride the bus, both of which I'm not very eager to do. I live a few blocks from here, too," she explained breathlessly.

"Join me then," I said, waving to the empty chair facing me. "Can I get you a drink?"

"I'm actually kind of hungry," she said. "My family's out of town for a few days to see a specialist for my sister, so I'm kind of on my own for dinner, too."

"I'm pretty hungry myself, that walk really worked up my appetite. You're welcome to come over to my house for dinner."

"Oh no, I don't want to trouble your aunt. Tell you what, we can get some take-out from the Chinese place around here and take it back to my place, if that's okay?"

"Yeah, sounds great," I said, my heart racing at the thought of going to Tamara's parent-free house. I tried to remain calm, grateful I could get my mind off my family for a little while. I threw away my untouched drink and didn't feel as bad about wasting it with my mouth still burning.

As we were walking out of the coffee shop, I recognized the middle-aged man holding the door open for us; he was one of my dad's co-residents at the hospital where he'd been doing his residency. We met him on a few occasions and he even came over one night for dinner about eight months ago. He recently moved here from Iran to advance his medical career. When Dad found out he was Persian, he befriended him right away and became a sort of unofficial mentor to him.

"*Salam aghaye* Jafari!" I said before he had a chance to go inside. I could tell he recognized me, too, but I was expected to greet him first since I was younger.

"Cyrus *jan, salam! Chetori?*" he cried in his booming voice and came over to give me a hug. He was stocky, short, and sported the bushiest mustache I'd ever seen.

"I'm good, how are you doing?"

"Okay, just here for coffee. I heard here is better than the Starbucks, no?" he said in his thick Farsi accent.

"Yes, their drinks are very good here," I said, then gestured to Tamara who was standing next to me and smiling politely. "This is my friend from school, Tamara, and this is one of my dad's co-workers, Mr. Jafari."

They shook hands and exchanged greetings.

"Tamara? What kind of name this is? Is Arabic name, no?" Mr. Jafari asked.

My dad had this running joke about how Mr. Jafari claimed anything sounding mildly exotic or foreign was either Persian or Middle Eastern in some way. On several occasions, Dad recounted one of his favorite memories involving Mr. Jafari, which was when he first went out to lunch with him during work and took him to the nearby Arby's.

As soon as Mr. Jafari saw the sign, he excitedly said, "Araby's? They have Arabian food, yes?" My father burst out laughing and then explained to a confused Mr. Jafari that Arby's did not in fact serve Arabian food. When he told us about the hilarious incident later that night, he had tears streaming down his face from laughing so hard.

"I don't know my name's origin, but I'll take Arabic!" Tamara said with a laugh.

"Yes, is Arabic, I'm sure of it," Mr. Jafari said, nodding his head in affirmation. "Well, I don't want to keep you, but it was so good to see you, Cyrus *jan*. Say hello to family for me."

I wasn't sure how much he knew about my father's long absence from work or what was going on with my family, but to my relief, he didn't say anything.

"I will, thank you. Take care."

Once he was inside, Tamara looked over at me with a wide grin.

"So, that was an example of someone with a thick Persian accent, correct?" she asked.

"Exactly, it's pretty similar to what my dad, uncle, and grandfather sound like, although Mr. Jafari's accent is much thicker since he's only been here for a year," I explained.

"Cool, well the accent is quite charming!"

I smiled. "It certainly grows on you."

After picking up two orders of shrimp lo mein from China King, we were too hungry to walk and took the bus to Tamara's house. This was the second time I was on a bus with Tamara and just like the first time, when she came over to interview me for her project, I was nervous. The greasy smell of the food wafted up to my nose and made my already-restless stomach feel queasy. I usually lost my appetite when I was nervous.

"So, what's your essay about?" I asked when the silence started to feel uncomfortable.

"Oh, it's for art class," Tamara explained. "We had to write a five-page research paper on an artist we admire, so I did mine on René Magritte."

"You had to write an essay for *art* class?"

"Yeah, Mr. Anderson's tough, but everyone likes him because he's so passionate about what he teaches," she said. "He wants us to first learn about the artist and then emulate the artist's particular style for our next project."

"Sounds interesting, so tell me about René – what was it?" I asked, a little embarrassed I forgot the artist's name.

"Magritte, he was a Belgian surrealist," Tamara said. "I love his work and I think he's a lot better than Salvador Dalí. Dalí's overrated."

"I have to admit I'm not very knowledgeable about art, but it's awesome you know so much and have artistic talent. You'll have to show me some of your work."

"Oh, I'm okay, but sure thing. So yeah, Magritte's most famous painting is called, "The Son of Man" and it's a self-portrait with a twist, where Magritte has a giant green apple painted in front of his face, hiding all his features except part of his eyes," Tamara said, her own eyes getting wide with excitement. "I just love the symbolism behind his paintings and in regard to this painting in particular, let me pull up his quote about it. It's so fascinating."

Tamara took her phone out of her backpack and starting typing.

"Okay, here it is, he says, 'It's something that happens constantly. Everything we see hides another thing; we always want to see what is hidden by what we see. There is an interest in that which is hidden and which the visible does not show us. This interest can take the form of a quite intense feeling, a sort of conflict, one might say, between the visible that is hidden and the visible that is present,'" she read, her face lit up by the phone screen in the dark bus. "So, I've basically based my paper on this painting and discuss what he means by this quote."

"That's really interesting, I'd love to see this painting and some of his other works," I said. "From what I understand, and correct me if I'm wrong, Magritte's saying everything's a facade hiding the real thing and that we always seek out what's hidden."

"Exactly, you got it. He was just so cool," Tamara said in her breathy whisper.

"I'd also like to read your paper about him," I offered.

"Sure, once I actually print it out," she said, giggling.

A few minutes later, the driver pulled up to our stop and as we made our way to the front of the bus, I heard an older white guy, who was giving us weird looks the entire time, say something under his breath as we passed him.

I stopped and turned around. "Excuse me?"

"I said, watch out for the terrorist!" he said.

"What the fuck did you just call me?" I clenched my fists and leered right at him.

"You heard me," the old man looked around to see if he had an audience and continued in a louder voice, "and I'm not afraid to use my Second Amendment right to help get my meaning across, boy."

"Cyrus, let's just go," Tamara pulled at my arm.

"Go to hell," I spat at him and then turned around to get off at our stop.

"That's right, get off the bus!" he yelled after us.

The bus pulled away.

"That was scary," Tamara said, her voice a little shaky.

"Yeah, what a nut-job! I can't believe people like him exist."

"It's awful, but this is Virginia, after all."

"Sadly, I think it's a universal problem."

After a short walk, we came to a neighborhood with rows of small, red-brick townhouses.

"This is us," Tamara said, walking up the steps to a house with neatly trimmed hedges and a colorful garden.

"You guys have a nice garden," I said.

"Thanks, it's my mom's thing."

Tamara unlocked the door and I followed her inside the dark house. It smelled like pine trees. Tamara turned on a switch in the hallway and I looked around, noticing how clean and organized everything was.

"Do you mind taking your shoes off? My mom is kind of a clean freak," she said, pulling off her own boots and placing them on the shoe rack.

"I thought only Persians had that rule about no shoes in the house." I took off my sneakers and sat them next to Tamara's boots.

She smiled and grabbing the shopping bags from me, asked me to follow her into the kitchen. To my surprise, I felt at ease. And hungry. While our food warmed up in the microwave, Tamara offered me a drink and gave me a quick tour of the ground floor, starting with the living room. Family photos and portraits lined the entirety of their small fireplace mantle and I thought about how I always wanted a fireplace just so my mom could decorate its mantle with our photos. I could tell they were a close and loving family just by being in their home. All of a sudden, a heavy longing grew inside my chest and rose up to my throat. A dense lump I couldn't swallow down. I'd almost forgotten what it felt like to have a complete family and being reminded of it made me ache for what I'd lost; for that feeling of security and contentment. I wanted to tell Tamara to be grateful for what she had every second.

Tamara pointed to a professionally-taken family portrait and introduced me to the still, smiling faces of her father, mother, and sister. Looking at them, I felt guilty for being alone in their home with their daughter.

"Hey, Tamara, you sure it's okay with your parents that I'm here? I kind of feel bad," I said, looking down.

"Oh, it's totally fine, they don't mind! But it's so thoughtful of you to mention," she said. "You're an absolute gentleman."

Just then, the microwave beeped and her eyes lit up. "Food's ready! Let's eat, I'm famished."

While we ate, Tamara showed me the René Magritte painting and let me read her essay. As we neared the end of our meal, she started telling me more about her sister's condition and the specialist her parents were seeing that weekend.

"My sister Lexi has a lot of trouble in school and sometimes her outbursts get pretty bad at home, so it's been really hard, especially on my parents. She's just the sweetest, most loving girl when she's calm," Tamara said, her eyes filling with tears. "I'm really hoping this specialist can help us. He's supposedly one of the best on the East Coast."

"I hope he can, too. How old is Lexi?" I asked.

"She's eight."

I was silent for a moment, swirling the uneaten greasy noodles around on my plate.

"Tamara, I think I'm ready to tell you everything that's been going on with my family."

"I'm all ears," she said. "And don't feel pressured to tell me every detail. Talk about whatever you're comfortable with."

I took a sip of my iced tea and told her everything that had happened since the beginning of school until now. Tamara listened with great patience, nodding her head every so often, her eyes soft and sympathetic – free of judgment.

When I finished, my mouth was dry and I could tell it was late. Tamara was looking at me with a mixture of wonder and sadness in her eyes.

"That's so much for one person to go through," she finally said. "I think it takes an incredible amount of strength and bravery."

"Not really, I'm just trying my best to keep what's left of my family together and take care of my little brother. He's only five and has to deal with something no five-year-old should have to go through. He's the brave one."

"Neither of you should have to go through it and I am truly sorry that you are," Tamara whispered.

"Thanks, Tamara, that means more than you know."

Her eyes were searching for something in mine – blushing, I looked away and stood up. "It's getting late, I should start heading out. Thank you so much for the company and for listening. I'm sorry if I upset you."

"Not at all, thank you for trusting me enough to tell me," she said. "And thank you for dinner."

"Anytime," I said. "Can I help you with the dishes?"

"No, thanks for offering, but I got it. I'll walk you out."

I put on my shoes and waited for her to open the door.

"I had a great time," I said.

"Me, too."

Tamara opened her arms for a hug, then slowly pulled away to look at me. With her face inches from mine and the same look she had in her eyes a few minutes ago, I knew she wanted me to kiss her. Tamara leaned in and I followed suit until our lips met. She moved her hands down from my arms to hold my shaking hands and pushed deeper into the kiss. I felt something tug at my insides, similar to how I felt the first time I saw her, but it was stronger this time and felt amazing. Like a sudden rush that flooded my entire body and had to be released. When I felt another stronger urge, I knew I had to stop her and pulled away gently.

In the dimly-lit hallway, Tamara smiled and looked down. "I'll see you later, I guess."

"See you, have a good night," I said, my voice a little hoarse. I cleared my throat and swinging my backpack over my shoulder, turned and walked down the porch steps. My heart was still racing and I could almost feel the blood rushing through my veins at warp speed.

It was almost 9 p.m. by the time I left Tamara's. Not wanting Aunt Maryam to worry, I texted to let her know I was heading home. Despite everything, after hanging out with Tamara and the sudden kiss we shared, I was floating.

* * *

A short bus ride later, I power-walked the rest of the way home since the temperature had dropped and my light coat wasn't doing much to keep me warm. I turned the corner toward my apartment building and keeping my head down to prevent the wind chill from stinging my eyes, I walked up to our apartment steps.

"And where have you been?"

Startled, I looked up and saw my uncle standing at the top of the steps, leaning on the railing. Per usual, a drooping cigarette sat at the corner of his mouth. He was taking his nightly smoke break.

"*Salam, Amoo,* I was at the coffee shop studying," I said.

"Good for you," he replied and pulled on the cigarette, the end glowing to life with the intake of breath. He didn't look too good – he was pale and his eyes were bloodshot red as if he hadn't slept in a long time.

I climbed the steps to hurry inside before he could say anything else, but then thought of something and reconsidered. I stood next to him on the top step and prayed the smell of cigarette smoke wouldn't stick to my clothes.

"Can I ask you something, *Amoo?*"

"Depends on what it is," he said, letting out a puff of smoke.

"What happened between you and *Baba?*"

Underneath the milky light of the streetlamp, his expression changed; he wasn't expecting me to ask him that. I rarely initiated conversation with Uncle Eskandar, but there was something different about his demeanor tonight. He finished off his cigarette and crushing it against the railing, flicked it into the bushes.

"What do you mean, 'what happened'?" he asked, collecting himself and looking at me with his red eyes.

"I mean, what created such a rift between you two that you're okay to testify against him?"

"I'm not okay with testifying against your dad, Cyrus," he said, pulling another cigarette out of the pack in his coat pocket. "I've been subpoenaed, which means I have no choice but to testify. It's not easy for me to go in front of all those people and tell them I witnessed my brother shoot his wife."

"That's fair, but I feel like you still have something against him and ever since we moved here, you two have always been in some sort of argument or fight."

"We have our differences and issues like many other siblings, but at the end of the day, I don't wish him ill," he said. "And those issues are between us and none of your concern, Cyrus *jan.*"

"It is my concern when my father is involved," I pushed back.

"It has nothing to do with this trial or my testimony. Long story short, your father owes me a good deal of money and he isn't willing to give me his share of the restaurant to settle his debt, so you see, we're in a bit of a stalemate situation."

Uncle Eskandar explained that according to Muslim law and tradition, which most Persians follow, the eldest sibling in a family receives a larger share of the inheritance. In their case, however, my grandfather did not follow this rule for two reasons: one, he lived in the U.S. and two, he tried to be fair by giving an equal share to both of his sons. His plan didn't work out so well.

"When Sohrab first came here, he had more time to work at the restaurant and things were so good for a while that Dad eventually stepped aside and I made Sohrab my partner, but he doesn't have time anymore because of his hours at the hospital. Not to mention, he's in jail now. Since we're partners, I have to ask for Sohrab's input before making any decisions, but your father was never available to talk about the restaurant because he was so busy trying to be a doctor. If *Baba* Behruz didn't help out, we'd probably be out of business by now. Still, the restaurant is hurting because of it. I'm hurting because of it," my uncle said. "Your father has his career as a doctor to fall back on if the restaurant fails. Me? I only have the restaurant. It's my life."

"Well, now he may never become a doctor," I said with a heavy sigh. "But I understand where you're coming from, *Amoo,* and I sympathize. I'm sure if he had the money, he'd pay you back. I don't know what his reasons are for not wanting to give up his share of the restaurant, but I'm certain it's not his intention to hurt you."

For the first time, I commiserated with my uncle. Maybe he wasn't so bad, after all. Life hadn't exactly been easy for him, either, and I felt like I had misjudged him. I'd never bothered to ask my uncle's side of the story until now and as far as I could tell, he was being honest.

"Look, none of this really matters anymore," Uncle Eskandar said impatiently. "Like I said, our dispute has nothing to do with my testimony because I'm simply going to tell the court what I saw. I'll be under oath and to some people, a promise still means something."

I sensed some frustration and resentment in my uncle's tone, as well, and decided not to push my luck. I was glad I had this conversation with him.

Maybe I could actually have a genuine relationship with my uncle.

Feeling my phone vibrate in my pocket, I figured it was Tamara texting to make sure I made it home okay and took it as my signal to say goodnight.

"Well, it's getting late and I have school tomorrow," I said, turning to go inside. "*Shab bekheir, Amoo.*"

"Cyrus, what made you ask me these questions tonight?"

"It was just on my mind, that's all."

"Well, you can believe what you want and if you think what I've said tonight is a lie, then so be it. But there's one thing I want you to know as the truth, which is I'm here for you and Rostam no matter what happens."

I looked into my uncle's troubled, restless eyes and wished I knew what he was thinking.

"Thank you, get some sleep, *Amoo.*"

"Sleep? Only the dead sleep. The worries of the living won't allow us to truly rest until the moment mankind's ultimate liberator comes and puts our mind at ease."

"Mankind's ultimate liberator?"

"Death, of course."

* * *

The second day of my father's trial quietly snuck up on us much like the first, except this time I felt a little more prepared. I knew what was coming – to a

156

certain extent. I knew the evidence and jury were not in my father's favor. I knew my uncle was testifying. I knew the results of the trial would circulate at school again.

For some reason, the part about school angered me the most.

Nothing was private anymore. I was unable to accept the fact that my family's personal life was mere hot gossip for others. Persians are secretive about what goes on in their personal lives, especially if it involves family or has to do with their reputation. Your family life is a sacred circle you have to protect no matter what.

But now, I was the subject of my school's gossip; I felt their eyes judging me and my family, heard their whispers as I walked by. The fact that I was so different from them only fueled their fire, but I didn't even care what they said about me just as long as my family wasn't mentioned. I knew I couldn't bear to hear anyone bad-mouthing my father or worse, my mother. My *gheyrat* – the powerful sense of duty you feel when it comes to protecting your family's honor at whatever cost – wouldn't stand for it. All self-control would escape me.

The day before, I let Mr. Becks know I'd be missing school because of my father's second day of trial. He was understanding, assuring me that he'd let the office know so they could notify the rest of my teachers; that way, I'd be able make up any missed work. The only good thing about my school finding out about the trial was I no longer had to come up with various excuses for missing class.

I was wide awake by five in the morning, wanting to give myself enough time to get ready before it was time to leave for the courthouse. After I got dressed and forced a cereal bar down my throat, I paced around the apartment aimlessly in the semi-darkness, the beating of my heart pushing me on, almost as if it was guiding my legs to find a space where it could be calm. But no matter where I stood, I felt anxious and on edge. Aunt Maryam and Rostam were still asleep and not wanting to wake them with my restlessness, I grabbed my coat and headed out for a walk around the neighborhood.

When I stepped outside, I was surprised to find Grandpa Behruz standing on the top step, hands in his coat pocket, cane hanging on the railing beside him.

"*Sob bekheir, Baba-bozorg,*" I greeted him. "You couldn't sleep anymore, either?"

"I haven't slept at all," he said, patting me on the back.

I stood next to him and in the chalky morning light, his sagging, wrinkled face appeared to be melting.

"You need to think about your health and look after yourself more," I said. "We need you."

"I am not strong enough for this, Cyrus," he said, his voice shaking. "I am not ready for today."

I didn't know what to say. I couldn't imagine how hard this was for my grandfather. I knew he felt guilty and considered himself partly responsible for what his family was going through. How often did he ask himself what he could have done to prevent all this? Probably every day.

"Have faith, *Baba* Behruz, it'll be okay."

I cursed myself for not being able to come up with anything better than that.

"Our family has endured so much," he said, as if he hadn't even heard me. "I don't think it can withstand today. Or any of the days that follow."

"You've taught us all to be strong and I know no matter what happens, we'll face it and move forward the best we can."

"There are some things you can't move past. Things that break you."

I realized any consolation was futile; the best thing I could do was let my grandfather unburden himself as much as he could.

Perhaps then he wouldn't break.

Chapter Nineteen

Trial proceedings commenced as they had the first time. My father was brought in, wearing a suit too large for his thin frame, and sat down next to his lawyer at the front. His head was bowed and he didn't look up until he was seated. His lawyer started whispering in his ear right away, handing him paper after paper in an almost frantic manner.

The jury filed in one by one, their movements robotic. There was a restless hum in the courtroom until we heard the "All rise" and the old judge ambled in. The prosecution was asked to speak first and the district attorney rose with a pompous air, aware he already owned the room. He reviewed the details of the case, adding they had a witness – the defendant's brother – whom he would ask to take the stand shortly. I glanced over at my grandpa Behruz and uncle Eskandar, both their faces chalk-white, then at my dad. His back was to us and I couldn't see his reaction, but I imagined he looked just as shaken as my uncle and grandfather.

Next, the judge addressed my father's lawyer, asking if he had any statements to make before proceeding to the witness testimony.

"Not at this time, Your Honor," he replied.

I shook my head. Even when he did have something to say, it didn't help much; regardless, it seemed the judge and jury had already made up their minds.

The district attorney announced, "Your Honor and may it please the court, at this time I'd like to ask the witness, Mr. Eskandar Nezami, to please take the stand."

I felt the blood freezing in my veins. Everything started moving in slow motion. Compared to this one, the first day of the trial was hazy because I'd chosen to drown it all out. Now, all of my senses were heightened and no details or statements seemed to escape me. The reality of it had finally sunk in; my mind and body could no longer rebel against or deny it. This was happening.

My uncle stood up and shuffled over to the witness stand; he looked frightened. After being sworn in, the prosecutor asked him a series of questions, like his relationship with my father, his relationship with us and my mother, his job – it all seemed pretty innocuous, but my father's lawyer would interject from time to time by stating "irrelevant" or "lack of foundation," to which the judge would either say "overruled" or "sustained." I couldn't make much sense of it.

Then, there was a lull in the courtroom before the district attorney asked his next question.

"Now, Mr. Nezami, I want you to recount the exact details of the day you witnessed the victim, Mrs. Parisa Nezami, allegedly shot at point blank and murdered by the defendant, Mr. Sohrab Nezami. Please remember, you're under oath."

For a moment, I panicked, unsure if I wanted to hear any of it. Part of me wanted more than anything to listen to my uncle recount details of that day and part of me wanted to run as far away as possible. I wanted more than anything to escape to the days when I was a normal teenager, when my life revolved around catching the Monday night football game, playing the latest video game, or binging the popular new TV show. I no longer recognized the boy whose only major worry was whether he had studied enough for tomorrow's quiz.

My uncle looked around the courtroom, then cleared his throat. It was so quiet I could hear the thrumming of my heart, which hadn't stopped its wild racing since early that morning. Morning felt like a hundred years ago.

"I was taking care of a few errands at home before heading to the restaurant that day," my uncle began.

"And around what time would you say that was, Mr. Nezami?" the prosecutor asked.

"If I remember correctly, around nine in the morning."

"Okay, please go on."

"Before leaving for work, I planned to go up to my brother's apartment to ask if he had time to go to the restaurant with me before heading to the hospital," Uncle Eskandar said. "We were short-staffed and I needed him to look over the books for me while I helped out the wait staff."

"Is that the reason you went up there?"

"Well, initially it was, but then I became worried for my brother and Pari – Parisa. Earlier that morning, I heard a lot of strange noises coming from their apartment," my uncle said, straining his eyes in an effort to remember.

160

"What kind of strange noises?"

"A lot of yelling, doors slamming, and later on…" Uncle Eskandar paused.

"Go on, Mr. Nezami."

"A loud bang."

"Would you say this loud bang sounded like a gunshot?" the district attorney asked with relish.

"Objection! Your Honor, that's leading," my father's lawyer cried.

"Sustained. Counselor, please phrase your question differently," the judge ordered the prosecutor.

"Yes, Your Honor. Mr. Nezami, what did the loud bang sound like?"

"In that moment, I wasn't sure what it could be, but it scared me," Uncle Eskandar replied. "Now that I think about it, it definitely sounded loud and mechanical – like a gunshot."

"Were you aware the defendant owned a gun?"

"No."

This was news to me, too. Why would my father – a doctor who saves lives – own a gun? Most importantly, why didn't he tell any of us he owned one? I wondered if even my mother knew about it. It looked like my father was very capable of keeping secrets and lying to his family.

I glared at his back.

"So, you go upstairs and what do you see?" the prosecutor pushed with his questions. "And around what time was this?"

"The door to the apartment was slightly open, so I went inside and saw my brother standing over my sister-in-law's body, his hands covered in blood. This was close to 9:30 now. He was looking around, almost in a daze, and didn't notice me at first."

"Where was the gun?"

"It was on the ground, beside the body."

"Your Honor, let the evidence show forensics has confirmed the 10mm bullet that killed Parisa Nezami was in fact shot from the same gun – a 10mm semi-automatic pistol – found next to the victim's body, registered to Mr. Sohrab Nezami. The official cause of death, according to the autopsy report, was a penetrating cardiac gunshot, with the bullet found lodged in the victim's left ventricle near the mitral valve. The official time of death was approximately 9:25 in the morning," the prosecutor said, addressing the entire court.

161

I felt nauseous. This was the first time I was hearing the details of my mother's murder. Right after it happened, I decided I didn't want to know how or with what my mother was killed, and Aunt Maryam agreed. Knowing all that would've made it more unbearable than it already was. Now, hearing about it in such graphic detail was beyond traumatizing. And the most shocking part of all was that the murder weapon was my father's own gun. Grandpa Behruz reached over and took my hand into his own shaking one. He didn't look too good. He closed his eyes, face strained, as if willing this whole thing to disappear once he opened them.

Aunt Maryam was sitting to my right, staring in my father's direction, her mouth set in a straight line. She wasn't crying. Her dark eyes were still, unblinking – she wasn't going to betray any emotion to this room full of strangers. I knew my aunt well; she hated coming across as weak and she didn't want to give these people the satisfaction of seeing her cry over her slain sister. They – especially my father – didn't deserve her tears. Grieving for Pari was too sacred an act to be displayed in public. Even at my mother's funeral and fortieth ceremony, she hardly shed a tear. It was only in the privacy of her bedroom, during her nightly conversations with her sister, that she cried for her.

In the front row, I noticed my dad placing his head in his hands.

I couldn't imagine anything more humiliating than this; for a moment, I forgot I was angry with him and an overwhelming sense of pity settled in its place.

"Did the defendant say anything to you once he noticed your presence?"

"No, he was in shock, he just kept looking around as if he was searching for something or someone. I asked him what happened several times – in Farsi – but he didn't answer me, so that's when I called 911."

"What did you do until the police and ambulance arrived?"

"I walked over to Parisa's body and checked her pulse, but it was clear she was – deceased. I got up and asked my brother again what happened, but he was sitting on the sofa at this point, sobbing quietly and repeating his wife's name."

"You mentioned you also heard yelling and slamming before you went up to the apartment, is this correct?"

"Yes, that's correct."

"Did the defendant have a good relationship with the victim?"

"Objection, misleading," my father's lawyer exclaimed, sounding unsure this time.

"Sustained. Counselor, restate your question," the judge said.

"Yes, Your Honor. Mr. Nezami, did the defendant and the victim dispute often?"

"Your Honor, husbands and wives argue and fight often, but it's usually not grounds for murder," my father's lawyer spoke again, interrupting the ricochet of questions.

"Sustained. Counselor, either state your question differently or move on to another one."

I was beginning to have some faith in my father's lawyer, after all.

"Of course, Your Honor. Mr. Nezami, before the day of the incident, did any quarrels that you overheard or witnessed between the defendant and the victim concern you, especially for your sister-in-law's well-being?"

"Objection, leading!"

"Overruled. You may answer the question, Mr. Nezami," the judge told my uncle.

"No, they had a great relationship and rarely argued," my uncle said. "And when they did, it was like any other normal couple. Parisa sometimes complained about his long work hours and it caused a bit of tension between them, but that was about it. They were very much in love."

It was the first time during the questioning that my uncle said something in my father's favor.

"And there was nothing you knew of that could've led to an explosive argument between them?"

"Nothing, to my knowledge. There was the issue with my brother's long work hours that I already mentioned, and Parisa did complain about it from time to time, but I don't think that could've led to such an explosive argument. Or maybe it could, I can't say for sure."

I did recall my parents were arguing more often about two months before my mother died, but I didn't think anything of it until the question came up now. I remember sensing my mom's growing frustration with my father's long, late hours at the hospital. His increasing absence did take a toll on all of us, with Rostam often asking Mom where Dad was. For my part, I tried to be supportive and help lessen the tension at home by keeping Rostam occupied and out of Mom's way, reminding him *Baba* was working hard to make our lives better. But on top of that, Dad became forgetful and irritable from the mental and physical exhaustion of his shifts, which didn't help his case at home. Some nights, Mom didn't wait up for him or prepare his dinner like she used to.

"I'm sure he's already eaten at the hospital, his new home," she said one night after we finished dinner, a new bitterness in her tone that was never present before when she spoke of my father. "He no longer sees me or the things I do for him, anyway."

She sighed and went to her bedroom.

At the time, I thought things would go back to normal once Dad finished his residency. Maybe I was unaware of how bad it really was.

One night, I woke up to yelling and for a moment, thought I was dreaming. Blinking, I strained my ears and heard my parents' muffled, angry voices coming from their bedroom. I jumped out of bed and tiptoed to the door, putting my ear against it to hear better. My parents had never argued like this before and it scared me.

I caught the end of it and most of what I heard didn't make much sense.

"I'm getting tired of this, Sohrab," I heard my mother's distraught voice. "We never see you anymore because you're always at that damn hospital and when you are home, you're not yourself. You're too tired to make time for us."

"What do you want me to do, huh? I'm trying my best."

"Well, apparently your best means forgetting about your family."

"That's unfair, Parisa. I'm doing all this to provide a better life for us. I want to buy us a nice house so we can move out of my father's apartment, and I want to be able to give my family whatever they want. I'm tired of being frugal just to make ends meet."

My father only called my mother by her full name when he was upset or frustrated with her and until now, it was a rare occurrence.

"And on top of all this, I have to be the one who answers to him when he comes here almost every day asking about his money and the restaurant because you won't give him a straight answer. I'm sick of being stuck in the middle of you two!"

"I will deal with him, don't worry."

"Deal with him!" My mother scoffed. "If you wanted to deal with him, you would've done it by now. You'd stop being stubborn and give him what he wants after he's waited all this time."

"Oh, you're on his side now? So be it, but I won't turn a blind eye to what's rightfully mine and my children's."

"You've turned a blind eye to your family, what's one more thing?"

"Parisa, that's enough! I'm running on two hours of sleep and have to come home to this nonsense from my own wife who should be supporting me."

I heard a door slam and then silence.

My entire body was shaking. Hearing footsteps outside the door, I ran to my bed and pulled the covers over my head.

A second later, Mom peeked her head inside to check on us and when she shut the door, I heard her softly blowing her nose.

The following night, Dad came home earlier and brought Mom flowers. I figured they made up and forgot about the entire incident. But maybe they hadn't. Maybe they were just good at hiding it.

How could I have been so clueless? And now that I knew the whole story behind my dad and uncle's dispute, it occurred to me that part of my parents' fight that night had been about my uncle and the money Dad owed him. About how my uncle was trying to get *Maman* to somehow persuade her husband to give him his share of the restaurant to settle the debt.

It seemed my mother was getting tired of being their buffer. It was unfair of Uncle Eskandar to get her involved in his dealings with Dad.

But more importantly, was *Baba* angry at my mother for getting involved? Angry enough to hurt her?

I recalled his voice, tinged with indignation and disbelief, when he asked my mother, *Oh, you're on his side now?* and shuddered.

"Your Honor, that's all my questions for now. Thank you, Mr. Nezami," the district attorney lisped and sat down.

My father's lawyer stood up and walked up to the witness stand.

"Mr. Nezami, when you arrived at the defendant's apartment, did you witness him shoot the victim?"

"Yes, that's correct."

"So, you heard something that sounded like a gun go off and then you went upstairs to see what was going on. And that's when you saw the gun lying next to the victim's body when you got there, correct?"

"It was."

"As the evidence shows, Your Honor, forensics was unable to find any traces of my client's fingerprints on the gun," the defense attorney addressed the judge.

"Your Honor, the gun could very well have been wiped clean by the defendant, it doesn't prove anything, and even if it hadn't been wiped clean, it's normal to assume his fingerprints would've been on the gun since he owned it," the prosecutor stated. "It neither incriminates nor acquits him."

The judge nodded in agreement with the district attorney, perusing the pile of papers sitting in front of him.

"Counselor, the evidence could go one way or the way in regard to the defendant's fingerprints on the gun and therefore does not offer substantial proof," the judge explained to my father's lawyer. "If another person's fingerprints had been found on the gun, then you would have something. Is that clear?"

"Yes, Your Honor. Mr. Nezami, did you see anyone leaving the apartment on your way up to the defendant's unit?"

"I did not."

"You mentioned earlier you were doing errands around nine in the morning. What time would you say you actually headed upstairs?"

"Close to 9:30."

"And during that half-hour, you heard the yelling and disturbances coming from the upstairs unit?"

"Yes, that's correct."

"And the last thing you heard was the loud bang?"

"Correct."

"How much time would you say passed between you hearing the loud bang and then going up to the apartment?"

"About five minutes. I know that sounds like a long time, but because I wasn't sure what I heard, I waited for a bit to listen for further disturbances as I honestly feared for my own safety, but when I heard nothing else, I ran upstairs."

"That could have given someone more than enough time to escape."

"And to wipe the gun clean and leave without a trace?" the prosecutor interceded again in a mocking tone.

"If they were hurrying and knew what they were doing, absolutely!"

"The defendant himself has claimed he saw no one," the prosecutor cried, pointing to my father, his face red with excitement.

"Counselor, settle down," the judge said, waving his hand dismissively toward the district attorney. He picked up his pile of papers and continued, "I see here in the defendant's written testimony he neither saw anyone leave the apartment nor anyone inside the apartment. He claims he was on his way to work when he remembered he forgot his briefcase and came back home to get it. Upon

166

arrival, he found the motionless body of the victim lying face-up in a pool of her own blood, with his gun lying next to her. He tried to revive her, hence why his hands and clothes were bloody, but she was already deceased. That's around the same time his brother, Mr. Eskandar Nezami, entered the apartment and saw him standing over the victim's body."

"Thank you, Your Honor. Mr. Nezami, you and the defendant were not on the best terms, is that correct?"

"Objection! Leading!" the prosecutor cried.

"Sustained. Please restate your question, counselor," the judge said.

"Yes, Your Honor. Mr. Nezami, describe your relationship with the defendant."

"We were on speaking terms, but things were a little tense between us due to an inheritance dispute."

"Go on."

"Objection!"

"Overruled. Answer the question, Mr. Nezami."

"My brother owed me some money, but was financially unable to settle his debt, so I asked him to sign over his share of the family restaurant, which we owned together after my father gifted us equal shares, and managed it as partners."

"And he didn't agree to give up his share of the restaurant, despite your numerous attempts to convince him?"

"That is correct."

"Did this anger you?"

"Objection, leading!"

"Sustained."

"How did you feel about your brother's constant rejection to sign over his share to you?"

"Like I said, it caused tension and we argued, but I was hopeful he would consider signing over his share once he started working full-time as a doctor."

"But that wouldn't be until another two years."

"I'd waited this long, what was another two years? Besides, I was also going to ask my father to intervene and perhaps convince him."

"Did you ever ask the victim for her help in convincing her husband?"

"Objection!"

"Overruled."

167

"I did a couple of times, but there was only so much she could do and I didn't like putting her in the middle of it. She tried to be as helpful as possible, saying she would talk to him, but she understandably had to keep the peace at the same time."

"Your Honor, I have no further questions. Thank you," my father's lawyer turned to face us and walked back to his seat.

"Mr. Nezami, you may step down from the witness stand," the judge said.

My uncle thanked him and leaving the stand, walked back to his seat next to Grandpa Behruz.

"This court will review today's witness testimony, along with all evidence of this case, and reconvene for sentencing. Court adjourned," the judge announced and struck his gavel.

I was in such a daze that I didn't notice when they took my father away. The courtroom was nearly empty when I felt Grandpa's hand on my shoulder, pulling me away from my troubled thoughts and guiding me toward the outside world.

* * *

On the way home, sitting in the backseat of Grandpa's Chevy next to *Khaleh* Maryam, I confronted them both about whether they knew my father owned a gun.

"I did not," Aunt Maryam said. She hadn't spoken a word all day. "I knew Pari was shot, but I didn't think to ask where Sohrab had gotten a gun from, or whether he actually owned one."

"Me, neither," Grandpa Behruz replied with a sigh.

"It was horrible finding out this way and having to listen to all the details," I said. "Right after mom died, I decided I didn't want to know how it happened. I didn't realize I'd eventually find out during Dad's trial."

"I'm sorry you had to hear all that, Cyrus," my uncle said. "And I'm even sorrier it came from me." Uncle Eskandar was driving and he shot a glance at me in the rear-view mirror with apologetic eyes.

"Why would Dad even want to own a gun?"

"I don't know for certain, but he wanted one ever since he was a teenager," Grandpa Behruz explained. "He used to go to shooting ranges all the time in Iran."

"I'm pretty sure Pari *khanoom* didn't know about it, either, otherwise she wouldn't have let him get it, or she would've convinced him to get rid of it, especially with you and Rostam around," Uncle Eskandar said.

"She never mentioned anything to me about it, so that very well may be true," Aunt Maryam agreed.

I didn't know who to believe at this point. The more I found out, the less I trusted.

Chapter Twenty

A few days following the trial, I got home from school to find an unexpected email from my father. I hadn't emailed him and thought it best to cease communication with him for a few days until I worked through my feelings.

Heart beating, I clicked on the email:

Cyrus,

When we were young, Eskandar and I, we had a persimmon tree in our backyard. I remember Eskandar would climb the tree almost every day to try and save the persimmons at the very top from the hungry crows pecking at them.

Our mother scolded him each time, saying there were plenty of ripe, juicy persimmons closer to the bottom for him to pick and eat. She filled a fruit bowl to the brim with plump persimmons, but he wouldn't touch those. Instead, he climbed the tree to scare away the crows and pick a persimmon from the very top for himself. In his mind, those were the best persimmons and he didn't want the crows to have them. Or anyone, for that matter. When he finally did manage to grab a persimmon from the top branch, he wouldn't share it with anyone. He greedily ate the whole fruit, the sweet juices running down his mouth and hands.

One day, Eskandar fell from a loose branch and broke his arm.

My mother thought he learned his lesson, but once his arm healed, he climbed the tree again. She would tell me, "Your brother is a high-flyer – he wants to fly high with the crows. He's not satisfied with staying on the ground. He's not satisfied with the persimmons on the lower branches. He's too ambitious and that will get him into trouble one day, you mark my words, Sohrab."

She told him, "Let the crows have their daily meal, it's not for you to decide whether they can eat God's bounty or not. There's enough fruit on that tree for you and the crows." But he wouldn't listen. He wanted the persimmons at the very top of the tree for himself, at whatever cost.

Cyrus, ambition is a good thing, but when it consumes you to the point where nothing will satisfy you anymore, that's when it becomes dangerous. That's when it will hurt you and those you love.

– Baba

After I finished reading, I sat back in my chair to figure out what my dad meant by all this. Was he trying to discredit Uncle Eskandar's testimony and in his subtle, indirect way tell me my uncle wasn't telling the whole truth? Was there more to the restaurant story? What did my uncle's ambitions have to do with all this?

I did know one thing – I was tired of all these stories and lessons and hints. This circuitous way of skirting around what was really going on was frustrating. I wanted the truth, simple as that.

I took out my father's gold coin from my pocket – where it almost always resided now – and feeling its weight in my hand, weighed my own words before replying to his email. I didn't know for sure whether Uncle Eskandar was being honest or lying, but things weren't looking good for my father, no matter how much he insisted otherwise. Though it pained me to admit this to myself, I was seriously entertaining the idea that perhaps my uncle was telling the truth. Either way, I had to be honest – both with them and most importantly, with myself.

Baba,

As you can imagine, I'm very confused. I'm also angry because I don't know who to believe anymore. Somebody is keeping the truth from me and I don't know who it is.

But I don't want to hide anything, so I'm going to tell you one thing I've kept from you and it's been weighing on my conscience: I've been reading you and Mom's letters from when you were dating. I found them in your drawer when I went to look for the coin. I don't know whether you meant for me to find them or not, but I did and I've been reading them.

I'm actually glad I found them because they're honest and genuine. They're from a time when there was no doubt about how much you and Mom loved each other. They're from a time long before any of this happened. A time when Mom was alive. A time when you weren't accused of killing her.

Dad, I really appreciate what you're doing with these Cyrus stories and your memories and how you've tried to teach me important life lessons with each of them. But maybe it's time to take a page out of these stories yourself and be truly open and honest with me, your son.

I don't want to keep hearing tales and memories from the past. I think I've heard enough for now. Instead, I want to hear from you. I want to hear about you. About right now. About what's happening with our family. About the truth.

Can you do that for me?

– Cyrus

I read over it before sending, making sure it didn't sound too harsh. At the same time, my dad had to realize how I was feeling and that stories weren't what I needed right now.

I hit "send."

* * *

That night before bed, I overheard Rostam talking to our mom. Ever since the day I told him Mom could see and hear him, he never missed a night of talking to her. He usually told her about school and his day, about us, and how much he missed her. His night terrors had stopped completely, to my and Aunt Maryam's relief. I tried my best not to eavesdrop on or interrupt his conversations, but what he said this time caught my attention.

"*Mamani*, please forgive Dad so he can come home," he said.

I sat up in bed and turned on the bedside lamp.

"What do you mean by that, *Dadashi?*" I asked. "Why are you asking Mom to forgive Dad?"

"Oh, because of what he did to her."

I got out of bed and went over to him. He looked at me as if he had done something wrong.

"What did you say?" I asked, trying not to alarm him.

"He's the one who made her go away, but that's okay because he didn't mean to," Rostam said.

Stomach dropping, my breath caught in my chest.

"Who told you that?"

"Uncle Eskandar said it, I heard him," he replied innocently.

I knew he heard my uncle the night of my father's first day of trial and I could've kicked myself for not sending him to his room.

"Rostam, it's rude to eavesdrop on adult conversations, especially when you don't know what they're talking about," I said. "You misheard *Amoo*."

"So, why can't Dad come home? Why do we have to visit him in that place where bad people live? People in school keep saying he did something bad."

Of course all this would spread around my brother's school, too.

I was angry with my uncle and anyone else insensitive to the fact that I was trying to protect my little brother from all this as much as possible. I looked up and noticed a small crack in the ceiling right above Rostam's bed.

No matter how much you paint and plaster over the cracks, they're still going to be there. There's only so much you can do to protect something.

"Because sometimes people believe you did something you really didn't do, and they think the same about Dad, so he had to go away to that place and now has to prove to everyone he did nothing wrong and didn't hurt Mom like they say he did, so they can let him come home," I explained, unsure if what I said even made sense.

"Those people won't let him come home? It's not because Mom is mad at him?"

"Right, she has nothing to do with him not coming home."

I didn't want to mention police or the law and make it too complicated. I tried to be as vague as possible, for his own sake.

"And you think he can make them believe he didn't do anything wrong?" Rostam asked, scrunching up his forehead.

"I hope he can."

"And what if he can't? He has to stay away forever?"

I sighed.

"Let's not think about that, buddy."

"Well, I know he didn't do anything wrong and that's why I'm telling Mom she should forgive him, too."

"I'm sure she will, and what makes you so sure he didn't do anything wrong?"

"Because he loved her!" he cried, throwing his arms up. "You don't hurt someone you love."

"That's right, now say goodnight to *Maman* and go to bed," I said, pulling up his covers.

"*Shab bekheir, Maman,*" Rostam whispered. "*Shab bekheir*, Cyrus."

"*Shab bekheir.*"

I had a restless sleep that night, the dream world and the conscious world tossing me between them until the faint light of dawn. I dreamt about Cyrus the Great, except it felt like I was him in the dream. The images and events were all jumbled together, but I remember feeling burdened and distraught.

The only vivid part of the dream I could recall was when I sat in a room similar to the courtroom where my father's trial took place. There was a large, angry crowd surrounding me and it felt like I, as Cyrus the Great, was on trial. The short, lispy district attorney was there, listing my crimes, the nature of which were at first unclear.

I kept yelling it wasn't true and insisting on my innocence, but the mob's shouting drowned me out. The district attorney kept pointing his finger at me and calling me a liar. There was something about murder and treason.

I told them to ask her, she knew I didn't do it. She would forgive me.

"She's dead!" they shouted at me. "You killed her."

It became apparent that as Cyrus the Great, I was on trial for having murdered Cassandane, my wife and the queen.

I knew with an absolute certainty I didn't kill her, but no one believed me.

"I loved her! I wouldn't hurt her."

Then there was mention of the Cyrus Cylinder and how the slaves were never freed, as I had promised.

"Liar! Murderer! Traitor!" the crowd shouted.

In a short matter of time, I was discredited of all my accomplishments, dethroned, and accused of murder and treason. No one listened to my pleas of innocence.

I was to be hanged.

"Cyrus the Deceiver!" the mob yelled over and over again.

I noticed Rostam in the crowd and begged him to tell them I was innocent. For some reason, I was convinced he knew I was telling the truth.

Rostam looked at me with tear-stained eyes, turned his back to me, and walked away. He was lost in the sea of people.

I jolted awake and looked around the dark room. Rostam's still figure was sleeping peacefully across from me, unaware of his presence in my disturbing dream.

Perhaps his night terrors had passed on to me now.

Chapter Twenty-One

On the last day of my father's trial, he was asked to take the witness stand and offer a final statement in his defense.

Everything seemed to be leading up to this moment.

I could finally hear what my father had to say and like Uncle Eskandar's testimony, I wanted to both hear it and run away at the same time.

Earlier, the defense and prosecution had asked several other witnesses to testify, like my father's co-workers and boss. The judge referred to them as character witnesses.

For the most part, his co-residents said they enjoyed working with him, but didn't really know him because he kept to himself and didn't talk to them unless it was work-related. One of his co-residents even called him a "loner." That didn't look very good. I also noticed his friend, Mr. Jafari, wasn't one of the witnesses. Perhaps he didn't want to involve himself.

My father's boss, Dr. Hamilton, was the last of the character witnesses to take the stand. He started off by stating he never had any issues with Dr. Nezami – that he was a diligent, honest worker and a good doctor. When asked about the day my mother died and if my father was scheduled to work, Dr. Hamilton said he wasn't scheduled and if he had gone in, it would've been a violation of his work hours restriction. He explained this was something every resident, including my father, is aware of and very careful about.

This excited the prosecutor. "Then, why would Mr. Nezami feel the need to go into work that day knowing full well he wasn't scheduled and could violate his work-hour restriction?"

"I can't say for sure – perhaps he confused the days on his schedule or thought he could make up work on an off-day," Dr. Hamilton replied.

The prosecutor asked a few more questions and then Dr. Hamilton was asked to leave the stand.

A few days earlier, I received a call from my dad's lawyer, who introduced himself as Mr. Nathaniel Moors, asking if I would like to testify in my father's favor. He explained I wouldn't be subpoenaed, so he was giving me the choice to testify. I thought about it for a few minutes, with Nathaniel Moors' heavy breathing keeping time on the other end of the line; he sounded like a smoker.

Eventually, I made a decision.

"I'm really sorry, Mr. Moors, but I can't do it," I said. "I'm so confused right now that I wouldn't be able to give a fair or favorable testimony. I would only get in the way of your defense, so I'd prefer not to get involved."

"I understand," Mr. Moors said in a grave tone. He was probably banking on my statement to build up his defense; the disappointment in his voice was palpable. "Thanks for your time."

"Again, I'm really sorry I can't help you," I said. I felt like a coward.

He hung up without another word.

When it was my father's turn to speak, he stood up, his entire frame shaking, and took a few slow, reluctant steps up to the witness stand.

It felt surreal, seeing him up there now. I wanted to both look at him and also look away.

He seemed so alone and lost sitting up there in his oversized suit. After he was sworn in, the district attorney was asked to go first. I could tell he couldn't wait to interrogate my father – to make him crack and confess to everything. He was prepared for the takedown.

"Mr. Nezami, I'm not going to waste your time, my time, or the esteemed court's time," he began. "I'm going to cut right to the chase and ask you to tell us exactly what happened the day the victim, your wife, Parisa Moghadam Nezami, was found dead, shot point-blank with your handgun and with you standing over her lifeless body. Remember, you're under oath."

"That day, I left for work around nine in the morning," my father began, speaking at a slow pace. "As mentioned, it was my day off, but I had some work I needed to get caught up on. I was aware of the work hours restriction, but wanted to ask the attending doctor's permission if it would be okay to stay for a couple of hours and catch up. Sometimes they allow it, depending on which attending is working at the time."

"Did anyone witness you leaving for work?"

"My wife."

"Anyone who is present today?" the prosecutor asked in a snarky tone.

"I don't believe so, no. My kids were both already at school and my father had left for the restaurant. At the time, I thought my brother had gone to the restaurant along with my father and didn't know he was home."

"Did anyone even know you were going to work that day since it was your day off?"

"No, I didn't tell anyone specifically."

"Your brother says he heard you arguing with your wife and believes you were home around that time."

"I had already left by then, but he was probably not aware," my father said. "And I did not argue with my wife at all."

"You then came back home after you presumably left for work to fetch your forgotten briefcase, correct?"

"That is correct."

"How much time do you think passed between you leaving for work, realizing you forgot your briefcase, and coming back home?"

"I would say around thirty minutes, so I came back home around 9:30ish."

"Now, that doesn't quite match up with the timeline your brother gave us. According to him, that's when he entered your apartment and found you standing over your wife's body. You're sure you're not mistaking the time?"

"No, I distinctly remember it was 9:30 in the morning."

"Very well, and when did the arguing between you and your wife occur?"

"Again, my wife and I did not argue at all that day."

"So, you're saying your brother is lying? And that he also didn't hear what according to him was the sound of a gunshot?"

"Objection! Leading," my father's lawyer cried.

"Overruled. Go ahead, Mr. Nezami," the judge said.

"Obviously, he heard someone shoot her, but I did not shoot that gun, nor did I argue with my wife. She was already, uh, dead when I got home."

"Why did you own a gun, Mr. Nezami?" the prosecutor suddenly asked, changing course. I leaned forward to make sure I heard every word of my father's reply.

"Both for protection and because it's my constitutional right as an American citizen," my father said. "I bought it on a whim three years ago, as I'd always wanted one ever since I was a teenager. My wife wasn't happy about it at first, especially since we had two young kids, but I convinced her to let me keep it as long as only the two of us knew about it and I kept it under lock and key."

"Forensics found a key which was used to open the safety lock box that held the gun, hidden in a credenza. Besides you and your wife, the only two people who knew you owned a gun, could anyone else have unlocked the box? Or even known where it was?"

"No."

"So, you're saying you and your wife were the only two people who could've possibly unlocked the safety lock box to access the gun, correct?"

"Yes, but I did not access the box or take out the gun. I assume my wife realized there was an intruder and took out the gun to protect herself."

"Your wife retrieving the gun to use in self-defense against a possible intruder is likely, but according to evidence, there were no signs of forced entry and no substantial fingerprints on the key to figure out which one of you last accessed the box," the prosecutor said. "And that's not really the point here – the main point is only you or your wife could've taken the gun out of its box that day, regardless of there being fingerprints or not, because only the two of you knew about its existence and therefore only one of you could've used it. And I think we know who that person is."

"As I told you before, I neither accessed the safety lock box nor used my gun that day. When I got home, my wife was already dead and the gun was next to her body."

"Mr. Nezami, do you know how to properly handle and shoot a gun?"

My father's lawyer shot up from his seat, "Your Honor, please note that the evidence shows my client tested negative for GSR." The judge looked over his pile of papers and nodded.

The prosecutor scoffed and said, "Your Honor, that doesn't prove much here. Gunshot residue can be washed off and traces of it only last for a few hours."

"Noted," the judge replied impatiently. "Please continue with your questioning, counselor."

"Yes, Your Honor," the prosecutor said and turned to face my father again. "Mr. Nezami, do you know how to properly handle and shoot a gun?"

"I do, I often went to the shooting range as a young adult in Iran."

"So, it was more of a hobby?"

"Yes, but it's also a useful skill to have in case I ever needed to use a gun to protect my family."

"Very well, and what happened when you came home to fetch your briefcase?"

179

"I noticed the door slightly open, walked inside, and saw – saw my wife lying in a pool of her blood with my gun lying next to her. I looked around the apartment and found no one, then I went over to her to try and revive her, but she was, um, already dead. I was in a complete state of shock by then," my father explained, his voice breaking and tears filling his eyes as the traumatic memory came back to him.

"And that's when your brother showed up?"

"Yes, although at first, I didn't even realize he was there. Seeing the state I was in, he called 911."

"Mr. Nezami, forensics evidence shows your wife had been dead for almost an hour – 50 minutes, to be exact – when the ambulance and police arrived at 10:15 in the morning," the prosecutor said. "That means she was shot and instantly killed at 9:25 in the morning, which is close to the same time your brother claimed he heard the loud bang."

"I had absolutely no reason to kill my wife, we were very happy together," is all my father said.

"Mr. Nezami, sometimes there's no rhyme or reason for the things we do and yet we still do them," the district attorney said coldly.

My dad said nothing in response, so the prosecutor continued.

"Mr. Nezami, do you have any reason to believe someone would want to hurt you or your wife?"

"None that I know of, but with all that's happening in the world, we were always a little nervous about being discriminated against for our religion and nationality."

"But you never received a direct threat?"

"No."

"So, here we have no other suspects and a defendant who has nobody to corroborate his story. I have no further questions, Your Honor."

As the prosecutor walked back to his seat, the judge looked to my father's lawyer to see if he wanted to question his client, to which Mr. Moors shook his head no. I guess he figured there wasn't much point to it.

"At this time, I would like to ask the prosecution to offer the court their closing statement," the judge announced. "Mr. Nezami, you may step down from the witness stand."

My father nodded his head and quietly made his way back to his seat next to Mr. Moors.

For almost twenty minutes, the district attorney addressed the court, reviewing every detail and evidence in the case against my father. Addressing the judge and jury, he concluded by stating, "And so, with the overwhelming evidence and witness testimony provided in this case – again, to review, the defendant was witnessed, by his own brother, Mr. Eskandar Nezami, to be standing over the body of the victim, Parisa Nezami, hands covered in her blood; the 10mm bullet that penetrated her heart and killed her was directly shot from the 10mm semi-automatic pistol registered to the defendant, Mr. Sohrab Nezami; no one else knew about or had access to the defendant's gun besides himself and his wife, the victim, and according to the witness testimony provided by the defendant's brother, Mr. Eskandar Nezami, the two were allegedly quarrelling right before the victim, Parisa Nezami, was shot and killed – it is beyond a shadow of a doubt that Sohrab Nezami cold-bloodedly shot and murdered his wife, Parisa Moghadam Nezami, on September 22, 2016, at precisely 9:25 in the morning at point-blank range following a heated argument with the victim during which he lost his temper and control.

"Perhaps the victim was feeling the strain of her husband's long work hours, confronted him about it, and the fight escalated. He was leaving for work on his day off, after all, and we know this was an issue that caused tension between them. Perhaps it was money-related, specifically in regard to their debt to Mr. Eskandar Nezami. The victim may have felt stuck in the middle and again, after confronting the defendant, a fight escalated and got out of hand. However you look at it, when the evidence of this case points to only one person – Mr. Sohrab Nezami – then our duty is to no longer ask why he did it, but to prove that he did in fact do it and punish him for this deplorable act against his own family. And make no mistake, motive or no motive, it is nevertheless an action we will not tolerate and will seek a justifiable punishment for. Thank you."

With a dramatic flourish, the prosecutor ended his statement and sat down.

There was no way my father's attorney could match that.

When he was asked to offer his closing statement, Mr. Moors stood, cleared his throat, and said, "Your Honor, ladies and gentlemen of the jury, even with the evidence presented, this was clearly a case of tragic timing. My client found himself in the wrong place at the wrong time. There is no clear evidence to suggest he had a motive for killing his wife and even the witness, Mr. Eskandar Nezami, testified to the loving relationship between the victim and the defendant.

Let us not just look for someone to place the blame on for the sake of placing blame and reaching an answer.

"Sohrab Nezami should not have to take the fall for someone else's crime against his wife – whom he loved – and his family. We cannot place the blame on him just because he was there and we have no one else to place the blame on. Simply put, my client had no motive or intent to murder his wife, especially in such a brutal manner, and is therefore innocent. We may never know who shot Parisa Nezami that September morning, but that does not give us the right, in good conscience, to point fingers at an innocent man whose only crime was being present at the traumatizing scene of his wife's murder. To close, in absence of proof beyond reasonable doubt, you simply cannot rule that Sohrab Nezami is guilty of murdering his wife, Parisa Nezami. Thank you."

The judge then gave my father the opportunity to present a final statement in his defense. The court grew silent when my father stood up, and the sound of him clearing his throat echoed around the room.

"The only thing I can say is no matter what the jury decides today, part of me will be at peace knowing I am innocent and that I did not murder my wife. But the other part of me will not rest knowing there are some who believe I am guilty of this crime and that I may not be able to prove my innocence. Your Honor, as a physician, I've always endeavored to save lives, not take them – much less the life of the person most dear to me.

"I wouldn't even know how to take a life, either with a gun or anything else. Yes, I do have an interest in guns and have gone shooting as a hobby, but that does not make me a killer. My desire to own a gun and keep it in my home was solely to protect my family if need be.

"I've said it before and I'll say it again, I did not kill my wife. She was – and still is – the love of my life and the day I lost her, my own life ended. Your decision on whether to end my physical life or not does not matter in the grand scheme of things because the life and happiness I knew is gone forever – it ended the minute my wife's life did.

"My only hope and reason for living are my two sons and I pray to be found innocent so I may go back to my family – to my sons who need me more than ever. I pray I do not get blamed for this heinous crime, forever known as the man who murdered his wife, ashamed to look into the eyes of my own children who will think I took their mother from them. That'll be worse than a thousand deaths. I'd rather die and not see that day become a reality. And so I humbly beg you to weigh everything and know it is not just a human life on the line – it is also a man's honor and reputation. It is what will follow his name like a shadow long after he is gone, what he will be remembered by. Please do not tarnish my reputation. This is all I humbly ask of you today. Thank you."

My father's face glistened with tears.

Grandpa Behruz was leaning forward, both hands gripping his cane so tightly, his knuckles had turned white. His head rested on his hands, shoulders undulating with silent sobs.

Even Uncle Eskandar had his head bowed and was probably regretting ever going up on the witness stand. I knew he didn't have a choice, but I'd still feel guilty if I were him, having played a part in possibly indicting my brother.

Aunt Maryam displayed her usual poker face, placid and calm, waiting to see what would happen next. She was as stone-faced as the jury.

Following my father's statement, the judge started addressing the jury and going over the details of the case, the evidence, and each party's closing statements. He said a number of technical things I didn't understand, no matter how hard I strained my ears to catch everything being mentioned.

* * *

After almost three hours of deliberation, the jury finally reached a verdict. I could hardly breathe as we heard the "All rise" and the judge entered the room. Once we were seated, he ordered the jury to enter, for which everyone stood up again. When we were asked to be seated for a second time, the judge asked a jury member he referred to as foreman if the jury had reached a verdict. The foreman replied that they had, then he stood up and handed an envelope to the bailiff. The judge opened the envelope and read the piece of paper in silence – a silence that roared throughout the courtroom. After what seemed hours, he finally spoke and said, "Will the defendant please rise?"

I watched my father's back as he slowly stood up, and tried to imagine what was going through his mind in that exact moment. I wished I was standing next to him and holding his hand. Standing there, waiting with bated breath to hear how his fate was decided, he looked like the loneliest man in the world.

The judge read the jury's statement, "We, the jury, find the defendant guilty of two counts of first-degree murder." Each ugly word out of the judge's mouth seemed to echo throughout the courtroom before falling on our unwilling ears that didn't want to hear them.

I closed my eyes as the entire weight of the world crashed over me. I should have seen this coming, so why was I shocked? From day one, it was obvious the jury pegged my father as guilty and there was nothing his defense could've done about it. There was nothing my father could have said that would've worked in his favor.

In the jury's eyes, he was guilty from day one.

Grandpa Behruz looked as though he was going to pass out; his hands shook more than usual and I took his cane from him so he wouldn't drop it. Uncle Eskandar massaged his shoulders and helped him take a sip from a water bottle. I wondered if the announcement of the verdict was his breaking point, but he was beyond broken. He was shattered.

The judge continued, "Each member of the jury that concurs with this verdict, will you indicate it to me by raising your right hand?"

All the jury members raised their right hands to show their unanimous agreement, to which the judge then replied, "The court will accept the verdict and order it filed."

In the Persian culture, a person's reputation is a life-or-death matter and many would rather die than have a bad reputation. It does not, however, play such a significant role in the American way of life and wouldn't usually be touched on in a case like this; obviously, mentioning it did not work in my father's favor.

If it felt like the world crashed over me after hearing the verdict, I couldn't imagine what kind of weight was crushing my father. How could one calculate the burden of a ruined reputation? A reputation that was collected little by little over time? A reputation that took years to build up, but a mere minute to collapse. I knew Grandpa Behruz felt the same weight on his shoulders – a father's reputation is linked to that of his children's. Their downfall was his downfall; made no difference.

"At this time, I call this session to a close with the sentencing hearing to follow in a week's time, during which I will consider the jury's verdict to reach a final decision on the sentence," the judge announced, banging his gavel.

Just like that, my father's fate was decided by strangers. It took them only three hours to end a life that had taken over thirty years to build up. Thirty years of working hard, struggling, dreaming, hoping – to end up somewhere better.

So, how did my father end up here?

But maybe it wasn't the jury or the prosecutor who ended it – maybe my father ended it with his own hands by the wrong choices he made. Maybe Uncle Eskandar was telling the truth.

Maybe he did kill my mother.

Maybe there was a side to my dad I didn't know.

Were the Cyrus stories just meant to serve as a distraction? It felt like I had woken up to find out the person I thought I knew better than anyone – the person who raised me – was a complete stranger.

A complete stranger who had taken both my mother and father from me and ruined my way of life. Someone who made me doubt and lose trust in everything I knew.

So, why should I feel bad if this stranger is sentenced to death?

Looking back, it was easier to emotionally detach myself from my father than have to deal with the pain of possibly losing him. It hurt less to be angry at him and believe he was guilty; to pretend as though I didn't know him.

Maybe that pulling away was wrong, but it's what I needed to do in the moment to cope with it all and survive. Otherwise, I would've fallen apart and I couldn't do that to Rostam.

Immediately after the verdict was announced, an initial, more nagging feeling washed over me before the sense of complete devastation came on, followed by the numbness of denial, then detachment.

It took me a long time to shake it. Years, in fact.

It was guilt. A deep, intense feeling of guilt for refusing to testify in my father's favor. Maybe it would've made a difference? Maybe they would've seen him in a better light? I felt like I had failed him. My dad had always been there for me, but I denied him my help the one time he needed it. His own son, the only person he could count on to believe him and defend him, had turned his back on him.

How could I possibly have expected the jury to show him any mercy?

Chapter Twenty-Two

After the trial, Uncle Eskandar drove us home. No one spoke during the somber car ride until my uncle stopped at the restaurant to pick up dinner.

"I don't have much of an appetite, but I want you and the kids to join us for dinner at our place," Grandpa Behruz told my aunt. He still looked and sounded shaky. "It's better for us to be together tonight."

I said I would go, but Aunt Maryam excused herself.

"That's very kind of you, *Hajj-agha,* but if you don't mind, I'd like to go home after we pick up Rostam," she said. "It's been a long day and I think it would be best for Rostam to come home with me. I don't want to expose him to any of this just yet."

I nodded my head in agreement. God knows Uncle Eskandar was incapable of being discreet in front of Rostam.

"That might be for the best," Grandpa mumbled. "Just remember to take your and Rostam's food along with you."

"*Mamnoon, Hajj-agha*, I will.*"

About half-an-hour later, I sat down to eat dinner with my grandfather and uncle in their apartment. I hadn't been there in a long time; since before my mother died.

The layout of their apartment was identical to ours. When you enter the apartment, it opens up immediately to the living room and to the left of it, the dining room area and kitchen. There's a narrow hallway to the right that leads to the three bedrooms, bathroom, and linen closet. The living room also has a sliding door to the terrace, but since they were on the ground floor, they had a patio.

I had to give them credit – for two older men living together, they were both very tidy.

We sat at their small dining room table and I helped Uncle Eskandar set the table, passing out the Styrofoam containers of hot food.

Even the tantalizing aroma of kabob did nothing to tease my lacking appetite, but I still forced a few bites. Tasting nothing with each spoonful, I washed down the food gathered inside my mouth with gulps of water.

"Do you think Sohrab will ever sit down to eat a meal with us?" Grandpa asked all of a sudden, his own meal untouched.

"Eat your dinner, Dad," Uncle Eskandar gently chided him. "These kinds of thoughts will only torture you."

"Let them, it can't be any worse than the torture I went through today," Grandpa Behruz said. "Witnessing my youngest son being convicted of murder, our family name forever tarnished. I wish I were dead and didn't see this day."

I tried to change my grandfather's mood by recounting happy memories of my parents. It almost felt like I was talking about two different people and not my mother and father. With everything that had happened to them, it was impossible to think they had seen happier days.

Eyeing the Persian rug in the dining room, I recalled the first time I went to the bazaar in Tehran with Dad. The first store we visited belonged to a friend of his; a renowned and wealthy rug merchant. Later, we had tea with him and he told me all about rugs and how they're made. I'd never seen so many rugs in one place before. The store wasn't that big and wherever you looked, there were rugs of all shapes and sizes rolled up in corners or sitting majestically on large platforms. Rugs in every possible color and design adorned the platforms in thick piles, which one of the salesmen flipped through with gusto so his customer could inspect each intricate, hand-woven work of art.

The customer ran his hand tenderly over each rug and asked about the number of knots and if it was made of silk or wool or both. Dad's friend explained you can tell a rug is all silk or contains silk if it's pricier and gives off a subtle sheen. I overheard the salesman as he rattled off numbers, measurements, and what region of Iran the rug was from. Every region has its own special design, like an artist's signature. If you look at a rug made in Isfahan, for example, it'll have a specific shape and pattern that sets it apart from the others. With just a quick glance, a seasoned rug dealer can tell you what region a rug is from.

Persians have a love affair with their rugs and if you walk into any Persian home, no matter how modest, you're bound to find at least one Persian rug adorning the living room, dining room, or bedroom floors of their home. More lavish households will have them covering the floor of every room. The more, the better; rugs are not only an investment and a status symbol, but also a point of pride. Even if your house is furnished with almost nothing else, a rug will redeem both your home and your honor. And if a rug is machine-woven or from another country, it's considered almost a betrayal. We'll not be unfaithful, however, as we consider only our hand-woven rugs to be the best in the world. They're a legacy; an homage to our homeland. Each one tells the story of the region it's from and the person who wove it. They're the colorful, woven maps of our country and culture.

Hundreds of miles away, in a small village in Isfahan, Shiraz, or Tabriz, living in a humble mud hut on a scenic hilltop, is a masterful yet humble artist. After spinning wool and silk into yards and yards of yarn, she will bathe them in big boiling pots of dye. They'll be reborn from the water with gorgeous, vibrant colors – the colors she needs to create her masterpiece. Once she has all the necessary shades, she will attach them to her enormous loom and sit down to paint with yarn.

Her fingers will work with incredible speed and precision, convincing you she could do this in her sleep. It may take months – even years, depending on the size and pattern – of sitting at that loom in her secluded hut, hands fluttering over it like frantic birds until she completes one rug.

Rug weavers have the patience of God.

"I remember when we were still living in Iran, Dad took me out for a guy's day, just the two of us," I said after a stretch of silence. "He took me to the bazaar to visit his friend's rug shop and then we went to the *zoorkhaneh*."

The *zoorkhaneh*, which literally translates to "house of strength," is a traditional gym in Iran where men gather to work out their bodies and their spirits. The practice of exercising in a *zoorkhaneh* is called *varzeshe-pahlevani* or "heroic sport," and is an ancient ritual. Originally, it was a traditional system of athletics used to train Persian warriors in Iran and surrounding regions since the Achaemenid Empire. It's a combination of several forms of sport, including martial arts, wrestling, and strength training mixed with traditional music and prayer.

Similar to yoga, *pahlevani* is one of the world's longest-running forms of training and marries various aspects of both pre-Islamic Persian culture, such as Zoroastrianism, along with Shia Islam and Sufism. I read a lot about the *zoorkhaneh* and *pahlevani* practices when I was younger, having fallen in love with it after that first visit with my dad. Before we came to the U.S., I begged him to take me on the weekends. If we still lived in Iran, I probably would've considered training at the one near our house.

I remember the scene clearly; muscular men gathered in the ring, awaiting the *morshed's* bell. The *morshed* – meaning "master" – is in charge of singing the traditional songs and prayers, playing the *zarb* – a goblet drum – and ringing the bell that signals the start and end of the exercises. Several special equipments are also used during the exercise ritual. The most popular and recognizable are the *meel* – large wooden clubs that originated from India.

To my amazement, the men swung the *meels* high above their heads, which takes an incredible amount of strength and practice. Just like with other types of weights, the *meel* varies in heaviness, with the heaviest one weighing 66 pounds. The thought of lifting something that heavy with one hand made my wrists ache.

The men continued their exercises by doing push-ups, running around the ring, and even spinning around rapidly, dervish-like, which takes a lot of practice to do without losing balance or getting dizzy. A number of other equipment are also used, like the *kabadeh*, or "bow and chain" and the *sang*, meaning "rock" in Farsi.

Meanwhile, the *morshed* sang atop his special seat, a respected and sacred place called the *sardam* – *sar* translates to "place" and *dam* refers to "speaking" or "chanting" – beat on his drum, and rang his bell. When the exercise ended, he rang the bell again and said a prayer. The men filed one behind the other to climb out of the ring and as they did, they touched the floor of the ring with their hand, put it to their lips to kiss it, and then raised it toward the ceiling as a thanks to God for a good training. It lifted my spirits just to watch them.

I continued telling Grandpa Behruz and Uncle Eskandar about that day, despite their quizzical looks. I don't really know why I was telling them all this, but it was comforting in a way.

After our trip to the *zoorkhaneh*, we went to one of the public bathhouses – a *hammam* – located in the older neighborhoods of Tehran. During my dad's childhood, most of the homes in Iran weren't yet equipped with the luxury of indoor plumbing, so people visited public bathhouses for both a shower and a deep-tissue massage. It was one of my dad's favorite places to go as a kid. I found that silly since it was just a place to shower and I told him it probably wasn't all that comfortable with other people around.

Dad explained that obviously the men and women's *hammams* were separate and undressing in front of other men wasn't a big deal; it was like a locker room.

"It's not just a place to shower, it's an experience," my father said. "The workers there are called *dalaks* and they come over upon request to wash and exfoliate your back with a special loofah called *kisseh* and a white-colored, chalky body scrub called *sefidab*. Your grandmother once told me it's naturally made from animal fat, sheep's spinal cord, and the fine powder from a kind of stone called *mel*. After you're nice and clean, the *dalak* gives you the best massage of your life. And the even better part is the ice-cold bottles of Coca-Cola they hand out to everyone. I'm sure you can imagine how refreshing and delicious it tastes after a hot shower. It was the best way to relax and such a treat every time we went."

I finally understood what my father meant when I went with him that day. I'll never forget how he tipped one of the *dalaks* and asked him to make sure I got the best treatment.

"It's my son's first time here," he kept saying with a proud grin.

To wrap up our day and keep to our theme, Dad took me to a nearby old-style, traditional restaurant – *restaurant-e-sonnati* – for some *abgoosht*, or lamb and chickpea stew cooked in special clay or stoneware crocks called *dizi*. It's usually made with lamb, chickpeas, white beans, potatoes, onions, tomatoes, and seasoned with turmeric. The ingredients are all combined in the *dizi* and cooked until the meat is tender. But we don't just ladle the stew into a bowl and eat it, oh no. Some important steps have to be followed before serving and enjoying the meal. First, once the strew is done, we strain the broth in a separate bowl. Then, the meat and half of the vegetables are mashed together in the *dizi* to create *goosht koobideh*, or "mashed meat," which is served alongside the broth.

Next, we break apart some type of flatbread, such as pita or lavash, into smaller pieces until they fill up a large serving dish or bowl. And then comes the fun part of pouring the piping hot broth and the rest of the vegetables over the little pieces of bread – called the *tilit* – until they nearly soak up the broth. Once all these steps are done, it's finally time to dig in. In fact, this hearty meal was created for digging in, and it's one of my favorite dishes – after kabob, of course. Once we had our fill of the *abgoosht*, Dad ordered some *Akbar-Mashti bastani* and *faloodeh*, my all-time favorite dessert. The ice cream, or *bastani,* is made from rose water, saffron, pistachios, and chunks of fresh frozen cream. Served on the side, the *faloodeh* are thin, frozen rice-noodles soaked in rose water syrup that get drizzled with either a layer of fruit-flavored syrup or lime juice and complement the *bastani* perfectly.

Dad told me ancient Persians invented *sharbat*, from which the word "sorbet" is derived. It's a syrup made from fruits or flower petals with which refreshing drinks are made. This invention aided in the creation of the earliest frozen dessert, the sorbet, created by both the Romans and Persians, and it traveled to other regions, gaining popularity throughout the centuries.

"In short," my father said, taking a big bite of his *faloodeh*, "Persians invented ice cream."

Leave it to my dad to credit Persians for every important discovery and invention in history.

He then dipped his index finger into the bowl of the melting *bastani* and touched the tip of my nose with it. I laughed and let it stay on until we finished our ice cream; even though it felt sticky and I probably looked ridiculous, I didn't want to wipe it off.

That day with my dad was one of the best days of my life and I recall that a deep sadness settled in the pit of my stomach on our way home. I thought how no other day could compare to it and in a way, I was right. I rarely experienced another day like it, when I felt pure happiness and nothing else. The older we get, even our good days are tinged with worries and everyday anxieties. Pure joy doesn't follow us into adulthood; we grow out of it like our childhood clothes.

"We spent the whole day together and I was so happy just being there with him, learning about all the things he knew, like he was letting me in on all the secrets of the universe. Secrets that only he and I knew."

"Why are you telling us all this, Cyrus *jan*?" Uncle Eskandar asked.

"Because I want to remember the good times I had with my parents," I said. "Because I'm tired of talking about the trial and what will happen, I'm tired of feeling miserable and anxious all the time."

Grandpa Behruz nodded and looked down at his untouched plate of cold meat and rice.

"Your dad was knowledgeable about almost every subject and he knew how to turn anything into a story," Grandpa said. "Your grandmother used to say he was born with a gift."

We spent almost an hour talking about our fondest memories of my parents.

"I hadn't thought of these memories in a long time, it's nice," Uncle Eskandar mused.

He mostly talked about their childhood and playing soccer with my dad in the dusty, narrow streets of their neighborhood, before their differences drove them apart.

"We used to buy these purple and white-striped plastic balls from the local convenience store for just a few cents," Uncle Eskandar said with a smile. "They were of a cheap quality and deflated after a few kicks, but those balls were everything to us – they were our entire source of joy and entertainment. I think more than anything else, they represent childhood in Iran and whenever I see one, I still get nostalgic."

I nodded my head in agreement, having played with those purple plastic balls countless times myself when we still lived in Iran.

"At the *zoorkhaneh*, I remember Dad telling me something that really stuck with me."

"What did he say?" Grandpa asked.

"When I tried to pick up one of the *meels* that was too heavy for me, Dad laughed and said, '*Pesaram, loghmeye bozorgtar az dahanet baar nadar.*'"

"Son, don't take a bite larger than your mouth."

"Of course, at the time, I had no idea what he was talking about, but now I know he meant I shouldn't take on more than I can handle."

"That's good advice," Grandpa Behruz said. "I used to tell him the same thing."

Persian parents and grandparents pass down the vast wealth of Farsi idioms and expressions to their children and grandchildren like verbal inheritance. We grow up hearing these familiar phrases, unsure of their true meanings when we're young, but they still manage to guide us and teach us everything we need to know. Then, as we grow older, we adopt them as our own mottos, our own truths that we hold within us like a precious organ. We use them to parent and guide our own children. The moment we start using them in regular conversation is the moment we realize we've stepped into adulthood; when we finally understand what those strange expressions mean. When we know them like we know our own name.

These words and phrases eventually become as familiar as breathing. They become part of our identities. They comfort and caress us like a mother's touch, as they are uttered in our mother tongue. They are as sacred as prayer.

"How can someone with so much knowledge, stories, and good advice be guilty of the worst possible crime? It just doesn't make sense!" I exclaimed.

I couldn't bring myself to say, "Murder."

My grandfather and uncle were both silent because there was no answer to that question.

After a few more silent seconds passed, I sighed and stood up to begin clearing the table. I didn't take Grandpa's food in case he got hungry after I left.

"Thank you for dinner, but I should get going," I said, looking at my watch. "It's getting late."

"You're welcome anytime, Cyrus," Uncle Eskandar said.

"Give Rostam a hug and kiss for me," Grandpa said.

I nodded and went over to hug him. To my surprise, my uncle opened his arms, too, and I leaned over to give him an awkward side hug. It was the first time we'd embraced since I was a child. The bitter, pungent scent of tobacco on his clothes filled my nostrils and I had to hold my breath a little. His smoking habit was worse than ever and I knew he'd go outside to smoke cigarette after cigarette once I left. During dinner, I noticed his hands nearly vibrated from the nicotine withdrawal.

I pulled away and seeing his face at such close range frightened me; his cheeks were hollow and the dark circles underneath his eyes had deepened. His bloodshot eyes made the subtle yellow pallor of his skin stand out more. I felt like I was staring too long, so I dropped my gaze and wished them both a good night.

Uncle Eskandar cleared his throat and mumbled a goodbye.

Grandpa Behruz only nodded, playing with the uneaten food on his plate.

When I got to the door, I heard my uncle asking Grandpa to eat something for the second time.

"*Siram,* Eskandar, *ghose siram karde,*" he said.

I couldn't get my grandfather's words – "I'm full, Eskandar, I'm full from sorrow" – out of my head the rest of the night.

* * *

The next day, I skipped school. I was too drained to face my teachers' looks of pity, Mrs. Krasinski's endless questions, and the swirling rumors.

I couldn't bear the hostile, judgmental looks and whispers, so I followed my father's advice and decided not to take on more than I could handle, if only for a day.

Most of all, I couldn't face my friends. What would Yiannis and Tamara say now that my father was found guilty? I wanted to believe they wouldn't judge me and my family, but I also wouldn't blame them if they did.

I didn't want to be identified as a murderer's son or the boy whose mom got murdered by his dad for the rest of my life. The more I matured, the more I understood the importance of reputation and saving face, especially after going through this experience. I understood why it was so crucial in my culture and almost sacred to Persian families.

Because it takes years to collect, like raindrops, and it's impossible to get back once it's lost, like an overturned bucket.

Even Aunt Maryam was sympathetic and thought it was a good idea for me to stay home.

She made me chicken soup before leaving for work and had to almost drag Rostam out of our room because he didn't want to go to school, either.

"How come Cyrus gets to stay home?" he whined, throwing his backpack on the floor.

"Rostam Nezami, you pick that up right away and march to the door," Aunt Maryam ordered, hands on hips. "We're late."

"I don't wanna go!" he cried, on the verge of tears. "I wanna stay home with Cyrus."

"Your brother is sick, that's why I'm letting him stay home," my aunt said with a sigh, looking at her watch. "Otherwise, he'd have to go to school, too."

"He doesn't look sick," Rostam insisted, running over to my bed to scrutinize me.

I faked a cough.

"I am sick, my body hurts and I have a fever," I moaned, putting my hand to my forehead.

Rostam mimicked my cough. "If my *dadashi* is sick, then I'm sick, too."

"Nice try, Rostam, *Khaleh* and I both know you're not sick! Now, stop arguing with us and go to school like a good boy. Maybe if I'm feeling better, we can play some basketball when you get back."

"Promise?"

"If I'm feeling better by then, I promise we can play."

"Okay," he mumbled and picking up his book bag, shuffled out of the room.

"Thank you. You sure you don't need anything else?" Aunt Maryam asked before following Rostam.

"No, thanks, I'm okay," I said. "Have a good day."

She smiled and hurried out of the room.

I could hear her fussing with Rostam until they left. Once the front door shut behind them, silence filled the apartment.

Not yet ready to leave the warm haven of my bed and face the day, I drifted in and out of sleep.

I slept through the first half of the afternoon; my body felt like it had been hit by a bulldozer and I couldn't even get out of bed to eat.

Around two-thirty, I heard a knock at the front door. Puzzled, I bolted out of bed and checked my phone. I had a couple of texts from Tamara and two missed calls from Yiannis.

Ripping my pajamas off, I hopped into a pair of dirty jeans lying on the floor and wrestled on a clean T-shirt I fished out of my drawer. After hearing a second series of knocks, I ran to the bathroom, splashed water on my face, squeezed some toothpaste into my mouth, and ran a comb through my matted hair.

I finally made it to the door and looking through the peephole, saw Tamara and Yiannis standing in the hallway with concerned looks on their faces. When Yiannis raised his arm to knock again, I reluctantly opened the door.

"There you are!" Tamara said, relief washing over her face. "We were so worried about you."

"Yeah, man, how come you didn't show up to school today?" Yiannis asked, pushing past me to come inside.

Tamara hesitated and looked at me, so I stepped aside and gestured for her to enter, doing my best to hide my annoyance.

Once they were both inside, I faced them with my arms crossed over my chest.

"Cyrus, are you alright?" Tamara asked.

"I'm fine, I just wasn't feeling up to school today."

"Are you sick?" Tamara came up to me and placed her cool hand on my forehead.

"Come on, guys, you both know why I skipped today," I said, jerking my head away from her hand. She dropped her arm to her side, a hurt look on her face.

"Well, we just wanted to make sure you're okay," Yiannis said, looking around the apartment.

"I'm fine."

I was surprised by how hostile I was acting toward them.

"Someone woke up on the wrong side of the bed," Yiannis said with a grin.

"What of it?" I cried. "I didn't ask you guys to come here."

"Look, Cyrus, we're sorry for barging in on you, but to be honest, we heard about your father's verdict and wanted to see how you're doing," Tamara explained.

"Of course you heard about it, and while I appreciate your concern, it's really nobody's business," I said. "I'm trying to deal with all of this the best way I can and don't need all this pity bullshit being thrown at me. How would you feel if your family's whole business was the talk of your school?"

"Dude, relax, we were just checking up on you," Yiannis said, raising up his arms defensively. "Nobody's trying to get in your business."

"This was clearly a mistake," Tamara said and grabbing Yiannis's arm, headed for the door.

I knew if I let them walk out the door like that, I'd lose my only friends for good.

"Wait, I'm really sorry, you guys," I cried. "I don't know what got into me."

They stopped walking and turned around; Tamara still looked upset.

I suddenly remembered the last time I hung out with her outside of school, we'd kissed. Now I was kicking her out of my house. If they weren't judging me or reconsidering their friendship with me before, I wouldn't blame them if they were giving it serious thought now.

"Tamara, I'm so sorry," I said, going up and taking her hand. "I'm just in a weird place right now."

Her expression softened. "I know," she said. "We're here for you."

"Yiannis, I'm sorry, man. You're great friends and I appreciate you both."

Yiannis's grin found its way back to his face and he gave me a playful punch on the arm.

"You really freaked out there for a second."

"I know, I'm sorry. Can I offer you guys a drink to make up for it?"

"Actually, I'm going to be late for a thing with my mom, she's picking me up," Yiannis said. "But Tamara, you can stay if you want."

I felt a pang of jealousy and tried to recall the last time my mom picked me up for something.

"Gee, thanks for giving me permission, Dad," Tamara mocked him.

"You're welcome, my child, and remember what we talked about, absolutely no monkey business."

I whacked him on the head with one of the couch pillows. Yiannis grinned and gave me a wink.

"You're so subtle, Yiannis," Tamara said, folding her arms and jutting out her hip. I realized how badly I wanted to place my hands on her hips. My face burned at the thought.

"Oh, look, he's already blushing!" Yiannis said, sticking his index finger in my face.

"Get out of here, you dingus!" I cried, opening the door.

Laughing, he sauntered out. "Be good, you two."

I shut the door behind him and mumbled, "Good riddance."

Tamara giggled.

I walked her toward the dining room table and went to the kitchen for some drinks and snacks.

"My aunt made me some chicken soup, if you'd like some," I offered, my stomach grumbling once I removed the pot lid and took in the fragrant, cozy aroma of homemade soup. "Her chicken soups are famous in our family."

"I already ate lunch, but if your aunt can make chicken soup smell that good, then I'd love some!" Tamara said.

When I ladled some into a bowl and handed it to her, she cupped her hands around it appreciatively and breathed in the steam with her eyes closed.

"Mm, I'm going to have to ask your aunt for the recipe!"

"And the trick to making it taste even better is squeezing some fresh lemon juice over it," I said, holding up a small plate of lemon wedges.

"There's no doubt about it, when it comes to food, you Persians got it going on."

"Just food?" I teased her.

"Among other things," she said, giggling.

After we ate, Tamara asked me about the trial and I told her as much as I could. It felt good to talk about it with someone other than family.

"I meant what I said, I'm here for you. Whatever you need," she said.

"Thanks, I know."

She smiled and took my hand in hers.

After a moment's silence, Tamara stood up. "Well, I should get going. I'm really glad you're okay," she said, pushing in her chair. "And thanks for the delicious soup!"

"Thanks for checking on me, and again, I'm sorry for acting so crazy," I stood up to walk her to the door.

"You're going through a lot, it's totally understandable, so don't worry about it."

"Oh, do you have a ride home?"

"Yeah, my friend Sarah said she'd swing by to get me," Tamara said. "She's at the nearby coffee shop."

My heart started beating as we got to the door. I didn't know whether I should kiss her or not.

"Okay, great," I said, my mouth dry. "Be careful, and thanks again for visiting."

"Sure thing. Will I see you at school tomorrow?"

"I'll be there."

"Great."

We stood there awkwardly for a second until Tamara pulled me into a hug. As she let go, I got a bit too eager and leaned in for a kiss, like last time.

"Oh," she muttered and gave me a quick peck on the lips. I had misjudged; it was not the right time for a kiss.

Mortified, I pulled away.

Without making eye contact, she turned and hurried off.

Closing the door, I leaned against it and closed my eyes, wishing I'd never answered it in the first place.

Chapter Twenty-Three

I didn't want the day of the sentencing hearing to arrive.

I busied myself and my mind with schoolwork, chores, hanging out with Tamara and Yiannis, reading – any mundane, everyday activity that would distract my mind and allow me to forget the impending date. Perhaps the more I did, the further the date would be pushed back.

As soon as there was nothing left to do, the reality crept into my consciousness and dug a sinkhole in my stomach. The thought that this event alone determined whether my father would ever come home, whether he would live or die almost knocked me off my feet.

I was surprised I could still function and live in a world where nothing made sense anymore; where I had to dodge the impossible scenarios reality flung at me. How am I – the product of the love between my parents – able to breathe and survive in the same world where my mother – who pushed me into existence from her own flesh – was killed at the hands of my father?

It's amazing what human beings condition themselves to get used to and endure. All the atrocities throughout history – how did we survive it all? How did the knowledge of what we're capable of doing to one another not kill us off long ago? Is our will to survive that strong? That we endure war, murder, rape, betrayal, and heartbreak just to carry on and preserve our guilty race? To what end? Are we trying to prove ourselves to our creator – the one who banished us after the Original Sin – knowing all too well we were doomed from the start?

Like arrogant, chastised children we scurry and stomp about on this planet causing chaos and still expect forgiveness and salvation. We don't learn from our mistakes. God knew this all too well – otherwise, He wouldn't have punished us so severely after the very first act of wrongdoing.

6,000 years of civilized human history and our mistakes have taught us nothing. We continue to repeat the same wrongs previous generations promised would die along with them.

And when our instinct to survive kicks into full gear, a totally different beast takes over us. If the judge gives my father the death penalty, will his instinct to survive take over? What will it drive him to do?

It was hard to grapple with these thoughts and not lose my mind. I considered talking to Aunt Maryam about seeing a therapist, but it wasn't cheap and I didn't know how much it would help. There was always Mrs. Krasinski, but if I shared some of the thoughts I had with her, she'd probably refer me to a psychiatrist anyway, admitting my case was beyond her expertise.

* * *

As with all the other days I dreaded, the day of the sentencing hearing arrived at warp speed to mock me.

It felt like I was living the trial on a loop; I couldn't escape it. It was like déjà-vu at first – that is, until the moment the judge entered and we all rose.

After that, everything happened too fast and left me reeling.

Six minutes.

That's all it took to change the lives of six people forever.

The judge reviewed the history of the case, the evidence, and the jury's verdict.

The only sentence I heard was the last one:

"I hereby sentence the defendant to life without parole. Though I respect the jury's recommendation for the death penalty, I do not believe it's warranted for the nature of this crime, the evidence provided, and the defendant's background. The lack of a clear motive is not sufficient to comply with the purposes of sentencing. Therefore, I believe the sentence of life without parole is sufficient, but not greater than necessary, to comply with the purposes of sentencing."

The judge continued, rattling off laws and codes and addressing both the prosecution and defense in that technical courtroom speech of which I understood very little.

"Life without parole."

Three words.

It took me a couple minutes to comprehend what that meant. Instead of "death," which is the word I was bracing myself for since the start of the trial, I

200

heard "life." For a few brief seconds, I was even elated. My father wasn't sentenced to death. He wasn't going to be executed.

He was granted the very opposite: life.

Then, logic took over. "Life" still meant guilt. "Life" meant life imprisonment.

"Life without parole" meant my father, Sohrab Nezami, will remain in prison until the day he dies. With no chance of ever getting out. It meant the death of his freedom and the life he once knew. The only thing worse than death was this.

My father won't have his physical life taken from him, sure, but he can't come home or be with his family for as long as he lives.

When a person dies, you know it's impossible for you to physically see them and be with them, and no matter how much that hurts, you're forced to accept it one way or another.

Knowing my father is alive but can't be with us will be torture.

It was life without living. That was his sentence.

I didn't dare look in my father's direction. To my left, I saw my grandfather with his head in both hands as if checking to make sure it was attached and my uncle staring straight ahead, eyes wide with shock.

To my right, Aunt Maryam was stone once again. I had an uncontrollable urge to shake her and yell that my father was going to die in prison. That in the eyes of the court and the Commonwealth of Virginia, he was guilty of murdering her only sister. That his reputation was ruined and he would never come home to us or walk as a free man in the world he knew. That he would never fulfill his dream of becoming a doctor in this country. That I didn't know how to tell my baby brother his father wasn't coming home. I wanted a reaction from her. Anything. Anything to confirm what I was feeling.

With the resounding bang of the gavel, the salty taste of nausea coated my tongue. My blood pressure had dropped from the shock, so I rested my heavy, throbbing head against the wooden seat and closed my eyes. I felt too weak to breathe and for a second, thought I would die right there. Then, I felt a cold hand on my forehead and a plastic bottle pushed to my dry lips. I took a sip of the warm water. Opening my eyes, Aunt Maryam's face was looking down at me, no longer stone.

"Cyrus *jan*, are you okay? Do you want me to take you outside?" she whispered.

I shook my head. "I want to see *Baba*."

"You can't, *azizam*, they're about to take him away."

I shot up in my seat and realized the courtroom was emptying.

That's when I saw him, amongst the flurry of suits and ties and papers.

I will never forget the look he gave me as they ushered him away in handcuffs.

It was so many unspoken words in one look. So many regrets.

It was a look of apology and shame.

But worst of all, it was a look of defeat.

For a man who officially lost everything in as little as six minutes, there was nothing left to fight for or protect.

My father had given up and I was witness to it. A son witnessing his father give him that look shatters something inside him – it shatters the steadfast belief he's had since he was a little boy: that his father is invincible. It shatters the assurance that his father is his protector. I never felt so vulnerable and alone. I now realized what Grandpa Behruz meant when he said there are some things that break you. This was it.

The thought of going through the rest of my life without either of my parents terrified me. I felt as though someone had ripped all of my bones from my flesh, shattered them, and then dumped the crushed pieces back into a deflated frame.

I wanted to tell the judge I would testify, that he was wrong for keeping a father from his sons who needed him and who had already lost a mother.

In that moment of pure desperation, I realized I wanted him to come back even if he did kill my *Maman*. Having one parent, no matter how guilty of wrongdoing, was better than none.

What gave this stern, black-robed man the right to ruin my life more than it was already ruined?

What gave any of these people the right?

Unable to stand it any longer, I stood up and tried to move past Aunt Maryam to get to my father, while yelling at the judge and whoever was left in the courtroom that they had no right. A tangle of hands and arms held me back, covering my mouth.

It felt like I was underwater; my limbs were first heavy and then went slack.

A ringing overtook my brain, then total darkness.

Chapter Twenty-Four

The days and weeks following the sentencing blended together like one long, never-ending day.

I stopped going to school and had already missed so many days that it didn't really matter at this point. Seeing the state I was in, even Aunt Maryam gave up trying to convince me to go.

Yiannis delivered piles of schoolwork I didn't bother doing and it became apparent I would fail and be forced to repeat freshman year, or I'd have to retake some of the classes I failed over the summer. Yiannis tried to talk to me a few times and even offered to tutor me and help me catch up, but I treated him like such a jerk that he stopped visiting or bringing the piles of papers I neglected, which ended up covering my desk in white.

I didn't return Tamara's texts or calls and after a while, they stopped.

I ignored Rostam for the most part. I knew that if I looked into his eyes, I would fall apart. Because I still didn't know how to tell him his father was never coming home. Once, he tried to get me to play basketball and when I finally lost my temper and snapped at him, he got the hint and avoided me after that. He could tell something was wrong, but didn't know how to ask us, or what to ask. He looked at us with questioning eyes, hoping to find the answer somewhere in our distracted, distraught faces.

I felt hollow and numb. I didn't think I'd ever be able to feel anything again.

A few days after the trial, my dad emailed me. When Aunt Maryam and Rostam left for the day, I sat in bed, staring at the unread "no-subject" email, wondering whether I should open or delete it. His email address was different now, the at sign was followed by the name of the state prison he'd been transferred to after the sentencing.

Like everything else in my life, I ignored my father's email and forgot it was there.

That night, when the thought of spending another second in the apartment made me physically ill, I took the bus down to the restaurant after-hours to get away from everyone and think. I couldn't remember the last time I'd been out of the house and didn't even care how late it was. Even Aunt Maryam kept her distance and gave me space, no longer asking me about my whereabouts – not that she needed to since I hardly left the house. When I told her I was going out for a bit, she looked relieved more than anything.

After getting off at the bus stop, I walked around to the back entrance to look for the spare key we hid under a potted plant for emergencies. As I went to put the key into the lock, I noticed the door was unlocked and the alarm wasn't on. Afraid we were being burgled, I opened the door slowly and kept the lights off in case the trespassers were still in the restaurant, using the light of my phone screen to guide my steps in the dark.

As quietly as I could, I made my way through the kitchen and heard a distant cry coming from the basement. The restaurant basement was a large area that served multiple purposes; one side was used for storage while the rest of the open space served as a lounge where a lot of the restaurant regulars – mainly older men who were friendly with my uncle and grandfather – got together on the weekends to smoke hookah, drink tea – and sometimes even whiskey, which some of the men brought with them to share since my uncle and grandfather refused to serve alcohol – and play backgammon.

Backgammon is a cherished game and pastime amongst older Persian men. I never really understood it, no matter how much my dad tried to teach me and get me to play with him. If I'm being honest, I found it a little dull, though I never had the heart to tell *Baba*. One thing's for sure, though – it's not dull when experienced Persian men play it together. Indeed, when they play, rolling the dice with an expert flick of the wrist, eyes gleaming as the dice ricochet against the walls of the wooden board, it becomes as exciting as an Olympic tournament.

Tiptoeing toward the basement stairway, I suddenly recognized my uncle's voice and hurried down the rest of the stairs to make sure he was okay. Perhaps the burglars had walked in on him locking up and hurt him in order to make an escape. It was almost 11:30 on a weeknight and despite his workaholic tendencies, I'd never known him to stay so late past closing.

It was then that I saw him in the far corner of the dark room, surrounded by a few lit candles melting in saucers on a low table beside him. He was on his knees facing the direction of Mecca, opposite the bottom of the stairs where I was standing. The dim light of the candles silhouetted his body on the adjacent wall in a grotesque manner. From his shadow, I could tell he was holding something in his hand, but since he had his back to me, I wasn't able to see what it was. Just then, he tilted his head back, bringing the object he was holding up toward his face, and I realized he was drinking from it. An amber liquid reflected in the candlelight as he drank from the clear glass bottle. I was shocked; he was drinking whiskey. One of the patrons must have either forgotten or left it here for the next time they all got together.

Uncle Eskandar was a fairly religious man and I knew some nights when he worked late, he said his prayers here at the restaurant before heading home. But something wasn't right here. He normally didn't cry when he prayed and for as long as I've known him, not once has he touched a drop of alcohol, let alone during prayer. It was sacrilege. He criticized my dad all the time for drinking and called alcohol *zahremari*, meaning "snake poison."

My uncle even avoided the basement a lot of the time since they drank and gambled here. He once tried to convince Grandpa Behruz to shut down what he called the "extracurricular activities in the basement," but my grandpa refused, saying it didn't make sense for them to go through all the trouble of getting a tobacco license and hookahs set up just to shut it all down. Plus, it helped bring in some profit. Uncle Eskandar couldn't say no to that.

Instead of going over to him, I watched for a little while longer, stunned by his strange behavior.

He set the bottle down on the table beside him, placed his hands on his thighs, and in a sobbing, slurred speech, asked God for forgiveness. In his inebriated state, he was completely unaware of my presence. I shouldn't have eavesdropped and thought about leaving right then, but something kept me glued to that spot.

The next words he said surprised me, "Forgive me for what I've done."

What did he mean by that? I leaned in closer to hear him better.

"Forgive me for causing my family so much grief. I only wanted Sohrab's share of the restaurant, I didn't mean to hurt anyone. This restaurant has brought nothing but misery to this family. Oh God, forgive me, this is all my fault!"

He stood up from his prostration in a drunken rage and began throwing tables and chairs in random directions, nearly hitting me.

Afraid he would hurt himself and damage the furniture, I rushed over to him.

"Uncle, it's me, Cyrus," I called over the racket and put my arms around him. "What's wrong?"

He stood still and once I was sure he had calmed down, I let him go. His arms hung limp at his sides as he turned around to face me.

"What're you doing here?" he asked, slurring his words. His voice carried a tinge of suspicion and since I didn't have a good reason for being there, I made up an excuse.

"I was passing by the restaurant when I noticed the door was open, so I came in to check and make sure we weren't being burgled."

I could smell the alcohol on Uncle Eskandar's breath as he looked at me, his eyes glazed over and unfocused. He looked around him and started to cry again.

"*Amoo joon*, what's wrong?" I asked. I couldn't help feeling sorry for him; he looked so pathetic.

"I didn't mean to do it, Cyrus," he wailed. "I'm so sorry."

At first, I was confused, but then I figured he was talking about testifying against my father.

"You were just doing what you had to do. Don't feel guilty, it wasn't your fault."

"I wish it were that simple," he said, shaking his head as his tears made a trail from his eyes to his unkempt beard.

"What do you mean?"

"I didn't want to do it. When a man has his back against the wall and nowhere else to turn, he never makes the right choices because he is driven by desperation. We have to live with the choices we make, both here and the hereafter."

I no longer knew what he was talking about, but I figured it was the alcohol talking. He was almost delirious and it was best not to push him with further questions. He had sunk down to the floor and was crying softly, so I wrapped my hand around his frail arm and pulled him up. I'd never seen my uncle so distraught before.

"Come on, Uncle. Let's get you home."

I blew out the candles, then shifted his weight on me to help him walk as we stumbled up the stairs with only my phone lighting our way. After making sure all the lights were off, I turned on the security alarm and locked the main entrance door behind us. There was no way I could've cleaned up the mess my uncle had made; he could barely stand and I needed to get him home before he hurt himself. I'd have to tell Grandpa Behruz about it either tonight or tomorrow. He was most likely asleep already.

Just then, I felt my uncle's phone vibrating against my hip as we walked. Fishing it out of his pocket, I saw it was Grandpa. He must've gotten worried.

Answering the phone, I let Grandpa Behruz know I was with Uncle Eskandar at the restaurant, and we were on our way home. I could tell he was surprised I answered Uncle Eskandar's phone and was probably wondering why we were at the restaurant together so late, but he didn't say anything about it and hung up.

I called a cab to take us home instead of taking the bus. I didn't feel like getting judgmental looks from the passengers or risking any of his local customers seeing him in this state since we were so close to the restaurant.

When we got home, I paid the cab driver and helped my uncle out of the car. He was pretty much passed out by this point and I had to almost drag him to their apartment, thankful they lived on the ground floor.

Grandpa Behruz opened the door before I even had a chance to knock.

"What has he done to himself?" he asked, eyes wide with worry.

"He's just a little drunk," I said and dropped my eyes to the floor, feeling embarrassed to say something like that about my uncle. "I think he was upset over Dad's sentencing and felt guilty for testifying."

My grandfather sighed and shook his head. "Okay, help me take him inside."

Once Uncle Eskandar was in bed, I said goodnight to Grandpa Behruz and left. It was hard to bear the sadness in his eyes over what had become of his two sons. I couldn't fathom what he must be feeling – to raise two sons and give them all you have only to watch them fade before your eyes, unable to do anything about it.

On my way up to our apartment, I had an uneasy feeling over what I witnessed at the restaurant tonight. It felt as though Uncle Eskandar was trying to confess something.

But what?

A concerned Aunt Maryam greeted me at the door. "Cyrus, I was worried sick! Where were you?" It was almost one in the morning.

I told her everything; about how I encountered Uncle Eskandar at the restaurant and what I heard. "What do you think he could've meant by it?"

She brushed it off.

"Oh, Cyrus, this has been a hard time for all of us," she said. "I'm sure he feels guilty about testifying against your father, which is understandable, and obviously the alcohol made it worse."

I nodded my head, wanting to believe her, but something tugged at me.

I heard Uncle Eskandar's pleading voice in my head: "*I didn't want to do it. When a man has his back against the wall and nowhere else to turn, he never makes the right choices because he is driven by desperation. We have to live with the choices we make, both here and the hereafter.*"

What wrong choices did he have to live with and answer for? Was it the way he treated my father and fought with him over their inheritance? Was it testifying against him?

The look in his eyes was that of a man guilty of something far graver than just being a lousy and selfish older brother.

It was the look of a man who knew he had done something wrong and wanted to atone for it, but didn't know how or what good it would do.

Just then, it occurred to me I could no longer look into the eyes of the men in my family. Their eyes had one thing in common: The burnt out, empty look of hopelessness. As if all light and life had been sucked out of their eyes. The men who were supposed to guide, protect, and reassure me were lost and without hope.

And I was too afraid to look at myself in the mirror. Afraid that the reflection of the eyes staring back at me would have the same vacant gaze.

Chapter Twenty-Five

Sometime during the days I no longer kept track of, our home phone rang shrilly. Aside from telemarketers, no one called our landline and we seldom picked it up.

Thinking it might be a long-distance call from Iran – perhaps her father – Aunt Maryam picked up. Her mother's health was fast deteriorating and she still hadn't decided whether she was going to travel to Iran to visit her or not.

The conversation was brief.

"It was your father," she told me after hanging up. "He wants to see you."

This was the first time he'd called the house since his arrest, but because I hadn't replied to his email, he had no choice but to call. My face burned with guilt.

What could I possibly say to him? I didn't have the words because they didn't exist.

But I knew I needed to go and see him. Perhaps nothing needed to be said.

Aunt Maryam offered to drive me there over the weekend, but I couldn't wait till then. I had to see him sooner, so I took the bus to the state prison that same afternoon. The state prison building was so much bigger and more intimidating than the county jail. The thought of my father spending his life in such a place seemed impossible. He didn't belong here.

Because he was now convicted, visiting arrangements had changed and I had to meet with my dad behind a glass partition and speak through a receiver.

When he walked tentatively up to the glass and sat across from me, I barely recognized him. His cheeks were sunken in and he must've lost at least ten more pounds since the sentencing. His skin was pallid, his scalp thinning more than before, and the hair that remained on his head was whiter, like his beard. It no longer reminded me of Virginia Beach in December because there was no more gray left. It was nearly all white now, like the foaming waves of a stormy sea.

And his eyes…

I still couldn't look at them for too long. They were protruding and owl-like in his small, shrunken face. I hated seeing him in the prison uniform more than anything.

He picked up the receiver with a weak smile and waited for me to do the same.

Feeling all strength leave me, I lifted the receiver to my ear with both hands and croaked a "Hello" into it.

"*Salam,* Cyrus *jan,*" he said, his voice barely above a whisper. "Thanks for meeting me, I know it must not have been easy for you."

"It's okay, how are you? It looks like you're not eating."

"Ah, I don't have much of an appetite these days."

"I'm sorry about the outcome of the trial."

"Me too, but there's nothing anyone could've done."

"Is your lawyer going to appeal it?"

"I asked him not to."

"Why not?"

"Cyrus, there's no point," he said with a heavy sigh. "I can't fight this anymore. I don't have the strength or willpower."

"Dad, I'm sorry I couldn't testify for you," I said in a low voice. "I wasn't in the right mindset to do it."

"Son, I'm not blaming you and I'm not upset you didn't testify. You have every right to feel the way you do, but all I'm saying is there's no point to an appeal. It's a long and winding process and it'll make no real difference."

"Maybe they'll be able to find some evidence in your favor and change the ruling?"

"They won't do that," he replied. "It's over."

"But maybe there's a slight chance they will. Maybe you could come home."

My father looked down and was silent.

All of a sudden, my mind went back to a couple of nights ago at the restaurant with Uncle Eskandar, to his strange behavior. I couldn't stop thinking about the things he had said.

"So, a few nights ago, I ran into Uncle Eskandar at the restaurant after-hours and he was acting very odd," I said, hoping my father could shed some light on what Uncle Eskandar meant and why he felt so guilty.

"This is your uncle we're talking about, so you'll have to be a little more specific. Odd how?"

"He was drinking and crying, asking God for forgiveness for something he'd done."

"And why were you there?"

"I wanted to go there to be alone and noticed the main entrance was open, so I went inside to see if someone had broken in and found Uncle in the basement."

"He was probably just feeling guilty about our rocky relationship and his testimony," Dad said, shrugging his shoulders. Like Aunt Maryam, he didn't seem all too concerned about it. "Or maybe it had nothing to do with me. Only God knows what goes on in the hearts of men."

"It was specifically about you," I insisted.

"Then, he's most likely feeling guilty about testifying."

"Dad—"

"Cyrus, listen to me," my father interrupted. "We don't have much time and I wanted to tell you something before you have to go."

His tone alarmed me, so I nodded into the receiver and waited for him to go on.

"I don't want you to worry about me," he began. "Just promise you'll take care of yourself and Rostam. You're all he has now."

I looked down and nodded again, feeling choked up.

"Far greater things have frightened and saddened me during my lifetime that I am numb to this now. The biggest was losing your mother, being taken away from you and Rostam, and having everyone who knows me think I killed my wife. My ruined reputation. I think life should be feared more than death because everything in life is unexpected. You can never prepare for it. Death is the one thing we can always expect and be certain about. Even the hour and fashion of our death, except in rare cases, are a mystery, but not death itself.

"It's always there, hovering over us like a second, invisible shadow. Death should not be feared because after we die, there's no more worry. For once, time waits for us on the brink of our last breath and then stops. No more waiting, suffering, longing, or heartache. No more anxiety over what tomorrow will throw in our waiting laps. No more difficult choices to make. In death, we do nothing but sleep and that's comforting in a way. I know what you're going to ask – will I be at peace? I will be because I know I'm innocent and that someday, the truth will come out and clear my name. And your mom will be at peace then, too. What offers the most comfort is the thought of seeing her again. Cyrus, we have gained and lost since the day we were born and take this from me, loss is the greatest life lesson because death, the most certain of all things, teaches us about it."

I wasn't sure why my father was talking like he was going to die, but it frightened me.

"Dad, you're acting like they gave you the death penalty. Stop talking about death so much."

A strange smile formed on his dry lips and his eyes had a far-off glance. He recited a familiar prayer under his breath: "We belong to Allah and to Him we shall return."

I shuddered.

"This is kind of like death in a way, don't you think?" he replied. "Being away from you both, unable to watch you grow into men and experience life with you. It's worse than death in my eyes."

"Stop, we'll come visit you as much as we can."

"Thank you, Cyrus. I couldn't be prouder of the man you've become. Thank you for being my son. I'm sorry for everything, for failing to be the father you and Rostam deserved, and I pray you'll both find it in your hearts to forgive me one day."

"There's nothing to forgive," I mumbled, biting on the inside of my cheek to keep from crying. "You just have to be more hopeful and stop talking like this."

"I'm a physician, Cyrus, I'm well-acquainted with death. It does not frighten me," he said. "It's running out of time that frightens me – time to make up for everything and atone for my sins."

"You have time, Dad."

We got the two-minute warning from the prison guard.

"Well, it looks like I only have two minutes," he said bitterly. "Take care of yourself and Rostam."

"I'll bring him with me next time," I said. "He's been asking about you and I still have to find a way to tell him you, uh, won't be coming home for now. I just haven't felt up to it yet."

"I'm sure you'll figure out the right time and way to tell him and I'm sorry for putting yet another burden on you."

"It's okay, Dad. Just take care of yourself and please try to eat."

"I'll try my best," he said with a forced smile. "Don't forget the stories I've told you. Maybe one day, you'll tell them to your kids. Did you read the one about the Cyrus Cylinder? It was in the last email I sent you."

I looked down, embarrassed. "No, not yet. I haven't gotten around to reading it."

"Ah, I figured you hadn't read it yet. Just make sure you do."

"I will, and maybe next time I visit we can talk about it."

"Okay, sure."

"Bye, Dad."

"*Khodahafez*, my Cyrus, *halalam kon*."

Before I could reassure him a second time that there was nothing to forgive, he quickly hung up and looked over at the guard to take him away.

* * *

That was the last time I saw my father.

Two weeks after my visit, Sohrab Nezami passed away from malnutrition in his cell, where one of the guards found him unresponsive in bed.

After hearing the news, his words finally made sense. He must've known he didn't have much time left. He tried to tell me, but I didn't realize. I didn't understand that he had simply lost the will to live or take care of himself after the sentencing. Recalling my own reaction post-trial, could I even blame him?

I wish I had said something to change his mind or give him hope. Something.

I also discovered that one parent's death – regardless of the circumstances – doesn't prepare you for the other's passing. It doesn't make it easier or more bearable. It is just as fresh and painful and impossible to accept.

An uneasy feeling came over me when I emailed him about a week earlier to set up a time to visit with Rostam and received no response. I knew something wasn't right, but tried to convince myself he was just depressed and would come around, that I would eventually hear from him.

But another week passed and still, I received no response from my father, which took my anxiety to new levels. I had trouble sleeping and became obsessive about checking my phone and email for an update.

When I walked into the living room Sunday night after hearing muffled voices, a feeling that dug a bottomless pit in my gut confirmed what I had been dreading. I saw *Baba* Behruz hunched over on the couch, his shoulders shaking as he softly sobbed, just like in the courtroom. Aunt Maryam was talking to my uncle in a low voice, her left hand cupping her cheek as if making sure that half of her face was still there.

"What's going on?" I asked, even though I already knew the answer.

Before they could tell me, Rostam followed me into the living room and looked around at the distraught adults. I ordered him to go to our room and shut the door.

"But Cyrus, I wanna stay," he whined.

"Now!" I yelled.

He stood his ground. "Why is Grandpa crying?"

"I'm going to count to five and if you're still here when I'm done counting, you can kiss your basketball goodbye."

With a stomp and a whimper, he turned and ran to our room, slamming the door behind him.

Once Rostam was gone and out of hearing range, Aunt Maryam and Uncle Eskandar huddled around me, spoke to me, to each other, saying words that again made no sense. My ears only caught four words: *"Your father is dead."*

I shook my head. "No, I just saw him. You're mistaken." My own voice came from somewhere outside of me. I felt displaced.

"It happened a few hours ago," I heard Aunt Maryam tell me. "Your grandpa got the call from the prison. They said they didn't notice he wasn't eating until it was too late."

I searched her face for tears, any trace of sadness. I saw none. It sounded like she was a reporter giving the details of a news story.

I pulled at the skin of my arm and imagined it was my aunt's heart. Then I punched it repeatedly. It was infuriating not to get any emotional reaction from her. In that instant, I hated her and wholly believed it was what she wanted all along – for my dad to die. Maybe she prayed for it.

In that dark moment, I needed someone to blame.

"Cyrus *jan*, are you okay?" she asked, coming up closer to me.

"You got your wish," I spat at her.

"What?"

"You're happy he's dead."

My uncle looked at me with wide eyes and even Grandpa Behruz raised his head to stare at me with his puffy, red ones.

"Cyrus, there's no reason for you to attack your aunt," Uncle Eskandar said.

"Look at her, she doesn't even care," I cried. "She's not even upset!"

Aunt Maryam lowered her head and said nothing.

"What? You're not even going to talk? You're heartless!"

"Cyrus, that's enough," *Baba* Behruz yelled. "*Harfe gonde tar az dahanet nazan.*"

"Do not say things that are bigger than your mouth."

"*Hajj-agha*, please, let him continue. Let him speak like this to the person who stayed and cared for him and his brother while grieving for the sister his father took away. What do you expect me to do, Cyrus? How do you want me to act?"

I was taken aback; I hadn't expected her to lash out like this.

"Put yourself in my shoes," she continued. "I've made the best of an inconceivable situation. I stayed when many in my position would've left long ago and this is how you thank me? There's nothing keeping me here except you and Rostam. And I'm sorry I don't feel particularly devastated over the death of the man who took my sister's life.

"I am sorry you lost both your parents and have gone through so much pain at such a young age, and believe me, if I could somehow undo it all and protect you from it, I would, but don't expect me to grieve for your father and don't turn me into the bad guy. How dare you? *Khejalat bekesh.*"

Aunt Maryam said the last part, "You should be ashamed of yourself," in Farsi to make it sound that much more biting. But I felt no shame. Only anger. And hatred.

Looking at her, I felt like I no longer knew who she was. It was the first time I resented her for resembling my mother so much. It made it harder to hate her.

"Who could blame Dad for giving up and wanting to die? How could we expect anything more from the jury and the court when we – his own family – failed to give him the benefit of the doubt?" I said. "It's our fault he's dead."

I turned to walk out of the room, but then stopped and looked back at Aunt Maryam. Making direct eye contact with her, I said, "Now there's really nothing keeping you here. You can leave whenever you want because we don't want you here anymore."

"Cyrus, stop this nonsense!" Grandpa Behruz bellowed, the vein in his temple bulging out. "Apologize to your aunt this instant."

"It's fine, *Hajj-agha*," she said, her eyes welling with tears. "Let him be."

"Now you're crying?" I asked, exasperated, and walked up to her until our faces were only inches away. "Well, I'm glad I was the cause of it."

Before I knew what was happening, I felt a stinging blow to my right cheek as my lower lip vibrated with the sheer force of the strike.

I realized my aunt had slapped me, her eyes wild and red.

In that instant, she looked so much like her deceased sister that in my unstable state of mind, I thought she really was my mother and collapsed sobbing at her feet. "I'm sorry, *Maman*, please forgive me."

Then I felt her hands lifting me up and kissing the tender spot on my cheek where she had hit me. "I forgive you, *azizam.* I'm sorry, too."

Once again, she held me in her arms as I cried and grieved, but this time for the deaths of both my parents.

Chapter Twenty-Six

Two years ago in early April, when Aunt Maryam had recently moved here from Florida, *Maman and Baba* took us on a weekend trip to D.C. to see the cherry blossoms to celebrate Mom's birthday. They were in full bloom and it was Aunt Maryam's first time seeing them.

As we weaved in and out of the trees bursting with papery, pink flowers, my parents and aunt were in awe of their beauty and took tons of photos. I remember begging to go to the park to play soccer, indifferent to the cherry blossoms. What thirteen-year-old boy cares about flowers?

Aunt Maryam looked over at me and said, "You know, living in Florida, I never took the time to appreciate the flowers. The winters weren't cold enough for me to feel the change in the seasons and we had flowers there all year long. But after this long, gray winter, the beauty of these blossoms is magnified a hundred times."

Something about what she said stuck with me. Every year, the flowers came out as expected and I dismissed them because it was nothing out of the ordinary. For my aunt, who was used to seeing flowers year-round, the appreciation for them was tenfold when they were gone during winter and finally came back in the spring. It made her notice them on a whole new level – or maybe for the very first time. I suppose that means there's even more beauty in something as cold and gloomy as winter because it further magnifies the allure of the flowers in spring.

I doubt I could ever find anything beautiful or positive from my parents' deaths, but I had to believe it served a higher purpose. As I matured, I learned that it made me cherish the people and the lives around me that much more, as if they were fragile porcelain piled high on a delicately-balanced tray that could tip at any given moment, causing them to fall to the ground and shatter.

My mother died in autumn and now, a few months later, my father passed in the winter.

I wondered if that was some sort of sign.

* * *

The morning of my father's funeral, I knew I finally had to tell Rostam what happened. Despite how I was feeling, I didn't want anyone else to tell him except me. I went over to his bed and sat on the edge; he was just waking up. Yawning, he stretched his skinny arms and rubbed his curly head.

"Morning, *Dadashi*, I have to tell you something important." I said.

He was wide awake. He had been expecting this for the past three days, his eyes questioning me ever since I sent him to our room the night I received the news.

He gazed at me now, impatient, while I collected my thoughts.

"I know you've been wanting to go visit *Baba* for a while, but he's not here anymore. He's with Mom."

"What? You mean I can't see him again?"

I could tell he was close to crying, his bottom lip quivering. I took his hand, hating myself for having to put my little brother through this.

"Dad knew *Maman* was lonely in heaven all by herself and he missed her very much, so he went there to be with her."

"You mean he's an angel like Mom now?"

"Yes, she forgave him just like you asked her to and wanted him to be with her forever."

"And we can no longer see him? He won't come home?"

"No, but he told me to tell you he loves you very much and will always be with you, even if you can't see him," I said, taking his hand in mine. "Just like Mom."

"Why couldn't he tell me that before he left? Why couldn't he say goodbye?"

I was stumped and had to think for a second.

"He really wanted to, but he only had a limited amount of time to leave, and it was before he had a chance to see you. I'm so sorry."

"It's not fair! Why did they both have to leave?" he cried, throwing himself into my arms. I rubbed his back, rocking him back and forth as he cried.

"Their leaving was not up to them and they would've said goodbye to us if they could," I said. "It may not seem like it now, but they needed each other more than we need them. They're in a great place now and just think, Dad no longer has to be in that place for bad people."

"Did the people keeping him there believe he didn't hurt Mom? Did they forgive him, too?" he asked, looking at me with wide eyes, his long, thick lashes soaked from his tears.

"Yes, they did. And if anyone tells you otherwise, don't believe them."

I didn't have the heart to tell him the truth. Not yet, anyway.

"Okay."

"Even though Dad couldn't say goodbye to us, we're going to say goodbye to him," I said. "Today we're going to go to that same place where Mom's magic stone is to put one up for Dad, so we can talk to him whenever we want. Would you like that?"

He nodded against my chest and I wished I could just hold him in my arms and in our room forever, wondering how much more sorrow and abandonment his small body could handle.

My mother used to say, "*Adam che chizaee ro ba een dota cheshmash mibine.*"

"A person has to witness so many awful things in this world with his two eyes."

I wanted to protect Rostam from it all; I wanted to keep him anchored in the safety and lull of his childhood for as long as possible. But all this trauma threatened to jostle him, unprepared, and throw him into the world's vastness.

I was holding on to a thread.

The rest of that day was a haze of disjointed scenes.

I remember Tamara and Yiannis came for about an hour. Tamara wore a pretty black dress that hit just above her knees. She once mentioned she hated her knees and that they made her feel self-conscious, so she always wore long pants and skirts. I didn't understand what she meant; I thought her knees were lovely.

At one point, she held my hand and I recall feeling cold when she let go.

Other than my friends, no one else outside our family showed up, or was invited for that matter. As with most things in our culture, it was a matter of reputation and saving face, so Grandpa Behruz did his best to keep the news of my father's death and funeral quiet, at least for the time being. He was too ashamed to invite anyone from the Persian community. And even if anyone was invited, they probably wouldn't have come. They weren't going to attend the funeral of a man sentenced to life in prison for murdering his wife and on top of that, committing suicide. Refusing to eat and succumbing to death was no less than suicide and therefore, a sin.

Before he left, Yiannis said something that didn't resonate with me until a few years later. "You've been through one of the worst things anyone could ever experience and you're still standing. I don't think there's anything in this world that can knock you down and that's strength worth admiring."

I thanked him, dismissing what he said as mere consolation. I couldn't have possibly known then how much of an impact it would have on me down the road.

Throughout my life, I weighed the value of a person's character by the words they spoke, and how much their words impacted and moved me.

The words we say reflect the depths of our soul; the words we keep and don't keep measure our character. I've always believed the ability to communicate with words to be the most powerful of human qualities; our lives are made up of them, built on them. I was the son of a storyteller, after all. A man who collected stories and words and treasured them over all material things. That's why I've always done my best to take care in choosing the words I speak.

As *Maman* would say, *"Harfeto ghablaz goftan maaze kon."*

"Taste your words before you speak them."

She'd continue by saying, *"Harfe nagoftaro hamishe mishe zad."*

"There's always an opportunity to say the words that have not yet been spoken."

By this she meant you always have the chance to say something you haven't yet said, but when you say something without thinking or meaning it, then it's too late. You've already said it and cannot take it back. You'll end up destroying the thin veil of respect that cannot be mended. That's why it's crucial to choose your words with care.

Words have the power to both create and destroy relationships, people – entire lives. They are our legacies because we're best remembered by the things we've said. When we pass, just the echoing of our words by the living's voices keeps a part of us alive. Like my father's stories and lessons. My mother's advice. The expressions they both passed down to me and I now know as truths. They are the only priceless, lasting inheritance we pass down from one generation to the next; the collected stories of our family that survive long after us and give us a history, a permanent fixture in this vast world. The stories of our lives – our memories and all the ways we loved – are the only things that cheat both time and death.

At the cemetery, I kept Rostam close to me as the *imam*, whom my grandfather had hired from the local mosque, prayed over my father's body. He had requested his burial be performed in the Muslim custom, so earlier that day, Grandpa Behruz and Uncle Eskandar had his body given a special ablution bath known as a *ghusl,* and enshrouded in a plain white sheet called a *kafan*, at the mosque. He was then placed in a simple coffin.

"Is *Baba* inside that long box?" Rostam suddenly asked me.

I shuddered just thinking about it.

"No, that's just symbolic," I said. "Dad went up to heaven, remember?"

I didn't want my little brother to think of his father's body inside that box, under mounds of dirt. He'd know everything soon enough once he was a little bit older. But right now, I wanted to spare him the details of death.

"Where's his magic stone?"

"It isn't quite ready yet. It'll take a few days to finish, but once it's ready, they'll put it up and you can talk to him whenever you want."

He smiled.

"What's that man saying? Why can't I understand him?"

"He's praying for *Baba* in Arabic. I can't understand him, either."

"What's Arabic?"

"The official language of the Qur'an and how we say our prayers."

He nodded and became silent, listening to the *imam's* solemn prayers.

I wrapped my arm around his shoulders and with my free hand, played with the gold coin in my jacket pocket; as always, it centered me. The tighter I wrapped my hand around it, the more stable I felt.

I said a silent prayer for my father's soul.

I prayed for him to have peace.

I prayed for his soul to find its way to God. And to my mother.

I prayed for her to forgive him.

"We belong to Allah and to Him we shall return."

At one point, unable to bear *Baba* Behruz's loud sobs over my father's grave and afraid of how it would impact Rostam, I took his hand and told him we were going to visit Mom's magic stone.

221

Standing in front of her headstone, I had a silent conversation with her, hoping to unburden myself a little. I'd done my best not to cry all day, but standing here in front of my buried mother's grave while my father was being buried a couple of feet away, I could no longer control myself.

My grandfather's cries played in my head; each wail that escaped him more pained than the one before it. As if he was being pulled apart, limb by limb. And perhaps that's how it felt to lose a child – to have a being you created and brought into the world taken from you.

I wondered if God felt that pain each time one of His creations perished. Were we given the ability to create life so we could feel what God feels if we lose our children? Was this our highest form of punishment?

Following the burial ceremony, we led a somber trail from the cemetery to our two cars to drive to the family restaurant for dinner.

I thought back to Uncle Eskandar's words the night I found him drinking in the restaurant – about how the restaurant had brought nothing but misery to our family. Was it really true or was Uncle Eskandar just looking for something to blame?

Walking with Rostam a little ahead of the adults, I overheard Aunt Maryam mention to my uncle how she was relieved that Sohrab's grave was not right next to Pari's.

This angered me, but I didn't say anything until dinner, during which I made a loud comment at the table about how some people, including the prosecution, got their wish. My father sentenced himself to death, so they needn't worry anymore.

My aunt shot me a sour look across the table and I smiled, taking a big gulp of water. I didn't touch my food, not only due to lack of an appetite, but also because I couldn't get my uncle's words from that night out of my head.

I looked over at Aunt Maryam again and noticed her playing with her own untouched food, a sad look on her face. I felt bad and wished I hadn't said anything.

Aunt Maryam and I were okay for the most part, but ever since my confrontation with her the day Dad died, our relationship was not quite the same anymore. At times, I felt a deep resentment toward her and it was something I couldn't control, although it saddened me. I still respected her and was cordial to her, but that night something snapped inside me, causing cracks to form in our relationship. As my mother said, some of the things you say in anger cross a line and can't be taken back. They rip apart the thin veil of respect surrounding our relationships, and it can never be mended. That's why you should try to taste your words before you say them. Because unspoken words can always be said, but it's the ones you've already said that you can't take back.

While I couldn't take back what I had said to *Khaleh* Maryam and it caused tears in the veil, it hadn't completely ripped.

I wondered if there was a way to mend the tears.

But the truth was, I couldn't look at her with the same eyes. Her love no longer felt unconditional and it shouldn't have to because she wasn't our mother. I needed to remind myself of that fact sometimes. I felt as though she stayed and took care of us because she had to, not because she wanted to. Maybe I was wrong, but it's how I felt after that night.

To a certain extent, I could see her side and sympathize. She was still young and had to give up her way of life to care for two boys who weren't her own children. She didn't really have a say in the matter. Perhaps she still planned on getting married and having kids of her own, although she claimed a handful of times she had no interest in getting married. She was ever the independent sister; the wild one who couldn't be tied down…until we tied her down.

I told her numerous times she should get her own place and being a realtor, she could easily find a nice apartment. I claimed I was capable of caring for myself and Rostam, plus we had Grandpa Behruz and Uncle Eskandar downstairs. She was free to live her own life and shouldn't have to be hampered by us; she'd done more than enough and fulfilled her sisterly duty to my mother. But Aunt Maryam wouldn't hear of it.

"Not until Rostam is older, and besides, you've never been a burden to me," she'd say. I wasn't entirely convinced.

After a while, I dropped the matter altogether. I didn't want her thinking I was trying to kick her out, which certainly wasn't my intention.

I wouldn't forget what she'd done for us and I was forever grateful to her. Nothing changed that. My affections toward her had diminished a bit, but my respect and gratitude never went away.

Perhaps time would mend the tears.

* * *

About a week after the funeral, I received a call from a different lawyer asking to speak with me concerning my father's will and final wishes. I was glad he had finalized his will before passing away. Not because I was interested in my inheritance – not in the least. Knowing what it had done to my father and uncle's relationship, I wanted nothing to do with it. My only concern was to make sure I carried out his final requests.

I made an appointment the following morning to go to the lawyer's office, which was a few blocks from the restaurant.

Waking up early, I got ready and took the bus downtown, hoping to beat the Tuesday morning rush hour.

Getting off at my stop, I speed-walked to warm up in the late December chill. Christmas decorations were everywhere, reminding me of how much I loved this time of year. Not anymore, though. Winter and its festivities were also ruined for me.

Non-Christian Persians and those who don't live in Western countries don't celebrate Christmas, but we do celebrate the Winter Solstice, which we call *Shabe Yalda*. On December 21, the longest and darkest night of the year, we follow the ancient Zoroastrian tradition and welcome winter and its chilly months by setting up a table very similar to the *Haft-Seen* table for spring, except winter-themed. On it, we place a variety of foods including watermelon, pomegranate, nuts, and dried fruit. As with most things in our culture, each item on the table is symbolic. For example, many believe eating watermelon will ensure your health later in the hot summer months.

Families and friends stay up late into the night, snuggling up by the fireplace or the *korsi* – a traditional heater resembling a low table with a heater underneath it and blankets thrown over it. Many tell stories, read poetry, and play games.

Just as *Nowruz* was Mom's favorite holiday, *Shabe Yalda* was Dad's favorite because of its emphasis on storytelling. He'd let us stay up late, telling us story after story until his voice was hoarse.

Mom joked he was the male version of Scheherazade from "One Thousand and One Nights."

"She was Persian, too," he said, beaming. "Storytelling is in our blood." He then added that my mom fell in love with him because of his amazing storytelling abilities, just like King Shahryar did with Scheherazade in the story.

Mom would roll her eyes, planting a hand against her jutted-out hip.

"Yes, you fooled me with all the tales you spun."

"Fooled? You mean swept you off your feet!"

She'd then throw her head back and give a silvery laugh. Even if I somehow forgot everything else about my mother, I could never forget her laugh. It was as if she gathered every particle of happiness inside her and injected it into every laugh and smile.

A few people carrying shopping bags zipped past me on their way to the next store and I couldn't help envying them a little bit. They were busy buying presents for their families and making holiday plans. I hardly had anyone left to buy presents for. Or celebrate holidays with.

It was just me and Rostam. Sure, we had *Khaleh* Maryam and my grandfather and uncle, but it wouldn't be the same without our parents.

Nothing ever would.

Every year for Christmas, Mom bought a tiny, decorated Christmas tree for our apartment and stockings for me and Rostam. Since we didn't have a fireplace, she hung them on our bedposts and filled them with little presents and candy. She also bought presents and put them under our little tree.

"We believe in Jesus, don't we? So, what's wrong with celebrating his birth and letting our children experience Christmas? We live in this country now and have to embrace their culture without letting go of our own," she told my father when he asked her why she bothered celebrating a Christian holiday, teasing her about having secretly converted to Christianity.

"It's tough having to balance and identify with two different cultures," he mused. "I have a hard enough time with it as it is and there's so much about this culture we're still clueless about. How do you make room for an entirely new culture when you've lived with another for most of your life? How do you make sure you don't lose your own while adopting a new one? And don't even get me started on the language dilemma."

"Such is the plight of the immigrant. Yes, it's difficult, which is why we have to teach our children how to do it from a young age, so it'll be easier for them as they grow," she said, wagging her index finger at him. "As far as language goes, you should be thankful your wife is so good at English. Maybe if you listen to her more, you'll learn a thing or two."

He laughed and held up his hands in mock surrender. "Yes, ma'am!"

Lost in my memories, I almost walked past the lawyer's tiny office building. "McCormick & Sons," it read.

I went inside and climbed a set of narrow stairs to reach the small receptionist and waiting area. I gave the old, scowling secretary my name and she paged her boss's office to let him know his ten o'clock was here. After hanging up, she instructed me to have a seat and added Mr. McCormick would be with me shortly.

Before I had a chance to sit down, a tall, dignified-looking gentleman emerged from his office and walked over to shake my hand. "Mr. Nezami?"

He must have been in his mid-fifties, with dark features, salt-and-pepper hair, and a prominent nose. If it weren't for his last name, I would've thought he was Persian.

"Yes, nice to meet you," I said, taking his hand.

"Likewise," he replied with a smile. "Please, let's go inside my office. Your uncle is already here."

"My uncle?" Why was he here?

"My apologies, did I forget to mention that over the phone? Your uncle is also mentioned in your father's will."

"Oh," was all I could manage and followed him to his office.

Uncle Eskandar nodded a greeting as I sat down next to him, facing the lawyer's desk.

"Okay, gentlemen, thank you for coming," Mr. McCormick began. "First of all, I offer my sincerest condolences for your loss."

We thanked him in unison.

"I want to do this as quickly and smoothly as possible, so if neither of you have any questions, we can get started."

We shook our heads no.

"Okay, first, Mr. Sohrab Nezami had a statement for Mr. Eskandar Nezami that he wished me to read aloud: '*To my older brother, Eskandar, I leave my share of our family restaurant to settle the debt I owe you. Please forgive me for taking this long to repay you and for being so stubborn. Forgive me for allowing this to come between us and for all the arguments and bitterness over the years, for which I am equally to blame. Please know I forgive you. I only ask that you forgive yourself.*'"

Uncle Eskandar pinched the inner-corners of his eyes and mumbled, "Thank you" to the lawyer.

Mr. McCormick pushed a box of tissues toward him and nodded sympathetically.

"And now, Mr. Cyrus Nezami, your father requests you read the last email he sent you, in which he has explained many things for you, but there's also a short statement here in regards to what he's leaving you that I will now read:

"'To my dear son, Cyrus, I leave everything in my name – including the money in my checking and savings accounts, which are now both under your name, as well as my life insurance money. My lawyer will explain all the necessary details for you. The money should be enough for you and your brother to live on comfortably for a while. You can also count on Baba Behruz for your expenses. I leave you the apartment here, as well as our home in Iran, the details of which you can finalize with my lawyer in Iran whenever you decide to make a trip back. I've included his contact information along with these documents. The last worldly possession I leave you is my car, once you are of driving age. My only request is that you remember these are merely things and to never let them get in the way of your relationship with your brother. Or anyone else who comes into your life. Do not make my mistake. Be generous to your brother and teach him to be generous, as well. Take care of each other. Lastly, the final and most important thing I leave you are my stories. Never forget them or the lessons they taught you. And don't forget to pass them down to Rostam and to your children. I ask that you don't forget me and try to find it in your heart to forgive me one day. I love you and Rostam with all of me.'"

"Thank you," I whispered, my mouth dry.

"My pleasure."

I couldn't believe I'd forgotten to read my father's last email. If it wasn't for this reminder, I might have never remembered. Was my dad upset at me for never replying to it – maybe that's one reason why…

Unable to finish the thought, I turned my attention back to the lawyer to distract myself.

"Now, Mr. Nezami also requested his father, Mr. Behruz Nezami, be present today, but due to him being emotionally unprepared for it, I have included everything relevant to Mr. Behruz in a sealed envelope that I kindly request one of you to deliver to him."

"I will do it," my uncle said.

"I appreciate it," Mr. McCormick said with a smile. "I want to thank you gentlemen both for coming in today. I'm going to take care of all the paperwork in the next few days and will be in touch. Any questions for me before you leave?"

Again, we shook our heads no.

"Alright, then we're all set. My condolences, again."

We shook hands and he walked us out.

Once we were outside, Uncle Eskandar asked if he could offer me a ride home. He averted his eyes, probably still embarrassed about the incident at the restaurant.

I thanked him and said I would take the bus. "Grandpa probably needs you at the restaurant right now. It's going to be lunch hour rush soon and I'm sure you've been busier since the restaurant was closed last week to mourn Dad."

"You're right, it's been pretty busy today. How about you come and have lunch at the restaurant, then? I can give you a ride home afterwards and that way, you don't have to take the bus."

I considered it for a few seconds. "Okay, that sounds good."

He smiled and led the way to his car. "I could've walked here from the restaurant. It's not even a two-minute drive."

"Yeah, I noticed it was really close."

My uncle cleared his throat. "Cyrus, I wanted to uh – thank you and apologize for – for that night. I wasn't in a good place, as you can imagine."

"Oh, it was nothing," I said. "I understand."

He grunted and patted my back. "You're a good kid."

For the first time since the incident, he met my gaze and even though he had apologized, I still noticed a look of guilt in his eyes.

Chapter Twenty-Seven

When Uncle Eskandar dropped me off at home after lunch, I ran straight to my room and opened my laptop. Scrolling through my inbox, I found my dad's unopened email, sent when he was alive. If only I'd responded then and said something to perhaps change his mind, give him hope. The email's bold, highlighted letters taunted me.

Taking a deep, shaky breath, I clicked it open:

Dear Cyrus,

As you know from your own studies and what I've told you about Cyrus, he is most famous for having decreed the first charter of human rights, known as the Cyrus Cylinder. When Cyrus conquered Babylon, he liberated the Israelites and all others who had been enslaved there, allowing them to return to their homelands and re-establish their religious temples. In fact, Cyrus' edict and Cyrus himself are mentioned several times in the Hebrew Bible.

Cyrus states in the Cylinder, "My numerous troops marched peacefully into Babylon. In all Sumer and Akkad I permitted no enemy to enter. The needs of Babylon and of all its cities I gladly attended to...and the shameful yoke was removed from them. Their dwellings which had fallen, I restored. I cleared out their ruins." He continues to state that he restored the people's religious temples and allowed them to worship freely and in peace. I cannot think of a greater act of justice, equality, and humanity.

Nowadays, we seem to forget the true meanings of "justice" and "human rights." We judge blindly and point fingers, merely looking for someone to blame, someone who can take the fall, especially if they're different than us. It doesn't matter if someone is innocent anymore. As long as we can prove them guilty and blame them for a wrongdoing – as long as we can put them away and feel better and safer about it – what does it matter if they're innocent? But I know

I am innocent and I hope that one day, the truth will come out and prove my innocence to everyone. I have faith that it will.

That's why I thought it was so important to teach you and Rostam about people like Cyrus the Great – to know people like him once existed and did great things. To know we humans can be capable of decency and honesty and goodness. To know I named you after a man like Cyrus the Great because I wanted you to follow in those same great footsteps, adopt the same values, and be an honorable man. To know it's possible to be good in a world that has gone bad.

To be honest, when this tragedy befell our family and I got arrested, I felt so helpless and the shame of failing you and Rostam as a father – well, I cannot put into words what that felt like. So, once again, I turned to one of the things in my life that has always been a constant source of fulfillment and comfort for me, aside from my family, of course. Something I've relied on and enjoyed on my happiest days and something that's gotten me through some of my most difficult and darkest days: storytelling.

Even on occasions when I felt like I had nothing else, I had my stories.

And when I felt helpless, knowing I couldn't physically be there for you and Rostam, and knowing there was nothing I could do to console you, I turned to my stories. Maybe my stories are a gift or maybe they're a curse, but they're all I have now.

They're all that will be left of me when I am gone. They're all that I leave you. It may not seem like it now, but they're one of the most valuable things I've given to you because aside from our love, our stories are what remain and get passed down long after we've gone. Some may call them memories, but I like to refer to them as stories.

Son, now you know why I named you Cyrus. After learning about Cyrus the Great, do you see any similarities between our lives? Our family is built on resilience. We have handled adversity in the most severe forms. Life is struggle. Life is chaos. Life is unexpected. The beauty is how we respond to it and move forward. The beauty is how we continue to love despite it all.

Obviously, back when we named you, we never dreamed we would be going through all of this. We had different struggles back then, but compared to now, they were our happy days. What I mean by struggles is your mother and I were not supposed to be together, you were not supposed to be born, and we were not supposed to come to America. But we fought hard for what we wanted, accepted the things we could not change, and held our heads high.

We tried to raise you to be hard-working, honest, fair, generous, and loving. I admit I was not the best role-model in some aspects and that's why I want you to learn from my mistakes. I want you and Rostam to be better to each other than Eskandar and I were. Being your father and raising you is one of the few things I did right in my life. You are my pride and joy. Whatever your mother and I have done in this life was for you and Rostam, to give you a better life than we had. And I know I am leaving Rostam in great hands – I know you'll raise him right and pass down to him the good things I've taught you, like Cyrus' stories.

My final request is that you live. Live the best life you can. Enjoy it. Do great things. Be successful. Be ambitious, but not over-ambitious. Don't allow anything to cost you your integrity, even your goals. Fall in love. Create a family of your own one day and pass down the same values to your children. I am sorry I won't get the chance to witness any of it, or meet my future grandchildren, but I know I would have loved them with all my heart. Protect your family with everything you've got. Don't ever forget where you come from. Don't ever lose sight of your roots, your culture, your language, and your family traditions. Lose that and you'll lose yourself.

Cyrus, I know it may be difficult for you right now, but please do your best to finish and graduate from high school. It was always our dream for the both of you to go to college. Don't take education lightly – it's one of the most important and powerful things you can own in this life. You are extremely smart and it would be a waste not to further your education. But don't forget to do what you love and are passionate about.

Let that always be your guiding light when choosing a future career. I know you'll both be great at whatever you decide to do. I only wish I could witness it alongside you and offer as much help and support as I could and tell you often how proud I am of you, the way a father should. I am sorry and ashamed for not being the father you and Rostam deserve. I truly am.

Lastly, naming you Cyrus was also an embodiment of our family's values: hard-work, love, faith, resilience, fairness, and honesty. These are the same values upon which Cyrus the Great built an entire empire and the reason I've always admired him and named my eldest son after him. I know I instilled those same values in you and they'll be the foundation upon which you'll build your own life, your own goals and dreams. Carry them on and pass them down to your brother and to your own children. Wear your name with pride for, aside from my stories, it is the greatest gift I ever gave you. No matter what happens, remember my love for you, your brother Rostam, and Maman Pari is eternal. These dark, difficult days will pass – you must have faith and move forward. You have to be strong – you're my pahlevoon, after all. Be strong for me, and especially for Rostam. He needs you – you're all he has now.

Don't ever forget me or how much I love you. And remember…

"Only love has power over lovers, death has none." – Rumi

Forever Yours,
– Baba

* * *

We buried my father two weeks ago, but it didn't feel like he was actually gone since he'd been away for a couple of months before his death.

I didn't know whether it was a good or a bad thing.

Sometimes I'd forget for a brief moment, thinking he's still in prison and would soon send me an email with another story. But then I'd remember and stop refreshing my inbox.

And then there were other things to remind me, too.

I received a call from Mr. McCormick, letting me know the paperwork he'd promised to send regarding Dad's will and accounts was all ready and asked if I'd like to pick them up or have him mail them to me.

I said he could mail them.

After a brief pause, the lawyer cleared his throat and asked if I'd recently seen or spoken with my uncle.

"I haven't, actually. Is everything alright?"

"Everything's fine, it's just after you both left my office that day, he called after-hours and left a message saying there was an urgent matter he wished to discuss with me. I called his cell phone the following morning and several times after that, but haven't been able to reach him."

"Hm, I assume he's just really busy with work, but if you'd like, I'll pass along your message and have him contact you when I see him."

"I appreciate that, thank you," he said.

232

"You're welcome. Is there anything else I can do for you, Mr. McCormick?"

"No, that's all, and please don't hesitate to contact me if you have any questions regarding the documents I'm mailing over."

"I won't, thank you."

When I hung up, it occurred to me that I actually hadn't seen Uncle Eskandar since the day at Mr. McCormick's office. I wondered if he was sick.

An uneasy feeling layered my stomach and I made up my mind to visit him and Grandpa Behruz later that evening. Come to think of it, I hadn't really seen my grandfather, either.

Maybe they were giving me space to grieve for my father in peace or maybe they were busy with the restaurant.

I prayed it was either of those scenarios and nothing bad had happened. At this point, I came to expect bad news on a daily basis, especially regarding my family.

I was so preoccupied with my own thoughts and grief that I had ignored my surroundings; I tried to swallow down the guilt, but it sat like a lump in my throat. I had to be stronger – like *Baba* had asked me to be in his last email. My grandfather, who was well in his seventies, was still managing the restaurant while grappling with the sudden deaths of his daughter-in-law and youngest son, the poor health of his eldest son, the aftermath of the murder trial, and his family's tarnished reputation. He had to live with the fact that he had failed to fulfill his wife's dying wish. The fact that everything he worked his whole life for was falling through his fingers like sand.

How do you face failure in old age, when you know you don't have much time or any chances left? How do you come to terms with that loss?

I was young and didn't carry these burdens, except for my grief, and already I'd stopped going to school and being there for my family – for my little brother. I felt ashamed of myself and vowed to do a better job of caring for the family I had left.

Around 9 p.m., I heard a car door outside and from the living room window, saw my grandfather shuffling toward the apartment building with his cane. He was alone, but that wasn't anything out of the ordinary. Uncle Eskandar usually stayed at the restaurant later than Grandpa, who couldn't stay past 8:30.

I waited about half-an-hour for him to get settled and then descended the stairs to their unit. I knocked softly at first, and then remembering he couldn't hear very well, knocked louder.

A whole minute passed before Grandpa Behruz opened the door.

"*Salam, Baba-bozorg,*" I greeted him. "May I bother you for a few minutes?" He didn't look very well.

Without saying a word, he stepped aside and gestured for me to enter.

The dimly-lit living room was in unusual disarray.

There were articles of clothing strewn about on the couch and the floor, papers covering the coffee and living room tables, with half-empty glasses and dirty dishes sitting on them like paperweights.

I eyed the mess in disbelief. "Is everything okay, *Baba* Behruz?"

"Not really," he said in a raspy voice. "Your uncle left for Iran two days ago."

"What?"

"There was a short note explaining he had to leave right away to be with his family."

"But why didn't he wait to say goodbye? Did something happen to his family?" I asked, sinking down to the cluttered couch.

"I don't know, Cyrus, he didn't give a reason why," Grandpa replied with an impatient sigh. "I was blindsided, too. Woke up in the morning to find out he'd left in the middle of the night."

Then it hit me that my uncle must've made this mess in his hurry to pack; the clothes all over the floor and couch were probably what he couldn't take with him.

"Does his note say when he's coming back?"

"He's not coming back," Grandpa Behruz said.

I was so confused – and a little hurt Uncle Eskandar didn't say goodbye. I was just getting to know him. We were becoming closer. It didn't make any sense.

"He also mentioned in his note he's giving back his share of the restaurant, plus the share your father gave him in his will. He asked me to follow up with the lawyer. After everything he did to get your father's share and all the sacrifices he made for the restaurant, God only knows why he would do this."

I now understood why he'd contacted Mr. McCormick following our visit to his office. He wanted to relinquish his shares of the restaurant. But why?

After so many years of doing everything he could to try and convince my dad to give him his share of the restaurant, why would he leave now that it was finally his? Why give it all up after everything he put himself and my father through, not to mention going so far as getting *Maman* Pari involved?

Something didn't seem quite right.

"I don't understand," I said, more to myself than Grandpa Behruz.

"Maybe he finally realized his family is more important than the restaurant and that they need him," he said. "Frankly, I'm surprised the poor woman's still stuck by him, taking care of two children by herself and trying to make ends meet with her husband on the other side of the world. Then again, he had me as his role-model and I did the same thing to your Grandma Afsar. Maybe I'm paying for that sin now with everything that's happened." His voice shook with a lifetime's worth of repressed anger and remorse.

"Why didn't he ever try to bring them here?" I asked, trying to shift the focus back to Uncle Eskandar.

"God knows he tried," Grandpa said, sitting down on the couch with a sigh. "But you know the immigration process has only gotten tougher for Iranians, and his family didn't show much interest, with his kids already in high school and college and his wife not wanting to leave her family."

I nodded, unsure of what to say.

Or maybe whatever he was feeling guilty about and asking forgiveness for that night he got drunk at the restaurant became too much for him to bear and he had to run away from it.

It hit me that with Uncle Eskandar gone, if we hadn't yet felt my father's absence, we'd really be feeling it now.

"What are you going to do with the restaurant now that Uncle isn't here to help you?" I asked.

"I might look into selling it soon, or maybe partnering up with someone. I'm not sure yet. If I do sell it, the money I receive from your father's share would be yours and Rostam's, of course."

"Thanks, Grandpa. In the meantime while you figure things out, I can come and help you since I'm not going to school right now," I offered.

"School is much more important," Grandpa Behruz said, his voice stern. "Why have you stopped going? I wasn't aware of this."

"I fell too far behind," I said, looking down. "I'm going to retake classes over the summer and next year to catch up, don't worry."

"Cyrus, since your parents are no longer with us, God rest their souls, your aunt and I are your guardians. You can't just do whatever you want or make such big decisions without discussing it with us first."

"I'm sorry, *Baba-bozorg,* you're right. I promise to talk to you and ask your permission next time."

"It's not about asking permission. It's about guiding you to do the right thing."

"I know."

"God knows it's been a difficult few months for all of us."

Before I left, I convinced Grandpa to let me help out at the restaurant for the time being until he figured out whether he wanted to sell the place or find a permanent replacement for Uncle Eskandar. In turn, I assured him I'd look into figuring out what classes I needed to retake.

At the door, I hugged Grandpa Behruz and thought I heard his bones cracking from the pressure.

I worried about him living all by himself from now on.

"Let us know if you need anything."

"I'll be fine, don't worry," he said.

But the look in his eyes said otherwise.

Chapter Twenty-Eight

I planned to take Rostam to visit Dad's grave that weekend.

After working long hours at the restaurant all week, part of me wanted to stay in and catch up on my sleep, but I already promised we'd go and I didn't want to disappoint my little brother. Luckily, Grandpa found someone to cover for me the whole weekend, so I figured I could sleep later.

I dragged myself out of bed and got dressed.

Rostam's bed was empty, his high-pitched chatter coming from the kitchen.

I followed the sound of his voice and found him eating cereal and telling Aunt Maryam about the latest art project he was working on in school.

I said good morning and grabbed a teacup to pour myself some tea.

"Rostam, hurry up and finish eating," I said. "I want to be at the cemetery before noon."

"Why?" he asked with a mouth full of cereal.

"I have plans later with Yiannis and Tamara."

"What are you going to do with them?"

"We're just hanging out, now stop asking questions and finish your breakfast."

I ate half a blueberry muffin and gulped down my tea. Rostam put the bowl up to his lips and slurped the rest of the milk.

"You'll both get stomachaches eating that fast," Aunt Maryam scolded.

"We'll be okay," I said, standing up. "See you later, *Khaleh.*"

"Did you want me to drive you?" she asked.

"Nah, we're just going to take the bus," I called over my shoulder.

"Okay, well call and let me know when you're done and I'll pick you guys up."

"Thanks, *Khaleh*, I will. Bye!"

On our way to the cemetery, my mind drifted back to the events of the past couple of days.

The day after I found out Uncle Eskandar left, I told Aunt Maryam. To my surprise, she got angry.

"Well, he couldn't have left at a worse time," she fumed. "Leaving his old father and two orphaned nephews in God's hands and not thinking twice about it."

"Maybe his family really needed him?" I offered, sounding unconvinced.

"He realized just now they need him? And why all the secrecy? Leaving in such a hurry in the middle of the night without bothering to say goodbye? It's not right."

"I was pretty shocked, too," I said. "It's the last thing I expected, especially after Dad gave him his share of the restaurant in his will. He finally got what he's wanted all these years, then gives it up just like that."

Aunt Maryam shook her head and then looked up with a strange expression on her face.

"By the way, your father's lawyer called yesterday and wants to meet with me," she said in a low voice. "Apparently, he's left something for me in his will, but whatever it is, I want you and Rostam to have it. I don't want anything."

I was silent for a moment, thinking of what to say. My dad was always a delicate subject with us, especially after our confrontation the night he died. We were in a better place, but there was still some tension whenever his name came up.

"I don't think it would hurt to go and see what it is," I said. "Then, you can decide what to do with it."

She thought for a while.

"That's fair," she replied at last with a smile. "I'll go."

I smiled back. It was the first time in a long time we had agreed on something regarding my father.

Later that week, she kept her word and visited Mr. McCormick's office. I couldn't wait to get home from the restaurant later that night to hear about it.

Once Rostam went to bed, we sat in the living room and she told me what happened.

It turns out my father gave her the small portrait painting hanging on our living room wall. It was one of my mom's most treasured belongings and she had it since she was a little girl. One year on their wedding anniversary, she gifted it to Dad and he hung it on the living room wall when we moved in. It was a portrait painting of an aristocratic English woman he claimed resembled her.

"It's you in another life," he once said.

"Then it's something to remember me by every time you look at it," she replied.

When my mom died, Aunt Maryam took it off the wall and placed it in one of the trash bags with *Maman's* other belongings. It was probably too painful for her to look at it.

"I remember how jealous I was of your mother's painting when we were girls," Aunt Maryam said. "Dad bought it for her from an old antique shop when she was around twelve and I cried myself to sleep that night because I didn't get one. Now it's mine, but I don't have my sister anymore. Life's just cruel that way, I guess."

"Are you going to put it back up on the living room wall?" I asked.

"Yes, he said he wanted me to remember her like that, carefree and regal, like the woman in the painting. He also said it's up to me what I want to do with the rest of her belongings."

"That's good, *Khaleh.*"

"He asked me for something, too."

"What?" I inquired, puzzled.

"Forgiveness."

"Will you?" my voice was barely a whisper.

"Oh, it's not up to me."

"Who's it up to, then?"

"*Zaman,*" she exclaimed, as if it was the most obvious answer. "As with most things, time will tell."

She now appeared calm when she spoke about him; the underlying rage was no longer present. Whether he was guilty of taking her sister's life or not, whether it was an accident or intentional, he paid for it with his own. The painting was just a formality; the ultimate thing my father gave my aunt was his life to atone for her sister's death. She'd never admit it and I hated to think it, but I knew it offered her some consolation.

Despite what I said to her in anger the night we received news of his passing, I don't think she rejoiced in or wished for his death. She did, however, want him to be punished and to somehow pay for a crime that in her mind, only he could have committed.

The next day, Mom's painting was back up on the living room wall. As for the bags filled with her clothes and belongings, I helped Aunt Maryam take them down to her car to donate to Goodwill.

"It's better I give them away without really looking through them," she said. "But you're welcome to look through and see if there's anything of hers you'd like to keep."

I found what I was looking for in the first bag I looked through – the silk red and blue scarf Mom always wore, especially in Iran. It was her favorite accessory and permanently smelled like her. When we came here, she usually wore it around her neck. As a kid in Iran, I looked for that familiar pattern bobbing up and down in the crowd whenever I went out with her. It was one of my earliest memories; one of those items that becomes a vivid emblem of your childhood.

I folded the scarf carefully and put it in my pocket.

The only other things Aunt Maryam kept were Mom's engagement and wedding rings and a few other valuable pieces of jewelry.

She donated everything else.

I sent a small prayer along with those seven bags. I prayed they'd be placed in good hands. That whoever wore and used them deserved the honor. I prayed for them to be good people who'd unknowingly keep her memory alive by living in and with her things.

"Sometimes, it's easier to let go of some things than to hold on to them," Aunt Maryam said and with that, she climbed inside her car and drove off to give away her dead sister's belongings to strangers.

When she was gone, I thought about her words. Maybe she was talking about more than just my mother's things. Maybe she was also hinting at her anger and resentment, and that she was finally ready to let them go.

* * *

At the cemetery, Rostam was quiet.

When we reached Dad's grave, he placed his hand on the headstone and closed his eyes. I followed suit and recited the prayer for the dead in silence.

There were a lot of things I needed to say to my father, but I didn't know how to say them or where to start. Besides, it was a conversation I had to have alone. This time, I only prayed.

After about ten minutes went by, my voice broke the stillness.

"Did you say all you wanted to say to *Baba?*"

"Yes, you think he heard it all even though I didn't say it out loud?" he asked, tapping the headstone with his hand.

"Every word. Remember, the stone is magic, it can hear all your thoughts and then sends them to Dad, or Mom. Kind of like an answering machine on a phone."

"So, the stone is an answering machine for heaven?"

"Exactly."

He smiled, content with what little consolation I could offer him.

Content to speak to his dead mother and father through a stone. Or at night in his bed, staring up at the ceiling.

Content it was just me and him from now on.

After paying Mom's grave a quick visit, I realized it still bothered me that my parents weren't buried next to each other, but there was nothing I could do about it, so I followed Aunt Maryam's advice and let it go. I then called her to pick us up.

When we got home, we saw Grandpa Behruz's Chevy parked in front of the building and checked to make sure he was okay. He said he wasn't feeling too well and left the restaurant earlier to rest. Aunt Maryam invited him upstairs for lunch; he thanked her and said he'd come up in an hour or so.

I excused myself and said I had plans with friends, then hurried upstairs to shower and get dressed. Yiannis and his mom were picking me up in twenty minutes or so; we were getting lunch and then seeing a movie with Tamara. They were on winter break and I was grateful their families hadn't made any plans to go away for vacation. Now that I wasn't attending school, we didn't get to hang out as much.

I still felt bad about how I treated them after the sentencing hearing, shutting them and everybody else out. But they were still there for me – calling and texting no matter how many times I ignored them. They attended my father's funeral and comforted me the best they could. Later, I apologized several times for my awful behavior, but they acted like they didn't know what I was talking about or why I was apologizing. I don't think I fully realized how lucky I was to have them, especially at that point in my life.

After the lunch and movie, Yiannis's mom offered to drop me and Tamara off at our homes.

On the way, I told them I'd made up my mind to retake the classes I failed over the summer so I could move on to becoming a sophomore, that I was going to work extra hard to catch up and graduate with them on time.

Yiannis joked it was about time I stopped being lazy and Tamara feigned a shocked expression, but I could tell they were happy for me.

"And who knows, maybe we'll even end up going to the same college," I said. "That is, once I make it through a few sessions of summer school to catch up."

Tamara squealed with joy.

"College? I always knew you were a nerd, being Persian and all," Yiannis said, chuckling. "So, what's it gonna be? A doctor? Engineer? Lawyer? Those are like the only degrees you Persians go for, right?"

"I plead the fifth, sir," I answered with a smirk, folding my arms across my chest.

"Well played, my man."

"Wait, I don't get it," Tamara said.

Yiannis and I howled with laughter.

For the first time in a long time, I felt like an actual teenager. A teenager whose only worries were what classes to take next year, who to take to the homecoming dance, and final exams.

For the first time in a long time, I felt my own age.

Chapter Twenty-Nine

Long after his death, I continued sending my father letters to his personal email, and I addressed a lot of them to my mom, as well. His inbox had probably accumulated hundreds of my emails from over the years.

I talked to them whenever I went to the cemetery, but sending them emails felt more intimate and real. They were mostly updates of how Rostam and I were doing. It was therapeutic and cathartic; it made them more a part of our lives. I knew they'd never respond, but I often asked in the emails for a sign that they'd received my messages.

Dear Maman and Baba,

Today is the first Nowruz we're celebrating without the two of you. Every day without you is hard, but holidays are harder.

Today was the hardest.

Rostam and I tried to make the best of it and cheered each other up with your memories. Like when Mom would bustle around the house getting everything ready and doing her spring cleaning. What did we call it? "Pari's Annual Spring Cleaning Brigade"? Something like that. I remember how much Rostam and I used to complain, but now...

Do you guys remember last Nowruz when Dad was working late and couldn't get white fish for our Nowruz eve dinner of herb rice and white fish? Mom, you got so mad at him. It was too late to go to the grocery store to get one, so you had no choice but to make chicken instead. I remember your look of disappointment as you cut up the chicken and said, "Well, at least it's white meat." You said it wouldn't be a lucky year because it had started off without a sabzi-polo mahi dinner. We laughed it off, but maybe you were right, after all. Maybe it wasn't superstition, but intuition.

Maybe the symbols we place on the Haft-Seen table for luck are more than just for luck – perhaps they're really used to safeguard us against the dangers

243

and bad things that a new year may bring. Perhaps our ancestors, like Cyrus, knew better.

Mom, remember how much you enjoyed reviewing the symbolic meaning of each item on the Haft-Seen table with us? You explained with great patience what Haft-Seen means and how the seven main items on the table all start with "s" – or "seen" in Farsi. You taught me well and would be proud of our little Haft-Seen table this year.

We've made one addition to it: a picture of you both, sitting beside the mirror – ayenneh – for light and reflection. It doesn't start with "seen," but it's still a crucial part of the table. Same as the candles – sham – which symbolize light and warmth.

Let's see, what else is there?

I gave Rostam the task of painting the eggs – tokhme-morgh. When I was younger, it used to be my favorite part about the table because it was most similar to Easter. As a child, I clung on to the similarities between our culture and the one we had adopted, pulling at the ends to somehow tie them all together and bridge the gap between the two. It made me feel less different. Do eggs symbolize birth or bounty? Perhaps both.

Hajji Firuz was another Nowruz favorite of mine because in my mind, he was like a Persian Santa Claus. Much like Santa Claus, Hajji Firuz is a fictional herald of the holiday, bringing gifts and joy along with him, dressed in red from head to toe.

I bought two goldfish – mahi – and named one of them Tala, just for you, Mom. Again, they don't start with "seen," but they're important because they symbolize life and vitality.

And now for the items that begin with "seen":

I've placed the apples – seeb – next to the eggs, for additional bounty at the table. I remember you always made sure they were the reddest apples you could find, Mom.

Did you know garlic cloves – seer – symbolized disinfection and health in ancient times? Perhaps during Cyrus' time, Dad. As a child, I used to think it was used to keep vampires away from the table.

I don't know why sumac – or somagh – stands for patience and tolerance. How did that come about? Probably because you had to have a lot of patience with me when it came to the sumac and vinegar – serkeh. Remember when I was around six or seven and used to dip my finger into the vinegar bowl and then in the sumac to pick up the tiny maroon flakes with my vinegar-soaked finger? Licking it off, I loved the sour and salty flavor combination. It used to drive you crazy, Mom.

You kept having to refill the dishes with more vinegar and sumac almost every day. Vinegar symbolizes satisfaction. Again, I don't know why, but I'm sure there's a good reason or story behind it. Like the satisfaction you no doubt got when I got sick one night after one too many tastings of vinegar and sumac and learned my lesson. I didn't go near the stuff again. Even now, the smell of both makes me a bit queasy.

Dad, the Pahlavi coin – sekkeh – you gave me is also at the table, symbolizing wealth and success. I'm sure you're glad to hear I haven't lost it yet.

I did my best to grow the wheatgrass – sabzeh – like you once showed me, Mom. I failed miserably. A few sparse blades sprouted and then the whole thing died. I used lentils, just like you said. I'm not sure if I watered it too much or too little, or perhaps the morning chill killed it. Since our wheatgrass – the symbol for nature and growth – did not in fact grow, we settled for the hyacinth – sombol – instead. It stands for spring and renewal, so I figured it was close enough.

And the last two items: the dried lotus tree fruit – senjed – for wisdom, and in the same dish, sweet wheat pudding – samanoo – for power and bravery.

See, I remembered them all.

But something is still missing and it'll forever remain missing. Items and symbols are just half of it. Sure, they may safeguard us, but when there's nothing to protect, then what's the point? When you've already lost so much of what needed to be saved, why should you even try?

I know I have Rostam and I am beyond thankful. I'll double the amount of each item I place on the table to protect him, don't worry.

I had an interesting thought today – I realized half of my relationship with you has consisted of letters (emails). I've lived with you both through words. Sometimes I have whole conversations with you in my head or I imagine what your responses to my emails will be. Perhaps I've gone crazy, but it's the only way I know to cope.

We miss you both so much. No matter what we place at the table, nothing will ever fill your missing spots.

Love always,

– Cyrus (and Rostam)

I never got the chance to ask my father if all the Cyrus stories he told me were true, but I held them to be true in my heart and that was enough. It was my belief that the experiences of Cyrus the Great that my father told me about in his stories led him to create the Cyrus Cylinder, his greatest legacy.

It took a few years for me to truly grasp how much these stories impacted and helped shape me. They were my compass when I was lost and needed to be guided – when my parents weren't around to offer advice. My father may have made mistakes, but he couldn't have been more right with the Cyrus stories. In a way, they saved me.

Cyrus the Great saved me.

Years later, as a senior in college studying toward becoming a lawyer, a lot of Cyrus the Great's values that my father taught and instilled in me, specifically about being just and fair, influenced and helped mold me into the kind of lawyer I turned out to be.

I wanted to seek justice and truth above all else. I wanted to fight for people like my father; I owed him that much. I tried to follow Cyrus the Great's example in every aspect of my life, but even more so in my career.

I worked hard to get myself through law school and even harder to pass the Bar exam.

After practicing criminal law at an established firm for a few years, my boss hinted at wanting to make me partner, but that depended heavily on my performance on a new case the firm took on. After reviewing the details of the case, I concluded that our client was guilty and we were being immoral by defending the wrong side, and at great cost to the opposing party.

I made several attempts to convince my boss to reconsider, insisting that winning this case would ruin an honest man's life, but all he saw was the money we'd make if we won. Our client was an influential businessman; someone who could easily buy his innocence. I wanted no part of it and resigned two days later.

Eventually, I made up my mind to start my own law firm. It was the only route to take if I wanted to practice law my way – or rather, the right way. It's the only way it should be practiced, without letting money and power blind me or influence my decision in the cases I took on. I even ended up taking the case of the man my old law firm was going up against – and won.

There was no bigger proof than that to convince me I had done the right thing. That all the hardships and struggles I went through to get my law firm off the ground were worth it. When a client didn't have enough money to match my rate, I told them to pay me whatever they could. I defended some clients pro bono.

While I was in the process of finalizing the rental of my office space with a landlord who was proving to be a headache, I came across a website about Cyrus the Great one night. The website was created by a Persian history professor and scholar of the Achaemenid Empire.

Over the years, I researched and read about Cyrus as much as I could, even though there wasn't a whole lot written about him, either online or in books. Even so, I was always in search of more information. That night, while scrolling through the search results of websites I'd already visited, an unfamiliar page popped up on the list. Excited, I clicked on it and that's how, by pure accident, I discovered the Persian history professor's website.

On the homepage, in bold letters, was a quote by Cyrus and as I read it, it felt as if he was directly speaking to me about my current situation:

"You cannot be buried in obscurity: you are exposed upon a grand theater to the view of the world. If your actions are upright and benevolent, be assured they will augment your power and happiness."

I stared at the screen for a long time, tears flooding my eyes.

As always, Cyrus the Great had found a way to teach me, guide me, and speak to me.

I copied and pasted the quote in a Word document. After playing around with fonts and formatting, I finally printed it out and planned to buy a nice frame for it the next day. It was the first thing I would hang up on my new office wall, even before my law degree.

Chapter Thirty

Persians have a way with words.

We're all natural-born storytellers, in our own right. We gesture and articulate to get our point across. To tell our tale. Make you understand.

We have thousands of colorful expressions and idioms, some of which get lost in translation.

Our poets and writers are world-renowned.

Our Hafez, Saadi, and Rumi.

We memorize lines from their poems and have stanzas on the ready for whatever circumstance and occasion calls for it because we're always prepared.

When we're unsure of something in our lives, we ask Hafez. Almost every Persian owns a Hafez poetry anthology somewhere in their home and whenever there's a question on their minds or an important decision to be made, we consult our poetic sage and fortune-teller.

We place the book in front of us, think of our question or decision, say a prayer, and then with closed eyes, run our index finger along the side of the closed book once. When our finger lands on a spot, we open the book to the page and read the poem like a fortune. It'll either be a good or bad fortune based on the poem's tone and meaning, and that ultimately answers our question or helps us make our decision. This practice is called *"estekhare"* or *"fal-e-Hafez."*

And so, I found myself searching for my copy of Hafez to seek his wisdom on something I was uncertain about.

It had become somewhat of a habit of mine to seek out the words and guidance of my culture's historical and literary figures. I read and researched about them heavily, buying whatever books and translated, annotated works I could get my hands on. And it all started with Cyrus, of course.

Life passes as quick as the turning of a page. One day, you're on the fifteenth page and then find yourself at page forty without knowing how you got there.

Twenty-five years later and here I was, on my fortieth page, consulting a page in Hafez about whether I should visit my sick uncle in the hospital.

Uncle Eskandar had been sick for a while with stage four lung cancer. After exhausting every cancer treatment option in Iran, he came back to the U.S. to try his chances here.

I hadn't talked to him since he left so many years ago without so much as a goodbye or an explanation and only heard updates about him from Grandpa Behruz while he was still alive. Now that my grandfather was gone, Uncle Eskandar contacted me – his only remaining relative here – to announce his return, which was as unexpected as his departure.

The day he called, I almost ignored the unfamiliar number on my phone screen. Then I reconsidered, thinking it might be a new client.

I was shocked when I heard his voice on the other end, not recognizing it at first due to his labored breathing and intermittent coughs.

He told me he'd been here for about five months now and staying with a friend while he underwent chemotherapy. Unfortunately, the chemo treatment was unsuccessful and the cancer had spread to his brain.

His doctor gave him two months to live – at most – and he wanted to see me before he died.

"Why didn't you call sooner?" I asked, trying not to sound accusatory.

"I didn't think you or Rostam wanted to see me," he replied in his raspy voice. "How is Rostam doing, by the way?"

"Rostam's good, he's finishing up his doctorate in biochemistry at Virginia Tech."

"Wow, good for him. And what do you do now? Are you married?"

"I'm a lawyer," I replied and hoped he wouldn't ask me to go into too much detail. "And yes, I'm married and have two children. A boy and a girl."

"Two children? The last time I saw you, you were a child!" he said with a half-laugh, half-cough. "May God bless them both. What are their names?"

"Thank you, *Amoo*," I said. "My girl's name is Soraya and my boy's name is Dariush."

"Beautiful names. Well, it seems you're both doing really well for yourselves, I'm proud of you," he said. Then after a pause, "So, will you come see your old uncle?"

I told him I would go, but had to check my work schedule to find out which day was best. When I said, "work schedule," I really meant Hafez.

When I opened to the page my finger landed on, it read:

249

Resist your temptation to lie by speaking of separation from God,
Otherwise, we might have to medicate you.
In the ocean, a lot goes on beneath your eyes.
Listen, they have clinics there too for the insane who persist in saying things
like: "I am independent from the sea; God is not always around gently
pressing against my body."

Unless you were a Hafez scholar, it often took a while to grasp the meaning of a Hafez poem and although I didn't fully understand the meaning of this one, I regarded it a positive sign to go.

The poem was titled, "We Might Have to Medicate You."

Close enough, I thought.

I knew I'd regret it if I didn't go see him one last time.

And after all these years, I still had questions only he could answer.

* * *

At a hospital, the dividing line between life and death hardly exists. New life is born into the world in the same building and at the same moment another life leaves it. As infants are thrusted into life, crying, the dying's loved ones cry them into death. And the dying are probably laughing as they go. Laughing at the workings of it all, wondering if we would ever agree to any of this if given the choice.

I think the cruelest irony and the biggest sacrifice of all is a mother dying during childbirth. Life and death intermingled at the same moment, within the same body. Pushing a whole life into this world with her last breath of departure from it.

Why do these things happen? What do they all mean? Maybe if we had the answers, we would be worse off.

Or, we would no longer be human – we would be God.

A few days after he called me, Uncle Eskandar's condition worsened and he had to be hospitalized. His friend called to notify me and tell me which hospital he was staying at.

I took the elevator to the third floor and headed in the direction of the oncology wing.

The nurse told me his room number and with a pounding heart, I headed toward it.

The door to the room was open, emitting a constant purring and beeping of machines attached to the motionless body of my uncle.

I walked over to the bed and after a moment, Uncle Eskandar's eyelids fluttered open. He was wearing an oxygen mask, but I could tell he was smiling. He looked around the room expectantly.

"It's only me, Uncle," I said. "Rostam's still away at school, but he really wanted to come and sends his love."

He nodded.

He looked older than Grandpa Behruz at the time of his passing, the effects of both the cancer and chemotherapy apparent on every inch of his body. His scalp and facial hair were gone.

Uncle Eskandar removed the oxygen mask.

"It looks like the cancer decided to expedite things," he gasped. "I wish our reunion could've taken place somewhere else and under better circumstances."

"But would you have even called if you weren't sick?" I asked him.

"I would have, eventually," he answered. "As difficult as it is, there are a few things I have to explain, and it's been weighing on me ever since I left years ago. Somehow, it's been worse than the cancer."

"It felt like you ran away."

"In a sense, I did. I didn't know what else to do, I couldn't face what I'd done," he said and he was about to continue when a coughing fit wracked his whole body.

I helped him place the oxygen mask back on his face while he took deep breaths. After a minute or two, the coughing stopped and he removed the mask. "I didn't have any other choice, otherwise I wouldn't have just left you and Rostam and least of all, my poor father."

"What do you mean by you couldn't face what you'd done?"

"It's all in here," he said, taking out a tattered, yellowing envelope from under his pillow. "I wrote this letter years ago, but didn't have the courage to send it to you or *Baba* Behruz."

"What is it?"

"It's everything you need to know."

I took the envelope from his shaking hand, my own trembling.

"I just pray one day you'll be able to forgive me."

251

I started to open it, but my uncle raised his IV-free hand to stop me.

"I think it would be best if you waited to get home to read it," he wheezed, straining to hold back another coughing fit.

I pictured his ravaged lungs, blackened and withered, with the cancer spreading from all sides like moss.

"Okay, if you don't need anything, I'm going to go and let you rest," I announced, tucking the envelope in the breast pocket of my blazer.

"I know this is asking too much, especially after you read the letter, but please come back one last time," he said. "And try to bring Rostam. I don't know how much longer I'll be here."

"I'll try."

Uncle Eskandar nodded. "Thank you, you're a good man, Cyrus," he gasped, taking in a sharp breath of air before speaking again. "Just like your father."

"I have to go, *Amoo.*"

"Okay, *khoda be hamrat.*"

"God be with you."

He was more in need of God than I was.

Once I was inside my car, I knew I couldn't wait until I got home to read the letter. Taking the ragged envelope out of my pocket with care, I undid the masking tape on the flap with my index finger; it was no longer sticky and easily gave way.

Pulling the frayed pages out of the envelope, I unfolded them and began reading the messy handwriting:

Baba and Cyrus,

I don't know why I'm writing this to you. As of this moment, I have no intention of sending this letter, but I'm afraid if I don't get it out somehow, even on paper, I'll suffocate.

I am sorry for leaving, but I couldn't bear to stay a minute longer and look into your eyes. I would sooner be dead than have to tell you this and I pray you can forgive me someday.

The truth is – I killed Pari. It was not intentional, but everything we have gone through is because of me. May God forgive me, I am a brother the likes of Cain, perhaps even worse.

On the day Pari died, I went over to the apartment after Sohrab left for work. I wanted to convince her to have him sign over his share of the restaurant. I was under financial strain and becoming the restaurant's sole owner would've solved a lot of my problems. My patience had run out and I was in a terrible mood. Our conversation escalated and at one point, while peeling an orange, I pointed the fruit knife at her and started yelling and making threats, saying her and Sohrab were going to be sorry if I didn't get either my money or his share of the restaurant. I obviously wasn't going to do anything and had only lost my temper, but she truly thought I was going to hurt her.

Then, Pari turned around to take something out of the credenza behind her and at first, I thought it was paperwork to the restaurant. Before I knew it, she pulled out Sohrab's gun from the hidden safety lock box in the credenza and pointed it at me. She told me to put the knife down, which I didn't even realize was still in my hand. I set it down and approached her slowly. By this point, she was hysterical. I'll never forget her words: "You're threatening your sister-in-law while she's home alone with a knife? Over money? Shame on you, Eskandar. I don't want you setting foot in my home ever again! Get out!" I tried to convince her to put the gun down, but when she wouldn't, I panicked and attempted to take it from her, afraid she would either hurt me or herself. In the struggle, I pulled the trigger by accident.

Pari was shot in the heart and died on the spot. She collapsed on the floor and for a few seconds, I stood there, unable to process what had happened – that I was responsible for it. I was a terrible coward, but I panicked and wiped the key to the lock box clean of any fingerprints, followed by the gun and fruit knife. I guess I was trying to make it look like a break-in, but I wasn't really thinking straight. All I wanted to do was erase any trace of me being there that morning. Making sure there was no blood on me, I left and hurried back to our apartment. When I heard the sound of Sohrab's car, I waited about five minutes or so, then went upstairs and saw Sohrab standing, in shock, over Pari's body.

I didn't want to believe I could be guilty of such a crime, especially against my own family. For a while, I actually convinced myself, along with everyone else, that it was Sohrab who killed Pari. It's amazing what the human mind can convince itself to believe as the truth.

But the guilt caught up with me. Little by little, it nibbled away at my conscience. It wasn't until I heard the verdict at the trial that the reality of what I'd done eventually settled in.

After my false testimony, the sentencing, and Sohrab's sudden death – I couldn't bear it anymore. Hearing his will at the lawyer's office was the last straw.

I know what I've done is unforgivable and I will be burdened by the guilt – both in this life and the next.

I don't know when I'll have the courage to confess the truth and I don't know with what words I can tell you how sorry I am. If I could give my life to take back what I did, I would do it gladly.

Now you know why I had to go – why I could no longer look either of you in the face, especially after Sohrab gave me his share of the restaurant in his will. I was so ashamed and disgusted with myself I could hardly stand it, so I just ran as far away as I could.

I've been a horrible son, brother, and uncle. And I haven't treated my own wife and children any better, either. I've been cruel and selfish, allowing my ambitions and greed to blind me.

I admit, I've even thought about suicide, but I haven't forgotten God that much to be able to carry out such an act – sin upon sin.

The list of my wrongdoings is endless and I know I will one day pay for them all. Maybe when you find out, you can take comfort in knowing I will be punished for my crimes – crimes against my own blood.

I don't know how else to say how sorry I am. I hate myself for what I've done. And Sohrab...

I marred my brother's good name. Ruined his reputation. Ruined his life and his family's life. He was always a better, more honorable man than I could ever be. He didn't deserve me as a brother.

Baba, if you ever read this, if I ever see you again – I don't know what to say. I was a terrible son and I am sorry for taking both Pari and Sohrab from you. I am sorry for all the pain I've caused you. Even if you do forgive me, I will never forgive myself for what I did to you.

Cyrus – I deserve whatever curse you wish on me.

You have every right not to forgive me. I took both your parents from you and from Rostam.

But if you're ever capable of forgiving me, it will be my only comfort.

I am sorry for everything.

– Eskandar

I leaned back against the car seat and the hand holding the wrinkled pages dropped to my lap, weighed down with their impossible words.

I looked around the empty hospital garage, unsure of why I was there. Unsure of whether I was breathing or not. Unsure of everything I'd ever known up to this point.

After a few minutes of looking around like a sleepwalker who had woken up in an unfamiliar place, I found I was able to move and managed to fold the letter, placing it back inside the envelope. I imagined it was tattered and yellowing because of the horrible truth it housed for so many years. It's a wonder the pages of the letter itself hadn't shriveled up yet. I had a strong urge to burn it and turn every word into ash, wishing they'd evaporate from my mind like smoke and erase what I had just read from my memory.

I knew I couldn't drive in this state, so I got out of the car and exited the garage.

I paced the hospital grounds for close to an hour, rereading the letter twice to make sure I hadn't hallucinated it all somehow. But how could I possibly have imagined something like this? And yet, it explained everything; his strange behavior that night at the restaurant when he got drunk and tried to confess to me, his discomfort every time he came over to our place. Looking back, it all made sense.

It was all here, twenty-five years later – or more like twenty-five years too late – revealing what really happened that horrible day and proving my father's innocence. The innocence he insisted on until the day he died. When I thought back to my father, to how much he suffered and how everything that happened broke him, I broke down.

Sohrab Nezami had been wronged and let down in every possible way by everyone he knew, including the people he loved.

And so, right outside the hospital building, in front of the patients and visitors and doctors passing by, I sobbed along with those infants being born in the hospital's maternity ward at that very moment.

And then I thought maybe infants cried because they were somehow cognizant of all the terrible things mankind was capable of, wondering if they would grow up to do those same awful things. Maybe they cried for the innocence they knew they'd lose along with their umbilical cords.

When I calmed down a bit, I thought about my uncle's plea for forgiveness.

Was I even capable of the thought of forgiving him, let alone the act?

He had wronged us all in every possible way. How could I forgive him?

Would Rostam forgive him if I told him the truth?

Would *Khaleh* Maryam, who was so sure of my father's guilt?

Would *Baba* Behruz be able to forgive him if he were alive?

Would my father and mother, the two people he had wronged most of all?

With his return and a single letter, my uncle had disrupted my life again, hurtling me back to a time in my life I was still trying to make peace with. I didn't want to forget what happened, but I was doing my best to let go of all the pain and regret and somehow move on from it. It was something I struggled with every day. Now, Eskandar decided to come back and undo the stitches I'd painstakingly sewed over each wound to try and close them, help them heal.

He had fooled us for over twenty-five years; leading me and everyone else to believe my father had somehow killed my mother. He had made us believe – or partly believe – the impossible. Twenty-five years of not knowing why or how. More than half of my life.

My grandfather went to his grave not knowing what happened, broken and alone. His youngest son dead and his oldest son abandoning him without so much as a goodbye. There's no place in one's heart for that kind of grief, no space anywhere in the body to put it. My grandfather died drowning in the grief he could no longer make any room for.

I will never forget how much he suffered the last remaining years of his life. I will never forget the look in his eyes the few times I had the courage to look into them. Even if I were to somehow forgive Eskandar for everything else, I wouldn't forgive him for that.

Now he thought he could come back, confess the truth, and be forgiven. And of course he'd use his cancer to incite pity. Of course he'd confess only when he was certain he had nothing left to lose.

If he wasn't dying of cancer, would he have confessed? If he was healthy and successful, would he have come back, much less told the truth? Otherwise, why wait twenty-five years to say anything? Even now, he was being selfish. He wanted to die with a clear conscience.

Well, I wasn't going to give him that. I should've known he would never change; that some traits are ingrained in a man's bones. I should never have trusted him or allowed him to get close.

I wasn't going to be fooled again. He didn't deserve my pity or my forgiveness. Not now, at least.

I walked back to my car to go home, almost certain I wouldn't be coming back to the hospital to see my uncle again. And even if I did come back, what could I possibly say to him?

* * *

That night, I dreamed I was Cyrus the Great again, but for the last time.

Throughout the years, I had recurring dreams in which I was Cyrus the Great and in every single one of those dreams, I was searching for something. I knew it was the answers to questions I still had. The past was unsettled and no matter how much I tried to make peace with it and let go, I didn't have closure. I couldn't move on. Part of me was stuck in the past.

In this dream, I was in the old Tehran bazaar shopping for artwork. I came across a painting of a young woman that looked vaguely familiar. It was the same portrait painting that resembled my mother; the one my father gave to Aunt Maryam in his will. I fiddled with the coin in my pocket, tempted to buy the painting. It was all I had on me and I couldn't believe I was willing to spend it.

Yet I was mesmerized by the painting, especially with the woman's resemblance to my mother, who in the dream I referred to as Shahbanu. I eventually gave the vendor my father's coin to purchase the portrait. When I looked up, it was Uncle Eskandar taking the coin from me, looking as sick as he did in the hospital.

Shocked and angry, I snatched the coin from him. It was one of the few keepsakes I had of my father and he was trying to take that from me, too. However, in a moment of clarity, I heard my father's voice, which I hadn't heard since our last meeting in the prison, reciting the closing line of his final email, a line by his favorite poet, Rumi, "*Only love has power over lovers, death has none.*"

That quote stayed with me all these years, reminding me of what matters.

Reminding me that for those who truly love, their love goes beyond everything – even beyond death. That they only answer to love and nothing else, not even death. It was one of the most comforting things my father could've ever taught me, and it got me through so much.

I gave back the coin to my uncle and walked away, leaving him the portrait, too. He had taken my parents from me and he could also keep their keepsakes. I didn't mind; in fact, I felt unburdened. While the coin was a source of strength for me when I was in a dark place, it was almost as if I was carrying my anger, hatred, and confusion along with it. Giving it away meant those feelings no longer had power over me. In a way, I was letting go of the resentment and bitterness that weighed on me for years. My heart had been hardened for so long, but now I only felt love and acceptance. Love for my family and for myself. Acceptance for everything I'd gone through because my pain, experiences, and the things that have haunted me also molded me into the man I am today.

I even felt love for the guilty man asking me for forgiveness.

The next day, I called Rostam to ask if he could make it down that weekend to visit Uncle Eskandar with me one last time. I told him everything that was going on with our estranged uncle – except his confession. That was something I couldn't tell him over the phone; it would have to be done in person because even though we were both adults now, I still felt the need to protect him. He, too, couldn't believe Eskandar had come back after so many years or that he was dying of cancer.

His voice sounded sad. Even though our uncle had been absent from our lives for so long, it was still a small comfort knowing he was alive in a corner of the world, unlike our parents and Grandpa Behruz. Besides Aunt Maryam, we didn't have any other close family.

But would Rostam feel the same way if he found out about Eskandar's confession?

Since he was in the middle of finishing up his dissertation, Rostam apologized and said he wouldn't be able to make it down. He told me to give Uncle Eskandar his best wishes and promised he'd try to come next weekend.

Since I didn't have Rostam for moral support, I took my son Dariush with me the following Saturday. I told him a little bit about who Uncle Eskandar was and why we were visiting him at the hospital, but kept the rest of the details to a minimum.

At the hospital, Dariush was a good sport, granting me the strength I needed to go back there a second time and face my uncle. At first, Uncle Eskandar thought Dariush was Rostam, having inherited my brother's curly crop of hair. When I explained Rostam couldn't make it, he looked disappointed, but it was soon replaced with delight when I introduced Dariush as my son.

Eskandar kept searching my face with anxious eyes, looking for any signs of anger or scorn, but I smiled politely and looked down each time.

I didn't have much to say to my uncle, but I knew the dream meant something. I took it as a sign to forgive him. I took it as a sign that my memory of my father were his lessons and stories and love, not his possessions, so I gave Dariush the coin before leaving for the hospital. I realized you only keep the coin until you need it, but once it's served its purpose, you must pass it down. I wanted to continue the tradition, explaining to him that it was passed down from father to son, like a thread that connected one generation of our family to the next. I told Dariush the coin was lucky and I hoped he would someday pass it down to his son. Or daughter. It didn't matter, just as long as it stayed in our family.

When he asked if it was real gold and how much it was worth, I smiled at him and said, "The true worth of a family heirloom isn't how expensive it is, but that it's a memento of those who are gone. It's a symbol of that family's bond and values. That's what makes it priceless."

Dariush nodded, but still weighed the coin in his hand. I smiled again; he had a lot to learn and I was looking forward to teaching him.

After about half-an-hour or so, during which Eskandar did his best to hold a conversation with my son between coughing fits, I stood up and signaled to Dariush it was time for us to leave. I was quiet for the most part and let Dariush do most of the talking, telling his great-uncle about school and the sports he played. When he said goodbye to Uncle Eskandar, I asked him to wait outside of the room for me.

Once we were alone, I leaned over and giving Eskandar's frail hand a gentle squeeze, told him I forgave him. He looked shocked, but I could see tears of relief and gratitude filling his eyes.

He turned his head away from me and said, "Living a life of guilt and torment for a crime so heinous was a million times worse than confessing to it. I thought I could emotionally get away with it, too. I thought the guilt would eventually subside and I could continue living a normal life, but my conscience caught up with me. I let my health go, my mind go, my family go.

"In Iran, I basically went mad with guilt and after a while, my wife and children left me. They gave me plenty of chances and I let them down each time, so I don't blame them for leaving. All my life, I didn't do right by anyone and that's why I've been alone. I've beaten myself over the head with the stick of my own wrongdoings. Now, I am on my deathbed and all I wish for is the one thing I don't have. The one thing I don't deserve. Time. Time to make things up to you and our family. But I know my time is up and I am ready for Azrael to take me."

I recalled my father saying the same thing the last time I saw him – how he didn't have time. Time to make up for everything and atone for his sins. But what sins did my father need to atone for? Being innocent and unknowingly taking the fall for a crime his brother committed and then lied about? I felt a slight prickle of anger and knew I'd have to wrestle with these conflicting feelings for a long time.

Eskandar continued to stare at the empty chair next to his bed. It felt as though he was speaking to someone else in the room.

"*Khosh amadi*," Uncle Eskandar said to the chair. "I am ready for you."

Then Eskandar Nezami's eyelids closed and his last breath fogged up the oxygen mask. The heart monitor flat-lined and emitted that final resigned beep.

A nurse hurried in to check on him and realizing he'd already passed, gave my shoulder a gentle squeeze and said she'd call the doctor to pronounce him dead.

"I'm sorry about your uncle, hon," she said before leaving the room.

"Me, too," was all I could say.

When my uncle's doctor entered the room, I left and went out to the waiting room to sit with my son. One look at my face and he knew; saying nothing, he took my hand into his own.

A few minutes later, the doctor came out to give us his condolences and said I was allowed some time with my uncle before they took him away. Dariush hugged me and said he'd wait for me. He didn't want to see death up close; he was still too young. I nodded and knew I was on my own, that I had reached an age where I could look death in the face because I was closer to it myself. The older we get and the closer we get to it, the easier it becomes to at least face it. I don't think we ever fully accept or come to terms with it, no matter what age.

When I re-entered the room, the first thing I noticed was the silence. All the life-monitoring machines had gone blank and quiet. Death had defeated them.

Uncle Eskandar looked as though he was having a sound nap, but would wake up at any minute. I thought it was strange that even though I had lost two parents, this was the first time I was seeing a dead body. I never saw my parents' bodies and I thank God for that because even though it looked like my uncle was napping, I knew he was no longer there. His soul had left his body; it was empty. I wouldn't have been able to handle seeing my parents in such a state, especially at so young an age.

All of these features, once used for the functions of life, would now be buried in the earth, turning into dust and mingling with the soil.

The nose, once wrinkling in disgust at the smell of something foul and decaying, would now itself decay.

Those two eyes that once took in the sights of the living world and inspected restaurant tables for dust would now be forever shut, lying underneath piles of soil.

His dry, purple lips were set in their usual straight, stern line, as if he was chastising me for these dark thoughts. Though for the first time in a long time, he looked content. It helped to know I had a part to play in him leaving this world with a lighter conscience, knowing he'd been forgiven by at least one member of his family.

I couldn't do the same for my father before he died. Maybe this was my chance to make up for it.

"We are of dust and to dust we shall return."

The bright late-morning light emphasized the signs of death on Eskander's body in a crude manner. I walked over to the window and pulled down the blinds, thinking he'd disappear or turn into dust right then and there as soon as I took my eyes off of him.

But he was still laid out on the bed, unmoved and completely surrendered to death.

Epilogue

We buried Uncle Eskandar at the same cemetery where both my parents and Grandpa Behruz were laid to rest.

It was a beautiful March day and even though *Nowruz*, which always fell on the first day of spring, was a week away, everything was already in bloom.

Spring was here.

My uncle's funeral ceremony was small, with only Rostam, my wife Bahar, my children, my uncle's long-time friend, and myself in attendance.

After the short ceremony, we said our prayers and moved on to Grandpa Behruz's grave, which now conveniently sat in the middle of my father's and uncle's graves. I figured they had a lot to talk about; Uncle Eskandar had much to explain and apologize for.

Five years after Uncle Eskandar fled to Iran, Grandpa Behruz passed away from a heart attack. I don't think his heart could take any more loss and disappointment. He did his best to hold on for as long as he could for me and Rostam.

With my help, he was only able to run the restaurant for another two years. When he sold it, he put aside some of the money for his funeral arrangements and gave the rest to me and Rostam in his will. He also left me the apartment building, which I sold after Aunt Maryam moved away. I wrote a check to Rostam for half of what I made on the sale of the apartment and the money helped both of us get through college and our post-graduate studies.

Grandpa Behruz owned an additional real estate property in the area that he rented out to various tenants; he left that for us, too. I decided against selling it and instead used the rent I collected to cover me and Rostam's expenses until we could both get through school and become a little more financially stable. I also didn't want to sell off all of my grandfather's investments. Investments he worked his whole life to grow and leave behind for his family.

I always wondered why an ounce of the generosity that flowed so deeply in my grandfather's and father's veins wasn't present within my uncle.

Grandpa Behruz died about a year after I graduated from high school and while taking college classes, I had two part-time jobs on- and off-campus to support us; Dad's life insurance money only covered so much and I put about half of it in a joint CD account for us. However, my financially-savvy grandpa made sure his grandchildren were well taken care of long after he passed. Otherwise, I don't know how we would have made it during those lonely years, when I was just out of high school and had no idea what I was doing.

Kneeling in front of his headstone now, I tapped on it with my index finger to say a prayer. It was customary to tap on the gravestone, as if to make sure the dead were aware of our presence, that our words and prayers reached them. Almost like a friendly tap on their shoulder.

Next, I stopped by my father's grave, tapping on it and saying a prayer. Before moving on, I told him how sorry I was for finding the truth out so late. I promised I would clear his name, no matter how long and difficult the process.

In Muslim tradition, an additional stone called *sang-e-lahad* is put directly over the body before the gravestone is placed; it's plain white and separated in two or three pieces. We believe that on the first night a body is buried, the soul awakens and causes the body to rise, unaware that it's in fact dead and not just sleeping.

However, upon rising, it bumps its head on the *lahad* stone and only then will it realize it's no longer part of the living world. Only then does it accept death and remain in the ground forever.

Following Eskandar's death, my children, especially Dariush, became curious about my past and our family history. I hadn't told them very much; granted, Bahar knew everything, but I wanted to wait until my children were a bit older. Now, standing together in a place filled with endings, it seemed like the right time to start at the beginning – the beginning of our family story.

My mother's grave was the last one we visited and as we stood in front of it, praying in silence, I began to tell them about their grandparents.

* * *

About a month after Uncle Eskandar's passing, I made up my mind to start the process of clearing my father's name with his brother's letter of confession.

My family supported my decision, as well. At first, I felt a little guilty for Uncle Eskandar's sake, but I knew it was the only way my father's soul could finally rest in peace. I knew it was the right decision.

I'm sure it's what my uncle would have wanted, as well. It's the least he could do for the brother he wronged. That's why he gave me the letter in the first place – a final act of redemption and righting his wrongs.

I remembered my father's words to me the last time I saw him at the prison, *"I know what you're going to ask – will I be at peace? I will be because I know I am innocent and that someday, the truth will come out and clear my name."*

Those words haunted me over the years.

My father's reputation meant so much to him, and this was the only way I could exonerate him. This was going to be the most important case I would ever work on, and I refused to put it off a second longer than I had to. While it was already twenty-five years too late, it was still happening.

It was still something.

I planned on going to court the following Monday to get the process started.

As for Rostam, I still hadn't told him about Eskandar's confession and as much as it pained me to be the one to do it, he had the right to know. I needed to talk to him before the news went public and it had to be done in person, so I waited to tell him once he came home from grad school. I already knew he'd support my decision to go public with the letter.

I was going to call Aunt Maryam and let her know, too. I wondered how she would react and if she would deem it the right time to forgive my father.

Aunt Maryam moved back to Florida two years after Rostam went off to college. It was with my insistence that she agreed to stay in our apartment after Rostam moved out, and we often visited her or she visited us. But when the loneliness and memories within those walls became too much for her to bear, she announced she was moving back to her home state. She never got married and kept busy with her job, although she did have a brief romance with a wealthy Persian businessman who was one of her clients. He wanted her to settle down and have kids, but she told him she wasn't ready for that and broke it off after only a year of dating him. She claimed she was too old to have kids, but I knew the truth – she refused to be tied down. More so than that, the thought of having children reminded her of her painful past.

She never did go to Iran to visit her parents one more time and to say goodbye to her dying mother, who passed away only a couple of months after being diagnosed with severe-stage Alzheimer's. I don't think the grudge she held against them ever went away. She couldn't forgive them for sending her away, for thinking of her only as a disappointment and a shame.

Years later, she told me what really happened with her parents before she came to the U.S.; it seems I only knew parts of the story. Maryam was four months pregnant with her lover's baby when her devastated parents forced her to make plans to leave for America. She broke into tears telling me how ashamed she felt and how her father never looked at her the same again. Her mother made her an appointment to get an abortion even though she begged them to let her keep the baby. But they wouldn't hear of it – it would ruin their reputation among their family and neighbors. Maybe that's why she's never wanted to marry and have children again. Maybe that's why she's had an aversion to tradition all her life.

"My only crime was being young and in love and wanting to live my life the way I wanted to live it, not how others dictated it for me," she said. "For that, I was punished and banished from my home and family. I was forced to get rid of the beautiful life growing inside me – my baby that I loved – like it was some dirty secret. And so I vowed to never set eyes on my parents again because if I saw them, then I knew I wouldn't be able to forgive them for making me go through such a horrible experience. So, I stayed away, carrying the pain with me all these years and allowing time and distance to heal what they can."

Every Persian should take care to protect the delicate balance of their reputation, but not at the cost of something much more significant – love. Unfortunately, some choose their reputation over all else and sacrifice everything else to preserve it – even their family. Much like Maryam's parents, they choose reputation over love and it costs them everything. The only relationship Maryam had with her parents was one of distance and it was the only way she could learn to forgive them. Seeing them again would have ruined that.

Now that she told me what she'd been through, I felt I knew my aunt on a deeper level; it explained a lot about her.

The night before Aunt Maryam left to go back to Florida, Rostam and I held a small goodbye party for her at her favorite restaurant. She promised she would come see us often and insisted we visit her in Florida, where the weather was actually nice, she joked.

But aside from a phone call every year on *Nowruz*, we haven't seen her since. I don't really blame her. Everyone has their own ways of moving on and coping; she already did her part. It's more than I could've asked for. We've had our disagreements over the years, but I'll always be grateful to her for being there and raising us the best she could under the circumstances. She stayed when most would have left.

It astounds me how gracious my dad was during the darkest, most difficult time of his life, putting everyone's needs before his own. He accepted the punishment he didn't deserve and said nothing. Even though he was certain of his innocence, he still asked for Aunt Maryam's forgiveness, appointing her as his children's guardian and giving her sole custody of his wife's belongings. He never once complained about the way she treated him, or how convinced she was of his guilt from the start.

He gave his share of the restaurant to Uncle Eskandar, unaware his own brother was the sole cause of all his misfortunes. He gave me stories and wisdom to help me understand and heal instead of accusing me of being a bad son for not fully believing in his innocence. Sohrab Nezami gave selflessly his entire life. Now it was my turn to give him something in return.

During my years of researching Cyrus the Great's life, I found there were very few honest, accurate accounts both about his life and the Achaemenid Empire in general. They say the victors write the history books, which may explain why Persians are sometimes depicted as monsters or the bad guys. I planned to one day visit Shiraz, the city of gardens and poetry, with my family and learn everything I could at the birthplace of it all. Shiraz, the famed city that housed Persepolis – *Takht-e-Jamshid* – and the Achaemenid Empire, the first Persian Empire, founded by Cyrus the Great. Throughout my research, I learned Cyrus had many names…

King of Anshan; King of Persia; King of Media; King of Babylon; King of Sumer and Akkad; King of the World; King of Kings; King of the Four Corners of the World; King of the Universe.

But to me, he would always be Cyrus the Great – my savior. Cyrus the Savior.

While I couldn't offer the world a true portrayal of the Persian Empire or Cyrus the Great's life, though I planned on turning my father's Cyrus stories into a book someday, I could tell the truth about my father right now. I refused to allow others to write his story. He spent his whole life telling other people's stories in the most beautiful, honest way and I was going to make sure his would be told in the same manner.

Learning of my father's innocence gave me a newfound, deeper appreciation for my career, making it that much more worthwhile. I was further convinced I'd chosen a path that led to honor and integrity. It was all my father ever wanted for me.

Often, I think back to my early years of high school and how I came so close to dropping out and giving it all up.

I still keep in touch with Yiannis and Tamara through social media and email.

We didn't end up going to the same college and nothing came of me and Tamara's brief romance, but I always wished the best for her. She was the first girl I ever loved and for me, that's one of the purest connections you can have with someone, even if it doesn't end up working out. They're both married and happy and that's enough.

Love is always enough.

"Only love has power over lovers, death has none." I recite this line like prayer and believe in it like my own name.

In addition to his love and my name, his stories and words and lessons are the greatest gifts Sohrab Nezami gave me.

That night, I sent another email to my father's old account, addressed only to him this time.

Dear Baba,

I've taken up your case myself to make sure they give you the correct sentence this time.

This time, I'm going to prove your innocence to everybody. I'm going to tell them your story in the way it deserves to be told. I know it's a long time coming, but you've always been the patient one. As the expression goes in Farsi, "sange-saboor" – "patient rock."

Thank you for being patient with me. Thank you for being my rock. Thank you for your love and for everything you taught me in the short time we had together. It was more than enough. I don't think I ever told you how proud I am to be your son, and I hope you'll forgive my shortcomings.

Remember when you told me that after I hear Cyrus the Great's story, everything will make more sense? That I'll understand why you named me Cyrus. That stories were all you could give me, but they will end up being enough?

You were right, as always.

May you now be able to rest in the peace you so deserve. I pray it will be enough. Say hello to Mom and Baba Behruz. As for Uncle Eskandar, I know you have much to say to one another and much to forgive. I hope in time that you do. And remember, "Only love has power over lovers, death has none."

Your loving son,
– Cyrus